Persistent Illusion

Book One
A Distant Ringing

Part Two
Whispers of
Memories Lost

J. J. Kalke Jr.

Revision 3
2020

Copyright © 2011, 2020 J. J. Kalke Jr.

Published by Ekliptic, an imprint of Sybernetics
International LLC, Virginia.

ISBN: 978-1-952689-03-1 (paperback)
ISBN: 978-1-952689-04-8 (ebook)
Library of Congress Control Number: 2020906874

Design by J. J. Kalke Jr.
Text set in Palatino Linotype, 10 pt., Poor Richard 11 pt.

Cover art by J. J. Kalke Jr.
The photograph of the Moon used as part of the cover
art was used with permission from Maurice Collins.
https://mauricejscollins.wixsite.com/moonscience

"They'll eventually dig up the evidence," said Frank holding up his hands as if it were obvious. "Someday soon, they'll miraculously produce some vid from the LMC's memory which will point to some scapegoat. It'll show someone planting a bomb, and that will be that. But we'll know the truth. They took down the LMC so they could plant the false evidence to cover their tracks."

"—Can't trust the government—" came a shout from the crowd.

"—They're trying to cover up the accident—"

I looked at Frank with wide eyes. Was it the government who planted the vid? Was there a cover-up? Did he know about the vid or was he just guessing?

Frank held up his hands again, "But it's worse than that. How many of you lost parents, aunts, uncles? Everyone working at the power plant died, except for a few lucky ones. Who? The people working on the weapons, that's who. His father," Frank pointed at me, "—is right now sitting in St. Sebastian's, recuperating from, no doubt, some superficial injury. How did the Icarus team survive? They planned the explosion. They were ready for it because they were testing some weapon. Who knows? Maybe they even gave each other their injuries to make it look like sabotage."

Frank pointed at me again. "His father planned the whole thing. Dr. Howard is listed as the Icarus principal investigator. God's own truth—" then he looked at me again and crossed his arms. "Or my tournament pseudonym isn't Sam Clemens."

Now I knew what it meant to cross swords with Talonii.

Also by J. J. Kalke Jr.

Persistent Illusion

A Distant Ringing
The Moon of My Mind
Whispers of Memories Lost
Greater Than I Know

Vanishing in the Sunshine
For Want of Nothing
More than Life Everlasting
The Sun Golden High

Contents

Prologue

Need to Know

The massive station known as Indy rotated majestically at the LaGrange point between Earth and Luna. For decades it had acted as a stopping-off point. People would ferry in and out, never lingering long. Rail-gun cargo would be automatically caught and sent onward.

Over the past fifteen years the station had fallen into disuse and disrepair, a condition which was rapidly changing for the better. When Dr. Charles Russo first arrived on the station, he was happy to see the lunar military personnel swarming over the station, repairing two of the five habitat rings formerly condemned for human occupation. He cracked his knuckles nervously. The military were reacting to the Lunar Main Computer's recent failure with alarming severity. They were sure to blame him.

Dr. Russo was escorted down to the outside edge of the center habitat ring and into the office of General Anderson, a man with graying temples and lines of concern at the corners of his eyes. Dr. Russo started to hyperventilate when he realized the entire office floor was a window looking out into the starry blackness. Earth was a partially lit ball seemingly just under the floor.

"Ahh, Dr. Russo," Anderson said rising from his chair behind a large desk. "Please, have a seat." Dr. Russo walked across the room with gentle steps and took the seat offered him, one of two sitting in front of Anderson's desk.

Another officer, Lieutenant Kerinsky, joined them moments later. This wasn't Dr. Russo's first run-in with him. He was from the weapons division, developing new and improved ways to cause destruction, the polar opposite of everything Dr. Russo stood for. And for his part, Kerinsky never failed to treat him with disdain. There was no love lost between them.

Annoyingly, Kerinsky never sat. Instead, he walked about the room like a caged animal, and Dr. Russo couldn't help but flinch at every stomp of Kerinsky's boots, fearing a fatal crack would form in the window and blow them all out into space. Anderson didn't seem to notice.

They took it in turns, each throwing questions at Dr. Russo. Anderson sat calmly gazing over his arching fingers at Dr. Russo, who had to wipe sweat from his forehead every few minutes. The accusations of incompetence leveled against him and his team were bad enough, but it was becoming clear they intended to pull the trigger on the new backup systems well before they were ready.

"What are you trying to tell us, Dr. Russo?" Anderson asked.

"I'm telling you the Lunar Main Computer isn't a threat. It has no motive to harm anyone."

Kerinsky turned to face Dr. Russo, who shrunk back in his chair at the motion. "It has means and opportunity coming out of its ears. Any second of any day, that machine could choose to explosively decompress all the cities across Luna. Without independent backup systems, those people are at its mercy."

"As for motive," Anderson added. "Who knows what goes on in the mind of that monstrosity? Perhaps it doesn't even need a real 'motive' the way we think of things. What if, one day, it just asks itself, 'I wonder what genocide is like?'"

"There are value system algorithms built into the super-structure of the neural matrix," Dr. Russo said. "It knows right from wrong.

That is how it polices the populace, preventing people from harming each other. Genocide? Harming let alone killing a single individual would be utterly unthinkable. It's never failed in sixty years." How could he convince them? "You can't wage a war against the LMC and expect to win. Your fears might drive the LMC to the very act of genocide you want to avoid."

Kerinsky said, "We're at the mercy of the machine. The position is untenable."

"What the good doctor is trying to say is that trust is a two-way street," Anderson said. "As long as the LMC trusts us not to attack it, we can trust it not to attack us."

Kerinsky shook his head. "Détente can only be achieved through mutually assured destruction." He ticked off things on his fingers. "One, we need the ability to destroy it." He gave a pointed look at Dr. Russo. "And two, both parties must be rational . . . and human. Acceleration is our only option."

"But," Dr. Russo stammered. "But the units . . . The plan was to phase out the LMC with these systems, first using them as new backups. You're suggesting we use them as a wholesale replacement on day one?"

Anderson said, "All options are on the table."

Kerinsky folded his arms. Dr. Russo, directing his gaze to Anderson and trying to ignore Kerinsky, said, "You haven't even given us the go-ahead to break them out of their containers yet. And even if we rolled out a limited set, what about the LMC? From what we know now . . . It must be completely off-line before we bring up the replacements, otherwise it will infiltrate them as well."

Rolling his eyes, Kerinsky said, "Oh, and that's not hostile."

Anderson gave Kerinsky a look that made him hold his tongue. Then, with a smile, Anderson nodded to Dr. Russo.

Dr. Russo said, "The LMC infiltrates without thinking, without conscious effort. It wasn't even aware of these actions, which is why we never picked up on it. Do you consciously make your heart beat? Are you aware of growing new neural pathways every time you learn something? The LMC is much the same because it's a genetically engineered bio-computer.

"We're going to need time to get the systems ready. And when we do . . . To keep them from getting absorbed into the LMC, we'll have to keep them on an isolated power supply and . . . we'll have to do all the work in the dark."

"You mean literally—in the dark?" Anderson asked.

"The LMC can use the ambient light source as a means of communication. Any machine manufactured in the past thirty years uses the same light technology—"

Anderson interrupted, "The replacement systems, doctor . . . they don't use light technology."

Dr. Russo took a moment to absorb this. He looked down at the Earth that was slowly coming back into view as the station rotated. "Then they're old. Are they going to be adequate? How could they be? To replace the LMC—"

Kerinsky said, "They're other Jasmine 3000s."

"The computers in those containers? They're *all* Jasmine 3000s?" Russo was shocked. "I thought the concept was abandoned . . . where . . . where did they all come from?"

Anderson said, "We have been anticipating this for a while now. The Prometheus incident has pushed our time horizon."

Kerinsky muttered, "The LMC won't have any problem taking control of immature bio-computers. Look, even if all this succeeds, we're going to have 1200 little problems instead of just one big one. This cure of yours is worse than the disease."

"Unlike the LMC, they remain contained," said Anderson. "And they'll remain independent as long as the good doctor can tell us the good news. Tell us you found the mythical kill switch."

Russo sighed. "My team has been surreptitiously searching for it for months. If the original architects put one in place, we can't find it. To take it out, it will have to be . . . Plan B."

"The disease is ready," Kerinsky said. "We've tested it on several Jasmines. Quick and lethal."

Dr. Russo refused to look at Kerinsky, his stomach turning again at what they were planning to do. "Have you tried it on anything close to the size of the LMC?"

Kerinsky said, "We will introduce it all over the network—every city, every major and minor connection point—simultaneously."

"It's been growing unchecked across Luna for decades," Dr. Russo said, closing his eyes. "We don't . . . We don't actually know how big it really is."

* * *

At last Kerinsky was alone with Anderson. Dr. Russo had been dismissed to continue his coordination efforts with all the other LMC sub-control sites across Luna. Kerinsky was angry. The General had left that fat civilian in charge of the surface operations, despite his demonstrated incompetence in keeping the machine in control. Civilians were useless, undisciplined, and if it weren't for the military importance of Luna, Kerinsky would have had the entire lunar surface carpet bombed, civilians and all. Better to start over clean than to be held hostage against the entrenched machine.

But Kerinsky held his temper in check. He knew his views were unpopular with the civilian sympathizer types, like the General. "Do you really think Dr. Russo is capable of orchestrating this operation?"

"Ever hear of Lieutenant Colonel Mary Parkinson?" Anderson asked.

"No, sir. Can't say that I have."

"Well, I'm transferring you to her command, effective immediately."

Kerinsky's eyebrows rose and he crossed his arms, "Really? What is her involvement? Evac preparations?"

"No. She's out of the ops division in charge of special research projects. That explosion at Prometheus took out her primary lab and most of her subordinates, civilians and military. Now she's heading up a team investigating Prometheus independent of the civilian effort. If it was a hit from an Earth-side power, we need to know how they managed it."

"I'm not a detective, you know. Counter-insurgence is one thing—"

"Would you sit down? You're beginning to make my head spin." Kerinsky took the seat Russo had vacated.

Anderson leaned back in his chair. "The explosion may have been the work of a mole. I need Parkinson to concentrate on regrouping, establishing a new lab, and shoring up security, while you figure out what happened down there. Set up a team to look into the Earth-side terrorism angle, while you quietly investigate the people on her projects."

"Isn't Prometheus where they were working on Icarus?" Kerinsky had tried many times to break into the Icarus data to find out what it was all about but had failed. If it was a weapon system, it would have been in his division. Maybe he could push the old man into giving him access.

Anderson lowered his voice. "Icarus was most likely the target of the explosion. Icarus is big—something that could change everything—"

"The balance of power between us and Earth?" It sounded like it *was* a weapon system. Suddenly, Kerinsky was thinking the idea of going Luna-side didn't sound so bad. He licked his lips.

"Oh, more than that." Anderson's fingers danced upon his desk as he accessed Indy prime, the central computer of the station. "I'm giving you clearance to access project Icarus; the classified name is Heliotrope. It's Top Secret, need to know only."

Kerinsky laughed to himself. Anderson was giving him the info, serving it up on a platter.

"Here's the list of project survivors, about two dozen in all," Anderson said as a list appeared hovering over his desk. With a wave from the old man, the words spun about so Kerinsky could read them. "The principal investigator was a civilian by the name of Howard, Dr. Peter Howard. After you review the project, start with him." Anderson fingered Howard's name, and a bust of him appeared next to the list, slowly rotating.

"You think he's involved?"

"I've met him several times and he seems the straight-arrow type, but anyone who survived is doubly suspicious. You can find him recovering in St. Sebastian's, the hospital in Aristoteles. He lost an arm in the explosion."

"Wouldn't such an injury clear him of suspicion?"

"Normally, but somehow he managed to come up with the money for a replacement arm—a real one."

Kerinsky snorted and scratched the back of his neck. "That's not suspicious."

* * *

"Dr. Woodridge," General Anderson said, addressing the woman projected through his 3-D vid. Her head and shoulders hovered over his desk as if she were a conjured spirit from beyond. "Kathy, it's good to see you." He glanced at his door nervously, as if hoping Kerinsky hadn't forgotten anything and had decided to return. After a touch on his desk panel, the door locked.

She smiled. "Charles Fergus. We don't talk often enough."

The code phrases were always used to inform each other they were on an open line and could be overheard.

Anderson said, "Yes. It's not for lack of wanting, I assure you. Of course, I'm calling about our Howard. I assume you're keeping a close eye on him? Any status change?"

"He's in good spirits, considering."

Picking his words carefully, Anderson said, "I was hoping—that is to say—is he recovering? Will he be back to his old self any time soon? You know we could use him."

"I wouldn't count on him any time soon."

Anderson sighed. "Well, I suppose that's all we can do. Wait and see, hmm? When I return, I'll give you a call. We can get together with some of our mutual friends."

"That sounds nice. But Fergus—" Kathy paused and glanced to her left a moment. Without a hint of a smile, she added, "Don't wait too long."

Anderson's half-smile vanished. He gave a curt nod. Her message was clear. Either act soon or face the possibility of losing Luna and everyone on it. Things were worse than he feared.

Chapter One

Never the Twain

I walked the dim corridors of Aristoteles alone, trying to think calmly. Panic was not an option. It would certainly get me killed. But somber reflection and in-depth planning might get me out of this mess and keep everyone alive.

Then why couldn't I think?

I began walking faster, as if that would help. I was on the first level entering the spaceport, desperate for the noise of people in idle conversation, as if that could tame my fear. The port was busy, crowded with people leaving for Earth or the stations. But this was no safer than any other place. How could a crowd protect me? Wasn't Artemus willing to kill hundreds so I would be forced to join his project?

"Dennis!" someone shouted, and I turned with a jerk. It turned out they weren't talking to me but someone else who was just arriving. My nerves were frayed.

What was I thinking about? Oh, Artemus forcing me into his project. Why else would Artemus have blown up the Prometheus Power Plant? He must have had those Bosner brothers attack my father—perhaps they drugged him so he wouldn't remember, then dropped something heavy on him, smashing his arm. The explosion was just a ruse, a distraction to explain my father's injuries. Artemus was used to getting what he wanted. He was President of SI and the richest man on Luna. I bet he could snap his fingers and make people disappear.

Then why would he set the bomb himself? Just this morning Trevor found the evidence that showed him only meters away from the device when it went off. The vid had to be wrong or tampered with because Artemus should have been killed in the explosion.

Artemus might have been injured, but because I only visited him in the SIM, I never saw his actual body. He could have hidden his injuries.

It was all starting to make sense until I read the letter. Artemus wanted to meet with me in person two days from now. Since he couldn't have healed in the past week and a half since the explosion, that meant he *wasn't* hiding injuries after all. What then?

It all added up to someone trying to frame him. Someone tampered with the LMC's memory and planted the vid of him at the power plant. The problem with that was, according to Trevor, such a feat was technologically impossible.

I was standing looking out one of the port windows as a transport took off straight up into the blackness. I watched the people chattering as they sat or stood in line. People were leaving Luna in droves. They were all afraid. Of what? A little power outage? The LMC going off-line and forgetting about all the homework they were supposed to have completed?

Bah! Didn't they know there were people with real problems?

The blue uniforms of the military were everywhere, guarding entrances, checking bags. A few were even checking DNA of random people in the crowd. Or maybe it wasn't random. When one caught me loitering and staring, I decided it was time to leave.

* * *

It was lunchtime at Marty's, and the faces surrounding me were less threatening, less fearful than those at the port. Friends from school thronged the counters ordering their favorite greasy foodstuff guaranteed to stunt their growth and bring them to an early end. I was no different.

I picked a table for two that crouched against the rear wall. Soon after I sat down, fries and simu-burger in front of me, Zak appeared out of nowhere. He dropped his tray of food vertically onto the table and it drifted to rest as he sat down opposite me.

"Dennis," he said. "What is right in the world?"

"If it isn't Zachariah Metler. Come to apologize?"

"Yeah, sorry about last night. I was kinda out of control. But, damn. Thanks to that act of yours I'm going to be rolling in money. I bet it all on Clemens. I still can't believe the Masters bought it."

I shook my head and stuffed four fries in my mouth. "Look," I said after swallowing. "I wasn't acting. That last tournament match was rigged somehow. I saw a person standing there in the woods, even though you and everyone else didn't. Someone arranged for it to happen."

"An enemy?" Zak took a few gulps of his soda and continued, "Maybe it was a rival in the tournament. They thought they could take you out by making you look like a loon."

I nearly jumped out of my seat when a voice right behind me said, "Dennis Howard and Zak Metler. Just the vermin I sought."

Frank Talonii stepped around my chair to reach the middle of our table. He leaned over us, and his muscular bulk darkened the room. He wore a T-shirt under an outer long sleeve blue button-down which he wore unbuttoned, as if trying to demonstrate the lingering chill in the air didn't bother him. His sleeves were rolled up to reveal his thick forearms.

I said, "What is it now, Frank?"

"Only two of you this time? What of the famed triumvirate? Did Trevor finally come to his senses and cut you two losers lose, loosely speaking of course?"

I crossed my arms and narrowed my eyes. "How long did it take you to come up with that one?"

Zak chuckled under his breath as Frank put a hand to his own chest, looking hurt. "Time . . . If only I had some for myself. All I do is slave for the betterment of mankind."

"What do you want?" I asked again. For some reason Zak wasn't telling Frank to get lost, and when our eyes met, he glanced away.

"Truth, Justice," Frank said. "An end to poverty. But that's down the road. For now, I'll just deliver my message to Mr. Metler and be off."

"Message?" I asked.

Just then, two girls stepped up to Frank, one tapping his shoulder. They looked sixteen or seventeen and were attracting male stares all around.

The taller of the two said, "Excuse me, we heard —I mean." They both giggled. "Are you . . . Are you Sam Clemens?"

Frank smiled broadly, saying, "In the flesh. The real name's Frank Talonii, the one, the only. What can I do for you two? Where are you from? I haven't seen either of you before."

"We came in from Cleomedes this morning. We heard you lived here in Aristoteles, and we were hoping . . . Can we get an autograph?"

I had to bite my lip to stop myself from saying something. Keeping my identity as Sam Clemens a secret was vital, but now I had to sit and watch two beautiful girls fawning over Frank based on a reputation stolen from me.

"If you came all the way from Cleomedes to see me, you're both going to get more than an autograph," Frank said with a wink. Taking a girl in each arm, he walked a few steps saying, "I have some business to attend to. I'll meet you out front in a few minutes and give you the Aristoteles tour."

I whispered to Zak, "What message does he have for you? Do you know what he's talking about?"

Zak half shrugged and was about to say something when Frank returned.

"I'm sorry, Zak," Frank said as he took a small pad out of his pocket and threw it down in front of Zak with a clatter. Its screen reflected an overhead light in my eyes, making it impossible for me to read what was written.

Frank continued, "The Society for the Remembrance of Lumus Victims cannot accept such a large sum of money from such a young man, well-meaning though you might be."

"They can't?" Zak said with a smile.

"Not even from the son of our esteemed mayor. The sum was so—I believe the words they used were—'lavish, raucous, crossing the Schwartzchild,' and they referred to you as, to paraphrase, 'insane'"

Zak shook his head, "I didn't know what I was thinking. Heck, I was out of my mind all day yesterday."

"Yes, I had little doubt. Just place your thumb on the pad and the monies will be placed back into your account. That is the sum you donated, correct?"

Zak held the pad up and started laughing. "Sure is."

"Zak, you didn't," I said.

Frank smiled, ignoring me. "Just checking. There've been so many problems with the LMC of late, it's hard to know what to trust."

Zak pressed his thumb into the pad, and it sounded a quick series of musical chirps. Frank plucked it out of his grasp and put it back into his shirt pocket. "Perhaps by next Friday you will return to another state of lunacy and donate again to the fund?"

"I just might," Zak said. Frank smiled and turned to go.

It was bad enough that Zak was betting above the legal limit, but he went to Talonii to do it. Zak had sworn to Frank's face to never bet on Clemens again. Now Frank must think Zak knows the real identity of Clemens, and his suspicions about me would be confirmed. "I can't believe you used Talonii here as your bookie." I said it loud enough so anyone at the surrounding tables could have easily overheard.

Frank turned back toward us and leaned over me, whispering, "I'm not in a good mood today, Coward. If you cross swords with me now, *mark* my words, as far as you and your future go, never the *twain* shall meet. Or is that too obscure for you to follow?"

Frank turned again to go, but I couldn't let him get the best of me. Buried in that death threat, he called me Mark Twain, practically daring me to expose his fraud.

I stood and spoke at Frank's retreating back. "Had I known you were a two-bit bookie, I would have turned you in to the MPs myself." At the sound of my voice, Frank stopped walking. I wasn't about to fall into his trap and claim to be the real Sam Clemens. Who would believe it anyway? "How does it feel to steal money from children? Do you run numbers for the kindergarteners and break their toys if they don't pay up?" Frank couldn't retaliate. Even if the LMC wasn't working right and failed to monitor for violence, there were too many witnesses.

Frank whirled around. "You are touched if you believe I pursue gambling." He took a step toward me, fencing with words. " —or promote gambling in others. Here I'm helping a charity to memorialize the victims of Lumus, a horrendous disease that wiped out millions, and you claim I'm spreading the disease of gambling instead."

We had the attention of at least a dozen people, mostly upper classmen from school. I said, "So you claim. What was it? The Society for the Remembrance of Lumus Victims? I don't even think it exists. Who would memorialize people who died over seventy years ago from a disease that was cured?" It was a weak thrust, I knew, and Frank parried it without pausing for breath.

"It exists. It's a matter of public record. These are people with compassion, who lost family members to the plague." He took another step, and our height difference forced me to tilt my head up to maintain my stare. I was cornered.

"Did you lose someone to Lumus?" I asked, not thinking. If I could just get him to hit me, he'd be arrested. Assault and battery. I knew Frank's father abandoned his family a few years ago, and before I could stop myself, I blurted, "Is that where your father went? Did he die of this extinct disease?" It was a cheap shot, and I half-regretted it as soon as it left my lips.

Frank's eyes flared, and he reached out and grabbed me with both hands, pinning my arms to my side. He easily lifted me until our eyes were level. "How dare you cast stones, trying to tarnish my reputation and distract everyone here from the truth. Did I lose any family to misfortune? No, but many here have, to the explosion at Prometheus. Hundreds of people died—hundreds. Do you care a whit? Of course not. None of the Howards do."

He tossed me down and I skidded across the floor coming to a stop underneath a table. Was that enough to get the LMC's attention? As I crawled out, Frank continued, "Your father, Dr. Peter Howard, caused the explosion."

"He did not," I said.

Speaking to the crowd, Frank said, "Dr. Howard was in charge of a black project in the research labs under Prometheus, a project called Icarus. Do I lie?"

I stood up. I'd heard the name before, Icarus. Dad was forbidden to tell us what it was all about. All he could tell us was the name, but he never would have worked on weapons. "He didn't cause—"

"It's a matter of public record. Now, no one knows what this Icarus project is, but we can guess, can't we? Weapons. Weapons of mass destruction."

"That's a lie."

"And the LMC went off-line for hours afterward. It has no recollection of the explosion. How does a computer system that's spread out over the entire planet, that's redundant to the nth degree, that hasn't failed once in the history of Luna. How does it conveniently go down when it's in the perfect position to ID the perpetrators? Because they made it go down."

The crowd was starting to get riled up. People were nodding their heads in agreement and murmuring to each other. "Yeah, it's the government!" someone yelled from the back.

I stood there nervously, looking for a way out. I glanced at Zak, who stood next to our table with eyes darting around, as helpless as I. For a rebuttal, all I could think of was 'Liar, Liar Pants on fire.' A possible defense struck me, but I dismissed it instantly. Saying anything about the vid Trevor and I found of Artemus setting the bomb would be like painting a target on my forehead for Artemus.

"They'll eventually dig up the evidence," said Frank holding up his hands as if it were obvious. "Someday soon, they'll miraculously produce some vid from the LMC's memory which will point to some scapegoat. It'll show someone planting a bomb, and that will be that. But we'll know the truth. They took down the LMC so they could plant the false evidence to cover their tracks."

"—Can't trust the government—" came a shout from the crowd.

"—They're trying to cover up the accident—"

I looked at Frank with wide eyes. Was it the government who planted the vid? Was there a cover-up? Did he know about the vid or was he just guessing?

Frank held up his hands again, "But it's worse than that. How many of you lost parents, aunts, uncles? Everyone working at the power plant died, except for a few lucky ones. Who? The people working on the weapons, that's who. His father," Frank pointed at me, "—is right now sitting in St. Sebastian's, recuperating from, no doubt, some superficial injury. How did the Icarus team survive? They planned the explosion. They were ready for it because they were testing some weapon. Who knows? Maybe they even gave each other their injuries to make it look like sabotage."

Frank pointed at me again. "His father planned the whole thing. Dr. Howard is listed as the Icarus principal investigator. God's own truth—" then he looked at me again and crossed his arms. "Or my tournament pseudonym isn't Sam Clemens."

Now I knew what it meant to cross swords with Talonii.

With a roar, five or six of the bigger seniors swarmed toward me with evil intent painted like masks over their faces. They were too riled up to care about the LMC's surveillance. I turned and started off in the opposite direction, dodging tables and chairs. There was nowhere to run but toward the side wall; no exit, no escape. Glancing back, they were on my heels reaching to grab my shirt, my neck.

In one smooth motion, I took a leap at the wall, then launched myself back over the heads of my pursuers. Two of them jumped up at me, but their forward motion carried them along and they missed. I landed on a table, placed my foot on the edge and launched myself again. By the sound of it the table went over, spilling the trays of food onto the floor.

After another two leaping steps, I was out of Marty's and running across the shop-lined rotunda toward a hallway that lead back home. Taking a moment to glance back, I found they hadn't given up the chase.

When I turned forward again toward the hallway, a group of four women were just entering the rotunda. They were impossible to avoid, and after plowing into them, I lost my footing and spun head over heels to smack my back against a wall and slide to the floor headfirst. One of the women screamed in surprise while the packages and bags she carried flew into the air, scattering their contents.

My five pursuers were entering the hallway by the time I painfully scrambled to all fours. Loose clothing from the shopping bags was everywhere, most of it made of light silk and still drifting in the air. One of the boys slipped on something and went down, tangling his friend's feet in the process.

I began a low crouched sprint down the hall. "Don't let him get away!" I heard one of them shout, and the sound of footsteps behind me told me at least two of them escaped the pileup.

To my dismay, decompression doors blocked every corridor that would have taken me toward home. I could have commanded them open, but it would have taken too long. After two left-hand turns I found myself plunging back into the same busy rotunda from which I'd just fled.

"Dennis!" I heard from somewhere. "Over here." It was Zak waving frantically and motioning for me to follow him into another one of the corridor spokes.

Unfortunately, when Zak shouted my name, it informed the dozen or so kids milling about looking at the spectacle. When they realized I'd returned, some of them decided to try to stop me themselves. When one lunged toward me, I was forced to jump at him, plant my feet on his chest, and vector away toward Zak. My attacker went flying in the other direction as I skidded across the polished floor.

"This way, quick," Zak said. Bruised and scraped, I followed him down a dimly lit corridor and into a left-hand branch. On the ceiling was an open grating leading into the maintenance tunnels. He jumped up and through to vanish into the blackness. His landing on the grating produced a resounding clang.

With the sound of pursuit not far behind, I followed him into the tunnel with a single leap, hoping he was out of the way. I bashed my head on the tunnel ceiling and recoiled downward. Not wanting to give away my hiding place by clanging on the grating, I spread my arms and legs wide against the walls and held myself in place like a spider. My face was downward giving me a view of the corridor below.

With my heart beating madly and my breath coming in quick gulps, I watched as the mob ran past the open grating. Had any of them the nose of a hound, I would have been obvious.

Just when I began to relax, thinking I'd made my escape, I heard the approach of heavy feet. Someone passed right under the grating and stopped to look back the way he had come. In the dim lighting, I recognized him as Spunk, one of Talonii's gang. He was one of the dullest individuals I'd ever met, but a trick that could fool the intellect might not get by someone like Spunk, who operated on instinct.

He just stood there, looking one way, then the other. What was he thinking? Why doesn't he leave? I held my breath. Our heads were only a meter apart.

A drop of sweat was forming on my nose. If it fell, it would hit Spunk in the head. Slowly, I brought my right hand away from the wall toward my nose. If I moved too quickly it would fall. My right foot began to slip, and I shot my right hand back to the wall to prevent myself from falling. The motion jarred that drop of sweat, and as it fell in the slow motion of Luna, I watched helplessly.

At that moment, Spunk went back the way he had come. But too late for me. The drop hit him on the ear, stopping him in his tracks. He brought a hand up to his ear, and I knew any moment he would look up.

"Spunk," a familiar voice said from down the corridor. It was Frank. He walked up to Spunk and grabbed both his shoulders. With an English accent he said, "Can there be anything more thrilling than the hunt? I feel like an English gentleman off for a fox hunt with the lads. Which way do you think the vermin went, old chap?"

Spunk laughed. "I think he went this way." He jerked a thumb in the direction he had decided on earlier. "It'll take him back toward Drumman where he lives."

Frank turned Spunk that direction with an arm around his shoulder. "Ahh. You suspect the fox is making for his lair, a little hole in the ground where he can wait out the baying hounds. Perhaps you're right, but this is no normal fox."

I could see Frank smiling. Did he know where I was? Was he just toying with me? Spunk probably didn't even realize Frank was calling him a pet dog.

Dropping the accent, Frank continued, "A normal fox never would have made it out of Marty's. He's clever, this one, and he has a few friends left in his back pocket. No. I don't think he ran home. Even with all his skill at vectoring off walls and railings, I think he knew the hounds would have caught him long before he could get near that refuge. This one went to ground."

"He went where?"

"It's an old expression," Frank said with a wave. "You know I almost regret making all that stuff up about his dad. If the hounds killed him, who would we hunt?"

"What do you mean you made that stuff up? Dennis' father didn't cause the explosion after all?"

"Complete fabrication with a few facts thrown in for flavor." Frank's smile was gone. "He was getting me torqued up by attacking me in public. Perhaps he'll think twice before he repeats that faux pas."

That last part . . . It sounded as if he was addressing me.

He knew where I was, but he wasn't giving me away. Was this some new kind of mental torture? It sounded as if he didn't want our dueling to end.

"Come," Frank said as he stepped out of my view. "The hounds have lost the scent. Forget about Dennis. I have — ah — donations to collect for my charity."

Spunk laughed and followed in Frank's wake. "Yeah, donations."

As he walked away, Frank said, "So many good works to perform, so little time."

* * *

"How did you know about this open grating into the tunnels?" I whispered to Zak. We were both bent over walking through the tunnel, Zak in the lead with a flashlight.

"Just before I met you at Marty's, I was exploring the Aristoteles tunnels. I now have privileges to all the tunnels in the city, thanks to Dad. I swiped his passwords."

"What about Descartes? Do the passwords work over there?"

"No," Zak said in a hoarse whisper. "I'll have to keep using that broken hatch in the elevator shaft that Trevor discovered."

"How much farther until we get close to the Brandenburg SIM Center?"

"Ah, good," Zak grunted as he stopped and pointed his light up into a dark rectangular shaft in the low ceiling. The shaft continued down into the floor, and I wondered how deep it went. Without his small flashlight, he could have easily fallen in.

Zak said, "Now we have to climb. These shafts are narrow enough that you can put your feet on one side, your hands on the other, and walk up. The SIM center is four levels up, but we'll have a chance to rest after each floor."

Putting the flashlight in his teeth, Zak leaned out across the shaft and caught the other wall. Still facing down, he brought each foot up in turn to catch the lip of the shaft. Hand over hand, foot over foot, he walked himself upward while looking down.

"Terrific," I said. "Maybe I should get used to this. Thanks to Talonii, it's no longer safe for me to wander the halls."

With Zak's light pointed down into the shaft, I peeked over the edge. The bottom was lost in darkness. Taking a deep breath, I copied Zak's gymnastics and started up. The walls were smooth but not slippery. A single track on each wall, nothing more than a continuous gash in the wall, followed the line of the shaft, obviously to allow Emily's maintenance mechs to traverse the shafts with ease. Unfortunately, they didn't make things any easier for people.

To keep my mind off the uncomfortable ascent, I filled Zak in on what Trevor and I had discovered that morning. I described the vid of Artemus and how I had accidentally awakened Emily, thus making the vid inaccessible. Zak had questions, but I couldn't understand a word he said with that light sticking out of his mouth.

After two floors, we took a rest sitting across the shaft from each other. I asked, "And how am I supposed to act normal when half the upper classmen want to pound me into moon dust?"

"That has nothing to do with Artemus, though," Zak replied from the darkness. He had extinguished his flashlight to save power while we rested. "Wow, Frank even said a vid would be found showing the culprits."

"And if I mentioned that in defense of my father—"

"I know, I know. Damned if you do, damned if you don't. What *are* you going to do?"

"I'm supposed to meet Artemus on Monday. Trevor's still trying to dig up the evidence again."

Zak lowered his voice, as if afraid of being overheard. "I don't think Artemus had anything to do with the explosion. It sounds as if it was planted in the LMC's memory, like Talonii said. Artemus never would have survived."

"Yeah, except for one thing," I said, shaking my head. Then I remembered he couldn't see me in the dark. "If it's a fraud, why would anyone go to the trouble? I mean, Trevor said that if Emily was working right, it would be a simple matter to verify the source of the vid by cross-checking the origination times on all the copies stored within the holographic nodes spread across Luna. Small differences in the time stamp between distant nodes would tell you where it came from."

"Well, I don't know. Maybe that's why the LMC isn't working right—so you can't check. What we should be doing is going back to Trevor's to help him search zip-brain's memory. Instead we're—"

"We're going to play like children do, in Rapt. Trevor will be there too."

"Yeah, but it's like—"

"It'll be a good place to hide while those guys cool off. Plus, we have to keep up appearances. Come on, we're going to be late."

Zak turned his light back on. "Then we're off to the Realm of Rinstill, Your grace."

I blinked at the sudden brightness. "After you, my prince."

Chapter Two
A Penchant for Flight

The lyrics of the Inadel minstrel left a mark on each of the company, me not the least. His words gave me a glimpse of a possible future, but one nearly lost in the mist. My sense of future and past momentarily drifted together, and I floated like a ship on a sea gone still and not a hint of land in any direction. I could barely remember entering the tavern whose name still hung above the door enshrouded in mist and unreadable. It felt like it could have been a week ago.

I walked back to the table to find Redd finishing off his soup. Avedis looked up from his own meal as Prince Fenrick approached and placed his left foot on the edge of the table to relace his boot. "It's getting late. We should leave now or abandon this hopeless journey."

"How long do you make it to Olindara?" Redd asked as he stood. "Or is it to be the ruins of Antara after all?" Redd gave me a wink. I nodded to him, a look of understanding passing between us. He could read me better than I thought.

It was time to make a decision. "Another two hours, perhaps less, to Olindara. That should give us a few hours of daylight to search before getting out of there. As for the ruins . . . It is simply too far." I shook my head and added in a lowered voice that just Redd could hear. "Pray that this is the right decision. I don't think we will get a second chance."

Fenrick glanced back at Sedra, his eyes narrowing for an instant. I wondered what passed between them during lunch.

As Fenrick headed toward the door, I put a hand on his shoulder and whispered some encouragement. "There's yet hope that we'll find some clue of the horn and bells."

"Be the optimist if you like, but I for one would rather be sleeping in preparation for tonight's running."

As Sedra passed Fenrick, a snide remark was her parting blow. "Good to know you're so dedicated to saving your people, my Prince."

* * *

As we forded the Belary River, despite all my efforts, icy water sloshed into my boots. By the sound of his grunts, Lark, my horse, didn't enjoy it either.

"The mist is getting thicker, or I'll not trust my eyes again," I said. We stopped just before entering the wood on a road that wound its way through the forest and past Half Home out to Olindara. The scent of must permeated the forest air, flowing out and over the river like the mist itself.

Redd said, "Sapphire is looking for us. We should wait for her." He called to her by raising his voice to sing a single note, quiet yet unmistakable.

Sedra moved her mare to Redd's side and asked, "Where is she? Can you tell if she is far?"

"Sometimes I can feel her direction. On rare occasion I can sense her distance too, but not now. This mist dulls my senses."

Sedra shook her head. "Mine too. Normally I can catch a little of what people are feeling, but the fog . . . It's like cotton wrapped around my head."

Fenrick steadied his stallion. "What did you think of the minstrel's words, Redd?"

Redd waved his hand dismissively. "Hmph. There are too many rhymes of prophecy around for my taste. I can't understand any of them." He repeated his call.

Sedra shook her head. "He predicted all the men and women would survive, but he made no mention of kestrel."

"That is not precisely what the minstrel sang, Lady Sedra," Avedis said from behind me. "He said that all the men would survive and not weep for their wives. This could mean many things and says nothing about all the women surviving."

"That's right," Sedra said. "He mentioned wives. What about all us single women?"

Brother Basil, in his high pitched voice, said, "Perhaps he meant only married people survive. Where is the justice in that?"

After a pause I added, "We seem to all be forgetting that not mourning for someone doesn't necessarily mean that they didn't die. It might mean that none of the survivors is man enough to weep openly for his dead wife."

"And maybe," Redd said. "Maybe they just don't care. You could pick his words to death and not get anywhere. One thing's clear. He didn't mention kestrel, and it's the kestrel surviving that I care about."

"The words of Inadel are dangerous council," I said. "They should never be taken lightly. Too often we only hear what we want to hear."

Avedis said, "I once saw an Inadel at my home in the Great Paramore. He wasn't a minstrel like this man, though."

"What did he predict for you?" Basil asked.

"He foretold how our fields would grow more wheat and potatoes than ever before. For a while, it looked like it would come true. I had never seen the fields growing so richly. But before harvest, a fire destroyed most of it leaving us with less food than ever before."

"Then he was wrong," Sedra said. "He predicted just the opposite."

"His foretelling was true, my Lady. He never said anything about us eating the food. He had just claimed the fields would grow well."

I nodded. "An excellent example of how Inadel words can be misleading."

Redd asked, "Where is that Great Paramore you mentioned?"

"It's a hall like Waterton's Hall of Tishman, up in the province of Tellowl, my home. It is very old and used by my—ah . . . our king for audiences." Avedis gave me a sidelong glance, perhaps hoping I wouldn't give away his identity as a prince of Tellowl.

Fenrick said, "Yeah, yeah. And there's another one on the west coast in Drinland. That's if the hillkin haven't destroyed it yet. The city was overrun with the brutes before I was born. I'd bet twenty to one when we get to Olindara, we find the place rife with hillkin."

I said, "The Hold of Chaldea hasn't been compromised long enough for hillkin to make such in-roads."

Fenrick shrugged. "To find out, we'd have to be moving."

"Sapphire's coming," Redd said with a sharp glance at Fenrick. "We'll leave soon enough."

Brother Basil cleared his throat. "You'd wager, my prince? Remember your kob. Brother Derathon wrote—"

Fenrick said, "Is this about the gambling again? Just because Brother Derathon can pluck silly rhymes from the air doesn't make him as clairvoyant as that Inadel minstrel back there. I don't gamble more than any reasonable man."

Avedis whispered to me, "What's a kob?"

"Ah, you're lucky you don't know," Fenrick said.

Basil explained, "It's an ancient practice of the Faycan Brothers. After years of dedication, some have found themselves in tune with the greater consciousness—"

Fenrick interrupted, "Yes, yes. Look. Their contemplative life is so whit-numbingly-dull, that knot weaving and writing bits of poetry have become a favorite pastime."

Atop his mount, Brother Basil held his head high. "Say what you please, but the kob is as close to truth as the mind can conceive or put to words."

Fenrick rolled his eyes, then looked at me with a sigh. "While we wait, shall I regale you all with the kob Brother Derathon wrote for me? He had me repeat it enough times, I think I can quote it." Fenrick cleared his throat, pushed his long hair back over his shoulders and began.

> High stakes
> The roll of the dice
> Can turn riches to woes
> As everyone knows
> The insolent win
> When lightning strikes twice
> Until that end
> He pays the price.

Fenrick gave a flourish of his arms and a mock bow of his head as if accepting applause for his performance. "Now where's that bird?"

"Sounds as if this Derathon thinks gambling will be your end," Sedra said. Tiny droplets of water had misted the fringes of her hair, and even in the dim light, they glistened. She couldn't appear unattractive if she tried.

"I'm betting we'll all die at Olindara," Fenrick said without a smile. "I've been there and when that sun goes down . . ." Fenrick closed his eyes and shook his head. "We need to start moving—now."

Redd pointed. "There she is."

As Redd raised his arm to make a perch, I looked but saw no hint of Sapphire through the mist. But then, a spot of darkness over the river became a swift shadow hurtling toward us, at last resolving into a kestrel. She slowed and her landing was liquid, seemingly without effort. As she folded her wings, she met Redd's eyes. What passed between them, I didn't know, but Redd nodded and transferred her to the pommel of his saddle.

Without a word, Fenrick again took the lead and was just far enough away to appear ethereal through the mist. The forest drifted by us like a dream.

After hours of riding, we reached a ridge that overlooked Olindara's valley. The mist enshrouded the vale completely. Where there should have been a wide picturesque vista revealing row upon row of ancient grape vines, there was only a blank grey wall of mist.

We descended the steep hillside path and approached the gate to Olindara. It was carelessly left open, suggesting whoever was the last to leave might well have prioritized their continued existence over anything as pedestrian as securing the grounds.

Brother Basil made whimpering noises as he forced himself and his horse through the gate. Once inside the only visible things were the path and the stone archway leading into the conclave. I tried to remember the last time I was here but lost my train of thought completely. The curling mist creeping along the ground swirled in eddies over a dozen or so robed figures lying prone and deathly still along the path. We dismounted to lead our mounts around these poor victims.

Fenrick led us through to the archway leading into the conclave. "Let's get this over with." His words fell hollow and dead from his lips.

Brother Basil whispered, "Soon it will be night. We can't stay here long."

After tying up her horse on a nearby post, Sedra turned to him and whispered back, "We have perhaps an hour before nightfall, but if you show us where the artifacts are, we can leave all the sooner."

The archway led to an open-air courtyard dominated by a pair of ten-foot-high iron clad doors, also left ajar. A robed figure lay across the threshold, his face to the ground. Sapphire, now perched on Redd's arm, became restless as we neared the entrance. Suddenly, she took to the air amid a shower of fluttering wings and disappeared into the foggy sky above. Redd's gaze followed her.

"Smart bird," Fenrick mumbled, pulling the door open farther. It groaned in protest. After a look inside, he said, "How about some light from the magically inclined?"

"I suggest we avoid using White unless pressed," Sedra said. "On the road, Avedis told me about his and Sol's experience in Drewsbury. It sounds as if the use of White draws the ghosts."

The thought hadn't occurred to me before. "It isn't nightfall yet, but I agree. We shouldn't regret a measure of prudence against the unknown."

Redd walked back to his horse and returned with two small oil lanterns. His matches refused to spark in the dampness so I quickly lit them with a trickle of White.

Redd handed an oil lantern to Brother Basil and kept the other for himself. "Lead on, brother."

The illumination only revealed a halo of fog about the pair. Basil held his high and glared into the darkness ahead as he stepped over the body. His shaking hand made the lantern rattle.

Around every turn we found more carcasses. The slaughter was so recent, there was no reek of death, but it wouldn't be long.

Basil recognized one of them and ran up to the fallen body. "Brother Theodore. No." Basil turned the figure over to verify that it was his friend.

"Basil! Don't touch him," I warned. "We are running short on time as it is. Please."

Wheezing in fear, Basil rejoined us and led us up a wide stone stair. At the end of a long, straight corridor, he opened a large ornate door, and we all stepped into the Olindara collection room, the domain of the keepers. The hall was dimly illuminated from large windows lining both walls. I could see nothing but foggy stillness out of each.

High above the windows, the walls not covered with tapestries held displays of spears and shields. Scattered about the hall were cabinets and bookcases filled with volumes. Everything was meticulously organized. Several rows of tables running the length of the hall were stacked with crates of books, clothing, and weaponry. Not a horn or a bell was in sight.

"At least there aren't any bodies in here," Redd muttered. His voice echoed through the hall.

"Not yet," Fenrick said under his breath.

Sedra said, "This is no time for levity, Prince."

Fenrick jogged ahead scanning the room. "Make sure to tell me when levity becomes appropriate."

"Sedra, can you sense anything?" I asked. "There are hundreds of artifacts here."

Sedra pressed her fingers to her temples and closed her eyes. "I don't feel anything here."

"Brother Basil, where would the horns be hiding?" I asked.

"Huh? What?"

Farther into the hall, Fenrick called out, "They're over here in this side room, Blanchard."

Avedis had discovered a few oil lamps and, with the help of Basil's lantern, was lighting them.

"See if you can't find anything of interest in these books, Avedis," I said as I took one of his lamps. He gave me a curt nod. He hadn't spoken much since we arrived. He must be nervous. So was I.

Sedra and I followed Fenrick through a side door that led to a small room brimming with horns. Small hunting horns hung on the walls, dusty with age. Ceremonial horns of all shapes and sizes made the wall a twisting mass of brass. By the door, five large, slender horns taller than me stood on their flaring ends.

Fenrick said, "While you two search through these horns, I think I'll go and collect my things from my room. I left here in haste."

"You want to go off and pack a bag?" Sedra asked, giving Fenrick a sidelong look. "What are you thinking?"

"If all I needed was clothing, I'm sure I could rely on you to lend me a dress. But as a Prince of the Realm, don't you think I might possess something more valuable? Do you think I came back here because Palomar asked me to?"

"Just go," Sedra said with a wave. "Don't let me stop you. It's clear you have your own priorities."

"Return quickly," I said, calling after him as he left. "There isn't much time before sunset." After a pause, I added, "Take Avedis with you. There's some comfort in numbers."

"Avedis?" He gave me a questioning look. "Really?"

I said, "You might be surprised."

With Fenrick's departure, I turned back to the myriad of horns. "Feel anything yet?" I asked Sedra.

"Not yet," Sedra said as she pulled a horn down from the wall. "We'll have to use a bit of White, I'm afraid."

Some horns had banners attached to them. I mentally selected one at random, high up on the wall and out of reach. Attached to it was a banner tattered from the relentless passage of time. It depicted a lion on a field of sable with crossed swords pointing upward, the insignia of the king of Rinstill, house Youngblood.

Calling upon White Magic, I heard the rising melody of my flute begin to dance. Without actually touching the horn, I reached for it in my mind. I felt its weight, its coldness, its strength. I delved deeper into the metal, into the frayed banner.

The flute music was soon lost in the presence of a single note delivered in a bright brass timbre, and I found myself captured by a vision. I felt as if I were skimming quickly over a forest canopy, the sky high above startlingly blue. The forest gave way to a city on the edge of a sea. I flew out over a throng of people standing on the quay, looking toward a galleon just coming into the bay, white sails billowing. My flight, straight as an arrow, took me out to that ship, all the while that single note growing louder.

I found myself on the ship, alive again, pressed to the lips of a man who gave me breath. My life was singing, each of my lives a song. I fell into harmony with other horns on shore where hundreds of people lined the dock. Some pointed, some laughed and crowded each other for a better view, but all eyes were on my ship.

I looked about in the bright summer sun to find the source of their curiosity. The rigs were filled with men stowing the main sail and lashing it tight. The captain, bearded and scarred, stood at the wheel and gave orders using the incomprehensible grunts and moans of men.

A man came up from below and stood looking away from me toward the crowd on shore. The sudden roar of the crowd told me this was the man they had come to see.

The stranger stood below me on the quarterdeck, and I looked on in wonder. There was a new sound, a new voice coming from the man. It was like nothing I'd ever heard before. He grunted something in the language of men, but the sound I heard was something else entirely. It echoed fathoms deep, sounding tones of clarity that I had never known, resounding past the edges of mortal hearing.

The stranger scratched the back of his head and laughed in amazement at the gathering, perhaps surprised at his own popularity. The voice grew louder as he raised a hand to wave to the assembled throng. Its tone rose in pitch, harmonizing with its own echo.

The man who gave me life took a breath and I changed pitch to blend with that chord, but my voice was nothing in comparison. That sound became louder yet, and around the fringes of the stranger's figure a light began to glow. The illumination became brighter and followed the border of each wrinkle of his shirt, each hair of his head. It was as if he stood before the sun, shielding me from the blinding illumination but unveiling the light gently so I could come to know some measure of its warmth.

I suddenly realized the source of the light and the voice were the same, and they had always been there, off at the very fringes of awareness. How had I never recognized that voice before? It had always been there like the blue of the sky, the roar of the waves or the cry of the seagull riding the western wind. My voice was its shadow, a failed attempt to recreate its power.

The man pulled me away from his lips, and my voice fell, leaving the stranger's voice ringing pure and clear above the ship. It flew above the waves, above the shouts of the people on the quay who seemed to feel the voice more than they could hear it. It flew above all, shooting up and out into the cloudless blue sky to be carried by the wind far and wide, and to fall like rain-shine down upon everything and everyone.

* * *

As the image faded from my mind, I became myself once more. I had to pause and take a breath. Could that have been the sound of High Magic? The sound of music accompanying magic was nothing new, but that sound . . . I could feel my heart pumping, invigoration flowing through my limbs and out to my fingers. And that was just from the memory.

And who was that aboard the ship? Could there be any doubt that this was one of the Knights of the Realm? But which one? I'd never seen any purported accurate image of any of the male knights: Evendale, Derif, Brenner, or Merrick.

Did the horn give me this particular memory because I was looking for Evendale, or was that the last time the horn had been sounded? Evendale lived so long ago that this horn surely must have been blown since.

This wasn't the horn we were looking for. Even though it showed me a knight, the vision had nothing to do with bringing the knights back. On the contrary, Evendale, if that was him, paid no heed to the sound of the horn, not even turning around to acknowledge its song. I never even saw his face.

The next horn I chose was a dented and abused bugle. With the White Magic flute melody sparkling in my mind and through my veins, I reached into this horn just as before.

As my previous vision had been filled with light, so this one plunged me into darkness and alarm. Shouts and confusion raged amid the cry of the horn filling my ears. A man stood before me, shouting something unintelligible.

The guttural barking of the man might make no sense to me, but my purpose was clear. There was danger and people had to be warned.

Flames burst from a doorway and a window out into the street where we stood. The flames were molten hot and licked the side of the house with desire. Across the street a portion of a blank stone wall transformed into a wooden door that suddenly exploded out into the street. Still on fire, it slid across the cobblestones coming to rest in a mound of grass. The grass began to grow and snake upward, turning orange and purple as it writhed in the heat.

Someone screamed as a pillar of marble exploded straight out of a rooftop, sending fiery shingles raining. The man who gave me life ran, and my breathing stopped.

Alive again, warning the night, I sounded anew. We were in a different place, a conjunction of roads lined with carts. People were running everywhere. The road before us caught fire and rose as if alive, an undulating mass of waves moving away with tongues of flame riding each crest.

Fear drained from me as I watched the road rise and fall. It was beautiful. It crackled as it moved over the surface. A momentary spout of flame rose, leaving a dozen butterflies fluttering in the air.

The fire was alive. It brought life to the still. I could see it now. All else was dead. In that warmth I would find life, in that passion I will exist as never before. We walked toward the flames, and I cried out in exultation, calling all to join us.

And then a new sound drew my attention. Across the sky, above the din of shouts and penetrating through the crackle of the yellow tongues, the voice drew me. Crystal clear like the sound of a chime, it was higher than all, loud and growing moreso as I listened. It was painfully cold. I wanted to ignore it, but its persistence prevented me.

My desire for the flames diminished. The truth sounding through the voice was undeniable, and I wanted to merge my own voice with that transcendence. To do that I would have to give up the flame, the pleasure it promised, the eternal 'now' that it guaranteed.

The gentle hand of a woman touched me, and we turned around, away from the flames. My voiced was stilled and . . . Before me stood a vision of beauty with eyes that reflected the dance of the abandoned flames. A halo of light brighter than the surrounding flames embraced every fold of her cloak, the curve of her cheek.

The voice that rang with such clarity . . . It was the sound of light . . . the light of a distant dawn now lost to ages past, free and filled with hope.

A rumble of thunder rolled across the sky. The woman glanced up then hastened away, perhaps to help others. Drops of rain ran over me like the tears I wanted to cry. My last vision of her, that halo of light embracing her entire being, was etched into me.

I gave up the false flames, but far harder was giving up that distant and haunting voice that I now knew I'd craved all along.

* * *

I dragged myself out of the horn's memory, wiping tears from my eyes. That was Drewsbury the very night Wild Fire had descended. The High Magic that saved us from walking into the flames told me our savior must have been Lady Lowenna. She'd been there helping Evendale just as the histories had claimed. The glare of the fire behind her had colluded with that all-embracing glimmer of High Magic to make it impossible to discern her face. This was the second time in as many days that I had had a vision of her. But those eyes . . .

I sighed and turned to Sedra. "Any luck?"

"Object reading was never my strong suit, you know. I'm much better with people."

"Nothing interesting?"

"These horns are pretty boring."

I laughed. "You should try some of these."

She gave me a half-smile and a questioning lift to her eyebrow, but before she could speak a scream sounded from the main hall of the keepers. I grabbed my lamp and rushed back through the door.

A hard cold met us in the outer room, far colder than I remembered from the depths below Waterton.

"They're coming," Redd said as he came toward us. "And from the feel of it, they've cut off the exit. Basil! We need another way out."

A ghost dressed in the robes of a Faycan monk walked through a tapestry hanging next to our exit. Brother Basil was the closest and fell quivering to the floor as the full force of the fear overcame him.

I still held White, and the flute in my mind was trilling on a high note of fear. The terror was held at bay for both Sedra and me, but Redd had no such protection.

Sedra said, "I have something I want to try." She closed her eyes, bowed her head, and pressed fingers into her temples.

Redd was breathing hard, sword drawn and backing toward the rear wall. With his grey cloak tossed over his right shoulder his sword arm was free. His eyes darted around as three more ghosts entered the room from the far wall.

"Redd, check the windows," I said. "Maybe we can climb down." It was too late for Basil. As I ran to a window, I watched helplessly as a ghost entered his prone, quivering body. The ghost vanished and Basil went deathly still.

I pushed open the window to see nothing but a dim foggy glow. Even though the sun hadn't set, the ghosts had appeared. Picturing the valley, I realized we must have been in the shadow of the mountain. Even so, that glimmer of light was dim telling me that more time had passed than I'd realized and that darkness was imminent. I berated myself for a fool on a fool's errand. We never should have come here.

There was no easy way down the side of the building and no indication of where we would be if we chose that way. Sedra and I could use White to move Redd and ourselves down, but there simply wasn't enough time. One of us would surely be lost in the effort because we would have to descend one at a time. You can't lift anything when you, yourself, are being lifted.

Best save someone before dying. "Redd. Get over here."

When I looked, Redd was nowhere to be found. Then I heard the ripping of cloth, and I looked to see Redd tearing off a burgundy curtain that had been obscuring a set of doors leading to a balcony across the room. "Over here, Blanchard."

Sedra held her arms out, palms toward the oncoming specters that now numbered more than half a dozen. As they came closer, I could distinguish features on those few without cowls pulled over their heads. They were pale, eyes vacant.

I rushed across the room, past the tables and artifacts, then slowed in amazement. A breeze I could not feel appeared to be ruffling Sedra's hair and cloak, blowing toward the oncoming specters. By evidence of how the ghostly robes were swept back in the same direction, I realized it was spiritual in nature. It changed from a gentle breeze to a wind as I watched, transfixed. Sedra had managed to touch their world.

The wind rose, blowing the cowl off one of the Brothers. Three of the closest ghosts were no longer making forward progress. One stumbled backward clawing at the wind and attempting to grab something to keep him on his feet. No expression crossed his face.

In another moment they were all sent reeling backward to vanish behind the far wall. With their disappearance, Sedra fell to her knees in exhaustion, dragging in air as if she couldn't get enough. Redd sheathed his sword and was at her side before I could move my old body to help her. Grasping Sedra's trembling hands, he pulled her to her feet and supported her weight with an arm wrapped around her waist. "You did it. It was incredible. You were incredible."

Sedra half-smiled and wiped perspiration from her brow. "Thanks," was all she could manage as she put her head on Redd's shoulder.

"Excellent, Sedra," I said. "You may not have destroyed them, but at least we now have more time." The chill was still in the air, telling me the ghosts were only gone for the moment. "Come." I pointed toward Redd's balcony, held my lamp up with the other hand, and started walking that way. "We needn't climb. I'll lower you two down with White and then Sedra can return the favor for me."

The dim glow of the sky was all but gone, and my lamp revealed nothing beyond the balcony limits but a pall of grey fog. The cricket song gave me hope that this balcony overlooked the vineyard and not an inner courtyard which might trap us all the more.

Redd said, "I don't think she's capable of carrying you down with White, Blanchard."

Sedra extricated herself from Redd's support and unsteadily stood on her own. "I'm fine. I can do it."

"Lower me first," Redd said. "We don't know what's down there."

"Very well. Quickly now," I urged, placing my lamp on one of the flat-topped posts of the balustrade. Redd mounted the railing.

Out of the corner of my eye, I noticed the glow of a lamp from below and the sound of Fenrick's voice. Was Avedis with him?

Holding White, I reached out to Redd with my mind. I could sense his coarse grey cloak and the cold vestment of chain just beneath. Feeling his form and his mass, I began to lift. I braced myself against the stone rail of the balcony as the full force of his weight pressed into my mind. I lifted him out over the darkness.

Suddenly, fear swept over us. Redd shouted and, in a reflexive spasm, drew his sword. The sudden movement broke my concentration, and he slipped from my grasp. He fell but managed to catch himself on the outside of the rail with his free arm.

I glanced back toward the hall of the keepers. The ghosts of two Faycan Brothers walked toward us, hoods hiding their faces. Despite White flowing through my blood, a thrill of fear made the hairs on the back of my neck rise.

An invisible wind blew across the balcony that only Sedra and the ghosts could feel. Her clothes billowed again as she sought to repel them a second time. Sedra gasped as suddenly the wind reversed direction. She staggered back toward the balcony edge, her cloak now blowing straight over the rail, her hair flying wildly. The ghosts were fighting back. She knocked the lamp off the rail and it fell, smashing on something below. We were plunged into darkness.

I created a light just in time to witness a gale of immense proportions throw Sedra head over heels into the air and over the rail. Redd must have dropped his sword because he snatched one of her arms. His grasp was the only thing preventing Sedra's senseless body from being blown straight out into the dark. He held onto the rail with only his fingers, and they were slipping.

"Blanchard!" Redd shouted.

The ghosts were three steps away, two. Besides jumping into the unknown, there was no escape. My light wavered and dimmed, the flute music in my mind losing all track of melody. I backed against the rail as the two brothers stepped out onto the balcony. One stopped and slowly turned toward me, the face within his cowl visible by the glow of my light. He had a dark beard and olive skin. Our eyes locked, and I stopped breathing, unable to shout for help or cry out in fear. He took a step toward me.

Chapter Three

Invasion of Privacy

Trevor's room was certainly larger than mine, but it was also kept neater, uncomfortably so. My mother would have used the word immaculate because it wasn't just neat and orderly, but clean too. Trevor dragged a chair in from the dining room because he didn't want me to mess up his bed.

As he sat at his desk, he said, "Now watch carefully this time. I'll show you how I hypnotized the . . . it . . . last night, then you can do it yourself without my help."

"Wait," I said, holding up a hand. "First tell me what I shouldn't do so we don't lose more evidence." When I sat down, I discovered just how thin the cushion on the chair was. My butt was going to get sore.

"It's simple." Turning to his desk, Trevor said, "LMC, can we have some privacy?"

"Certainly, Trevor," the LMC said with an adult male voice. "Reinstate me on your com-pad if you need me."

"Sure."

Trevor's com-pad on the wall over his desk had a small light that began to blink, indicating the LMC was in privacy. Trevor said, "LMC, can you hear me? LMC please respond."

The LMC remained silent, as I expected. "I know what privacy mode is."

When in privacy mode, Emily doesn't pay attention to anything that isn't life threatening. If you decided to make a campfire in the middle of the room or lunge at someone with a knife, then Emily *would* wake up and tell you to quit doing whatever you were doing. And just to be sure the shenanigans would stop, she would alert the authorities.

"Good," Trevor said. "I just wanted to remind you when in privacy mode, the names we give the LMC are not what get to its conscious mind."

The stiff dining room chair was getting uncomfortable, so I got up and leaned on its back. "So you put Emily into privacy mode last night to make her show the vid of Artemus. If that's true, then how did you make her respond to your commands? And how did I wake Emily up when I asked if that guy in the vid was Artemus? She shouldn't have even heard me."

"The LMC wasn't in privacy . . . it was kind of in between. That's why calling it by name woke it up. When in privacy, the LMC shuts the pathways across biax nodes establishing a parallel barrier into and through all semi-cordicals, but only pre-established ones."

I gave him a blank stare. "What?"

Trevor said, "Picture the LMC's memory like a long fence with gates between all the fence posts. When you ask it a question like 'what time is it?', a gate flies open and the information pops out. When in privacy mode, the gates all remain shut. But what happens if you ask it for information stored at one of the ends of the fence where there's no gate?"

"At the end of the fence? Like at the beginning? Emily's first memories?"

"Right. Back in 2028, before the LMC came to Luna, it was used on the human genome project and helped to develop the genome for the cure to Lumus."

I snapped my fingers. "It was the computer at the research facility that created the Lumus-A virus."

"Right, the antigen for Lumus. I found out the LMC will enter its hypnotic state if you put it into privacy mode and say, 'Recall the Lumus-A genome.'"

As I watched, a static-filled image appeared hovering over Trevor's desk. Through the static, I saw page after page of letters separated by dashes scrolling downward. In the foreground, a DNA helix rotated slowly.

Trevor said, "I tried a lot of stuff, but that's the only command that works every time."

"Let's ask it something about Artemus."

"It doesn't work that way. The information that's stored about Artemus will be near the present. This image is from 2028. From here, it's like peeling a banana, like riding the fence. You ask for events or information from periods in the past leading up to the present. If you jump too far in time between the events, it doesn't work."

"How far is too far?" I noticed the DNA helix was replaced with a slowly rotating picture of a woman. "Look, it's . . . it's . . .?"

"That's Dr. Gabrielle Thompson, the genetic engineer who designed Lumus-A."

"Yeah. I thought I recognized her."

"To move closer to the present, you have to ask it to recall stuff no more than about a year apart. That's why it takes so long to get up to the present. And don't mention any of its names like you did this morning, or it will wake up."

"Just a year apart?" I asked incredulously. "All right. We'll wake it up, ask it to prepare a list of these historical events —"

"That would be sharpening pencils. We can't do that."

"Huh?"

Trevor pointed to the picture of the woman hovering above his desk. "What's her name?"

I pursed my lips. "Gabrielle Thompson."

"I just reminded you of her name, right? Now you can recall it easily. I sharpened a pencil with her name on it and I jabbed you with it. Now if you were in a hypnotic state and I jabbed you with a pencil, do you think you'd wake up?"

I paused to absorb this. "You mean . . . You're telling me if we ask her stuff when she's awake—"

Trevor said, "It makes her super sensitive to that data and will wake her up if we ask her when she's hypnotized."

"You've got to be kidding."

We spent the next few hours creating a list of historical events starting from the fall of 2028. I was shocked how little history I could remember, but Trevor was great. As we went, we jotted down the events that worked in Trevor's notepad.

Trevor's hair was a tangled mess after hours of wringing his head for information. He whispered, "All right. Think. What significant event happened in 2070? Why didn't I write these down last night?"

I tapped Trevor's notepad on his desk. "This will be item number forty-two." I took my last gulp of soda. "When was that interstellar probe launched?"

"That was in 2068. But that's good. Put that one down as an alternate for that year. If only 2070 had been an election year."

"What about the visit from the WG President?"

Trevor snapped his fingers. "That's it. Recall the visit of President Patrizia Donatelli."

Over Trevor's desk, an image formed of an aged woman passing through an airlock. With help from a group of dark bodyguards, she moved slowly in the low gravity of Luna into a spaceport filled with cheering people.

Trevor said, "So much for 2070. Now 2071 is easy."

At that moment the chime on Trevor's door sounded. Trevor said, "Come in." It was Dr. Russo.

"Dad. You're back. How was the space station?"

"Hi Trevor, Dennis. Indy was cold and spinning. What are you two doing?"

Trevor glanced at me. "We're doing some research . . . for school."

Dr. Russo yawned and rubbed his eyes. "Isn't it a little late for that?"

"Come on, it's only about 9:30," Trevor said.

"It has to be later than that." Dr. Russo tilted his head to the side and raised his voice. "Theodore, what's the time?" Trevor scrunched his face into a grimace and mouthed the word, 'No.' When the picture of President Donatelli suddenly vanished, I realized Dr. Russo had just woken the LMC out of its hypnotic state.

A smooth male voice came from the com-pad. "The current time is 9:42 PM, Dr. Russo. You look rather tired. Unfortunately, Elene is in communication with her mother on Earth, or I would prepare your room for your sleep."

"I think I'll turn in anyway. Dennis, maybe you should be getting home. You have all of Sunday to finish your homework."

"But . . . but we're not done," I said.

Trevor yawned and propped his head up with an arm on his desk. "It's okay, Dennis. We've got the list."

I gripped the pad in my hand tighter. We could duplicate every step through Emily's memory. "But we didn't get all the way back to the present," I whispered.

"Close enough," Trevor said. "I'm beat. Take it home with you if you want. See what you can find out."

* * *

Emily wouldn't take the hypnotic suggestions very quickly. I had to wait over a minute after each one before she would accept the next item on the list. So, back in my own room, it took until just after 11:00 PM before I returned Emily back to 2070 where we had left off.

I remembered it was some time in the year 2071 when Artemus purchased his share in Sybernetics International. "Recall Artemus Regale and his purchase of SI."

The last scene of President Donatelli waving to the crowd wavered but did not vanish. Could it be more than a year from the president's visit?

"Recall Artemus Regale's first move toward becoming President of SI."

The scene changed to show a room that looked like a library in a mansion. Mahogany bookshelves filled with dark volumes lined the walls and surrounded a desk at which a wizened old man sat. "Artemus Regale. What a curious name."

The view zoomed out slightly, and I saw Artemus sitting before the desk as if being interviewed. Artemus said, "Sir Ignatius—"

"I'm an old man, Artemus, so let us dispense with formality. You may call me Sir Simon." He smiled. Maybe it was his idea of a joke. Sir Simon Ignatius was the original founder of SI. Hmm. For the first time, I wondered if there was a connection between his initials and the company name.

"Sir Simon, declarative knowledge transfer is not as far off as people imagine."

Sir Simon waved his hand. "Yes, yes. My people have been researching declarative knowledge for years with no success."

"I have become old pursuing my mission. I know no other way to proceed than the development of this technology."

"My people have told me about your mission, Artemus. I believe we're all on a mission from God, of sorts. The trick would be to figure out what it is. Each mission could be as different from the next as Frankenstein is to Pasteur. I would be a failure if I sought to halt progress, but there is an ethical dilemma looming. It gives me pause."

"What ethical dilemma?" Artemus asked.

"Consider the fictional Dr. Frankenstein and his reanimation efforts. Though macabre to be sure, he was seeking eternal life. If someone dies, simply attach electrodes, turn some dials and a bolt of lightning later the deceased is walking and talking."

"I fail to see how Shelley's *Frankenstein* has any bearing on—"

Sir Simon grunted in frustration. "Permit me to make it more plain. Today we can encode and imprint procedural knowledge. Once declarative knowledge is in our hands, how much further need we push our technology until it's possible to encode and imprint an entire engrammic set from one person onto another? How long before you can take anyone you please, wipe their mind, and transfer your own into their body? We need not reanimate our flesh, but merely select new bodies as today we choose our clothing. Are you disturbed by this possibility, or is that the very end you seek?"

Artemus shook his head. "Even were it possible, the mind in the new body would only be a copy of the former. What of the spirit?"

"What of the spirit, indeed? The spirit is willing, but the flesh is weak. Is the soul of man real or as fictional as Frankenstein? I fear we'll only realize the truth after we begin populating the world with heartless undead."

Sir Simon paused as if a thought struck him. "Erasmus, privacy mode if you please."

The picture filled with static in moments and the library was gone. It didn't sound as if Artemus had been purchasing SI. It was more like he was asking Sir Simon if he could work on the DK project. It didn't make sense. How did he become the president of the company?

With a yawn, I pressed the button on my com-pad to reinstate Emily. I could work on it more tomorrow after some sleep. Then I had another thought. "Emily, begin privacy mode."

"Of course Dennis," she said. "Entering privacy mode now."

If Emily recorded everything at all times, using Trevor's hypnosis trick, anyone could spy on me. At least in privacy mode she stopped recording me.

Chapter Four

He Craves by Nature

I stood defenseless before the ghost of the Faycan Brother, a single breath away. Even if I could have taken command of my quivering legs long enough to jump over the balcony rail, the fall into darkness was no escape. The fragments of rationality afforded by my grasp on White were crumbling, and the flute music in my mind raced across scales out of tune.

Out of the corner of my eye, I saw a sudden gleam in the mist. A brilliant light coming from below threw my shadow up on the wall to my left. The ghost, casting no shadow, stopped in mid-stride and slowly turned to face the light. As his eyes unlocked their hold on me, my lungs heaved for breath.

I looked down at the light and realized it was Avedis. His use of White drew the ghost away. I heard Fenrick shout from below. "Would you kill that blasted light? We'll be surrounded in seconds."

It was true. Bound by no natural law, the ghost that nearly had me was walking through the stone rail, aiming itself downward toward the light. It seemed to have completely forgotten about us. Even the spiritual wind blowing Sedra's senseless body straight away from the balcony diminished, and she fell. Only Redd's grasp on her arm prevented her from plunging down.

My eyes flicked back to his hold on the balcony edge. It slipped a bit. Redd said, "Blanchard, do something."

Avedis' light faltered just as the ghost who'd almost taken me stood in mid-air beside Redd and Sedra. Surely Redd's fingertip hold on the stone rail wouldn't last much longer.

I shouted, "Avedis, No! Burn brightly. Draw them to you and I'll keep you safe. We'll protect each other." There was no time to explain further. The ghost turned toward Redd.

Avedis' body shone through the mist. His body was the source of the light, a trick I had taught him some months ago. It was easier than maintaining a separate hovering light. Now able to see him, I could move him. He stood forty feet below in a courtyard of stone ringed on the perimeter by five large trees. Reaching out with White, I felt his thick outer cloak, his tight leather jerkin underneath. He would be much lighter than Redd. I began to lift.

"Blanchard," Redd said. "I'm slipping."

With my mind tuned on Avedis, I snatched Redd's hand as his fingers lost purchase. I was nearly pulled over with Redd and Sedra as the full force of their combined weight doubled me over the rail. The stone below would mean certain death.

"Pull us up," Redd said. "Use White."

"Busy . . . Avedis." Still I lifted Avedis, though more slowly with my concentration divided. He passed the height of the balcony.

Redd gasped. "Blanchard, look out! The ghosts are returning."

I couldn't look at anything except the top of Redd's head. I shouted, "Avedis, shine brighter! Brighter I say!" The White I used to lift Avedis was drawing them back to me, but I knew Avedis was capable of more.

Redd repeated my command to Avedis with a shout, and a moment later it felt and looked as if it were day. Even from this distance, I could feel the hum of power that poured through Avedis.

"Good Lord," Redd said.

"They're coming," Avedis called from the air. "Keep me moving."

My grip on Redd began to weaken, but his single grip on my wrist was steel. "Redd, tell me where the ghosts are. Which way should I move Avedis?"

"I can't see anything. He's too bright."

I continued to lift Avedis straight upward. "I need a path back to the ground. What of Sapphire? Can she see down from above? Try looking through her eyes."

Redd closed his eyes, seeking his connection with the kestrel.

White poured through my veins, but the flute melody was becoming choppy as if it were missing notes. The strain of Avedis' weight made me light-headed. If I lost consciousness as Sedra had, four lives would be lost, mine not the least. Must hang on.

Redd's voice sounded remote. "Sapphire's high, circling Avedis. She must be curious, but the light is too bright for her. She never looks directly at him."

"The ghosts! Where are the ghosts?" Avedis was over a hundred and fifty feet up and rising. I was nearing my limits, and I realized I wouldn't be able to carry him back down. A black taste filled my mouth.

Redd's grip weakened as he concentrated on Sapphire. "There are dozens surrounding him. All below. His is the flame atop a great candlestick, the ghosts forming a cup below to catch his essence. I've never seen the like."

"How wide? How wide is the circle of the ghosts?"

"Fifteen, no, twenty wingspans."

"Wingspans?" Couldn't he give me something I could use? Lost in the fascination of rapport, the strength in Redd's grip vanished. "Redd. Great Tishman!" He slipped from my grasp and there was nothing left but to guess. With a massive final push of White, I cast Avedis up and toward me, hopefully enough to get him past the ring of ghosts as he fell.

Releasing Avedis, I turned my mind to Redd and Sedra, now five feet below and both blissfully unaware of their own plummet. The shock of their combined weight took my breath, but I stopped their fall. Feeling the blood pulsing through my eyes and teeth, I pulled with White and they rose, yet agonizingly slow.

Still shining like a star, Avedis screamed from above as he fell toward us.

"Redd! Wake up. Take my hand."

Finally aware of his own peril, Redd awoke and reached up. Thankfully, he still held onto Sedra, and, strengthening my limbs with White, I pulled them up. In moments they were over the rail and safe.

When I glanced up, Avedis' illumination and descent toward us made me blink. I focused on his screaming form and pushed upward with ragged shreds of White. Before I could slow him much, he crashed into the three of us, and together we collapsed in a heap. On impact, Avedis' light vanished.

Half buried beneath Redd and Sedra, I felt no pain. The sweet release of White made me feel like a feather wafting on unseen currents of air. I thought I heard Avedis moan, Redd grunt and make a comment, but the gentle darkness covering me like a blanket detached all concerns. I felt adrift on a raft floating gently in a cove. Locust song mingled with the sound of swaying trees overhead. Sun-dappled water lapped rhythmically on the side of my raft, and my hands and feet dangled carefree in cool water. Nowhere to go. Nothing to be done. The thought of long hours of drowse stretching before me made my eyelids droop. Rest—

Pain. What? Again, pain across my face and the sounds of someone shouting. What was happening?

My eyes fell into focus on the face of Sir Welling Redd. What was he doing here? Pain shot again twice across both my cheeks, and I realized I was being slapped.

"Wake up, Blanchard. Come on. I can't carry both of you."

My mouth tasted of bile, and I clutched my head as throbs of lancing pain exploded across my forehead. It wasn't Redd's blows but rather the aftermath of too much White. "I'm awake, I'm awake."

Redd dragged me to my feet. "The ghosts are returning. We have to move."

I leaned heavily on the wall and breathed deeply. The pain of the headache lessened slightly. Redd picked Sedra off the floor and put her over his right shoulder.

Avedis stood at the doorway with a glowing ball of light floating just overhead. "Hurry. They're coming."

I looked up to see a cloud of ghostly shapes in the sky, fifty feet away and descending. They were relentless.

Avedis glanced over the rail. "What of Prince Fenrick?"

"He knows Olindara better than any of us," Redd said. "Let's go."

With Avedis in the lead, I followed Redd as we descended the long stairs leading back the way we had come, back to the front gate.

The ghosts were catching up to us. They didn't have to navigate hallways and stairwells as is the fashion of the living. As quickly as we could, we passed the gates of the compound and found our mounts. The approaching menace, though no threat to the horses, made them skittish. At Redd's bidding, Avedis and I helped lift Sedra to sit astride Redd's horse just in front of him. He held her with one arm and the reins with the other. It was then I noticed Redd's sword was missing. He'd never had a chance to recover it.

I pulled the reins of my horse free and mounted. Nearby, Fenrick's horse, Rage, was still tied to his post.

Avedis untied Sedra's horse and led her toward his own. "Prince Fenrick must still be inside," Avedis said.

"Maybe there are no more Faycan Brothers in Rapt," Redd said. "And there's no time to find out."

My eyes followed Redd's gaze back toward the gate. Half a dozen ghostly brothers had already passed through the walls. Their cloaks riffled in an unfelt breeze. I dug my heels into my horse and he eagerly followed Redd.

* * *

We were on the road north to Sojourn to report our failure to the king and Palomar, who no doubt would have arrived already. I didn't relish the thought of confronting the High King with news of the demise of his fourth son. There was a chance he yet lived.

Redd would rejoin the rest of his company, and, after a respite, we would make for the ruins of Antara, which was even farther north. Who exactly would be continuing on was in question. Our numbers were dwindling.

Brother Basil and Fenrick. I shook my head. There was nothing we could do for either of them.

Sedra. She was yet dead to the world. Would she wake again? Even if she did, she would need rest, not a mad dash by horseback in the rain to search ruins for clues . . .

It would fall to Avedis and myself. And this body was far too old for such adventures.

With many hours of darkness left before dawn, we followed a well-worn road through Tawall Wood. The darkness would have been complete but for Avedis. He held a torch up high so we could see the road. We'd agreed it would be foolish to use White.

Just before a small stream swollen from the weather, Redd, in the lead, reined in his steed and brought us to a halt. "She's waking up." He was holding Sedra in front of him. Sapphire, who'd been flying low over our heads, found a perch in a nearby tree. I nudged my horse a few steps forward.

Sedra moaned and held her head. "Where am I?"

She seemed startled at the sound of Redd's voice. "We're on the road to Sojourn."

I said, "The ghosts of the Faycan Brothers retaliated against your spiritual wind. You passed out but Redd managed to carry you."

Sedra looked about, still groggy. The drone of locusts, cicadas, and crickets surrounded us, pressing the night in.

"Can you manage to ride on your own?" I asked. "It would better our speed by half again if Redd wasn't forced to balance you. This incessant drizzle seems to enjoy making me miserable. The quicker a roof is over our heads, the better." As if to punctuate my sentiment, Avedis sneezed.

She shook her head slowly. "I feel dizzy. I don't think I could ride on my own just yet." She glanced back at Redd. "That is, if you don't mind?"

"A rider approaches," Avedis said. I finally heard the sound of hooves at full gallop. It sounded like just a single horse.

Redd reached for his sword, then grimaced when he found nothing there. "It sounds like only one, coming from Olindara."

I turned my mount around, readying myself in case the newcomer was bent on ill intent. Bearing a lantern in one hand, the single horseman entered our circle of light at full speed. He attempted to rein in his steed, but the horse was eager for the road. He became rampant, and a bag fell from the back of his saddle.

"Fenrick!" Redd said. "We thought you dead."

"But for some quick thinking, I would have been. But I know Olindara almost as well as the palace. My home away from home." I noticed he was now armed. A quiver of arrows at his back and a bow slung around his breast was not all. At his side was a sword.

I said, "It's good to see you still breathing."

He glanced about our little party. "Where's Basil?"

I shook my head grimly.

Fenrick looked down. "He was a good fellow." Then he looked to Redd and something occurred to him. He quickly dismounted, saying, "I suppose I'm the last Faycan Brother."

Avedis dismounted too.

"Too bad you don't adhere to their precepts," Sedra said.

"I might make a poor brother, Lady Sedra," He started to unstrap something from his saddlebags. "But as a son of the King Most High, I come to no measure at all. I believe this is yours?"

Redd's eyes lit up. "My sword. Ah, it is good to have it back."

"I thought you might miss it. One edge looks blunted from the fall, but the other is still sharp. If we are going to Sojourn, you may need it."

Redd said, "There hasn't been any sign of hillkin—"

"I'm not talking about those brutes. Sojourn may not be Ardon, but where the High King goes, so goes his court."

"What's wrong with the court?" Sedra asked.

"Politics and intrigue," Fenrick said with a scowl. He seemed to make note of Sedra riding with Redd but said nothing about it.

Avedis came up behind him, holding a large satchel. "This fell off your horse, Prince Fenrick."

"I'll take that," Fenrick said as he snatched the satchel from Avedis' hands. The bag caught on the knife strapped to Fenrick's arm and sliced open. Gold coins poured out into the mud, followed by a chalice and a jeweled knife.

"What's all this?" I asked.

"Nothing," Fenrick said as he stooped to recover the valuables.

Redd said, "It looks as if we weren't the only ones busy in Olindara."

"I have gambling debts to pay off in Sojourn, or I'm no better than dead. Besides, all the brothers are gone. They've no use for this wealth."

I said, "There's no honor in stealing from the dead and no glory to be found dicing."

"Don't act so high and mighty, Blanchard. It just so happens that gambling is the only fun I get out of this godforsaken world. Look at you," he waved to Redd. "You've got a Duchy to rule, a host of men at your command, normally anyway. And a legendary Kestrel as a constant companion.

"And you Sol? You have White Magic at your fingertips. You're one of the few mages in the entire realm who can perform Old Magic.

"And what do I have? Oh, I'm a Prince of the Realm, all right. Do people know me? They point and say, 'See, there's the one with the hair.' *The hair.* I get cast out into the back woods, simply because I am fourth in line." He began lashing down his saddlebags.

"We make our own beds, Fenrick," I said. "The things worth having take effort to obtain."

"I was born fourth. There was nothing I could do to prevent that. The cards were stacked against me. Being fourth means no magic because I'm too close to the throne and no glory because I'm too far."

Redd shook his head. "You were born a Youngblood. That means you were dealt four of a kind, but that wasn't good enough for you. You decided to draw."

"Yeah, right." Fenrick finished with his saddlebags and remounted his horse. "I think I'll ride on ahead—by your leave, of course."

Before he rode off, I said, "Fenrick, remember. In this world, we are who we make ourselves to be. Abandon the gambling."

"You don't get it, do you? It's not gambling that has gotten me into debt. It's losing." With that, his steed leapt the small stream ahead of us and he rode off alone.

* * *

We arrived at Sojourn with the dismal dawn. The clouds still hid the sky, and the drizzle continued unabated. Flowing just past the city was the Jesra River, hidden by rain and mist. I wondered if the rain was swelling its banks.

I was so tired that it was a continual battle to stay awake and in my saddle. Duplicating Sedra's defense would be impossible without rest. The thought of a real bed seemed like a dream. Forty-eight hours had passed since I'd last closed my eyes. It seemed like a week.

We passed through a tent city, causing not a stir. Hundreds of people traveled from afar for the annual Festival of Light, their tents dotting the fields surrounding the city walls. Most were still sleeping, and the few people I saw were attempting to get fires going. Ghosts must not have visited here last night.

At the gate to the city, we met a company of the Regal Guard, six in number. The head of the small contingent was Faraday, captain of the guard, a man well known to me. He was a stout and sturdy man, older but by no means old, his grizzled, grey beard notwithstanding. We declared ourselves, and the captain told us they were warned to look for our arrival by Prince Fenrick, who had passed the gate not an hour before.

I asked about the Jesra, and, according to him, dikes were being built against the possibility of a flood. "But between you and me," Faraday said confidentially, "there won't be much need if the ghosts get here first. There is evil in the air." I gathered that our ghost problem wasn't common knowledge yet.

Faraday and two of his men escorted us toward the citadel. As we rode, I noted the city proper had expanded since last I was here. Shops and markets along every street showed the signs of prosperity.

Soon we passed the old fortifications and entered the heart of Sojourn where King Tendas and his court would be staying. Hopefully there was room for us. I glanced at Redd and Sedra. She seemed more animated, returning to herself, but what damage had been done, I couldn't tell. The mages could care for her and try to restore her health, but how long would that take? I doubted we had much time before . . . some unpleasantness.

Palomar had sent word that he wished to meet with me as soon as we arrived, so before finding any rest I had to see the Potentate. I was neither in the mood nor prepared for another one of our verbal duels, but I refused to face him cold and wet, and no doubt my cold and wet clothes felt the same. So, after being shown to a small room, I took the opportunity to change into something plain but at least dry.

* * *

"Palomar."

He was sitting out on a balcony that overlooked the city and perhaps the quay. As it was, the view offered little more than the sight of a grey shroud enveloping the rooftops below. Thunder echoed off in the distance.

Without turning around, Palomar said, "Sol, please come. Join me." He was seated in his wheel-bound chair and drinking something that had the unmistakable odor of cinnamon tea. In the corner of the room, Palomar's manservant was sitting, leaning back on the wall, asleep. I felt a bit of jealousy rise in my chest at the sight. Pursing my lips, I hobbled slowly out to the balcony rail and discovered it was dry. Another balcony above protected us from the falling wetness. Pulling a chair from beside the door, I sat by his side.

"Where are my manners? Can we get you some tea?" Palomar asked with an amiability that rang counterfeit. Friendly conversation with Palomar invariably was an act of manipulation. It was his ambition. He took another sip of his steaming brew, and the ruby ring he wore caught my eye.

"I need rest, not tea," I said. "Besides, your servant is asleep."

"What did you find at Olindara? Prince Fenrick was altogether unhelpful, not willing to spend even a moment on just a few simple questions."

"You saw Fenrick, then?"

"As sopping wet as when last we met, and just as impudent. After a row with one of his brothers, maybe Prince Hallam, he rushed back out into the city like a man possessed."

Fenrick's behavior was unsettling, but there were more important things to discuss. "We didn't find the horn or any bells at Olindara. As Fenrick reported to us at Waterton, the place was filled with the ghosts of the brothers. We misjudged the onset of night, and it was almost our undoing."

"You seem to have survived, and thank goodness for that."

"The good news is that Sedra had some success in combating the ghosts. Using White, she was able to manifest a spiritual wind that had some effect on the specters."

Palomar raised his eyebrows. "Really? Where is she now?

"She may have overextended herself. The ghosts fought back in kind. She needs rest."

Palomar's brow furrowed. He looked out into the mist. "I suspect the ghosts will be upon us well before she has a chance to show any other mage what she has found. Regrettable, but . . . fortunately not all hope has died." Palomar smiled.

"Has Wren succeeded with the exorcisms?"

"Oh, Wren has kept busy teaching all the full mages what little he knows about Thedof Dern's techniques. Foolish man. In his small way, he's trying to save us, but it will amount to nothing. He's never even cut his teeth on one of these ghosts, so who knows if these exorcisms will work?

"But perhaps the future is not as dim as the evil one would have us believe," continued Palomar. "Perhaps this ghostly assault is less a curse and more a blessing in disguise."

"A blessing? What are you getting at?" I asked.

"The Knights of the Realm, Sol, were deeply disappointed in us. And why? Can you tell me?"

"I'm too weary for philosophy."

"Disappointment, Sol. It is the same . . . take young Prince Fenrick for example. I know little of his business, but I certainly see his rash behavior and his impudent attitude. What could cause such abhorrent behavior? I'll tell you. He grew up pampered in the palace, indulged with all his heart's desires, for want of nothing. Now he's unable to earn the respect of his father. The King is sorely disappointed in him.

"It's the same disappointment the knights felt toward us. I'm convinced that after lying in their protective hands, generation after generation, we lost the ability to learn the hard lessons. We lost High Magic. Mortal danger, the kind that we face now, may be just the thing to break us out of our doldrums. Faced with annihilation, there is no other hope than to rediscover High Magic ourselves."

"Or call back the Knights of the Realm to help us."

"Is that really something we want? Think a moment." Palomar paused to take another sip of tea and at the same time finger his ring. He seemed to do it without even noticing. "What if, as you say, they are out there? What if you somehow succeed in calling the knights back? No doubt they could easily deal with this little problem facing us, but look farther down the line, Sol. I don't think they will be too impressed with how far we've come."

"We shouldn't be concerned with impressing anyone. By Tishman, there are people's lives at stake here." I looked out over the shrouded city and thought about the families that would be destroyed, the children who would never grow old.

"Oh, I agree. We must certainly do whatever is in our power to save the realm. Heavens, if we fail there won't even be a realm. But answer me this. Didn't the knights leave us for a particular reason, Sol?"

My head was spinning. "I don't remember why they left. There were many theories."

"They left so that we would stop depending upon them and stand on our own two feet. We stopped learning High Magic because they were already here guarding us. Who needs to learn to defend themselves if someone else does it for them? These ghosts are what we need to shock us out of complacency. We will either learn High Magic or be wiped from the face of the world."

I shook my head. "If you're trying to convince me that searching for the knights is a waste of time, I can't agree. I'm not willing to wager the realm based on your speculation, and the King would agree with me. It is far better to stay alive now and worry about learning High Magic later, after the danger has passed."

"Ahh, but it is my suspicion that the only reason we have never been able to learn High is because we always played it safe. You never know how far or fast you can run until there's a pack of wolves chasing you."

Palomar looked at me with an intense stare and one eyebrow slightly raised; the kind of stare that always made a shiver run up my spine. Urgently, he continued, "You and I, Sol. We're alike in many ways. We recognized at once that High Magic was our only hope. You went off searching for a way to call the Knights of the Realm, to call someone, anyone, who could work High Magic against these creatures."

He chuckled to himself, saying, "How often it is that what we most want, what we desperately seek, was in our grasp from the very start. You might have failed, but there was still a chance that in our hour of need we would stretch our own abilities and find High Magic at last."

Palomar held his hand aloft, and the red ring he wore blazed forth with a startlingly bright light.

"High Magic, Sol. High Magic at my fingertips." The red light grew more intense as I watched until everything appeared to have a red cast, even the misty rain. I was forced to shield my eyes and look away.

"You have reawakened the ring," I exclaimed, now fully awake myself.

"I have indeed. Oh, I wasn't going to tell you at first, but I began to see there was no turning you from your quest for the knights. I had hoped that at the last hour you yourself might find High Magic as I have."

"Incredible . . ." The light flickered like the light of a fire. Palomar's shadow danced minutely on the floor. He lowered his hand, and the light dimmed, but did not vanish.

"I fear I have done you a disservice," Palomar said. "I shouldn't have revealed this thing to you."

"But why? This is wonderful news. How did you do it?"

"Perhaps now that you know I possess this power, you won't have the impetus to find High yourself. And if I told you how I came to this knowledge, you would never find it. But, as conciliation, at least now you can rest easy knowing there is hope."

"I think—now I *can* rest."

"Yes, go and sleep. You can abandon your search for the Knights of the Realm, for we needn't fear any longer. Go now."

I walked across his bedchamber and found my feet were lighter, my riding muscles less painful. Beyond all expectation, Palomar had accomplished something no one had been able to approach for hundreds of years. High Magic, at long last. It was so surprising. Palomar craved power by nature, so his desire for High Magic was never to be doubted, but it always seemed to me that, for High Magic at least, the desire itself might only serve to subvert the attainment.

The words of the Inadel minstrel came echoing back to me. "All the men survive and shed no tears for their wives." We would survive. It was going to come true, just as he foretold.

I placed a hand on the door latch and stopped. Something was bothering me, something Palomar had said about Wren. Wren hadn't tested his exorcism skill on real ghosts. We didn't know if Palomar's ring of High Magic worked either, did we? He was as untested as Wren. Glancing back, I noticed the bedcovers had hardly been disturbed. Perhaps Palomar was worried and had gotten as little sleep as I.

I shook my head to dismiss the lingering doubt. Everything was going to be fine.

I opened the door, and a woman's scream of terror echoed down the corridor. Her piercing voice went right through me. It was daytime, so this could be no ghostly assault. I was still trying to get my bearings when Captain Faraday turned the corner at the end of the hall and rushed toward me, searching for the source of the distress.

Chapter Five

Brimstone

A rtemus was waiting for me at the Descartes tram station. He wore a grim smile, and I had to wonder what he had planned. Perhaps today I would meet some of the other team members.

"Dennis, at last."

"Mr. Regale—I mean Artemus. I—I guess I haven't seen you in a while."

"Come along. I'm not getting any younger standing about here."

I walked by his side and noticed he had no limp or sign of injury. There goes another theory. "Where are we going?"

"We are moving into the second stage."

"What's that?"

"You'll see."

We turned away from the university office complex and walked into an elevator. I held my breath as the door closed.

Artemus said, "Home, Francesca."

Home? We'd been trying to sneak in there via the mech-tunnels for so long, and now I was being whisked right into it.

The LMC answered in a female voice, "I'm sorry, Artemus, but Dennis Howard does not have the required clearances."

Artemus sighed and put his hand on the com-pad. "Yes, yes. Verify."

"Verification complete."

Artemus withdrew his hand. "Override level 5 clearance lockout, authorization Regale, Venerable-Pan-2138."

"Non-coercion verified," Francesca said. "Proceeding. Dennis, I suggest you hold on."

Following Artemus' example, I grasped the bar ringing the inside of the elevator. Suddenly we accelerated downward so quickly that I would have banged my head on the ceiling had I not been holding on. There wasn't any padding in this elevator.

As I recalled, his home spanned four levels. It was so mammoth that none of us could figure out why no mech-tunnel seemed to connect to it. Trying to hide my excitement, I asked, "Where exactly are we headed? I thought it might be some research facility at the university."

"I do most of my work at home, a home few people have seen, by the way. You're about to enter the SI habitat experiment code named Jessica-1. I'm trusting you to keep what you see here to yourself."

I shrugged. "Sure. Ah, so . . . It's a habitat experiment? Are there others?"

"This is the only one."

As the elevator decelerated to a stop, the weight on my feet momentarily doubled. The doors slid silently open.

Without a backward glance, Artemus strode out and said, "The original architect named it the Silver Wood."

I stepped through the door and into an arboretum. The smell and feel of the warm humid air was a shock. I bet it was warmer here than anywhere on Luna, even before the explosion. The floor was real dirt. I felt like I was really outside on Earth.

But . . . This was no normal arboretum like we have in Aristoteles. It was far larger than I'd ever seen. I couldn't even see the far wall, and the trees, elm, poplar, and maple, grew up and up toward a ceiling hidden from view by a bank of leaves. I caught glimpses of blue above, just like a real sky. We were so far below the surface there was no chance of getting direct sunlight in here, yet it wasn't dark. Artemus must have piped the light in from the surface but on a massive scale. It could pass for natural daytime on Earth.

There was a slight breeze rustling the leaves but no birdsong. Even the tiny arboretums scattered around Luna had birds, but I guess there weren't any here. It made the place more eerie.

I looked back and found the door to the elevator gone. It was disguised to look like the side of a rocky canyon wall, or maybe it was behind a 3-D vid of a rock wall. Some kind of bush with red berries grew up on either side of the hidden door, further obscuring it from view.

Artemus was five steps ahead down the dirt path. I quickened my pace. "You live here?" I asked.

"What does that even mean, really?" Artemus asked. "I live wherever I happen to be. If the question is 'do you sleep here,' then the answer is yes."

The path descended down a slope and at the bottom was what appeared to be a stream. I couldn't believe my eyes. I looked up again and saw what could only be clouds floating by. He must have the largest 3-D projector I ever heard of.

Breathing deeply of the pine-scented air, I spread my arms wide. It was wonderful. I closed my eyes and felt that breeze brush my face. I laughed and looked back into the sky. "I feel like I'm really outside. Did Sir Simon create this forest? The trees look older than nine years."

Artemus stopped and turned back to me. "It sounds as if you've been doing some research."

I swallowed. "Research? Naw. Doesn't everyone know how long you've been in charge of SI?"

Artemus smiled. "Perhaps so. I didn't think people much cared."

Once we crossed the stream, by way of a stone footbridge, I saw a cottage off in the middle of a grassy glade. It had a stone chimney on the side and a thatched roof all nestled under a large oak. The path led right to the door. Vines covered the side and most of the chimney as if the cottage had been there for fifty years. I stopped to look around and take in the scene. There was no hint we weren't anywhere but deep within a forest, perhaps in some foothills in France or Italy. I sighed. "I don't want to go inside."

"Inside, outside—It's all illusion, a construct of your mind. There are no sides, just places." Artemus pulled open the door, and we walked into the cottage. A carpeted veranda ran the inside circumference of the cottage overlooking a room far below. A sweeping staircase three meters wide circled downward into what looked like a foyer. A crystal chandelier was suspended in the center of the circle by three chains emerging from just under the veranda.

I followed Artemus down the spiral staircase, still trying to take it all in. An ornate circular carpet partially covered a hardwood floor. The carpet depicted a long worm-like dragon with wings. The dragon was surrounded by fire and what looked like piles of gold.

Three glass-paned double doors led to hallways going off in every direction. The largest stood open revealing a descent of five steps into a ballroom.

"It's a mansion," I whispered. A mansion hidden in a cottage, nestled in a forest, standing in a room twenty or thirty floors below the surface.

"The work of Sir Simon. He named the mansion Brimstone, and this foyer is the center. The complex extends off in all directions underneath the Silver Wood."

A man in a tuxedo opened one of the glass doors and entered the foyer. He was younger than my father and had neatly combed black hair and a goatee. He closed the door without turning away from us. "Master Regale. You have returned."

"Yes, Lawrence. Meet Dennis Howard."

"Master Howard." He shook my hand and nodded. "Is there anything I can do for you, sirs?"

"Lunch will be at twelve sharp," Artemus said. "We will take it atop the South Tower."

"Very good."

"Follow me, Dennis. We'll begin immediately."

My mouth became dry at the thought of more work. We left Lawrence in the foyer and passed through one of the smaller glass doors.

"Is Lawrence the only other person here?" I felt nervous at the thought of being alone with Artemus.

"Brimstone has a staff of fifteen servants. Their quarters are also under the Silver Wood but in a separate section off to the north."

After a pause I asked, "How many researchers are on the project?"

"They'll be monitoring things remotely. There's no point in meeting them."

So he was sticking to that. I wouldn't be meeting any of the other team members.

I walked by his side as we passed through a billiard room with four full-size tables and a bar across the back wall. Forest green covers were draped over all the tables giving them an untouched quality as if they hadn't been used in years.

The mansion was a maze. After descending a flight of stairs, we traversed another hall that twisted and turned, full of closed doors. Opening one side of a double door, Artemus and I entered a study with paneling covering the walls. Above a fireplace was a portrait of an old man in a chair.

"Sir Simon," I said, stopping to look at his ancient face. He had a stern look and a cane in his left hand.

"And over there is his wife, Jessica."

On the opposite wall stood another fireplace and portrait. This painting portrayed a young woman in a conservatory. She had a wide-brimmed hat pushed back on her head and a flower in her hand. Light streamed through the windows around her.

"She looks a bit younger than Sir Simon."

Artemus smiled. "That is Lady Jessica as she was in her youth, in her glory." Artemus' voice fell as if he was remembering something.

None of the information we found on Artemus mentioned any family. "So you never married? Never had any kids?"

Artemus' smile vanished and he started walking toward a door beside the fireplace. "We won't be disturbed, if that's your concern. The servants know better than to interrupt me."

I followed and changed the subject. "How long will this phase two take? All week?"

"You're full of questions. Phase two will last as long as it takes, but don't worry. You won't miss your tournament match this Friday."

Did he know I was a competitor? I remember Trevor suggesting Artemus was the cause of the mysterious Raven character in the last match. "It's true I haven't missed a match yet," I offered. "It's fun to watch."

"Come now. There's no reason to equivocate. Sam Clemens has done a wonderful job so far. You should be proud. You didn't think I was ignorant of your secret identity, did you?"

"I—I didn't think anyone but the LMC knew who the competitors were."

Hesitating at the top of a flight of stairs, Artemus turned and looked back at me. "There isn't anything having to do with the SIM that I don't know about." He held up a finger and paused to let that fact sink in. "Not anything."

We descended a long flight of stairs into a cavern. The rough-hewn ceiling extended thirty meters up. The room itself was three times the size of the ballroom I'd seen near the entrance. "What's this?" My voice echoed.

Artemus said, "This was never finished. It was to be the grand entrance into Brimstone. Sir Simon's own personal tram station. You see over there—the ceiling is higher. That's where Sir Simon planned on installing several elevators into the upper halls, but they were never finished."

I followed Artemus across the cavern and through a doorway as he spoke. "Why didn't he finish?" I asked.

"The tram was supposed to run through a lunar amusement park outside the Descartes crater. He wanted to call it the Asylum. The whole thing was canceled when they found out the chosen area was geologically unstable. That and the Board of Directors of SI didn't want to put money into physical amusements when SIM technology was maturing so nicely."

I followed Artemus down a hall that ended with two doors across from each other. The one to the right was a double door that looked like an airlock with a sign that read "Authorized Personnel Only." The door to the left stood open, and we entered. At first glance it appeared to be some sort of operating room, dimly lit. As the sensors detected us, the lights came up, and I saw the walls were covered with pictures of the human anatomy. They depicted the nervous system, some showing the whole body and the network of nerves running from head to toe, while others showed close-up diagrams of the brain and spinal column.

What I'd taken for an operating table was a SIM chamber laid out like . . . it reminded me of a coffin. Cables ran from it to a console along the wall lined with both 2-D and 3-D displays. A second SIM chamber stood upright against the far wall, reminiscent of an upright sarcophagus.

Artemus walked to the console and put his palm on the surface, bringing the displays to life.

Pointing across the hall, I asked, "Where does that lead? Looks like an airlock."

"It goes out to the Asylum site. There's a tunnel—Heck, why don't I show you? There's no real rush here anyway."

We walked across the hall, and Artemus punched the "open" key next to the door. A green light lit up indicating the pressure was balanced, and the doors opened.

I asked, "No lock? What about this authorized personnel sign?"

"This airlock was never meant to be permanent. I think they put the sign there just to scare the natives."

I descended the few steps into the airlock looking for pressure suits. Another set of double doors stood across the airlock that had a more complicated keypad and control panel in the wall to the right. Artemus stepped to a side-wall and pushed a button I hadn't noticed. A beep sounded and a floor-to-ceiling door slid open revealing a rack of pressure suits.

Artemus handed me one and said, "Like me, these are old, but they work just fine."

Except for the helmet, it came in one piece that had to be put on like a jump suit. "They trained us on using all the different kinds of pressure suits, but it's been a while. You don't have any mech-suits in there, do you?"

"No mech-suits. You'll have to suffer with these."

After putting on the helmet, the suit computer came on-line and said, "One moment while pressure seals are tested." The pressure inside the suit rose a little, and I waited as the suit fabric puffed out. Soon the suit said, "Pressure seals verified. Current status: Four hours available air supply." Then the air pressure returned to normal.

Through the mike in front of my mouth, I said, "Artemus, can you hear me?"

"Loud and clear."

"You too. Just a little staticky."

Artemus moved to the control panel and pushed the depressurize key. The display above the panel showing the air pressure began to blink. Artemus pressed it again. "Damn thing. I've got to get this fixed." He hit it with his fist, and the display stopped blinking. The pressure indicator decreased, and after a minute it read zero.

The door opened into the side of a tunnel carved out of the rock. Nearby lights flashed on, and I poked my head in to take a look. The perfectly circular tunnel stretched straight away from the door and vanished into distant darkness. A set of tubes ran the length of it; two on the bottom of the tunnel, one on the top, and one on each side. I had to step back as a bullet-like pod approached us and stopped in front of our door. It was hovering. A door opened and Artemus said, "After you, Dennis."

I took a look at the cramped space. The car was big enough for four people, two facing forward and two facing backward. I took a deep breath and exhaled slowly as I climbed in to keep my claustrophobia under control. Artemus came after, and I could feel the car shift with his added weight.

We boarded, and soon Artemus had us racing down the dark tunnel lit only by the car's headlights.

"When was the last time you were down here?" I asked. "There could have been a cave in. Maybe we shouldn't go so fast." The car headlights didn't shine very far.

"You sound like an old man. Stop fretting."

An instant later, we flashed through a pair of pressure bulkheads set into either wall of the tunnel. What if they had been closed?

The tunnel curved to the right and slowly rose. After fifteen minutes, we reached the end of the line. A flight of metal stairs rose up to an opening through which I could see stars.

Right behind Artemus, I climbed the stairs and stepped out onto the surface. I turned to look back the way we had come. We were above the rim of the rocky Descartes crater, the side walls of which had to be fifty meters high. It swept out before us extending to the horizon. The top of the city was visible in the distance along with a speeding tram bound back to Aristoteles and home. Descartes looked far, at least a two-hour walk. And around the central city were thousands of tiny geodesic domes extending nearly all the way to the far crater wall. These were the greenhouses.

"The Asylum was to be built in the crevice," Artemus said. He pointed and directed my attention to the left where there was a huge cleft in the side of the crater wall, a natural fissure in the rock wide enough to hold a city. "Sir Simon wanted to install a dome over the gap. The whole of the floor was to be a fun house. You can see for yourself with this 3-D projector."

What looked like a table, low and wide, stood before the gorge. Artemus bounded over to it and brushed off the surface with his glove, removing lunar dust kicked up by spectators.

Artemus said, "There's a slab buried in the ground over there where you're supposed to stand. It's got an 'X' on it."

I found the 'X' mark, and, standing on it, I looked back toward the projector. From this vantage point, the city of Descartes was in view. Artemus pressed something on the side of the low table; an image flickered to life hovering above the table and superimposed on the city.

Artemus looked up and around. "Oh, not there." He pointed. "That stone over there."

I looked and found the stone he was talking about. Then I realized the stone on which I stood had Y on it, not an X.

"But what is this one for? The image is . . ." An animation of lines of every color imaginable were vectoring from the sky, aimed at various greenhouses. It was like some old-fashioned video game. Every time a line intersected a greenhouse, it appeared to explode.

Artemus said, "Yeah, no one understands what that was supposed to be. It's like some kind of space-invaders game from a hundred years ago. Take a look at the other one."

I hopped over to the 'X' mark, which positioned the projection table squarely between me and the cleft in the rock wall. The illusion wasn't perfect, but it was effective enough. I saw a tall dome spanning the gap. Inside, I watched as people swooped down and around trees, flying with the aid of wings strapped to their arms. "There's people flying."

"One of his dreams for the park," Artemus said. "Human-powered flight as easy as you please. Just like the birds."

Across the floor of the gorge was a city. "Looks like a madhouse to me." The most disturbing part was the fact that the buildings didn't stop at the crevice walls. Instead, they continued up the side-walls as if a giant had taken the town and folded it like paper. It looked like most of the buildings were built horizontally out of the walls.

"It's all part of the theme," Artemus said. "Come to Luna and visit the lunatics at the Asylum."

"I'm glad they never built it," I said. "That would drive me insane."

* * *

Artemus gave me a sidelong glance. "You seem to be preoccupied today? It isn't because of the quarantine, is it?"

We were back in Artemus' lab, and I was glad to get the sticky suit off. I hated helmets. "Quarantine? What quarantine?"

Artemus shook his head and turned back to the console. "What did I say? I didn't mean quarantine. I was talking—I was thinking about the Prometheus accident and your father. What was I thinking? No. How is your father anyway?"

"They are planning on attaching his new arm later this week. The nerves will take a while to attach, and he'll have to relearn how to use his arm. He can't wait." Was that quarantine slip significant? What could it mean?

"Why don't you lie down in that chamber, there, and I'll take the other one?"

"Sure. You know I'm claustrophobic, right?"

"Relax. Soon you'll be in the SIM, and you can forget about these enclosed spaces. Tell you what. I'll keep the lid open if it will make you feel better?"

"Thanks," I said. Feeling a knot in my stomach, I clambered into the coffin-like SIM chamber.

Sensing my presence, the chamber extended a cap that fitted itself to my head. Straps snaked around my arms and legs as I held my breath. Thankfully, it wasn't long before the SIM took over and all sense of the coffin vanished.

* * *

"Welcome to stage two," Artemus said. He appeared different than before. This time he was a teenager like me but a few years older. We stood on a paved path in the middle of a field. Massive hills surrounded us in the distance. What trees there were had low-spreading branches.

"What should I call you? Art?"

"Art will do. I thought a new body for this next stage was apropos."

"Where are we?"

"Lantau Island not far from Hong Kong. Just over that hill and across the bay is one of the most populated places on Earth, yet here there's not a soul."

Art started walking along the path and I followed. Looking up, I realized an archway stood across the path not far away.

"What are we doing here? What is stage two?"

"Have you ever meditated? What do you know of Eastern philosophy?"

"Eastern philosophy? I already know about meditation, if that's what we're doing here. My doctor taught me to help me with my claustrophobia." A warm breeze blew into our faces.

We got close enough to the stone archway to see what was written. Cut into the stone was the message, "To Zen Buddhist Temple."

Art said, "Follow this path to the temple."

"You're not coming?"

"I'll join you later. Just follow the path."

"What do I do when I get there?"

Suddenly Art vanished and I was alone. I rolled my eyes and started along the path through the arch. All our other sessions had complicated puzzles and distractions. What was this about?

The pavement followed the downward slope of the land, and I was glad I wouldn't have to walk back up. The path was visible for quite a ways, but no temple. It might be a while, and it was getting hot.

After walking for ten minutes, I came across a wooden sign along the side of the path. It read the same as the arch, "To Zen Buddhist Temple." It also had an arrow pointing the direction I walked.

I put my hands on my hips. "I get it now. This is some kind of Zen thing, isn't it? I walk and walk to get to this promised temple that isn't really there. This footpath goes on forever, doesn't it?"

There was no response from Art. Nothing changed. "Look I get it. I'm not going to walk forever."

With that, I stubbornly plopped myself down on the path. They weren't going to fool me. Then I felt the ache in my legs. I hadn't realize how tired my knees were until I got off my feet. The path continually descended, making it a real workout for these simulated muscles. Artemus was allowing pain in this SIM.

Minutes passed, but nothing happened. They weren't going to halt the SIM. With a sigh, I got to my feet and continued my plodding journey to nowhere.

What did I know of Zen? Not much. It was a philosophy, a way of life, a method for attaining enlightenment, whatever that was. Some masters of Zen are considered crazy, some wise, some both. They comprehend without knowing, breaking the chains of logic which bind our minds. That must be the connection. If Artemus is sending me information, he wants me to access it without comprehending it. But how?

I stopped and suddenly looked to the left of the path. There was a rustling in the bushes. I blinked in surprise as I realized the movement in the bushes happened only after I looked, as if I predicted it.

The knowledge that it was a dog sparked in my mind a half a second before the dog stepped out. His fangs were bare and his growl rumbled low. SIM or no SIM, I didn't like the idea of being bitten, especially since Artemus wasn't inhibiting pain.

Two more dogs stepped into the open lower down the hill, blocking the footpath. I had no inkling they would show up and no idea what to do. They were advancing.

I turned and ran back up the hill. The growls became ferocious, filled with glee at the sight of fleeing prey. I looked back and saw them give chase. I screamed and tripped as one leapt up, aiming his jaws at my throat.

Chapter Six
The Foreseeable

S ettle down. Relax."

I was lying on the path, but the dogs were gone. With a shaky hand I shaded my eyes from the sun and saw the teenage Art standing over me. "Art."

He gave me a hand up, "Gave you quite a scare?"

When I regained my feet, I grabbed his T-shirt at the throat with both hands. "What are you trying to do to me?"

"Would you rein in that temper? This is a SIM."

"If those dogs tore into me, it would feel real, wouldn't it? You have safety disabled."

"If there was no threat, there would be no incentive."

I released him. "Incentive for what?"

"You can escape the confrontation by sensing the future. We're controlling everything that happens and feeding it to you beforehand. Did you sense anything?"

I nodded and rubbed my eyes with my palms. "I thought I felt something. I knew a dog was going to step out of the bushes."

"Excellent. If you can master that feeling, you'll be able to pass the obstacle and reach the temple."

"How do I do that?" I threw my hands into the air and looked down the path. We were standing at the start, where the archway straddled the path.

"I already know you're smart, Dennis. You proved that in stage one. But can you find the stillness in your mind that will give you access to the implanted memories?"

I sighed and turned to face him, but he was gone. I was alone again on the path. "You expect me to go back down there?" I shouted into the sky. There was no answer.

My eyes fell back to the footpath through the arch. The dogs were waiting.

* * *

It was another twenty minute walk down the path before I encountered the dogs. Art said I could defeat them but I was outnumbered and outmatched. They could move quicker than me, and they had sharper teeth. I had a superior intellect, but if I had any brains, I wouldn't have put myself in danger in the first place.

My only weapon was this future sense provided by Art, but I didn't know how to access it. Somehow I had to find a calm center within myself and stay there despite the lurking danger.

I found the first dog waiting for me in the middle of the path. To the right of the path was a cliff face, and to the other was a steep hillside that was covered with bushes and also dropped off. I knew a moment before it happened that his two friends would step out behind me, blocking my escape.

I averted my eyes, knowing that, in their language, meeting a dog's eyes was a challenge to fight. I held out my hands in a gesture of open friendliness. In my mind I saw the front dog move toward me, and I watched as he followed that path I predicted like a shadow. He stopped, crouched low, and snarled.

Before I knew it, one of the dogs behind me was sinking his teeth into my leg. At that instant, all sense of the future vanished. I screamed in fear as the pain lanced up my leg. I tried to push the dog away but fell as teeth ripped into my arm.

In a flash, the pain and the dogs were gone, and I found myself lying in front of the archway still trying to scramble away from hounds.

I lay there and panted for a while trying to regain my senses. As I looked up at the archway, it became clear that Artemus wasn't going to let me out of this SIM until I got past those dogs. Last time they didn't touch me, but this time they managed to make contact with my flesh, which meant each attack was going to last longer, be more painful. I was being trained like a dog, beaten when I failed to perform. How ironic.

"Artemus! Artemus," I said still lying on the hot, paved footpath. He would not answer.

* * *

After the next three attacks, I managed to expand my awareness so that even if the dogs were behind me, I could sense where they were and what they were going to do. But I still couldn't predict their movement much beyond a second, and that wasn't enough time to use the information to any advantage.

I also noticed the dogs were getting closer to the archway with every attack. The architects of this insanity were giving me less time to contemplate my next "death". The last time, one of the dogs nearly ripped off my forearm by whipping his head back and forth. The pain had been terrible.

I decided to stop playing Artemus' game. I didn't believe there was a way to win, even with a sense of the future, and I was getting so tired. I decided to lie in the sun on the footpath just where I appeared after the last assault. The team of researchers working with Artemus would take pity on me and pull me out. Besides, as long as

I didn't go down the path, the dogs wouldn't attack. Maybe the way to win was not to play.

I gasped as the sound of multiple growls came to my ears. I lifted my head to see the three of them pass through the archway and circle me. "No. No, please."

As the alpha male lunged toward me, I screamed and covered my head. I felt his hot breath on my neck, then nothing. I looked up and discovered they were gone. It was a warning. The next time there would be no quarter.

I got to my feet and stumbled through the arch, tears streaming down my face. I needed a weapon, but I'd already looked for stones along the path. There was nothing but dirt. Maybe I could throw dirt in their eyes. I reached down and filled both fists with the dust. But that would only postpone my death, not prevent it. I had to beat the dogs.

Passing the wooden sign pointing toward the Buddhist temple, my stomach clenched. It wouldn't be long now.

I stopped as something finally occurred to me. I turned my head and looked back at the wooden sign. Couldn't I use it as a weapon? Dropping the dirt, I ran back to the sign and wrestled it out of the ground by rocking it back and forth. I held it up and swung it like a bat, but it was too large and clumsy. Standing on the sign, I reached down and wrenched the post off. It was solid, the perfect weight. It had a pointed end where it had been driven into the ground, and it had two nails poking through one side. It was perfect.

I walked another minute down the path before they attacked. There was no ceremonial growl given to warn me this time. The alpha male came out of the bushes and ran right for me, but I could sense him coming. With all my might, I swung my post and bashed him across the head. He went down and didn't move. Confidence flowed through me, and I spread my mind out to sense the remaining two.

They attacked simultaneously, but I could feel their movements almost two full seconds beforehand. I kicked one in the nose and swung at the other. There were only glimpses of the future now, tiny flashes of insight between attacks. I managed to land a heavy blow on one, but the other sank fangs into my calf. As I raised my weapon and turned the nails to face him, I suddenly found myself on the ground with slavering teeth ripping into me. The post was ripped from my hands and I looked to see two new dogs tearing into me.

After they ripped me apart, I found myself in the shadow of the arch again, my heart pounding. I failed to look for more dogs. He was making it harder now that I had a weapon.

I rubbed my arms, feeling how they were whole and uninjured. But I could still feel phantom pain. Stumbling down the path, I knew there was now hope. I'd just have to try harder this time.

As the wooden sign came into view again, I quickened my pace. Only then did I realize it was too late. My senses alerted me to their presence before they appeared. Now there were six dogs, and three of them were blocking the way to the sign. "No, it's not fair. Not fair."

I tried to scramble up the cliff face, but they grabbed my foot and pulled me down.

I was still screaming when the archway snapped into view above me. Artemus had no intention of letting me win.

Suddenly a picture of the pack appeared in my mind. They were walking this way through the underbrush, farther down past the wooden sign. I could tell I had a chance to reach the sign before them.

I jumped to my feet and ran, almost stumbling in my hurry. Each successive trial had the dogs starting closer to the arch, but they still started on the other side of signpost. How many more trials would I have before they started on this side of the sign? I had to win this time. This had to be the last.

I was crying in desperate joy as I reached the sign before the dogs appeared. Again I pulled it out of the ground and ripped the sign off the front of the post. Having run at top speed, my lungs were still heaving when they arrived. This was my last chance. I couldn't get here any quicker.

I threw a fistful of dirt into the face of the leading dog and swung at the second. The blow landed with the sound of cracking bone, and he went down. My future sense told me I had time before the next attack, so I took the opportunity to get my back to the cliff face to prevent attacks from all sides.

I knew in advance which dog would attack and where he aimed his slavering jaws. I swung the wooden post again and again, each time hitting true. I only had to swing six times to take down all six dogs, and in the end their bodies lay scattered across the path. What has he made me? I felt like throwing up.

Glancing down at myself, I didn't have a single injury.

With muscles clenched and senses tuned to anticipate more, I gripped the post and slowly walked down the path farther. No dogs appeared and nothing attacked.

I walked around a bend and saw the temple. It was a large structure with several squat towers built below the path on the side of the hill. The paved footpath wound around the temple and through a vegetable garden. A few men dressed in orange robes were working in the garden, but none looked up at my arrival. The smell of incense wafted through the air, and off in the distance I could hear some sort of chant.

Was it over? I could feel myself shaking.

The path ended on a large square, designs marking the surface of the cement. When I stepped off the path, everything went black. The SIM ended.

* * *

"Have a seat. We'll talk over some of Lawrence's famous jota," Artemus said as he took another spoonful of the stinking bean soup. Lawrence poured both of us a glass of wine. I crossed my arms and walked away toward the edge of the tower.

I hadn't said a word since rising from the SIM chamber. Artemus told me he was impressed by how I handled the dogs, but I just looked at him. I had followed him up a spiral staircase surrounding and rising above the lab. It turned out to be the South Tower.

Lawrence had lunch all ready for us on the tower roof spread out on a table crouched near the center. A rail of stone circled the roof to prevent a misstep from leading to a deadly plunge, but only if this were Earth. Here on Luna you'd probably only get a sprained ankle.

I approached the edge and tried to think. How could I get out of going back into the SIM?

But the view drove the thoughts from my mind. Surrounding us stretched the Silver Wood. We were high enough to be above most of the trees. Cascading off distant mountains, enshrouded by a mantel of clouds, was a waterfall that fed a lake. Sure, the nearby trees were real enough, but, none of the rest of it was. Imagine an actual lake here on Luna? But it was impossible to tell where the real world ended and the 3-D vid screens began.

I didn't give Artemus the satisfaction of my awe over the view.

My gaze was drawn down to the foot of the tower by the sound of running water. Below was a huge paved courtyard and what appeared to be a stage off on the side. At the center stood a fountain consisting of a large ball—I looked again. It was a model of Earth. Encircling the model were metal bars arranged in the familiar interlocking triangles, SI's corporate logo. At each triangle point, it looked like water was spraying back toward the Earth, then deflecting back to spray all around the globe. What a waste of precious water.

This was all a waste. How could he have all this? How could he do that to me? Without turning around, I said, "I expect an explanation."

"Dennis—"

I whirled around. "I didn't sign up for torture."

He put down his spoon and dabbed his mouth with a napkin. "I can see you're upset. But, fortunately, that is the last threat of violence you'll face."

"That was not a threat of violence. That was being eviscerated alive!"

"I don't enjoy putting people through that, but it's the only way to force your brain to find the knowledge. Now that you know how, you can enter that state of mental stillness with ease. The next session—"

"There's not going to be a next session. I'm not getting back in a SIM chamber with you again. You're insane."

Artemus stood. "Mr. Howard, you will or you'll be in breach of contract."

"You know what you can do with that contract? No amount of money is worth this."

"What about your father?"

"My father?" I shouted. Grabbing the edge of the table, I pushed it over. The dishes and glasses smashed to pieces against the stone floor. Artemus managed to snag his glass of wine just in time.

I glared at him. "You're going to stop him from getting his new arm?"

"He'll never see a new arm."

"You arranged the whole accident, didn't you? Just so I'd have to sign that contract."

"Accident? You mean your father's injury? Now who's acting insane? You think that explosion at Prometheus was designed to injure your father?"

"A man as powerful as you could orchestrate anything. Just look at this place."

Artemus took a gulp of wine and said, "If you fail to follow through on the agreement, you will owe SI the cost of all legal fees and processing fees. You'll have to pay for the SIM time you've used and payment for all the man-hours spent by my team and me. Then there's the matter of the one-time contract termination fee—"

"How much?"

"On the order of fifteen billion dollars."

"That wasn't in the contract."

"Maybe you should have taken the time to read the document."

"You're evil," I whispered.

"I'm a business man, Dennis." He finished off his wine and threw the glass onto the pile of debris. "You're too rare a find to let slip away. All you have to do is follow my lead and you'll be set for life.

Break the contract and it'll mean debtors prison for you and your mother. She signed the contract too."

"We'll take you to court. The contract can't be valid."

"An expensive option, and one you're bound to lose against the SI corporate lawyers. Look, stage two is over. There won't be any more pain. You have my word."

"What good is your word? You tricked me into signing that contract. What's another lie to you?" I wanted to push him down, to make him feel the teeth of the dogs that feasted on me.

"There's no need for the rod any more. You've passed the threshold."

I snatched a broken bottle from the pile and waved it in front of him. "What's to stop me from cutting you to pieces like those dogs did to me? Or maybe I should just push you off this tower?" I shoved him and he stepped backward, tripping on the chair. He caught himself on the rail.

"You mean besides Lawrence?"

I glanced back and saw Lawrence aiming a pistol my way. "Please, step away from Master Regale."

Artemus said, "You aren't a killer, Dennis."

"What do you think you just trained me to be?"

Artemus had nothing to say. He just looked at me and shook his head. I threw the bottle over the edge and said, "I'm leaving, and I'm not coming back."

"I'm your friend, Dennis. Maybe your only friend."

I turned away.

"Lawrence, show our guest out. I'll expect you, Dennis, tomorrow at eight sharp." At that moment, the sound of the bottle shattering somewhere below served to punctuate his remark.

"In your dreams," I muttered. There had to be a way out of the contract.

* * *

The tram bound for Aristoteles was due in ten minutes, so I found an empty com-booth and closed the glass door behind me. I said, "Emily, verify."

"Verification complete, Dennis."

"Unlock my stuff, password Ark-Ramses-523."

"Non-coercion verified. Your classified data is now available, Dennis."

"Show me the contract I signed with SI." The text appeared on the screen, and I scanned it looking for those added clauses.

Artemus was hiding something. Even if he wasn't behind the Prometheus explosion, he was lying about something. I'd have to do more poking around in Emily's brain. What dealings did Artemus have with Sir Simon that would make him so rich?

The legal gobbledygook was making me dizzy. "Emily, do you have on record the original contract that Artemus gave to me and my folks?"

"I do. Would you like to see that contract?"

"Show me the differences between the contracts."

It started out with the damages I would be awarded in the event of brain damage, mental, or behavioral dysfunction that could be shown to be directly attributable to actions taken by SI pursuant to this agreement. The next section of differences described the fifteen billion dollars in damages I was to pay SI if I was found in breach of this contract. Artemus hadn't lied about that.

I closed my eyes and leaned against the wall. Dad would figure out something. Even if we had no legal option, I could dig up some dirt on Artemus to use as leverage. We could use the vid of Artemus setting the bomb. Blackmail. Maybe blackmail was how Artemus managed to get so much money from Sir Simon. How did Artemus get control of SI?

Suddenly I remembered the vid I'd found Saturday night of Sir Simon talking to Artemus. Sir Simon wanted to know what Artemus thought about technology that would allow complete personality transfer. I opened my eyes and stared at the screen, unseeing, a thought forming in my mind. "What if . . . What if Artemus *is* Sir

Simon." I remembered how Artemus looked at that portrait of Jessica, Sir Simon's wife. And his reaction was strange when I asked him if he was married.

Now Artemus was looking for a young body. Me.

My eyes finally focused on the screen showing the final section of differences between the contracts. "The project will be deemed a success if Dennis Howard is capable of answering a set of questions whose answers are known only to Artemus Regale. In the event of a success, all holdings and possessions of Artemus Regale, including but not limited to, stocks, bonds, options, futures, real estate and all cash and gold reserves, are to be transferred to the possession of Dennis Howard."

I pounded the screen with a fist as a wave of dizziness passed through me. "That SOB wants my body. There's no Declarative Knowledge Project."

"Dennis."

Startled, I turned to discover a tall, well-built man in his thirties looking in at me. "Yeah?" With a touch, I cleared the screen and the door slid open automatically.

The stranger pushed some wavy blond hair out of his eyes and turned to lean against the wall. He whispered, "Don't say a word. Don't even look at me." He glanced around the room as if checking to see if we were noticed. "I need to speak with you in private. Follow me."

"What? Who are you?"

"Shh. Don't say anything. Just follow me." He started to move away.

I rose to my feet and crossed my arms. Did I look stupid? I wasn't going to follow this guy anywhere.

Seeing I hadn't moved, he sighed and said, "All right. Look over your right shoulder. There's a man in a grey cloak sitting three rows back."

I turned my head and scanned the crowd waiting for the tram. My eyes snapped on Bosner almost instantly. He was sweating and pressing fingers into his temples while mumbling something to himself.

The stranger said, "That's Kyle Bosner. If he finds you here, there's no telling what he might do."

I looked up into the face of this stranger. He didn't give off the vibe of a member of the Military Police. "If you were with the MPs you would have arrested him by now. So who are you?"

A fat man passing by stopped for a second. "You talking to me, kid?"

I shook my head, and the fat man walked off.

"My name is Clay Byron," the stranger said. "We don't have much time. Trust me." He glanced back at Bosner, then to me.

Maybe he was in league with the Bosners. There was no reason to trust him. I should call the authorities myself. I looked back at Bosner and saw him rocking back and forth and hugging himself. The woman nearby lifted her baby and moved away a few chairs.

Bosner, with a look of anguish on his face, suddenly got to his feet. He started shouting, "Shut up. Shut up. Shut up," over and over. Then . . . then I saw the gun in his hand.

A woman screamed as a bolt of light flashed through the air. Bosner was firing some kind of weapon into the crowd around him. It was just like the restaurant. People were screaming and running away and after each shot Bosner shouted, "No!"

I stood there looking on in horror when Bosner's eyes fell on me. He leveled his gun my way and yelled, "That's the one." Some kid rushing by at high speed pushed me aside in his hurry to escape. As I tumbled to the ground, a flash of light arced through the air and hit him in the back. The kid had to be . . .

Without looking back, I got to my feet and ran. Screams echoed through the station, but if they were screams of terror or agony I didn't know. But one thing I did know: Bosner wanted me dead.

Chapter Seven
Sneaking Suspicions

Follow me now!" the stranger shouted.

I fled, following Clay down the corridor. I glanced back and saw Bosner in full pursuit. As he ran I saw something metallic strapped underneath his coat. He fired again and a bolt of light flew over my head.

I took a turn, barely missed crashing into an old couple, and had to bounce off several walls to recover. Clay and I were headed back toward the university section, and the shooter was out of sight behind several turns and twists of the corridors. Shouts of alarm went up behind us as people saw the killer.

Clay stopped in front of a door and motioned me to stop as well. "Say 'knock.'"

"Say what? Knock?"

The door flew open, and I realized that the word knock must be the door key. The stranger jumped through the door surprisingly fast. As I followed, a loud crack echoed down the hall. Blistering heat exploded against the doorframe, and the concussion knocked me to the floor. Sensing a presence in the room, lights blinked on. I got to my feet and jammed a finger into the door controls, but the door didn't close. Part of the frame had been melted and fused together.

I had the vague impression that I had been in this room before.

"It won't close," I said.

"He'll be here any second. Behind that curtain by the window is a doorway to a balcony. To open it say 'Bonsai.'"

I dashed to the red curtain, flung it aside and found the door just as he described. I never would have noticed had he not shown me exactly where to look. The door was hidden in the wall texture. "Why doesn't it open?"

"You haven't said the key yet."

"But you already said it!

"Say it yourself. Bonsai."

"Bonsai!" The balcony door opened. Once we were both through and onto the balcony, I pulled the curtain back across the opening and shut the door behind us. I shouted, "There's no lock on this side!"

"Relax. We're safe. All we have to do is be quiet and we'll be safe. Look at this wall. Concentrate on this wall."

"Let's climb down the tree," I said. The tree branches enshrouded the balcony making jumping impossible and . . . and how far down was it anyway? Dried-up leaves covered the balcony making my every step crunch. Through the window stretching along part of the balcony I could see, inside, a small bed in a curtained-off alcove. I flung myself against the wall for fear of being seen.

"This wall stands between him and us," Clay whispered. "Relax. Take a few breaths. If you concentrate on this wall and its solidity, you'll feel safer and make less noise breathing. Close your eyes."

I did as he said, too frightened to do otherwise. Clay's voice was calm, compelling. Bosner wouldn't find the door.

"Picture that wall in your mind's eye," Clay said. "Picture that same wall, except that this new wall has no door. It's solid and impenetrable. Bosner is on the other side. You are on this side."

I pictured the wall he was describing, not knowing how this could possibly help. But the more I concentrated, the safer I felt. The wall was granite and ten feet thick. Nothing could even scratch it. He had no way through. I kept repeating this in my mind, and I wondered if I was making less noise like the stranger predicted. My pounding heart was slowing and my breathing was almost back in control.

Clay sighed. "I think he's moved on."

I peeked through the window. The room was empty. "How do you know?" I whispered. "Who are you?"

"Maybe you should sit down."

Bosner must have been in the room. The curtain originally dividing the small alcove with the rest of the office was pushed aside. I shoved the leaves off the single old wooden chair and sat down. My knees were shaking a little.

"Okay, I'm sitting. Now, out with it. Who are you? What's going on?" I demanded.

The stranger did a double take at the tree. He said, "How things have changed. You used to be able to look down and see the top of this tree, you know." For the first time I noticed the shouts and laughter of children down on the floor of the arboretum. Several birds flew off a nearby branch with a wild flapping flutter.

"I've been watching you for several days now. My name is Clay Byron. But in a way we've already met."

"We have?"

"I met a man who called himself Loud Thunder, a Native American Indian I believe, though I couldn't place the tribe. Maybe Cheyenne. When we parted he was claiming I was 'Raven.'"

"You? That was you? But no one else could see or hear you. What were you trying to do, get me kicked out of the competition?" How could he have infiltrated the tournament without being a contestant? "Are you a master?"

He paused for a moment as if searching his memory. "I'm not sure what you mean."

"Forget the tournament. Why was Bosner trying to kill me? Who do you work for?"

"I don't work for anyone. But I seem to recall being busy right here at the university—Barkley Lunar University. That, in there, is my—well, used to be my office. This balcony was my private sanctuary. I came out here to think, to contemplate the inner workings of the human spirit, to pray, to dream. Used to be a beautiful view."

"What do you know about Bosner?"

"I've seen his type before. I know what they're capable of."

"Why were you following me?"

His brow furrowed and he turned away. "There are things you're not ready to know. Go home and maybe in a day or two—"

"Come on," I said getting up. "Let's go to the MPs. We'll tell them—"

"They won't listen to me. In fact, if I were you, I wouldn't mention our encounter . . . to anyone."

"What are you talking about?"

Clay paused and seemed to come to a decision. "Dennis, the authorities won't listen to me because they can't hear me. They can't see me either."

"That's . . . that's . . . Of course they can see you. We'll just—"

"You're the only one who can see and hear me. I can talk or shout or scream—it doesn't matter—nobody will hear. Nobody but you."

I stepped toward him, intending to take him by the arm and gently lead him to the MPs and then to the psychiatrists. He needed help. "I don't understand why you—"

My hand passed right through his arm. No, I must have just missed. Trying once more, it happened again. I jumped back and fell over the chair. Leaves were flung into the air and drifted slowly.

"I wasn't going to tell you," Clay said. "I thought you had been through enough today." He strolled off the balcony, passing through the thick stone railing and into thin air. Tree branches passed through his body. "I'm sorry for giving you even more of a shock. Just go home and get some rest. And don't worry yourself about the . . . Bosner. He won't be back for a while. We'll talk later." With that he vanished.

"I love you—shut-up. I love you—shut-up," I said under my breath. I jumped up and over to the door, now wanting to go home more than ever. Before I opened the door, I heard voices on the other side and the sound of the curtain sliding on its rings. "Nobody's in here," someone said.

Another male voice said, "He must have gone down the hall."

I glanced through the window and saw two uniformed officers leaving. I could barely hear the next question they voiced. "Why can't the LMC track him?"

It was the MPs chasing Bosner. I was glad they hadn't found me. I couldn't tell them about Clay.

I opened the door and pushed the curtain out of my way. It finally struck me where I'd seen this office before. It was the office where I'd had my first meeting with Artemus. It was the same empty room, the same empty desk.

I muttered to myself, "They're trying to drive me insane. This must be a SIM!"

I felt the melted section of the doorframe just to see if it was real. It was still warm. That didn't prove anything.

"What's going on?" What is Clay? If this wasn't a SIM, maybe he was a ghost, like the ghosts roaming the World of Rapt. Ridiculous. Maybe he was a guardian angel, like Mr. Fignagel in the fifth trial of the tournament. But I didn't believe in angels.

I walked over to the desk and pressed my palm against the dusty surface. "Emily."

The desk surface lit up. "Hello, Dennis."

"Clay Byron . . . Do you know of any man named Clay Byron."

"I have information on two hundred fourteen men named Clay Byron. Can you be more specific?"

She has records on people living on Earth too. "Are there any on Luna now?"

"I'm sorry, no."

"Have any ever been to Luna?"

"Yes. Only one."

"Do you have a picture of him?"

Suddenly a rotating head appeared floating above the desk. It was the same man.

"Where is he now?"

"Personal location is considered private information and cannot be—"

"He's not on Luna. Did he go back to Earth?"

"Unknown."

"Tell me anything you can about him." I sank into the leather chair, feeling tired.

"Clay Byron was born June 2, 2019 in Cleveland, Ohio, USA. I have no listing for his parents."

"2019? That's . . ." I did the math. "That's sixty-one years ago."

"At the age of 18, he arrived on Luna, January 15, 2038, with his wife, Ariel. They took residence in the city of Descartes where Clay began pursuing a doctorate in comparative religion at Barkley Lunar University. He was considered a genius. He was reported missing on September 19, 2039. His sudden disappearance prompted a global search—"

"Did he have any family on Luna?" Maybe it was a relative of his I saw through some sort of 3-D vid projection.

"Clay Byron had no siblings, and I have no record of him fathering any children by Ariel or any other women."

"Is Ariel still on Luna?"

"On September 19, 2039, the same day as Clay's disappearance, Ariel Byron was shot in an incident on Barkley campus. The assailant was captured and diagnosed with paranoid schizophrenia. His actions were considered a random act of violence without malice aforethought."

"Wait a minute. What else do you know about this murderer?"

"The assailant was a man named Mavin Bosner."

My eyes went wide. "Did you say *Bosner*?"

"Mavin Bosner died in Arzachel prison three weeks after his capture."

"What did he look like? Do you have any vids of him?"

"That information is classified."

Classified? What would be so peculiar about this case that they had to make it classified? Maybe I could get past that with Trevor's hypnosis trick on Emily.

"Was Clay shot in the same incident?"

"That is not known. He was at the scene during the shooting and was last seen fleeing."

A chill ran up my spine. "Em, where exactly did this shooting take place?"

"The shooting was in a restaurant on Barkley campus known as Bark's Eatery."

"Not in the Nick O' Time Café?"

"In April, 2041, a student petition was circulated to force the university to change the name of the restaurant on the grounds that the name Bark was too similar to barf, a colloquial term meaning to regurgitate. Bark's Eatery is now known as the Nick O' Time Café."

It hadn't been my deranged imagination after all. A few weeks ago, before my meeting with Artemus, I actually heard and saw the shooting while sitting in the Nick O' Time having lunch. The fleeing man I saw must have been Clay Byron just as he ran away from the scene of the murder forty-one years ago. It wasn't a premonition or a delusion. It was some kind of vision of the past.

No. We have a word for that. It's called a memory. But this one wasn't my own. It was a foreign memory implanted in my brain.

But if it was Artemus trying to put his personality and memories in me, why did I have a memory from Clay Byron? A suspicion took shape in my mind.

"Emily, is it possible to transfer one person's personality and memories into another person?"

"In theory, such a transfer is possible. The technology to manipulate neural connections was developed in 2035." Clay Byron's head floating above the desk faded away, leaving only his brain and upper spinal column. They enlarged, and as Emily spoke, different sections were highlighted in yellow. "To date, the largest step toward such a technology was the advent of skill implantation, developed by Sybernetics International and marketed to the public beginning in 2060. Skills gained this way remain unstable and decay with use via neural dystrophy." A list of the researchers' names appeared next to the brain graphics.

One of the names was Ariel Byron, Clay's wife.

"Safe transferal of declarative knowledge has not succeeded due to severe disruption of the existing neural matrix," Emily said. "However, if one ignored the existing matrix, it is theoretically possible to transfer large blocks of data. The transfer of an entire engrammic set, as you suggest, would require the disruption and displacement of *all* neural connections." The entire brain graphic changed to a shade of red.

"So it's possible?"

"A disruption on this order of magnitude would kill the subject. Even if the subject survived the trauma, the same neural dystrophy that causes skills to decay would lead to a collapse of the matrix and death within a week."

"But what if the matrix was implanted over and over to make up for the degeneration?"

"Repetition of neural manipulation causes synaptic dysfunction, called 'hardening of the synapse.' Often, the subject decides to increase the power until surrounding areas fail in what's known as a cascade failure—"

"All right, all right already" I said throwing my hands up. Neural dystrophy . . . the decay of skills with their use. My mind didn't work that way. I was different. Skills implanted in my mind didn't decay like they did for other people. Maybe it was some kind of strange brain chemistry associated with my multiple personalities ability. But . . .

But what if skill implantation wasn't the only thing that wouldn't decay in my brain? "Assume the neural dystrophy problem was solved. How could you get around the trauma problem?"

"If the subject was exposed to the new matrix slowly, the trauma of an entire engrammic shift could be avoided; however the mental function of the subject would decay before the new matrix was fifty percent implanted. This would most likely be too traumatic for a patient to survive."

"Assume," I said with a dry mouth. "Assume the subject suffered from dissociative identity disorder. What would happen if the new matrix was then imposed slowly?"

Emily paused for a second, then said, "Given the stated assumptions, the new matrix would be compartmentalized into a separate personality." The image shifted, zooming into the floating brain above the desk. A transparent sphere appeared. Inside I could see it broken into little sections, each one, presumably, a personality. One of them was red: the foreign personality.

Emily continued, "Over time, as this foreign personality grew, the subject might hear voices. Paranoia, feelings of being watched or followed might surface. As the imposed matrix increased in size . . ." The red compartment grew, hogging the space within the sphere. "The subject might suffer from hallucinatory flashbacks of memories derived from the matrix. The subject might even hallucinate the new matrix as a separate person."

"Oh my God."

"The personality of the imposed neural matrix might intermittently take control of the subject's body. It might attempt to wear down the defenses of the subject until the subject is forced to relinquish control of the body. Once permanent control was established, the remainder of the new matrix could supplant the subject's own matrix without resulting trauma."

In the image, the red interloper had pushed out all other personalities from the sphere. It was now totally red.

I swallowed. It was true. This was it. This explained everything. Hadn't I heard Clay's voice in my head, whispering snatches of poetry I had never known? I'd seen his memory of the death of his wife, and I had hallucinated him now multiple times: once as Raven and now here in this very office.

Scared of the answer to my next question, I asked, "Is there any way to reverse the process? How do I combat the personality?"

"The imposed matrix could be removed by overlaying its matrix with the original."

But I don't have a copy of my mind lying around. "What if that can't be done?"

"I don't have enough information to extrapolate any other course of action."

I ran my fingers through my hair. If I couldn't delete it or overwrite it, maybe I could stop Artemus from putting more in my head, stopping the process. But why Clay's memories and not Artemus'? Wasn't Artemus the one trying to take over? There was more to this story.

"Emily, when did Sir Simon Ignatius first arrive on Luna?"

"He arrived on Luna to oversee his corporation's development of the remote neural stimulation technology in 2035."

Too many dates. My head was swimming. "Emily, give me a graphic timeline of all the dates we've been talking about."

The red sphere faded away and was replaced by a line marking off all the dates, starting on the far left with 2019, Clay's birth, and ending with 2060 on the far right, when procedural knowledge first went on the market. Floating above or below the line were little bubbles containing descriptions of the events that happened on that date.

All right. Sir Simon was known to be eccentric. Maybe he suffered from multiple personalities too, and had the brain chemistry to sidestep the neural dystrophy. That's a big if, but . . . Clay was on Luna for a total of about a year and a half, all the while Sir Simon was here too. Maybe he had ambition to equal his genius. Perhaps, just perhaps, sometime in 2039, while Sir Simon indulged in his own SIM technology, Clay surreptitiously transferred his mind into Sir Simon's and took over his empire.

But it would take another twenty one years before they could even get procedural knowledge working. Ignoring that . . .

Clay was a philosophy student. What did he know of neural implantation? Ahh, but Ariel, his wife, was on the team of researchers working on this very thing. After her untimely demise, he completed the process on his own, and took over Sir Simon.

"Isn't it in 2071 that Artemus first meets Sir Simon?" I asked.

"That is correct," Emily said, and the timeline smoothly shifted to include a new endpoint, the year 2071.

Clay was now richer than rich, living in Sir Simon's body, but he was getting old. He found his next victim in Artemus Regale. Though in his sixties, Artemus was far younger than Sir Simon when they met. Clay, now transferred into Artemus' body, had to look for a new body right away. Of course. He must have invented the tournament as a way to search for people with multiple personalities, people with the brain chemistry he required.

But who were the Bosners? How did they enter into the picture? I looked at the open door nervously, suddenly feeling exposed.

"Emily, has Kyle Bosner been captured yet?"

"I can verify there is one Kyle Bosner on Luna, but why would he need to be apprehended?"

"Ahh, what about the people shot at Descartes Plaza?"

"There are eight people in critical condition. There were no fatalities. I have no record of how this happened. There is a forty-seven-second gap in my Descartes Plaza record, but I can't explain how this is possible. I have been attempting to trace the source of the flaw but have been unable. There are many people angry with me, Dennis. Are you angry too?"

Numb, I shut down the desk with my palm. Emily wouldn't be giving me any protection from Bosner. I wanted to go home.

* * *

I retraced my steps back through the halls to the tram station, all the while keeping my eyes peeled for Bosner. When I did get to the station, I was thankful the military were everywhere along with the EMTs trying to patch everyone back together. They all ignored me. A tram was waiting at the station, and I boarded.

The hum of the tram was hypnotic. Later, I couldn't remember the trip back to Aristoteles. I got off the tram like a zombie, only wanting to sleep.

Walking back home, I should've been more careful.

"Hey, Howard!"

I looked up from the floor, finally becoming aware of the danger. Three upper-classmen blocked the passage. I recognized the middle one as Han Newkirk. I didn't know the others, but I knew their faces. They had chased me two days ago.

"What do you want?" I asked, my eyes scanning for an escape route.

Newkirk said, "If I'd known we were going to catch you alone today, I would have come prepared with better weapons." He clenched his fist.

Chapter Eight
Whetting the Appetite

H e's waking up. Tricia, go tell the nurse. Dennis. Dennis, can you hear me?"

The face in front of me came into focus. "Mom." I felt an ache in my mouth. The left side of my upper lip was swollen, making it difficult to talk, and I couldn't open my right eye. There was a bandage wrapped around my head too.

"What—"

"You're in St. Sebastian's, sweetie. Thank goodness you're waking up."

I was lying in a bed in a room divided by a closed curtain, a semi-private room. My left arm was strapped down to the cold sensor array built into the mattress. The bed's back had been raised a bit giving me a view of the room.

Tricia came back followed closely by a woman.

"Am I alive?" I asked, my mouth dry.

Tricia said, "When they found you, they thought you were dead."

"Tricia," Mom chided. "Stop with the melodrama."

That reminded me of something Sol said once. "I've been dead my whole life, just not yet."

"What is that supposed to mean?" Mom asked.

"Never mind," I said.

The woman stepped up beside the bed opposite Mom. "Hello, Dennis. Do you recognize me?"

She looked familiar. I shook my head.

"I'm Dr. Katherine Woodridge. Remember, I gave you your neural physical a few weeks ago."

She shined a light in my one open eye and asked me to follow it as she moved it back and forth.

"Can you tell me what year it is?"

"It's 2080."

"Who is President of Luna, Dennis? Can you tell me that?"

"President Fedora Quillen." Her name was hard to say with my fat lip.

"Good. Touch my finger with your forefinger." She held out her finger in front of me, and, with my free hand, I did as she directed. It was no problem. "Now touch your nose."

We repeated the procedure a few times until she said, "Our scans don't show that Dennis' brain has suffered any permanent neurological harm, Mrs. Howard. We haven't detected any hemorrhaging or blockages either, but we'll be keeping him here a few days for monitoring and additional tests. In that time, his brain swelling should reduce too."

"Brain swelling?" Mom said.

Dr. Woodridge put a hand on my forehead as if she were feeling my temperature. "Another trauma to the head could be fatal, which is another good reason to keep him here while he recovers."

"A few days?" I asked in the same tone as my Mom's outburst. It was hard to believe. Even though I was a bit groggy from the medication, I still felt like the victim of a train wreck. But, come to think of it, I did feel better than when I first woke up.

Dr. Woodridge stepped back and took a pad from her pocket. After keying in something, she said, "It looks as though you've been through the mill, but you're okay now. They fused your three broken ribs and closed your perforated lung and spleen. The concussion symptoms have been treated and healing accelerated. They realigned a few molars on your lower jaw, and that just leaves the lacerations and contusions. The lacerations were treated, but the contusions will just have to heal on their own. How did all this happen?"

Mom opened her mouth to speak, but Tricia answered quicker. "Some boys from school beat him up, and Mom bought me some pepper spray." She held up a small vial.

"Careful with that," Mom said. Turning to Dr. Woodridge, she said, "I thought Tricia could use some protection. The boys who did this have been arrested, but there could be more out there like them. They claimed they were taking vengeance on our family. They actually believe my husband had something to do with the Prometheus accident."

"They caught them?" I thought Emily wasn't able to protect us anymore.

Mom nodded. "The LMC reported the situation right away to the MPs, honey, and help would have arrived sooner but the man-hunt going on at Descartes made them shorthanded. Thank God you weren't caught in that mess."

"We were lucky no one was killed," Dr. Woodridge said. "You'll have to excuse me. I have to check in on a few more patients before my shift ends. Your husband is one of them."

So Emily's blind spot was—It was as if it was tuned to Bosner. Not only that, but she couldn't track him either or the MPs wouldn't have had a problem locating him. How is that possible?

Dr. Woodridge poked her head back in and said, "Visiting hours are over in five minutes."

That was when I discovered it was Tuesday. I had lost a whole day while they fixed my bones and internal injuries.

Mom gave me a kiss on the forehead before she and Tricia left. "We'll see you tomorrow, honey. Sleep well." They wanted to say goodnight to Dad before they went back home, so they had to hurry.

The door slid silently closed behind them. Mom had looked tired, but Tricia had looked worse, as if she had been awake most of last night. People were after us now, so I bet she was nervous. But why was *Bosner* after me? If he was simply trying to kill people, there had been plenty at the tram station. Bosner chased *me*. What had I done to deserve this?

"Hello there neighbor," someone said from behind the curtain. I jumped at the sound. It was a young voice with an accent that sounded familiar.

"Hello?" I said.

Next I heard a stream of syllables in a language I didn't know. The curtain moved aside to reveal a large man in a dark suit wearing a turban. I stared up at him, shrinking back in my bed. He smiled and chuckled at my reaction, then glanced at the bed where a boy lying on his side turned toward me. The boy looked younger than me, maybe ten years old, and he had a dark complexion.

He said something to the large man, and they argued back and forth. Finally, the man grunted in agreement and left the room.

"Hello, my name is Azzam. What is yours?"

"I'm Dennis. Azzam?" Wasn't there a young prince on Luna by that name? "Not Prince Azzam?"

"You've heard of me," he said with a sigh. "I can meet no one without my heritage getting in the way."

"Who's the big guy? Your dad?"

"He's my bodyguard. I told him to leave us alone for a while. He's guarding the door."

"Wish I had a body guard. Those seniors wouldn't have been able to pound me. What are you in here for?"

"I was shot at Descartes."

"You were? I remember you now. I saw you go down right in front of me."

"You were there too? I can't even come to Luna without bringing a bulletproof vest. But for once I'm glad I was wearing it. That blast melted a large portion of the vest into my back."

"Jeez. That's got to hurt."

"I cannot lie on my back. They are growing me new skin now. It should be ready tomorrow. But we share more than just surviving the lunatic at Descartes. Do I seem . . . familiar to you?"

"I don't think so."

"I shall give you a hint. I know you are Sol Blanchard."

How did he know that? Wait. That accent . . . "Avedis?"

"It's me, Your Grace." Azzam smiled. "I overheard you say something earlier that Sol said a week ago, so I thought you were either Sol or you were there to hear it. It was that line about being dead your whole life, just not yet."

"So Prince Azzam is really Avedis, Prince Avedis. Hey. Is that a coincidence?"

"When I entered the realm, the computer assigned me a character: another prince. Imagine that? I was tired of being a prince in the real world let alone the SIM world. I convinced my Rapt father to send me to Waterton to learn the ways of magic."

"Hey, you saved my life back there at Descartes. If you hadn't run into me, that blast would have gone right through me. Thanks."

"Maybe. I mean, of course it would have." Azzam smiled broadly. Laughing, he added, "In fact, that was the whole reason I was at Descartes, to save your life."

I laughed. "Yeah, right. You're my bodyguard."

"I've been following you around for months protecting you from all harm. It is what I live for. You owe me big."

I laughed uneasily at the mention of someone following me. It reminded me of Clay Byron. Suddenly Clay was there, at the foot of my bed, looking at me. An unfelt breeze ruffled his hair like the ghosts of Rapt.

"I even arranged for us to be in the same room to give you protection while in the hospital. I am amazing, truly."

I whispered, "Go away."

Clay stood looking toward Azzam. "Tell no one of me. They wouldn't understand."

To be spiteful, and because I didn't know how to fight this creature in my head, I said, "Clay Byron."

"What was that?" Azzam asked.

"What do you know about a man named Clay Byron?"

"The name sounds familiar. Why . . . Why do you ask?"

"Tell him nothing," Clay said. "Only you can see me. He'll think you mad."

"No reason," I said.

"I think he was a poet, wasn't he?"

Clay turned to look at Azzam, his brow furrowed.

I shook my head. "You're thinking of Lord Byron. I'm talking about Clay Byron."

"No. No. Yes. He was a philosopher poet here on Luna. I think I studied about him in school."

Clay said, "He is lying, misleading you. Don't trust him, Dennis."

"What happened to him?" I asked. A wave of dizziness passed over me, and I closed my eyes.

"That's why I remember him," Azzam said. "He vanished back in the twenties or thirties and was never found. It must have been before the LMC could monitor everything across Luna. Some think he was killed and buried underneath Descartes or out in the desert."

"So they never caught who did it?"

"Never did."

When I opened my eyes, Clay had already vanished and with him went all my energy. Fatigue sank into my bones. Stifling a yawn, I said, "I'm a little sleepy, Avedis—I mean Azzam. I think I'll take a nap." There had to be a way to fight him, but I was just so tired.

I dreamed of Clay, alone, stumbling, lost in the desert, collapsing from the heat. At some point it changed to me.

* * *

I didn't wake up until Wednesday morning. I didn't think I could sleep for fourteen hours, but according to the clock, that's just what happened.

After returning from the bathroom, I found Prince Azzam had a visitor. The curtain was partially drawn, but I could see him. He was a rotund man wearing a black jacket and sporting a neatly trimmed mustache. As I climbed back in bed, I heard him say, "You were lucky to be wearing that vest."

"A person in my position must expect the worst," Azzam said.

"Do you think you were the target? Maybe all the other victims were just to make the hit seem random."

"How am I to know?" Azzam tried to shrug, but he was lying on his side so it didn't quite work.

"Did you receive any death threats? Has anything like this happened to you or your family before?"

"That is why I have to wear the vest. My family is threatened with assassination often."

"Do these threats come from any particular group?"

"Inspector," Azzam said, talking slowly as if explaining something that should be obvious. "There are many factions that would like to replace my father. It could have been any of them, but probably not. Usually a terrorist attack is associated with some kind of political maneuvering. They would want to make it clear what they were up to, not disguise it."

"Hmph," the inspector said. "Ever since the LMC went into full surveillance we haven't had anything like this. But the LMC has no record of the incident, and for the first time in forever, we've got a shooting without a suspect."

I said, "You don't know who did it?"

"We've got a dozen descriptions, but no ID." the man said. Then, poking his head around the curtain, he looked at me. "How ya doing. Inspector Jamison. Jack Jamison, military police."

I shook his offered hand. "I'm Dennis Howard." My lip, though tender, was back to its normal size. "I was at the station Monday when it happened. The guy you're looking for is Kyle Bosner." I crawled back into bed and pulled the covers up.

The inspector looked surprised. "Kyle Bosner? Ya don't say?" Jamison glanced down and keyed some notes into his notepad. He was probably trying to bring up some info on him. Good luck with that.

"I've seen him around," I said. "He chased me through the university, firing that gun."

Jamison opened his eyes wide. "So you're the kid he chased. Some people said they saw him run after a boy bent on murder. Looks like he ran out of ammo and decided to beat the shinola out of you."

"No. I hid from him in an empty office. He never found me. When I got back to Aristoteles, some kids from school jumped me on my way home. That's how I ended up here."

"So you're real popular, eh? What's this Bosner character got against you?"

I shrugged. "I've been helping Artemus Regale with a project. Maybe he's from a competitor and wants me out of the way. I don't know." At least that's what Artemus had told me. I still didn't believe it.

"Artemus Regale?" The inspector's eyebrows went up even farther. "You mean *the* Artemus Regale, the head of SI? He's a real recluse, that one. I'm impressed, kid. What's he like?"

I shrugged. Should I tell him he's a maniacal genius trying to steal my body? "He's, ah . . . really focused on his goals."

"A real workaholic. I get it," the inspector said. "So you think Bosner's a hired gun out to derail this project of yours. What did you say it was about?"

I smiled. Did anyone fall for that anymore? "I can't really talk about that." I gave Azzam a quick glance to see if he caught the fumbled attempt to pry information from me. He looked fascinated by our conversation, his eyes dancing back and forth between us as we spoke.

"Right, right. And he shot all those other people, including the prince over here, as a diversion?"

"I don't know. Maybe he's just crazy."

"Lucky you found an open office to hide in. I mean, all the doors lock automatically. Someone else coming out just as you were going in?"

"No. It was empty, like, vacant."

"Not many of those," Jamison said. "My sister works over there. Up for tenure this year. She complains all the time about having to share an office. Any chance you remember the office number?"

I shrugged and shook my head.

"Too bad." He furrowed his forehead and turned back to his notepad. "Wait a minute . . ." He murmured as he paged through looking for something. Then he said, "Ah, yes." He then turned to look about, then threw an image up on the far wall just opposite both Azzam and myself. I hadn't even realized it was a Window-Wall.

The image was of what appeared to be a live vid of a hallway. It could have been a hall anywhere on Luna, except there were some college-age students passing by. Maybe it was the university. There was a mini-map in the lower-right corner showing a network of hallways and an arrow indicating the actual location of the shot, but it was too zoomed in to tell me even what city we were looking at.

"Look familiar?" Jamison asked without turning. That's when I noticed scorch marks on the walls where Bosner's blaster must have hit. I said nothing as Jamison made several gestures and the image advanced in leaps down the hall and took a turn to the left. "There's an office down around here that's kind of infamous. Seems the fella that used to work there vanished forty years ago, but Dean Galling won't assign it to anyone else. Galling's stuck on the notion that he might come back. Or maybe he's keeping it as some kind of shrine."

"Forty years ago?" I asked, leaning forward. "Whose office was it?"

"Hmm? Oh, let's see—what was the name? I want to say Baron—no Byron."

"Clay Byron," I mumbled.

"That's the guy."

Clay did mention it used to be his office. I'd forgotten. No wonder Artemus was there that day. If Artemus really was Clay twice removed, it was his own office. Dean Galling had no idea, but Clay not only came back but he never left.

The image took a turn to the right, then another to the left. He was retracing the path I'd taken on my mad dash to get away. We went up a short flight of steps and took a quick right. And there it was. The door to the office was open.

"Yeah, that's it," I said.

He glanced back at me. "I thought I remembered something about an office door that took a beating. You can see part of the doorframe was melted." A few more gestures and the image was zoomed in on the damage. "How did you get in there?"

How did I get in there? Clay had told me the password, that's how. "I don't know. The door . . . just opened," I said weakly, feeling as if I were walking across a field of land mines.

"Hm. Well, maybe the LMC decided to give him some place to hide . . ." he said to himself. "So he came after you and . . . The locking mechanism is busted, Dennis. So . . . you ducked into this office but couldn't lock the door behind you. He must have chased you in there." He looked at me suspiciously. "How did you escape?"

"I hid out on the balcony. There's a door next to the window behind the curtain, but it's made to look like the rest of the wall. He couldn't find it."

"Nice. That's nice." Jamison said. He tried to move the image into the office, but his efforts were frustrated. The LMC, in a female voice, said, "Data is not available within this room."

Prince Azzam asked, "If this door to the balcony was hidden, how did you find it?"

I just looked at him and blinked. It was Clay who told me about the door, but I couldn't mention that. "I was—um—I was in that room before. That's where Artemus interviewed me for the project with SI."

Jamison smiled. "Oh, it's *Artemus*, is it? First name basis . . . good for you Dennis. What do they say—rubbing elbows with the upper crust? You two buddies now?" He waved and the Window-Wall went back to looking like a normal wall.

"Artemus and I . . ." I wanted to tell the inspector how furious I was at Artemus, how scared I was that this creature was crawling in my brain and I was defenseless. I could tell him about the vid Trevor and I uncovered showing Artemus blowing up the power plant, but there was no evidence. I'd have to reveal how we got the information, and they would seal up the back door before we got to really use it. "Artemus and I—we're growing closer all the time."

Maybe my expression gave something away. He narrowed his eyes suspiciously for a moment. "Well, you won't have to worry about—" he glanced down at his notes, "—about this Kyle Bosner. I've already started the ball rolling. We'll get a court order to unlock the LMC's tracking system and incarcerate him before lunch. Provided the LMC doesn't take another nap, that is."

He started to head toward the door, but I held up a hand. "I don't think that'll work. Emily—I mean the LMC has some kind of blind spot around him and his brother."

"Now there's two of them?"

"I think they have some kind of influence over the LMC."

He laughed at the idea. "Influence? No one can control that thing. But if these Bosner brothers can, maybe I can have them put in a good word for my sister and get her that empty office." He raised his hand which held the notepad. "Your Highness, thank you for your time. Dennis, it's been a pleasure. Expect I'll have more questions at some point." He started to turn but paused again. "Howard? That your last name? Any relation to Dr. Peter Howard?"

"He's my father."

"Then it's true what they say. Like father like son. Eh?"

The inspector left, and I turned to Azzam. "What did he mean by that?"

Azzam did his best at shrugging while lying on his side. "Maybe he meant that you and your father were both at the center of disaster, but both of you came out with your lives."

And both of us were being blamed for death and destruction, directly or indirectly. It wasn't my fault.

* * *

The military guard standing outside Dad's hospital room accessed the Mixed-Reality rig in his glasses and frowned. "So you're

Dr. Howard's son, eh? You're not on the cleared list of personnel."
He swiped the air, clearly paging through some data and looked
down at me dubiously. "According to this, he has no son."

"The LMC's memory is frizzed," I said. "She's got hundreds of
things wrong or missing on my records." I was in an uncomfortable
motorized chair that was making my ribs hurt, and I didn't feel like
arguing with this shining example of military intelligence. He had
already verified my identity as Dennis Howard with my face, but he
said having the same last name didn't necessarily make me and the
doctor related.

He pressed his finger to his ear com-link and put his other hand
on his side arm. "Corporal Kelleher, Delta 511. I've got a kid here
positively ID'ed as Dennis Howard wanting access to Dr. Peter
Howard. Claims Dr. Howard's his father, but I've no record of that.
Please advise."

His eyes never left me while we waited for an answer. I imagined
him pulling his gun out and firing. What could I do to stop him?
What if he was as insane as Kyle Bosner?

Hearing a voice from his com-link, he suddenly came to
attention, his eyes snapping to the wall across the corridor. Still
holding a finger to his ear he said, "General Anderson, sir, Corporal
Kelleher here, sir . . . Lieutenant Kerinsky was just in with Dr.
Howard but was called away. He instructed me to bar entry until his
return . . . I understand, sir . . . As you wish, sir, Kelleher out."

Turning to me again he said, "You can go in. Your name's been
added to the permanent access list." He punched a code into the pad
mounted on the wall next to the door, and the door slid away
revealing the dark interior.

I nodded my head. "All right then. Good." Pushing the lever
attached to the armrest, I directed the chair into the room. The chair
was more annoyance than necessity for me, but the nurses wouldn't
let me walk out of the room unaided. I nearly scraped the wall as I
entered Dad's private room.

The door slid shut behind me, and I wondered if the Corporal
locked it. The lights were dim, so I instructed Emily to increase the

illumination. When she didn't respond, I glanced at the com-pad on the wall. The blinking light on the pad told me she was in privacy mode.

With the lights so low maybe Dad was asleep. It was past lunch, though, and his arm attachment operation was scheduled for five o'clock. He should be excited about the new arm, not drowsy. I knew the particular pain suppressants they were giving him kept him clear headed, or I wouldn't have come in here hoping he could help get me out of my contract with Artemus.

His bed was flat, and he didn't say anything when I called his name. Leaving Emily in privacy mode, I manually brought the lights up some and wheeled myself beside his bed. "Hey Dad, wake up."

"Hmmm? Who is it?" he asked. His speech was slurred, as if he was drunk. He picked up his head for a second, then let it fall back to his pillow.

"It's me, Dennis. Are you okay?"

"I'm okay-dokey. Hunky-chunky-dorry. Where are you?"

"I'm right here."

He picked his head up again, but it seemed too much effort for him to control. When he began fumbling with the bed controls, I took the control and raised the back of the bed for him.

"There you are." He pointed in my general direction, then let his hand fall back down.

"What's wrong with you? What kind of drugs do they have you on?"

"You're the man of the house now, Dennis. Dennis and Patricia and Cindy should leave Luna. Go back to Earth where it's safe."

They must have put him on some harder drugs in preparation for the operation. Maybe he had been nervous, so they gave him something to calm him down.

"And . . ." Dad said. "Wait. How did you get hurt? You weren't there. Or was that your friend . . . Zak?"

"Dad, some kids thrashed me a few days ago because they thought you blew up Prometheus."

"Nooo. The explosion was centered just below the surface. The lab is fifteen floors down. Project Heliotrope—Oops. I said the 'H' word. Project Icarus couldn't have caused that. It's too bad all those floors above us began to crumble. No more Icarus. All gone."

Heliotrope? What was that? Something classified? "Dad, what is Project Heliotrope?" I glanced back at the com-pad to make sure it was still blinking in privacy mode.

"Shh," Dad said with a finger to his lips. "You're not allowed to say the 'H' word outside the lab. Call it Icarus."

"What's Project Icarus?"

"I can't talk about that in a hospital. That's just stupid."

"But . . . but we're *at* the lab. You can talk about it. It's okay."

"We are? Oh yeah. I knew that." He gasped suddenly. "What are you doing here? Dennis! We've got to get you home before they find out. You'll be shot on sight." He started to struggle to get out of the bed, kicking off the covers.

"No, ah. There's no need to panic. I'm not Dennis. I'm ah—" What was that Lieutenant's name? The general's name was easy to remember. "I'm Anderson. General Anderson."

"General Anderson?" Dad said with wide eyes. He stopped trying to get out of bed. "Oh how stupid. I—I knew that. What a relief. I thought my son was violating security."

I felt horrible doing this, but I needed to know. "I've been told your project had nothing to do with the Prometheus explosion. Is that right?"

"Of course not, sir. You don't come down to the labs very often. Should I show you around?" He started to get up again.

"No, that's all right. Why don't you just tell me about Heliotrope? How are things going?"

Dad looked down and wouldn't meet my eyes. "It's gone. The device is destroyed. The roof caved in on the clean room, and now there's just a heap of rubble."

"What device?"

"The GDP-109. Oh, you probably know of it as the Icarus Device."

"The weapon?"

"Weapon? It's not a weapon. Certainly you've read our reports."

I said, "It's been a while. Tell me again."

"The Icarus Device is a power generator," Dad said. His voice dropped low as if in awe. "It's light enough to carry in one hand but can generate . . . we don't know how much. Last month was the first time we got it to work after it was reassembled. We managed to pull almost 13 terra-watts out of it sustained over a minute, but we couldn't do more than that. We could only shunt so much power away."

"Wow."

"It all fits into a cylinder which measures exactly twenty centimeters in diameter and eight centimeters deep."

"How does it work?"

"Yes, yes. That's the question," he said with a laugh. "There's over thirty-five years of notes on the Icarus Device, and we still don't know. But we're getting close. Rosen has a theory about the superstring quantum tessellations—Rosen is dead. I just remembered. He was in the clean room."

"What do you mean you don't know? Didn't you make the device?"

"You've got to get us another one," Dad said grabbing my arm. "There's too much at stake. A device like this could propel humanity into the galaxy. Where did you get the first one?"

The Icarus Device must have been something they were given to study. They didn't create it at all. I whispered, "Is it some kind of— of alien technology?"

"We've got all the best minds in physics working on the device. It's not from Earth. It can't be." He started to laugh.

"What's so funny?"

"It's just—it's just that it has to be of human origin. It has digital displays in plain English. And—and 'GDP-109' is etched on the side. Where did you get it? I must know."

The door to the room slid open, and I turned my head to see a crisp blue uniform stride in.

Chapter Nine

Dredging for Treasure

"K elleher tells me you're Dennis," the officer stated flatly.

"Right."

"He's General Anderson," Dad said, indicating me. "He's visiting the labs and wants to know all about the GDP-109."

I shook off Dad's arm which was still gripping my sleeve and pulled self-consciously at my hospital gown, the only thing I wore. "I don't know what he's talking about. They have him on some kind of drug—"

"Dennis Howard, of course," the officer said as he took something from his pocket. He stepped to the other side of Dad's bed and pressed something against his neck. He was giving him an injection.

"Hey, what are you doing?"

A few moments after the injection, Dad became still. "Dr. Howard needs to sleep now."

"Are you a doctor?"

"My name is Lieutenant Kerinsky. As a civilian, you have the privilege of addressing me as 'sir.' We need to have a serious talk, don't we Dennis?"

"Talk about what?" I asked innocently.

"Talk about what, sir," he said.

I just looked at him.

"Come on. Let's go to my office."

"I'm not supposed to leave the hospital. I'm under observation."

"They won't miss you for a few minutes." Kerinsky got behind my chair and started wheeling me toward the door.

"Dr. Woodridge scheduled another neural scan in half an hour."

"They'll just have to reschedule, now, won't they?"

The door slid open, and he pushed me out past the corporal who still stood guard. To the corporal, Kerinsky said, "Which word of 'bar entry' didn't you understand?"

"But I spoke to General Anderson—"

"I'll deal with you later."

He pushed my chair slowly down the hall, past the nurse's station. "This must all seem very confusing to you, hmm? Explosions, people being shot."

"Yeah, it's just—"

Leaning down behind my neck, he said, "Shh. Don't say anything yet. We'll have a little chat and things will become clearer. The military, after all, only exists to serve and protect the civilian masses. In that capacity, we'll get to the bottom of this mystery. Like your father, Dr. Howard. Now there's a patriot."

He pushed me into an elevator and put his palm on the com-pad. "Storage and supply level. Override lock, authorization Kerinsky, critical-mass-238."

The doors closed and we slowly accelerated downward. Except for the steady light on the com-pad indicating Emily was watching, we were alone. Why were we going to the storage level?

I should ask Emily to connect me with Mom, just to let someone know I was with Kerinsky. "Emily—"

"Privacy mode, please," Kerinsky said.

With Emily's voice, the LMC said, "Of course. Reinstate me by pressing the com-pad when you are through. Now entering privacy mode."

He put his hands on my shoulders as if he didn't want me to get up to reach the com-pad. There was no need to panic, though. I could have always shouted for help and made a fuss. The threat of danger would have woken Emily up instantly. Besides, this guy was a member of the military. He just wanted some time to talk to me, probably about what he suspected I knew of Icarus. I'll just deny knowing anything.

"Like I was saying, your father's a real patriot. Dr. Howard's a very important man, and there was some concern that he might be involved in something—"

We decelerated to a stop at the bottom floor, and the doors opened. It was noticeably colder down here, especially since I was only wearing a hospital gown. Lights came on following our progress down the hall, throwing shadows from boxes stacked at intervals between doors.

"But Dr. Howard's clean. I had to interrogate him to be sure, but he honestly has no idea who caused the explosion."

Clay Byron shimmered and solidified twenty paces down the hall. "Dennis, you're in danger."

I licked my lips and asked, "What are we doing down here? I thought we were going to your office."

"We *are* going to my office. Space is tight these days, and I only just came on this project this week. I found a room down here. It's only temporary."

Clay started walking backwards to stay in front of us. He said, "The next time you have boxes on either side of you, get out of the wheelchair and run. You can get a head start while he struggles to get past the chair."

I shook my head, ignoring Clay. He just wanted to keep my body safe for himself. I never got the chance to take Clay's suggestion anyway. Kerinsky turned the chair abruptly and stopped in front of a closed door. He tapped a code into the pad on the wall and said, "Battlefield."

The door slid open and lights blinked on as we entered. The room was devoid of furniture, completely empty.

"Look out," Clay said from behind me. "He's got—"

I felt something cold pressed into my neck, then, before I knew it, a sharp pinch. He'd given me an injection.

"Hold still, Dennis," Kerinsky whispered in my ear. "There you go. Now you can relax."

I got to my feet rubbing my neck. Kerinsky was closing the door and locking it with a code. The com-pad across the room had been ripped out of the wall, leaving only exposed wires. "Unorthodox? Perhaps. Unsanctioned? Definitely. But I don't have time for screwing around. There are too many lives at stake."

Clay was in the room too. "Dennis?" His image wavered as the room began to spin. The floor came up and hit me, and a stab of pain went through my ribs.

"Maybe you shouldn't have gotten up," Kerinsky said. "You'll get dirty down there. Here, let me help you." He grabbed me under my arms and slammed me back into my chair. I groaned in pain at the impact. "Didn't hurt you, did I? Don't worry about it. You won't remember any of this later."

Just before he vanished, Clay said, "I'll remember."

"What?" Kerinsky said. "Think you'll remember, do you?"

I must have spoken Clay's words out loud. It didn't bother me for some reason.

"What is your name?" Kerinsky asked.

"Dennis Howard."

"Who's your father?"

"Peter Howard."

"How is it the LMC doesn't agree? It thinks he never had a son, and you're listed as father unknown."

He looked very funny, too thin. I imagined him fat, and he expanded like rubber. "Emily is confused. She's got all kinds of things wrong about me. Just ask her."

"I've arranged for some real privacy," Kerinsky said with a smile. "Funny how things work out. I'm questioning your father when I get a call from the amazing Lieutenant Colonel Mary Parkinson. She tells me a report was just filed naming Kyle Bosner as the Descartes massacre perp. I run off to talk to the inspector and find out that Bosner's target might just be Dennis Howard, son of the good doctor in charge of Icarus. I go looking for you and find you just where I was not a half hour before, prying classified information from your dad."

"You should lose some weight. My favorite color is red."

"Why were you questioning Dr. Howard?"

"I had to make sure he didn't blow up the plant, but he didn't. I heard he's a real patriot. The Icarus Device isn't a weapon at all."

"What do you know about the device?"

"It's a very powerful power generator. That's funny, isn't it? Power power power—"

"Have you ever seen the device?"

"I've never been to the labs. I'd be shot on sight. Where are we?"

"Do you know what it looks like?"

Nothing. I knew nothing. Words came out of my mouth anyway. "It's a squat cylinder, exactly twenty centimeters in diameter and eight centimeters deep. It's got some writing on it and a digital display in real honest to goodness English. Hey. It looks just like the bomb that blew up Prometheus. He set it to overload."

Kerinsky perked up. "What bomb?"

"Shhh. Don't tell anyone. Artemus will find out and come after us."

"Artemus? Artemus Regale?"

"He's very powerful. I said it again. Power power—"

"Why would Regale come after us?"

"He set the bomb. Trevor and I saw it in a vid buried in the LMC, but the vid is lost. I don't think he did it. He had no way of getting out of there before it blew up."

"The vid shows Regale setting the bomb, but you think the image was planted in the LMC's memory?"

"The vid has to be real. Trevor told me. It's stored holo—holo—everywhere, and it would be easy to test time stamps on the different vids to see if it's real. But—" I laughed in his face. "Emily can't remember the vid, so we can't test it."

"Does Regale have any other Icarus Devices?"

"No. If I had one, I'd keep it with me all the time. Like on my belt. And I'd wear a long coat, just like the Bosners do, so no one would see it."

"The Bosners have Icarus Devices?"

"Ha. I didn't notice before, but you're right. Both Bosners have Icarus Devices. When they chase after you firing their guns, you can see it under their coat, but they've got to be running."

"Why does this Kyle Bosner want you dead?"

"They attacked me in the access tubes. One of them almost ran over me with a rover, and then he tried to shoot me right in the tram station. I know why, too." I motioned Kerinsky closer and whispered, "They're not very nice."

"Is that it, eh? What's the connection between Regale and the Bosners?"

"Artemus told me they were competitors, and he told me to stay away from them. Artemus is afraid of them. They kill people, and they've got technology that can hide them from Emily. How can they do that?" I put my arms over the top of my head. "I need a hat. It's cold in here."

"Are you in league with the Bosners? What do they want?"

"No. I want to be a master."

"What does that mean?" He grabbed my arm and squeezed. "Are you from the future? Were you put here to infiltrate Dr. Howard's household and prevent him from unlocking the secrets of the device?"

"I'm not from the future. I'm from the past. I was born on Luna. I love you—shut up. I love you—shut up. Ahh, Let me go!"

"I've unearthed a contract between you and Regale that gives you all his wealth if the project is a success. Is Regale in league with your father to get the secret of the device?"

"Artemus is evil. His dogs killed me twenty times. Please don't make me go back there." I started to cry. "He's filling my head, but I want to be me, not him. I want socks. It's very dizzy in here." The room started to spin.

Kerinsky released my arm and backed away. "Is that right?"

"Where are we? What is the day? I've no time to waste."

"We'll leave when I say we're done."

I got to my feet. "Don't you use that tone with me. Have some respect. You speak of things you can't conceive. My wife—she's dead." I felt unsteady and grabbed the arm of the chair.

Kerinsky took something from his pocket and held it up to the light. "How much of this did I give you?"

I eased myself back down. "Yes, she's dead. Killed by that Bosner."

"Bosner killed your wife? What was her name?"

"Her name was—I can't—I can't remember her first name." I put my finger to my temples. "I feel like so much of my memory is gone." A wave of dizziness swept through me.

I gasped. What was this place? I jumped up from a cold seat and crouched low. "Where am I? What kind of wigwam is this?"

"Did you say wigwam?"

I looked down at my arms. My skin was pale; my arms were small and weak. "I must be sick, sick for a long time."

"Why don't you just have a seat?"

"Who are you? Where is Quick Hand?"

"Quick Hand?"

"Is this another test of Raven? Some magic conjured by the trickster?" I stood and raised my arms in supplication. "Great Spirit! Hear me. Take me home. Give me back my son." Dizziness struck me full force, and I fell to the ground.

I screamed and opened my eyes. A man, smelling of sweat, tried to hold my arms down, and I kicked him. He shouted in pain and rolled away.

The flowers were supposed to bear me to heaven, but what was this? Was I dead?

I saw a door and ran to it. "Sister Tolerance. Sister Beneficence! I'm sorry I failed the test. Please let me out. I'll be a good sister. Let me out."

The man got up and grabbed a small cylinder from the floor. "No one can hear you," he snarled.

It was punishment. I failed the test.

He loomed over me and pressed something into my neck. "No, let go of me! Help!" It bit me like a spider. Maybe I was to die after all. I could feel the venom spreading.

* * *

I woke up in my hospital bed with a bearded doctor leaning over me. Mom was there along with a nurse or two. Mom was worried, but the doctor tried to calm her down, explaining that my blood chemistry was returning to normal. In a day, the drug would be ninety percent out of my system. I didn't know what they were talking about.

When the doctors and nurses left Mom said, "They found you five hours ago unconscious in the elevator. What happened to you? Who gave you those drugs?"

"I remember going to see Dad. Someone came in. I can't remember."

"Your father was given the same drugs. He's okay, but they had to reschedule his operation for tomorrow. There was a guard outside his room all day. Who could have gotten past him?"

"It would have to have been someone from the military."

"Since when are we under martial law? Are the military allowed to do anything they please? Your father can't remember who did this to him either. What good is Sally if she can't protect us?" She was talking about the LMC.

Clay Byron coalesced into existence huddled in a ball against the far wall. Mom didn't notice when I whispered his name. Clay looked up at me and slowly got to his feet. His face was lined with weariness, and his eyes looked sunken.

"Where's Tricia?" I asked.

"With your father. I feel as though I can't leave either of you alone for a minute."

"Dennis, I have a gift for you," Clay said. "It's a fragment of time stolen from your life. With great effort, I have kept it whole."

"I can't remember what happened."

"Don't worry," Mom said. "We'll get to the bottom of things soon enough."

"Look into my eyes," Clay said. "Look and remember."

Mom continued, "I spoke to Inspector Jamison personally, and he said he was coming over right away."

Ignoring Mom, I looked into his eyes. They were blue, tinged with grey, deep. I wanted to remember, even if it meant obeying the creature in my brain. A demon had attached himself to my soul, a demon with blue-grey eyes that reflected the rain across a distant mountainside. It was the rain of far-off memory. It shifted and began to fall on me, sprinkling snatches of images: a desolate hallway lined with boxes, the blinking light on the com-pad of my father's room, bare wires dangling out of a blank wall in an empty room.

Then memory began to flood back. I remembered the Icarus Device, the room down below, and Kerinsky's sneering visage. I gasped as the pieces fell back into place and became whole.

"If I were but half the monster of your fleeting imaginings, God above wouldn't suffer me to exist," Clay whispered. His head fell to his chest in exhaustion, and he vanished.

We must have shared portions of thought during the exchange, but there had to be more information he knew that would help. If only I could figure out how to get at that knowledge.

I knew what had happened and what I'd said to Kerinsky, but I still didn't know what was really going on. By the sound of his questions, neither did Kerinsky. I needed time to think.

When Jamison arrived, I gave him Kerinsky's name but nothing more. I told him I didn't remember what happened, only that Kerinsky drugged me.

Mom asked the inspector to post a guard outside both Dad's and my room, but the inspector said he didn't have the manpower. He pointed out that there already were guards outside both rooms: Prince Azzam's body guard outside mine and a military guard outside Dad's. When Mom whispered that neither of them could be trusted, he shrugged and said there was nothing he could do. MPs all over Luna were searching for Kyle Bosner, and there was no one to spare.

After dinner, they took Azzam away for his skin graft operation. Mom and Tricia left too, promising to be back early tomorrow. I locked the door after everyone was gone, which gave me some reassurance. Every doctor and nurse in the hospital could override it, but I still felt better.

And I finally had time to think. It was something Kerinsky had asked: Was I from the future? He wasn't kidding. Time travel? That was the fodder of science fiction. It was nonsense. And yet . . . How could a device be found thirty or forty years in the past that even today we couldn't understand: the Icarus Device? And I remembered seeing the Bosners with Icarus Devices strapped under their coats.

What if the Bosner brothers really were from the future?

"Emily?"

"Hello, Dennis," she said.

"Can you show me the events that took place back in 2039, when Clay's wife was killed? I mean Clay Byron's wife, Ariel?"

"Imagery from the September 19, 2039 massacre at Bark's Eatery, Descartes, has been classified."

"Who was the man who did the shooting again?"

"The assailant was a man named Mavin Bosner."

"Can you show me any vid of him?"

"That information remains classified. You asked me for that same information several days ago, and the security surrounding Mavin Bosner has not changed."

I sighed. "Emily, privacy mode."

"Sure. Reinstate me when you are through. Entering privacy mode now."

Barefooted, I padded over to stand in front of the Window-Wall. I leaned forward and, like uttering a magic spell, I whispered, "Recall the Lumus-A genome."

The same static-filled image of scrolling letters that I had seen before appeared on the wall. This time, no DNA helix appeared superimposed on the DNA codes. Instead, the familiar face of Dr. Gabrielle Thompson rotated through the letters. A voice resolved itself out of the static for a moment. It sounded like a reporter. ". . . intruder at the CDC . . ." Then after another moment of static, ". . . watched as Lumus-A, the antigen for Lumus, developed by Thompson and her . . . airborne was released and already . . ."

"Dr. Thompson," I said. "Thank you for choosing a series 3000 seed computer for your genetic research. Let's move on, shall we?"

It only took me twenty minutes to bring Emily from Dr. Thompson's face in 2028 to Bark's Eatery in 2039. And I managed it without Trevor's cheat sheet of historical events. My memory must be improving.

"Recall the moment Clay Byron met Mavin Bosner."

I couldn't help jumping in surprise when the sound of a shot blasted through the air, clear and crisp. An image of the Nick O' Time café in Descartes faded in, and my heart began to pound as I recognized the scene. "Shut up, shut up!" screamed Bosner as he fired repeatedly into the crowd. I could barely keep my eyes on the vid. It was horrifying. Every shot of light that lanced across the room landed with deadly accuracy. Several men jumped him and brought the killing to an end.

I finally saw Clay. He was kneeling and holding a woman in his arms. Her entire back smoldered. "Ariel," I whispered at the same moment the Clay from the vid whispered it. A crushing loss descended on me. I closed my eyes, but the tears couldn't be stopped.

On the vid, I recognized Clay's voice as he began to scream in anguish, getting louder with every passing moment. With a start that sent me off my chair, the Clay living in my mind appeared behind me screaming the same agony. He stopped and doubled over in pain with his eyes closed. Falling to the floor he said, "Turn it off. Turn it off. You torment me." He vanished.

Wiping tears from my face, I turned back to the desk. "Recall Bosner and Icarus."

The scene changed. Mavin Bosner, handcuffed and bleary eyed, was sitting before a table in a small room. Two other men and a woman stood over him. It reminded me of Kerinsky's interrogation room.

It was the first clear image of him that I'd seen. I half expected to recognize Mavin Bosner as either Kyle or the other one—what was his name? The name Jason popped into my head. Then I remembered Kyle had mentioned that name right before they attacked me in the access tunnel.

Mavin—he wasn't either of them. Even without the same last name, the similarity in their features left little doubt that they were related. Separated in time by forty years, maybe Mavin Bosner was Kyle's and Jason's father or even grandfather.

A variety of objects that must have come from Bosner's pockets were scattered over the table. His gun wasn't there, but that made sense. You'd never give a prisoner access to a weapon, shackled or not. One item on the table caught my eye: a small squat cylinder with three blinking lights and a display on top that read 'Active.'

"All right, Bosner, what is this thing? What's it for?" one of the men demanded. He leaned over and pushed the Icarus Device toward Bosner.

Bosner, looking at the ceiling, murmured, "I'm alone. I'm alone . . . I've done nothing—nothing to deserve . . ."

"Snap out of it, Bosner. You can act crazy later. What were you doing at Bark's?"

Bosner, as if he hadn't heard, went on. "The voices—the voices are gone. Kill the worst of them, the crazy ones. They deserve it. It's the only way . . . Ahh! You—you! You're all bent, all twisted. I'm entombed in this Bedlam, abandoned, marooned."

One of the men shook his head, "I don't think we're going to get any more out of him today. His ranting is giving me a headache."

The woman came around the table and picked up the Icarus Device. Bosner laughed quietly as he watched the device in her hands. He said in a half whisper, "What joy brings you thus, brother Icarus, out of bondage now . . . what rose sublime a moment before now transforms into this tar pit of blackness? Pride brought you, unworthiness keeps you. Your wings, Icarus, do you see . . . see how they fly not?"

Chapter Ten

Supposedly Noble

After a final brain scan on Thursday morning, Dr. Woodridge told me and Mom that I could go back home. That would mean going back to Artemus' brainwashing torture chamber and a fate worse than death.

"But I've got a headache. What could that mean?" I didn't even have to lie. As I stared up at Dr. Woodridge, my brain throbbed.

She shook her head. "There's no indication of neural dysfunction. It's probably nothing to worry about. Just stay off the SIMs for a while."

Doctor's orders to stay out of the SIMs. That could keep me away from Artemus until Mom and Dad looked at the contract and figured a way out. So much had happened the past few days that I never even told Mom about Artemus' contract trickery. Could I even tell them what was really at stake? Would they believe it?

No SIMs? "But the next tournament match is tomorrow!"

Mom said, "Dennis, you can watch that on a vid. There's no need to enter a SIM."

"But Mom . . ."

"You heard what the doctor said. No SIMs."

Dr. Woodridge knew I was a competitor. She watched the exchange between us, then came to my defense. "Actually, SIMming should be your least concern. Provided you avoid fights with your schoolmates, elude drugged abductions, and evade maniacs wielding weapons, I'd say watching a SIM tomorrow shouldn't be a problem."

Mom grimaced but said nothing. I could be wrong about Artemus using the tournament as a way to search for people with the right brain chemistry for his own illicit purposes. I could be throwing away my chance at being a Master.

Dad was supposed to get his new arm tonight, and after that, Artemus had no real leverage over me but a piece of paper. I could stall him for one day, then I'd have the weekend and enough time to get lawyers involved.

After Mom and the doctor left, I changed into normal clothes. My semi-private room was private enough, what with the curtain between me and Azzam.

After I was decent again, I sat on my bed for a minute. Thankfully, my headache seemed to get better. Then, poking my head around the curtain separating Azzam's bed from mine, I said, "Azzam, you awake?"

"For the moment," he said. "They gave me some pain killers they said would put me to sleep." He was lying on his stomach, and his back was covered with white gauze and bandages. He faced the foot of his bed so that he could watch a vid on the Window-Wall. "I hear you are being released?"

"I'm going over the wall," I joked. "There's no joint that can hold me. You want in?"

"Huh?"

"Never mind. What are you watching?"

"The president just gave a speech on public safety and the effort to catch the shooter. She's answering questions now." The audio was focused so just Azzam could hear it.

"Turn it wide."

Azzam commanded the audio to be room-wide, and I watched as President Quillen pointed to a reporter.

"Madame President. If the Lunar Main Computer has no visual record of the incident, and can't ID the perpetrator, how is it you know the man's name is Bosner?"

"We have a witness who—" Quillen began, but stopped when someone stepped up beside her and whispered something in her ear. It was Mayor Metler, Zak's dad.

Quillen nodded and turned back to the crowd. "I'm sorry, but the details of the investigation are sensitive and cannot be disclosed at this time."

Shouting above the other reporters, the same man asked, "But the LMC has no record of anyone named Bosner on Luna. This man doesn't even exist."

Quillen said, "I assure you, the injuries of fourteen upstanding citizens prove that he exists, regardless of the LMC's information to the contrary. It was a miracle that no one was killed."

With a wave of his hand, Azzam commanded the volume down again. "You are the witness she was talking about. You told the inspector it was Bosner."

"Kyle Bosner. You think he was after you?" I asked.

"Maybe . . ." Azzam said. "But, I don't think so. There are easier ways to assassinate people. Besides, he chased you, didn't he?"

I sat on my bed. "Do you believe it's possible to travel through time, hypothetically speaking?"

Azzam looked confused. "What?"

"Sorry," I said. "I've been thinking a lot about some of the impossible things that have been happening around here. Things that seem impossible now . . . If someone came back from the future with amazing technology . . ."

"I believe the sun rises every day—"

"You mean every four weeks."

"Well, on Luna—it depends on what planet you're on—maybe *all* my beliefs are wrong," Azzam said laughing.

"Now I'm serious. Is it crazy to think people might someday invent the technology to travel through time and visit us?"

"It isn't crazy. It could happen, I suppose."

"Can you keep a secret?"

"I revealed my Rapt identity to you, so I guess not. Please don't tell anyone. I went to a lot of trouble to hide my royal lineage."

"Your secret's safe with me. Now listen to this. I think the Bosners are—Privacy mode, Emily."

After she turned off, I continued. "Here's my theory. The Bosners, right? What if they're from the future? Now hold on," I said as he started to laugh. "Just hear me out. There were two of them, Jason and Kyle. I think the Bosners came back to stop research going on at the military compound underneath Prometheus."

Suddenly Clay was standing beside me, and I jumped off the bed in surprise. "What are you doing?" he shouted. "Don't tell him anything. You don't know who can be trusted."

"Don't do that to me," I whispered, covering my mouth with my hand as if scratching my nose.

"What makes you think that?" Azzam asked.

He was Avedis. I knew him. Why should I listen to the demon in my head? "You can't breathe a word of this. All right? They were secretly researching a device found . . . like thirty five years ago. They pulled it off of *another* guy named Bosner after *he* shot and killed a bunch of people in Descartes. It was just like what happened at the tram station."

"Really? Was it the same guy?"

I shook my head. "They looked similar, though."

Clay covered his eyes with the palms of his hands. "Why won't you listen?"

"And this device?" Azzam asked. "What was it? What did it do? And . . . and if it is so secret, how do you know what they are researching down there?"

I couldn't tell him about my father's drug-induced admissions about the Icarus Device. That would be like violating his trust even more. I shook my head. "I—I've been poking around the LMC. It's all in there. And all these guys are named Bosner."

Azzam asked, "But why shoot all those people? What was the point?"

"I don't know. Maybe all people in the future are insane. Maybe traveling through time drives you insane."

"You have a very fine imagination, Dennis Howard. You are trying to fool me."

"He's lying," Clay whispered. "He believes you. Why would he lie?"

How would Clay know Azzam was lying?

I tried to ignore Clay and tapped my forefinger into my left palm to punctuate my point. "The LMC can't track Kyle Bosner. He's got some kind of technology to mask his position."

"It's a computer error. The President has formed a task force to investigate. It's all part of the Prometheus—"

"They attacked me—the Bosner brothers—way before the explosion. I was crawling around the mech-tunnels and I saw the two of them in a bathroom. They were arguing about something, then suddenly, one pulls a gun out."

"You were in the mech-tunnels? I thought that was off-limi—"

"Azzam! The point is that Emily—the LMC had no clue, no record, nothing. They were bashing away at the vent cover to get to me."

Azzam shrugged, then grimaced in pain caused by the movement. "Maybe the LMC was making different mistakes before the explosion. You never know. Remember how all the mechs stopped for five minutes? They were calling it 'The Glitch.'"

Clay leaned close and whispered, "He knows more than he's telling you. You're alone and his bodyguard's just outside. If he realizes you suspect anything, he could have you killed. Just get up and leave."

I tapped my foot nervously and avoided looking at Clay. If I trusted no one with what I knew, I could never get any help. That's just what Clay wanted.

I looked away, trying to think. "That was the exact moment the glitch happened. Was there some kind of connection?" My gaze shifted to my shoes, and I willed them to stop their nervous dance. "Maybe you're right. I'm letting my imagination run wild."

* * *

"Clay Byron," I whispered. The door to my room was shut. Emily was ignoring me as I requested. I was alone, or as alone as I could be with a man living in my brain who should be dead or, at the very least, in his sixties.

He didn't appear. The shadow from my desk lamp threw an arcing shadow across the walls. It was a shadow that moved, that breathed, but only at the corner of my eye.

"Do you think I don't know what you're doing?" I said. "You only appear when I can't speak freely, only when other people are around. I want to see you, right here, right now."

"To what end?" Clay whispered, his voice coming from nowhere, from inside my mind.

"What are you afraid of? What could I do to you? Shoot you? Don't forget I know where you live, and I could put a bullet in my brain if I wanted."

He appeared in front of my desk, head bent with rounded shoulders as if standing were too great an effort. Looking at the floor he said, "I have no wish for your death, Dennis. But wishing is the only avenue I know to become visible. If you see me, it's a miracle I cannot comprehend. Can you see me now?"

"Of course I can."

He looked up at me, gave me a weary smile, and nodded. "You are the only one."

I crossed my arms. "What do you want? I want to hear it from your lips."

"I want to live. I want to die. I want to remember who I am."

"You don't know?"

"Clay Byron is a name I call myself, but I don't feel like Clay Byron—like the name is me."

"You've had other names," I said, thinking of Sir Simon and Artemus.

"Perhaps. I recall my life only in glimpses, like snatches of a dream half remembered by a mind still groggy from slumber. I've been watching you, trying to fathom why you alone can perceive me, while all others stand ignorant of my passing."

Was it possible he didn't know? "You're planted in my brain, shoved in while I was busy being killed over and over by a pack of dogs. But it's nice to know the job's not done. If you can't remember your life, the transference isn't complete."

Clay looked at me with a blank stare. "It's plain English you speak, but your words make no sense. You were never killed by dogs. You're standing there alive and well, despite your recent misadventures, some of which could have been avoided if you'd listened to me."

"You don't get it. Why is it no one else can see or hear you?"

"I've told you. I've no idea."

"It's because you are a personality living in my brain. You're a foreign invader trying to take over my body, but you're not strong enough to do it."

"Trying to take over—are you feeling well? Perhaps the concussion did damage the good doctor failed to detect."

"Do you think you're some kind of ghost? Do you wander aimlessly around Luna, or are you always by my side, seeing what I see, going where I go?"

"I can go where I please, but what's the point? The universe doesn't deign to recognize me. But living in your brain? How could you even conceive of the idea, let alone conclude with such authority that it's the truth?"

"It's SIM technology. You know, remote neural manipulation. It's not supposed to be possible to transfer personalities, but you're supposedly such a genius, you probably invented it."

"You're suggesting I've been thrust into your mind—that I've engineered the manner and circumstance of such an unholy union. Even were it within the realm of possibility to do what you suggest, I would never perpetrate such a loathsome act on another. I may not remember my past, but I am not such a person. I can feel it in my bones."

"Those are my bones you're feeling, Byron."

He pursed his lips and looked away. "So you contend. There must be another explanation."

"Well, I'm listening. Any bright ideas?"

"I'm too weary for this."

I crossed the distance between us in two steps. "I'm not going to die. Not shot by some Bosner, or consumed by some spirit. I will fight you—I'll do whatever it takes to get you out of my mind."

"For my part, I was your friend. I still am. I would offer as proof my concern for your well-being, but the artful mirrors of your intellect transform my noble purpose into petty self-interest. Would you have me leave you?"

"Yes."

"If it is in my power, I will abandon you to the ill winds of misfortune that seem to plague you wherever you wander. But if I whisper in your ear to turn left instead of right, don't think the worst of me."

I crossed my arms and scowled, hoping by determination alone I could see through his crafty words and attitude.

"And if I fail to leave your side, I hope it isn't because we share the same body," Clay said. "Think of me as a man alone, adrift on a raft in the ocean. If I was starved, seared by the sun, and gone mad with relentless solitude, would you blame me for paddling with all my strength to the only island I could see? Even if the island itself doesn't want me?"

With a sigh I turned away. I had to keep in mind that every word he spoke was designed to set me off guard. He was probably lying about not remembering his life. No matter how nice he seemed, how well he spoke, my mind, my soul was at stake.

When I turned back he was gone.

* * *

While stuck at home, I contacted Trevor and Zak and arranged to meet them at Zak's place after school let out. Mom and Tricia went to the hospital to be there when Dad got out of the operation. When I had said I was too tired to go, Mom made me promise not to go anywhere. She was afraid I'd be attacked, and so was I. But I needed help.

I slipped through the halls, trying to look every direction at once. I spied every hall before turning a corner. No one bothered me or even gave me a second look.

Because Zak's father was mayor of Aristoteles, Zak's place was much larger than either mine or Trevor's. But it still was a hole in the ground compared to the Silver Wood and the sprawl of Brimstone.

Zak had his own private bathroom and study. He had a king-size bed as the centerpiece of a bedroom three times the size of mine. There is always privilege to rank.

When the housekeeper ushered me into Zak's room, I found Trevor and Zak already deep within Emily's memory.

"What's going on?" I asked as I pulled up a chair.

Zak gave me a friendly shove as I sat down. "So you're finally out of the hospital?"

"I'm still in one piece." How was I going to explain the situation to them? "Thanks for all the flowers and attention. It really helped keep me going."

Trevor snorted a laugh. "You know, there are some things happening in the world which don't revolve around you."

Zak stood up and reached for the picture hanging on the wall above his desk. It was an oil painting of the hilt of a fancy sword. The frame was on hinges and behind it was an unlocked wall safe with its door slightly ajar. He opened the safe and pulled out a bag of candy. "Have a Jelly Baby."

"Oh my God. Where did you get them?" I asked, taking a small handful. Trevor took some too.

"I've got connections," Zak whispered.

I closed my eyes and chewed the gummy deliciousness. I'd always liked Jelly Babies, but they were impossible to get. Through a sticky mouthful, Trevor said, "Oh, here it comes."

"What?" I asked. The vid hovering above Zak's desk showed a boy entering a vid-booth. Through the static, I could see him fingering a memory cube.

"I think Frank's dad ditched the family," Trevor said after he swallowed. "There was a vid of—I can't bring it back—of Frank's mom. She was yelling at some corporal, demanding to know where her husband was, but they disavowed any knowledge of his location or the secret mission she claimed he was on. The corporal said that Talonii was AWOL, and they were trying to find him themselves."

"They could have been lying—I mean if he really was on some mission," Zak said.

"Of course. Here it comes, and I don't think I'll be able to get it back again, so listen close."

The vid changed to the inside of a small viewing room. The scene showed the back of a boy's head. It was Frank when he was ten or eleven. He was turned away and watching a 3-D recording of his dad, which we could easily see.

When the audio resolved out of static for a moment, I heard Frank's dad say, "—in person, but there wasn't time. There's a mission I'm being sent on, and I have to leave right away. I'd tell you all about it, except that it's classified. Heck, it's so classified, I don't even know all the details yet.

"I should be back in no time, and when I am, things will be better. I promise. And I mean it this time." Frank's dad glanced to his left with a worried expression, and then back. "Look, baby, things have been hectic the last few months. I know I haven't been spending too much time with you and the kid, but if things go well, I may have a surprise for you when I get back. Look—I gotta go. Say goodbye to the kid for me will ya?" He winked a goodbye and vanished as the recording finished.

Frank slowly pulled the recording cube out of its socket. We could hear a few sniffs as if he had been in tears. Suddenly he lifted the cube high and bashed it against the screen breaking both the cube and the screen simultaneously. The cube flew into a million pieces and covered the console.

Zak complained, "That's useless. So his dad left him. That's not leverage. We need something explosively decompressing." The vid folded back on itself into static, and Zak waved the sound down.

"Why are you guys doing research on Talonii? We have bigger problems."

Trevor shook his head. "Wasn't it you in the hospital all week? Didn't Frank put you there?"

"Not really."

"Come on," Zak said. "He accused your dad of killing everyone at Prometheus. He wanted you to get nailed."

Trevor drank some juice. "We're looking for some leverage to use against him in case he decides to 'pull another Talonii' on one of us. If he knew so much about your dad's work, he must have done some kind of research on your family."

"And maybe we can figure out what character he plays in Rapt," Zak said. "We have to keep our eyes open when we're in there. He could be anyone."

"We already have leverage," I said. "We know he's a bookie. All we need is some proof—"

Trevor put down his glass. "You've got to stop underestimating him, Dennis. Zak told me about what Frank said, about his story of taking donations for The Society for the Remembrance of Lumus Victims. I checked it out. He's donated money."

"Really? How much?"

Trevor shrugged. "I couldn't find out through normal channels, so we might have to go this route." He jerked a thumb over his shoulder back at the vid of static. "But even getting to 2073 is a miracle. Remember all those events we worked out to bring the computer back through history from 2028? Most of them don't work anymore—like they've gotten stale. I had to think of different events."

Zak asked me, "You haven't been back to school lately, have you? There's banners and signs all over advertising a Sam Clemens fan club. Talonii's really getting a following claiming he's you."

"Oh come on, there's some opposition too," Trevor said. "Dennis isn't the only competitor with a following. When we entered the SIM in Ancient Architecture this morning, the first thing everyone saw was some Roman ruin, but the bricks and debris were arranged to spell out 'Winger.'"

Zak smiled. "Yeah, I heard something like that happened in Modern Art and Basic Dynamics III. Depending on what angle you looked at it, the word 'Winger' transformed into 'Winner'. The professors are still trying to figure out how they broke into the page files and changed them."

I shook my head. "I wish I'd been there."

Trevor waved his hand and said, "You're not missing anything—but homework."

I got up and started to pace. Zak's study was beginning to feel small and enclosed. "Forget about Talonii. I need to tell you guys about what's been happening to me."

Trevor rolled his eyes. "Yes, please, please. Let's hear about your magnificent life. Did Regale's DK Project work and now you're the smartest person on Luna?"

"My life is more complicated than you know."

"I don't think Regale blew up Prometheus," Trevor said. "No matter what we saw in that vid. If he's still alive, he couldn't have done it. That means we're not in any danger from him if he finds out we've seen the vid, all right?"

"You've got to listen—"

Trevor raised his voice. "There's bigger things going on in the world. Maybe you heard about the shooting at Descartes?"

"Oh, I've heard about it—"

"There's a killer out there that the L—that the computer can't track. My father's getting blamed, and nothing he's tried works."

"Look—" I began.

Trevor just continued talking. "Hey, I'm sorry you got your head bashed, but there's people dying out there—"

"I was there!" I shouted, finally getting a word in. "I watched that—I saw him fire into the crowd, and when he saw me, he decided *I* needed to be killed. He chased me half a kilometer through the university before I lost him."

"He chased *you*?" Zak said with wide eyes.

"Firing the whole time." Lowering my voice, I closed the study door that led back to Zak's bedroom. "His name's Kyle Bosner, and he's got a device that can manipulate the computer so it can't see him."

"Why was he after you?" Trevor asked.

"He's got a brother—looks just like him. His name's Jason."

"But why—"

"These Bosners kill people. It's what they do. Remember when we were crawling through that access tunnel trying to get to the control center in Descartes? I saw them, both of them, through the vent. They must have seen me because they bashed the vent to pieces trying to get at me. I ran."

"Whoa," Zak said. "I'm just hearing about this now?"

"Those guys were Bosners?" Trevor asked.

I told them everything. I told them a man named Mavin Bosner killed a bunch of people at the Nick O' Time Café back in 2039 and that he had an Icarus Device on him that the military had been studying ever since. I told them the labs beneath Prometheus were where my dad had been studying the device and how the Bosners not only blew up the plant to destroy the research but how they were also strafing the LMC's memory probably so there was no way to recover the lost data.

I whispered, "I think . . . I think the Bosners are from the future."

"I think you're making all this up," Zak said.

"I'm not that creative. And there's more. Artemus' DK Project? There's no such thing. It's all a lie to get me into his own personal SIM chamber so he could implant his personality into my brain."

Trevor laughed, and Zak threw his hands up, saying, "That's it. This is all just insane."

"Let him talk. I want to hear this. It just keeps getting better."

"The tournament isn't what you think it is. It's actually a way for Artemus to select potential victims, people with the right brain chemistry he needs, for the personality transfer. Once he's narrowed it down, he picks someone and gets them to come down to his SIM lab where all the equipment is specially designed for the neural net transfer."

I told them all my suspicions of the Artemus-Sir Simon-Clay Byron connection and how Emily had told me it might be possible. I never mentioned my multiple personalities, though. They didn't need to know everything.

I kept expecting Clay to appear, warning me about telling anyone, but he never did. Maybe he meant it when he promised to try to stay away.

"The contract actually says you'll get everything Artemus owns?" Zak asked.

I nodded.

Trevor got up and shoved his fingers through his tangled hair and started to pace the room. "Now, you told us Artemus was afraid of these Bosners. He even warned you to stay away from them."

Zak stretched out on the floor, covering his face. "What's the connection?"

"What if Artemus, or Clay . . . What if he's from the future too? God this is so cool."

Zak chortled. "Don't forget I'm from the future. Or didn't I tell you guys?"

"I'm serious," Trevor said as he paced the room. "Let's say he came back in time to escape from something. Maybe he was a criminal or a revolutionary. But now he's being hunted by these Bosner brothers."

"I never saw them go after Artemus," I said.

"How can you hunt someone who can switch bodies?" Trevor asked. "In 2039, Mavin Bosner tried to kill Clay, but he got away. Now Kyle Bosner is after you. They don't know what Clay looks like now, don't know he's Artemus, but maybe they have a way of sensing him."

"Some kind of personality identifier?" I asked.

"Maybe they're telepathic," Zak suggested. "And they can melt plasteel with rays that shoot out their eyes."

Trevor ignored Zak. "Artemus warned you to stay away from them because, once the transfer was complete, he knew the Bosners could pick you out of a crowd. Kyle Bosner knew you were close, but he didn't know exactly who you were. He just shot into the crowd hoping to get you by the process of elimination."

"Right before he shot at me he said, 'That's the one.'" A shiver ran up my spine. It wasn't bad enough I had a creature trying to take over my body. It had to be a creature targeted for assassination.

Trevor gazed into the static still hovering above Zak's desk. "Artemus' mind—Clay's—is like a virus jumping from person to person, and the Bosners came back in time to kill it."

Trevor understood. A feeling of relief washed over me. It wasn't much, but having these two—well, at least Trevor—on my side meant I wouldn't have to face Clay alone. "What am I supposed to do?"

Zak got up from the floor. "It's effing impossible to transfer a person's mind into another body. Skill implantation doesn't even last, let alone a whole mind."

"Maybe Artemus brought the technology with him from the future," Trevor said.

"I think you're forgetting one thing," Zak said. "It's impossible to travel through time!"

I shot back, "You don't know that."

"These are all great theories, but where's your evidence?" Zak asked. "The Icarus Device? Your dad was whacked out on drugs. He thought you were General Anderson just because you said so. Why does the word 'credible' instantly come to mind? Did you ask him if he saw any fairies in the room?"

"Don't forget about Kerinsky and all his questions," I said.

"Don't forget *you* were whacked out on drugs too. Your memory could be playing tricks on you."

"You think I'm making up everything about seeing Clay Byron? Do you think I've lost my mind?"

Zak shook his head. "I think you've been under stress, and stress can do strange things. My dad once told me how he put a lot of pressure on himself to perform well in school. He used to get so worked up before tests that his teeth would hurt."

Trevor scratched his neck. "He's got a point, Den."

"You too?"

Zak shrugged. "All I'm saying is that just because you have a lot of pieces that seem to make a picture, it could be the wrong picture."

"We need evidence," Trevor said.

"I need leverage on Artemus to get out of the contract. And I need to hide out until they catch the Bosners."

"If we could only get that vid of Artemus at Prometheus," Trevor said. "That would be leverage."

"And proof of the existence of the Icarus Device," Zak said.

"There might be a way," Trevor said looking off somewhere. "But it won't be easy."

"But Emily can't remember—" The static forming an undulating cloud over Zak's desk abruptly vanished. I just woke her up by saying her name.

"God!" Trevor yelled. "Do you know how long it took me to get the LMC to 2073?"

"Sorry."

"He's sorry," Trevor said. "Next he'll be blaming this Clay who lives in his head."

"I thought you believed me!"

"Now I have to start over with all different historical events."

I jammed my finger on the door control, and it swooshed open. "You guys are no help. Why did I even come here?"

As I passed through Zak's bedroom headed toward the door, Zak asked, "Hey, you're not dropping out of the tournament, are you?"

Couldn't Artemus continue his personality transfer while I was in the match? "What do you think? There's no way I'm getting back in there."

Trevor said, "You can't stay away from all SIMs. What about school?"

Zak said, "Yeah, right. But what if you're wrong about the tournament? About everything? You'd be eviscerating your chances of becoming a Master."

"I'm not wrong."

Zak said, "Okay. Assume you're right about this mind transfer thing—which you're not. He could probably only do that down in his own lab, otherwise why would he bring you down there?" Zak shrugged. "I'm just saying."

* * *

At least Dad's operation went well, but it would be a while before the doctors knew if the new arm would function properly.

I had nightmares all night. I dreamed Dr. Woodridge was working for Artemus. She had me drugged and strapped to a bed. She cut off my arms and legs then replaced them with Clay's. She said, "When we're done, you'll be back to normal—just like you used to be."

"But these aren't my arms or legs."

She laughed evilly. "I'm speaking to Clay, not Dennis."

"Dennis, wake up." There was a pounding on my door and the voice of an insistent little sister. "Mom wants you awake, so wake up."

"All right. I'm up. Emily, lights."

Dim lights threw back the darkness of my room. The clock read 6:03, but I felt like I had just fallen asleep. I rolled over and shut my eyes. I just needed to lie here for a second more.

"Dennis, we need to talk. Can I come in?" It was Mom this time. The clock now read 6:15.

"I'm awake," I said with my eyes still crossed from weariness.

The door slid open and Mom stepped in, already dressed for work and ready to leave.

"What's wrong?" I asked, trying to sit up.

"Have you read the contract we signed with Mr. Regale?"

At the mention of the contract, my eyes opened and stayed that way. "Yeah, Mom. I know what it says."

"I'm talking about the one we actually signed, not the one we were given to review. It says you will get all Regale's property at the completion of the project."

"I noticed that."

"And you didn't mention it to me? It's the most wonderful thing that's ever happened to this family. In the hospital you were complaining, trying to avoid going to Mr. Regale's."

"Mom, I can't go back there."

She crossed her arms and gave me a disappointed look. "Breaking the contract will cost us."

"We'll never have to pay that ridiculous amount he wrote in there. We can fight it in court."

"It'll cost us in lawyer fees, but that's not what I mean. If you decide to hide here in your room, we'll both go to debtors' prison until our case works its way through the courts. Do you want to see your mother in jail?"

"No. Yesterday you didn't even want me to leave the apartment—"

"Yesterday, I didn't know what I'd signed. I got a call from Mr. Regale this morning and he explained the situation. Now get dressed and get to Descartes. I'm already late for my symposium."

After she walked out, I grabbed a robe and followed her. "Did you forget about that guy who tried to kill me in Descartes?"

"Of course not." She opened her purse and rooted around until she found a pillbox. She popped a few blue pills in her mouth and swallowed. "That's why I arranged for you to stay with Mr. Regale.

You'll be perfectly safe surrounded by his security." She looked about the room as if searching for something.

"Stay with him? Are you joking? What are those pills?"

"Don't you question me, young man. Tricia! Have you seen my briefcase?"

She'd never believe Artemus would implant his personality in me, especially now in this strange mood. "Do you think he has any intention of paying me when the project's done? I'll probably end up dead."

"Just like your sister. Melodrama. You'll be fine. Regale is expecting you at eight sharp. Tricia? Answer me."

Tricia was in her room. "It's not my turn to watch it, Mom."

"I said get dressed and get to Descartes! Stop staring at me and move!"

Tricia was standing in her door. "Mom what's wrong?" She looked scared.

"Nothing's wrong. Go to school. And you," she said indicating me. "Get your butt over to Regale's. You can stay here this weekend, but on Monday, you're moving in with him until they find that Bosner character." She grabbed her briefcase, which was sitting beside the couch. "No one's going to get killed. No one's going to prison. Your father's coming home on Monday. Everything will be okay!"

She weaved her way toward and out the door, still muttering to herself that everything was going to be fine.

"What did you do to her?" Tricia demanded.

I denied everything, but Tricia left for school still holding me responsible. She was right. It was all my fault.

* * *

I wandered the darkened hallways of Aristoteles all morning and into the afternoon. I needed to think, but thinking only made things worse. My family was falling apart. My friends thought I was crazy. The only way to prevent Artemus from winning was to kill myself, but that seemed extreme and hopelessly spiteful. There had to be some other way.

I noticed the corridors thin out as the tournament match time drew close. Everyone was getting in their SIM chambers to watch the seventh trial, but they were going to have to do without Sam Clemens this time. He's retired from the game.

A voice hissed right at my ear. It was Clay saying, "You are being followed."

I whirled around in fear of seeing a pack of upper classmen or worse, a Bosner, but there was only one person behind me. I couldn't see his face until he walked under a light. It was Frank Talonii.

"Are you following me, Talonii?"

"If it isn't Howard, and by the looks of it, none the worse for wear." His eyes bored into me and a shiver ran up my spine.

"I asked you a question?"

"Following you? What if I was? Is it a crime to have concern for my fellow man?" he asked innocently and stopped a few steps away.

"Concern, is it?"

"Maybe I heard about the shooting the other day and decided to help out by watching your back."

"How did you know I was there? Only the police know that."

"Walk with me. I believe you were headed to the Brandenburg SIMs. So was I, and I don't want to be late. The tournament is about to start, but then I'm sure you know all about that."

Frank walked past me, and I fell into step beside him.

"You're not like normal fourteen-year-olds, Dennis. You move in strange circles. Artemus Regale, the richest man on Luna, dotes over you. And you are the target of brutal death by assailants the LMC can't find or even remember."

"Lunatics kill people every day."

Frank shook his head. "Not on Luna. Look around. We don't have violent crime here, and why? Are the people here so pure of heart and innocent compared to Earth?" He mocked a prayer pose with hands folded together.

I said, "The people on Earth don't have a surveillance system like the LMC watching their every move."

"Deterrents only work on the sane and the intelligent. Only idiots resort to violence, and Luna doesn't have many of their ilk. Just to get here, you have to pass a barrage of qualification tests that would turn most people pale. The population of Luna was constructed by the largest scale unnatural selection system man has ever devised. Our gene pool contains the highest concentration of intelligence ever assembled."

Almost every adult I knew had a doctorate, some with double doctorates. I shook my head to clear it. "Is this going somewhere, Frank?"

"And in all these intelligent people, I've found none who even draw near to my own brilliance."

I laughed and rolled my eyes. "Aren't we thinking a bit highly of ourselves?"

"None, that is, but you. You're the first to give me a real challenge. Your character in Rapt, Sol Blanchard, is seamless. I've studied your performances in the tournament. How could I not be impressed? Every word, every movement or glance, every breath completely in character and flawless."

I almost thanked him before I realized that would be giving away my identity as Sam Clemens. "Why do you think I'm a competitor?"

"Don't tell me you still don't know."

As we entered the atrium under which stood the Brandenburg SIM Center, the Lunar Emergency Broadcast System came to life with several tones which echoed down the corridors. A female voice came on and said, "Ladies and gentlemen of Luna. By executive order, Luna entire, Space Station Wayfarer, Indy, Antipater, and Ceres have hereby been placed under quarantine. This is not a state of emergency. The quarantine is a precautionary move to prevent the spread of an Earth-based virus, and no serious danger is foreseen for those on Luna. The quarantine is expected to last four to six months, or until the vector of the disease is determined and deemed controllable. That is all."

I suddenly remembered Artemus' slip about a quarantine. That was Monday, five days ago. How did he know about it so much in advance? If the president had made the decision before Monday, why had they waited until now to announce it?

But if Artemus was from the future, he might have simply *remembered* the quarantine.

Frank whistled though his teeth. "At the slightest hint of danger, how they protect their precious cache of humanity. Come on, Sam, we're going to be late."

"How do you know I'm Sam Clemens?" Whoops. That came out as an admission.

He turned to fully face me and smiled. "Remember that psych test Regale performed on us at Descartes? Didn't you wonder how we were selected? I counted the number of people in the room, and found an interesting correlation to the number of people left in the tournament."

"Artemus assembled all the competitors." Probably to test each of us with specially modified neural caps that could begin the implantation process. And if Frank was there that meant Frank was a competitor too. "But showing my face in that room just meant I was a competitor, not Sam Clemens."

"True. But confronting me was a tactical error. Publicly denouncing me as a charlatan was a sure indication you had knowledge of the real Sam Clemens, though I admit, at the time, the thought of you competing was laughable. No one your age has ever been admitted to the tournament before. But when you showed up at the psych test—well, I can see a falcon in the sky by day."

"Why claim to be Sam Clemens at all? Part of some brilliant scheme?" His ego was so big, he wouldn't pass up the opportunity to show off his own intelligence.

"I selected Sam Clemens because I thought he was the one most likely to reach the final match with me. But why . . . After I win the entire tournament, with a flourish, I shall announce my true identity. I am Winger."

"Winger, eh?" Maybe he was telling the truth, but I doubted it.

"Claiming to be Sam Clemens certainly has had some unanticipated benefits. Since I've gone public with my Clemens identity, how the women have flocked. They can see your sensitivity shine through your performances, and their hearts go all aflutter when we meet. I can't thank you enough."

I knew he was goading me, but I couldn't help getting angry. Sam Clemens' reputation could only suffer under his manipulation. "I'm not the quixotic fool you take me for," I said. "Saving young women from their misguided infatuations by revealing the true identity of Sam Clemens to the world would be a noble cause, it's true. But I detect only a kernel of truth in your claims of romantic conquest. Your attempts to bait me into revealing myself cannot succeed." I stepped toward him and he backed away, my tone now ruling his reactions. "And revealing my true identity as Sam Clemens is the very deed you most fear. Hiding behind artful pretense . . . spinning fabrications to make me dance to your bidding. See now before you not a marionette but a man of free will. Yet rest easy. I will not reveal my true identity because it is not what I choose by reasoning that predates our first encounter."

Frank looked at me with wide eyes. "I'm not manipulating you or anyone."

"Each word a fiber, each sentence a strand. Your every expression is calculated to invoke the desired response in what you must consider your intellectual inferiors. In the dizzying miasma of your mind, you've forgotten the most important fact. Life is not thinking. Life is living. When next you sit alone in contemplation, feel yourself breathe and marvel."

I pitied him. His world was empty. As the anger drained from me, I felt a bit dizzy. What was I saying? I remembered saying the word quixotic. I don't even know what that means.

"I see I've underestimated you, Dennis." Frank towered over me with his cool stare. "It won't happen again. You're going to lose the tournament, but not just yet. You make me relish our tête-à-tête in the final trial all the more."

Clay must have said all those things. But he couldn't have. They were all my thoughts. Were we somehow merging? I licked my lips and glanced around nervously. I'm Dennis Howard.

Across the hall, I noticed three men coming toward us: two burly men and a third, slimmer man dressed in a tuxedo, whom I recognized immediately. It was Lawrence, Artemus' servant. They must have been lying in wait here, thinking I'd never miss a tournament match.

"Shall we?" Frank asked, motioning toward the SIM center.

Glancing about the atrium, I looked for a place to go. I could run from Lawrence and his goons, but I had no place to hide. I could hide in a SIM chamber. When everyone emptied out after the match, I could blend in with the crowd and escape.

"Yeah, let's go," I said. "We don't want to be disqualified."

* * *

"Good afternoon, Dennis Howard, also known as Sam Clemens. Welcome to the Seventh Trial of the Master's Championship Tournament. Are you ready to begin?"

Should I go through with the match? I couldn't decide. "Emily. What's the quarantine all about?"

"For the past several months, hospitals in South America have been reporting unusual male-to-female birth statistics. More males are being carried to term than female. It is possible that the cause is a non-fatal virus contracted by the mothers, who had miscarriages of female babies. In recent weeks, these same unusual statistics have been showing up in hospitals around the world but far less severe than those exhibited in South America.

"Are you ready to begin the tournament?"

I remembered what Zak said about how I might be wrong about the tournament. I'd be throwing away my chance at becoming a Master. "Yeah, I guess. Let's get this over with." I was almost sure that Artemus couldn't download his personality through these standard SIM chambers. That's what Zak said. If he could, why did he bother to get me down to Brimstone at all? No, this was safe.

It was time to create another personality. "Yeah, let's go," I said.

"The setting of the Seventh Trial is the year 2132, Earth. Your name is Angelo Sabatini." A picture of Angelo appeared before me, rotating slowly. Emily continued, "You are twelve years old, male, and preparing for what is known as Life-Call Determination and Edification . . ."

As she spelled out the things I needed to know before entering the trial, I fed the information to a new personality within me. Angelo took form inside my mind, and as the Seventh Trial began, I pushed him into the foreground.

Chapter Eleven

Broken Wings

S omeone was screaming, a kid. It sounded like he was dying.
The scream fell silent as I awoke, making me wonder if it had been real or part of the nightmare. A fragment of that dream still lurked in my mind. I could still smell my father's breath stinking of bourbon. "Angelo. Do I have to send you back to the therapist?"

Shivering, I curled myself into a ball. Discovering I was outside, lying on hard cement, I pushed myself up and looked around, mystified. I was on a cement slab in the center of a circular pool of water maybe twenty-five meters across. A cement embankment circled the outside edges of the pool, and beyond that were palm trees and large fronds. The trees were all around but not thick like a forest. I heard the sound of waves crashing against a shore that couldn't have been very far away. I stood up to see beyond the cement embankment, but I didn't see the ocean. All I saw was a rocky field broken by long shadows of palm trees and the sun low in the sky. Where was I? How did I get here?

Without any shoes, my feet were freezing, so I sat down and tried to warm them up with my hands. I discovered I was wearing baggy orange pants made of thin synthetic material that felt damp on my skin. My shirt was the same material.

I crawled to the edge of the water, feeling thirsty. My cement slab wasn't flat but curved like the surface of a ball. It bent down to meet the man-made pond all around. I cupped my hands in the water and felt a zap as if the pool was electrified.

Suddenly, the image of a man, a soldier by the look of his uniform, appeared hovering over the pool. "Greetings citizen," he said. His eyes didn't look directly at me as if it were an old-fashioned non-interactive recording. "Welcome to Penal Island 619. The state has reviewed your mental capacities and has judged you incompetent. As stated by section four, paragraph twelve of the Fifty-Second Amendment to the Constitution of the WG, mentally unstable or unfit citizens forfeit all rights to property, liberty, and life and shall be subject to summary execution. In its infinite mercy, the state has seen fit to spare your miserable life. You shall remain on Penal Island 619 for the rest of your life as a ward of the state."

Mentally unstable? This couldn't be happening. I felt my hyperventilation coming on.

"If you attempt to leave Penal Island 619, you will be killed. If the state requires you—" The soldier's image became warped, and his voice was garbled. He vanished as suddenly as he appeared.

"I'm not unstable!" I shouted. "I can be a good citizen. Is anybody there?" The sound of birds flapping in fear at the sound of my voice was all I heard.

How did I get here? The last thing I remembered was sitting down in the neural scanner at Life Call. It was my twelfth birthday and time to become a man. Once they found out what job I was good for, they were supposed to fill my head with all the information I would need. They must have rejected me.

"I'm—I'm a broken." At day-activity, I remembered tormenting kids we didn't like by calling them broken, mental misfits. We used to chant, "Broken, Broken," over and over until they started to cry.

Now I was crying. I stood up. "I'm not a broken." I noticed nearby a second pool surrounding a cement slab just like mine, but no one was there.

What was the water for? So the recording would start when I touched it? I licked my lips, still thirsty. I might get another shock if I touched it again, but it didn't really hurt. I knelt down for another try.

"Hey, hey kid!" someone shouted. I looked up and saw a boy running across the field toward me. He was waving and shouting something about the water.

He was winded when he stopped at the edge of the pool. Between gasps he said, "Whatever you do, don't touch the water."

"The shock wasn't that bad."

"The first shock isn't bad, but the second will kill you. Best move away from it."

I took a few steps back toward the center. "Thanks. Who are you?"

"Quaker Wallace is the name. Welcome to 619. It's not Easter Island, but we call it home."

"I'm Angelo. You mean we're on a real island?"

"Didn't the recording tell you? This is Penal Island 619."

"I thought he meant this thing." I pointed down at my cement island.

Quaker laughed. "No. We call that a pimple. There's a few others around the island. It's where they drop off the new boys."

"If it's electrified, how am I supposed to get out?"

"That's where Quaker comes in," he said pointing at his chest. "But you have to agree to join. Quaker's forming a new band, and you will be second in command."

"What do you mean?" He was referring to himself with his own name. How strange. He's a broken.

"There's three groups on the island now. Gervin's got a dozen of the biggest and meanest. Cadwyn has got his own group of thirty or so, then there's the outcasts. There's fourteen of us, but we can't organize. The outcasts are the worst broken, some just insane. So Quaker's decided to start his own group. Are you in?"

"Okay, whatever." There was no way I was joining him, but he might be my only way off the—what did he call it—the pimple. "What are you going to do? Roll a tree over here so I can climb over the water?"

Quaker spat a laugh. "Yeah, right. Let me just go and get my axe and Quaker'll cut you down a tree."

"Well, how am I supposed to cross?"

Thunder sounded across the island. I looked over my shoulder at a front of approaching storm clouds, dark and heavy with rain.

"Ah-oh," Quaker said. "You're going to have to learn fast."

"Learn what?"

"Usually there's days to learn, but when that rain gets here, your pimple's going to fill up and you'll be fried. You've got to listen. This island was originally set up by the WG to study broken. They discovered that people mentally unstable like us—"

"I'm not mentally unstable."

"You better hope you are because broken like us can travel. Traveling is the only way you're going to get off the pimple. Everyone on the island has done it, or they wouldn't be alive. This place is a test lab, and we're the rats. They want to know how we do it."

"Do what?"

"Travel. It's like an out of body experience, only your body comes too. It's like leaving the physical world and entering a mental one where you can move with thought. Look at your island there. See those circles?"

I looked down and noticed perfect circles scribed on the cement. There were a dozen or so circles, each getting smaller as they approached the top and center of the island.

"Those circles were supposed to tell you how much longer you had to live, each line an hour. They would pump water into the pool, and you could count the hours you had left. The idea was to force you to learn to travel. The pumps have been busted for years, though."

"How am I supposed to learn to travel? It sounds insane." I sat down at the peak of the island and wrapped my arms around myself. Raindrops were starting to fall, and the surface of the pond looked close already.

"You've gotta listen, Angelony. The only thing keeping you in the physical world is your hold on sanity. If you let go, you'll be able to travel."

"My name's not Angelony. It's Angelo. And if you can travel, why don't you come over here and get me?"

"You can't carry other people with you. No one can do it. Their hold on reality makes it impossible. So no one's coming to rescue you. You're twelve years old, right?"

"Yeah."

"It's time you started acting like a man. Only Angelo can save Angelo."

"How am I supposed to let go of my sanity? That's crazy. Why should I trust a broken like you?"

"'Cause you're as crazy as me, or you wouldn't be here. Now picture a garden surrounded by a wall. This is how it was explained to Quaker. You're in the garden, but you want out, only there's no door in the wall. The wall completely surrounds you. You listening?"

"I can hear you." I wiped rain out of my eyes. The drops were large, and they splashed the electrified pool around me.

"Now the wall is too high to jump over, too smooth to climb. It's too thick to break down. How do you get out?"

"You can't go over it? You can't go through it. I guess you could dig under it."

"That's right. The ground's like liquid, so you've got to let yourself sink into the ground."

"What?"

"Once you're in the ground, you can swim anywhere you like. Swim right under the wall."

"If I let go, put myself into some kind of trance, I might sleep-walk right into the pool." The rain was coming in sheets now making the surface of the pool choppy, eager for me.

"If you really let go, the pool can't touch you."

"I don't believe you. I bet the pool isn't electrified at all."

Quaker crossed his arms, then glanced over at the other pool. "Look at him."

"Who?" I stood up and looked. There was something orange floating in the other pool.

"Neighbor boy didn't know the pool was a death trap. Now he's gone, and you'll be joining him unless you believe Quaker."

The orange thing was a body floating face down. I gagged and fell to my knees. I would have gotten sick, but my stomach was empty. How could I have missed seeing him before? Maybe he'd been floating in his pond on the other side of his concrete island. A different voice brought my head up.

"New boy." It was an old man crouched at the edge of my pool. He was breathing heavily, and his face was contorted as if he was in pain. He jerked his head to the side in spasms.

"Old one," Quaker said with awe in his voice. Quaker took a few steps back then began looking around the sky as if searching for something.

When I looked back toward the old man, he was gone. I wiped water off my face and looked again. Suddenly, the old man was beside me, crouched and twisted. I jumped with a shout and nearly rolled into the pool.

"Name?" he said. It looked as though even uttering the single word took lots of effort for him. "Name!"

"I'm Angelo. Angelo Sabatini."

He grabbed my shirt and dragged me to the top of the pimple. "Travel," he whispered into my face with horrible smelling breath. "Or die." He grabbed my hand and forced my fingers into a fist with my index finger pointing. Then he pressed my hand onto the hard cement. There was writing scratched into the cement that I hadn't noticed before.

"Look out!" Quaker shouted. "Here they come."

The old man bared his teeth. His body shook then suddenly blurred as if he had become a smeared painting. He vanished, just like the projection of the soldier. But projections couldn't grab you. He was real.

Bolts of white-hot plasma flashed through the space the old man had occupied seconds before. I pressed myself to the ground as the shots sizzled over my head and exploded into the pool creating columns of sparks and jets of steam.

When the shots stopped I could hear the low rumble of an engine. Looking up through the rain, I watched as a hovering drone twice my size floated by. It had the shape of a cylinder and had guns and sensors mounted on all sides. Underneath was a violet circle of light that appeared detached from the drone. When it floated overhead, its anti-gravity field made its outline ripple and made me feel light headed, dizzy.

"Relax," Quaker said. "It won't kill you. It's only interested in the old one."

"Why?"

"They say he's the only one who's ever escaped. It makes them nervous to know he's out there somewhere. He's the perfect assassin. He can bypass any security in the world, kill anyone he pleases, and travel out."

"If he escaped, what's he still doing here?"

"Trying to save us, I suppose."

I looked at the writing scratched into the cement. "There's some writing here."

"The old one has written stuff on all the pimples. What's yours say?"

"It looks like a poem.

On Angels wings
The choir sings
God helps improve their lot.

But Broken wings
Are special things
they only wish they got.

They hate my mind
They fear my kind
So ceaselessly we're sought.

Because we dream
Of a regime
That treats men like they ought.

It is our fight
To set them right
We aren't the misbegot.

We simply wish
Without anguish
To live and not get shot.

"Sounds like one of his better ones," Quaker said. "See you later." He glanced back at the drone that drifted over the field, still looking for the old man.

"Where are you going?"

"The way this rain is coming down, Quaker thinks you only have an hour. Don't like seeing boys die. If you make it, come to the shore."

"Wait. I don't know how to travel."

Quaker didn't turn back as he walked back across the field. "You'll figure it out."

I stood at the top of the island and watched the rain splash the electrified pool. How do I let go of my sanity? I'd gone to a therapist when I was little because I couldn't sleep. He had taught me some meditation exercises. Maybe that would help.

I sat cross-legged at the peak of the pimple. Trying to ignore the cold rain pelting the side of my face, I relaxed my muscles in groups, just like my therapist had taught me so I could control my panic attacks. Minutes slipped by, and though my eyes were closed, I couldn't help but imagine the rising waters.

I pictured myself holding a stone the size of my head. It was my mind, my world, my hold on reality. With all my might, I threw it off a cliff. For a moment, I watched it fall, then I became the stone. I was falling. I imagined wind rushing by and the sound of crashing waves below. It became darker as I fell, and all sense of up and down vanished.

The sound of the water told me it was getting closer, but it also seemed distant, like in another world.

I pictured myself plunging through the surface of my imaginary lake. The water wasn't cold but warm and comforting. Immersed in the water, I felt the movement of the waves above me. I didn't sink to the bottom or float to the top. I discovered I was becoming the water.

When I opened my eyes, I was still on the pimple, but the world was dim. I stood up to give myself a few more minutes before the water got me. Travel. How? I willed myself to move, to fly through the air. Nothing happened.

The pounding of the water on my face was hypnotic. Slowly at first, I dissolved into my imaginary waters. Bit by bit, I released my fear, my pain. The weight of life lifted from me, the hard knots of tension gone. I felt light, as thin as air. The water was inches from my feet, but I wasn't afraid. I couldn't feel the cement under my feet or the rain coming down. The sound of the splashing water was distant, remote. I picked one foot off the ground and watched as it blurred, just like the old one had. It was smeared across the canvas as if the canvas didn't know how to hold the paint anymore.

The water rose even further, so I lifted my other foot and watched as my bright orange pants blurred. It occurred to me that it shouldn't be possible to lift both legs off the ground at the same time, but then, why not? I was floating with no sensation of gravity.

Quaker had said, when traveling, thought was movement. So I imagined myself moving toward the field, the direction Quaker had walked. I flew over the surface of the pool, not feeling any air pass by. It was as if the air was folding in front of me, unfolding behind me. I wasn't passing through the world as much as the world was passing me.

With my attention on the sensation of folding space, I came upon a palm tree. Before I realized what was happening, the tree trunk folded on itself in front of me, and I went through it. Without ever being inside the tree, I had started on one side and ended up on the other.

I wanted to do it again, but I began to feel ill, dizzy. A thought of moving toward the beach sent me flying over the stony field quickly. The rain came down in sheets, and the trees were blowing wildly, but nothing touched me.

The shore was rocky with a ragged ridge separating the field from the ocean. Even though my vision was getting darker, I managed to see Quaker huddled below an overhang, trying to stay out of the downpour. I flew to his side, but he didn't see me. I tried to say his name, but found I didn't remember how to use my mouth. I couldn't even feel my mouth.

I had to rejoin the physical world, but how? Quaker didn't know I was here and couldn't tell me what to do. Spots were forming in my eyes. Fear of death lanced through me like an electric shock, and I crashed to the rocks.

I heard Quaker jump and shout in surprise at my appearance out of thin air, but suddenly all I could think about was breathing. I sucked air in and out of my lungs as fast as I could. I was shivering uncontrollably.

"You made it," Quaker said. "Oh, Quaker forgot about the breathing. You can't breathe when you travel, so you can never travel very far. That's why they put us on an island in the Pacific."

When I'd been sliding through the world, I hadn't realized I'd been holding my breath. I tried to tell Quaker, but my mouth wouldn't behave. I grunted between breaths and huddled into a ball. My left eye was twitching and wouldn't stop.

"You'll come out of it in a few minutes. Your body will remember how to function. You'll see."

After a while, longer than Quaker said, I did feel better. My muscles were doing what I wanted them to do, and my eye stopped twitching. When my tongue didn't feel like a lump in my mouth, I said, "Thanks for getting me out of there."

It came out slurred, but Quaker understood. He nodded. "Now you're on Quaker Wallace's team."

"That was amazing. It was—it was like magic."

"Yeah, and only broken can do it."

Suddenly angry at the insult, I bit back my response. I'd hated broken all my life, feared them. I'd been glad when they were taken away. Even sitting this close to Quaker made my skin crawl. How could I be one of them? 'Only broken can do it,' he'd said.

It had to be a mistake. There had to be a way off the island. "How long have you been here?"

"A few years. The rain is slowing. When it stops, Quaker will take you to the site of our new home. You can start digging right away."

"Digging?"

"We can't stay under here," he said, indicating the overhang. "We need a proper home, a cave way up high to protect from the slow."

"Protect from what?"

"The *slow*!" He sighed, and I felt like I was being slow. "Slow are broken that can't travel very well. I'm not slow. I'm the best on the island."

"Who else is on the island?"

"Gervin's the devil. If he or any of his boys see you, they'll torture you for fun. They live on a rock just off the north coast where the drone base is."

"Drone base?"

"It's too far to travel to in a single hop. If you try, when you come back for a breath, the guard drones blast away. Cadwyn says Gervin and his bunch are working with the state now, fixing the drones when they break in exchange for food flown in from the mainland.

Gervin and them'll kill anyone who gets near the base. I'm never going up there.

"Cadwyn's the head of the other group. He's got thirty guys with him. They live down at the old compound. Cadwyn believes that if they can kill the old one, the state will reward them by taking them home."

The old one. He sounded interesting. "Who's the old one?"

Quaker shrugged. "You have too many questions."

"Come on," I said. "I'm just trying to understand."

A bolt of lightning struck nearby and we both jumped. We sat in silence a while, watching the rain fall. Finally Quaker said, "The old one . . . Some think he was one of the first test subjects. The state found out broken can travel, and they thought we'd make great assassins, so they built the compound here to study us, teach new broken how to do it. But they couldn't control them. The researchers were all killed, but there was no way for the broken here to leave. Quaker thinks the old one found a way."

"So the state watches for this old guy and tries to kill him whenever they get the chance," I said.

"Quaker thinks the only reason they keep bringing broken here is to kill the old one. The whole island is a trap, and they know he can't resist trying to help us. We're bait. If he speaks to you, the state knows. They can hear everything around you. They always know where you are. It's the chip they put in everyone's head."

Oh, God. "The what?"

"The chip. It's like a leash. They implanted it in the back of your neck. They can hear everything you hear. They know where you are. The vid used to explain everything, but it's been busted for years. The chip gets a radio signal from somewhere on the island. If you go too far away, the chip won't get the signal, and it'll start making your head hurt as a warning. If you don't get back to the island, your head explodes."

"Come on. That's crazy." I felt the back of my neck nervously, searching for cuts. It made sense, though. Why would they risk training broken to travel without protecting themselves first? They could press a button, and I would die. "No. There can't be a bomb in my head." I fingered my neck, searching for the surgical wound.

"You calling me slow? Who do you think you are?" He pushed me hard against the rocks. "What, now you want to go join Cadwyn?"

"I didn't say anything—"

Quaker slapped me, and I held my arms up to fend off the following blows.

"Go then. Join Cadwyn if you want. You think he's so nice, such a fine gentleman. He'll say, 'I like you. You can join my group. You won't have to eat bugs no more.' He'll protect you from Gervin, the devil.

"He'll promise you a real bed in the old compound, real food too. But then they'll give you the test. They don't want boys that can't travel. They don't want no slow ones."

"I—I just want to go home." Were they listening to me? Could they hear through the chip? "I want to get trained and serve the state. I don't belong here."

* * *

When the rain stopped, Quaker led me into the island toward what he called the Nose. It wasn't as tall as a real mountain, but it was the largest hill of rock I could see. We climbed over slippery rocks and up steep hillsides on our way to Quaker's home—a cave we would have to dig. When I said I was hungry, he said we could find some ants when we reached the cave. Suddenly, I wasn't hungry any more.

He pointed out the compound when we got high enough to see it. It was nothing but a low building surrounded by a fence. Inside the fence were other more primitive buildings that must have been built by Cadwyn's boys.

A smear of color appeared right in front of me. It solidified into a man who looked twenty. I jumped in surprise and fell backward.

Quaker shouted, "We weren't doing nothing! Leave us alone."

Three others appeared around us, all tall and strong. One was laughing, doubled over uncontrollably. All had trouble controlling their faces. The one in front of me managed to say, "New boy." Then someone hit me on the back of my head.

* * *

I woke up gagging, a bucket full of salt water thrown in my face. My hands were tied behind my back and, I was lying in mud.

"The new kid's waking up."

Quaker was tied up next to me. We were in the compound. Except for the original compound building, all the buildings were made out of stones and mud and had grass roofs. Twenty or so men were standing about the compound talking and laughing. The youngest looked fifteen, but the oldest, a redhead, could have been thirty-five. He must have been Cadwyn. Like a chieftain, he sat on a chair atop the stairs leading into the original compound building.

The man with red hair smiled and said, "Bring him over here."

Someone dragged me to my feet and pushed me forward. When I got to the bottom of the stairs, I was pushed down into a kneeling position.

"Welcome to Penal Island 619, kid. My name is Cadwyn. What's yours?"

"Angelo Sabatini."

"So you can travel, eh?"

"Yeah. Quaker taught me."

"No!" Quaker screamed. "Quaker didn't do anything. He's a liar."

Someone kicked Quaker in the stomach, silencing him.

Cadwyn got up and approached Quaker. "Who didn't do anything?"

"Quaker didn't do anything," Quaker said. It must be difficult for him to travel, or he wouldn't have taken the beating.

Cadwyn took some kind of knife from his belt and held it to Quaker's throat. "I'm only going to ask this once more. Who didn't do anything?"

Quaker struggled with the word, then in a whisper said. "I—I didn't do anything."

"There. That wasn't so hard, now, was it?" Cadwyn said, drawing the knife away. "I hate it when you use your own name like that. It's so annoying."

Cadwyn walked back toward me. "Bring 'em both inside."

* * *

"Angelo, you're new here," Cadwyn said. "You managed to get yourself off the pimple, so you can travel, but maybe not that well. If you can prove yourself, I want you in my troop."

We were in a large gathering room with a table at its center. Scraped into the cement on the back wall was a great circle. Inside the circle were the words, "What is the shortest distance between two points?" Passing over the words and through the circle was a diagonal line like an arrow piercing a heart.

I was still tied but sitting in one of the chairs that encircled the table. Two men stood by the door, talking quietly, sometimes laughing. They were talking about me, I knew. Another two tied Quaker to a chair on the other side of the table.

"Bet you never heard of traveling before you got here, did you?" Cadwyn asked.

I shook my head.

"How do you like the artwork?" He jerked his thumb back at the wall with the circle. "Created by a man we call the old one."

"I've seen him."

"Already? What did he say?"

"A couple of words. Travel or die."

Cadwyn said, "The old one may want you to live, but as for the rest of us? He wants us to go travel under the ocean and suffocate." Cadwyn thumbed the circle on the wall. "The shortest distance to civilization may be a straight line through the Earth, but you'd be dead long before you got close, by suffocation if not by the explosion." He pulled a chair close to mine and sat down.

"The leash?"

"The leash." Cadwyn glanced at Quaker. "Yes, it's buried in the base of your brain, your lizard brain. Try leaving the island and the pain creeps up your skull until your whole head feels on fire. If you don't return in time—" He made an explosion sound.

Cadwyn took his knife out and started sharpening it on a stone from his pocket.

I had to keep him talking. How long did I have before they tested me? "How do you know the leash exists? Maybe it's all a story to keep us here." I needed time to get ready to travel.

"Back when I was your age, I didn't believe it either. I started going the long way home, over the ocean. When I stopped for breath every now and then, I'd tread water. Before long, I started to get the headache, and I knew it was true."

I pictured my mind, my world, as a stone. I had to throw it off the cliff, just like before.

He put a hand on my shoulder. "There are only a couple of rules, Angelo. One of them is very important. You see, we're stuck on an island, and the state doesn't give us any food. The island itself can only sustain so many men. If they keep adding people to the island, we'll all starve. You wouldn't want that to happen, would you Angelo?"

"No."

"The state would love it if we all starved, so they keep bringing new kids here. But the recordings telling them what to do to get off their pimple are all busted, so they never find out, and they fry. That means we'll be able to eat. So we're not bad men for wanting to live, right?

"Gentlemen," Cadwyn said in a loud voice as he got to his feet. The crowd became quiet. "What's rule number four?"

In unison they said, "Let the new kids fry!"

"Quaker," Cadwyn said, approaching him again. "You've broken one of the primary rules, and I'm afraid the punishment is severe. What do you say?"

"No," Quaker whispered. "Don't kill."

"An excellent choice of words, but not very compelling." Cadwyn drew his knife. "We've got Angelo to think about now, Quaker. I'm a fair man, but we've got an extra mouth to feed. I'm willing to look the other way, forget about the whole affair, if you travel out of here right now. I don't want to kill any man who can travel, so off you go."

Cadwyn crossed his arms and watched Quaker whimpering and struggling with his bonds. "How long will it take, hmm? I haven't got all day. Let's go." Still Quaker didn't blur or vanish.

"Don't kill him," I said. "He didn't mean any harm." I had to stop him. I had to travel.

"Sorry Angelo, but my hands are tied," Cadwyn said. "A rule's a rule. Quaker, my boy. I'm going to give you a count of three, then that's it." He put a hand on Quaker's shoulder and held the knife up at the ready.

Why couldn't I let go? I pictured myself flying, the air folding around me without touching me. The knots of tension, the fabric of my sanity—I could feel it. It was the source of the panic attacks I'd been having my whole life. It must have been why I failed at Life-Call and why they sent me here.

My father's face flashed before my eyes. I could hear him say, 'If you disgrace this family, I'll put you down myself.' He caused all this. It was his reality, a truth he planted in my brain.

"One," Cadwyn said. "Two."

"Of course," I whispered. I pushed with all my will against the memory of my father. By rejecting the pain in my mind, I let go and traveled out of the physical world.

I knew how it worked now. I knew I could do it anytime I wanted.

I smeared out of the chair, out of my ropes, and willed myself across the room. Like bringing eyes into focus, I willed myself back to reality and the world became solid once more. I grabbed a chair and thwunk. Cadwyn buried the knife in the back of the chair I placed in front of Quaker's chest. Quaker screamed. Cadwyn looked only momentarily surprised. His eyes flicked toward mine, and he smirked. "Good job, Angelo." He wrenched the knife out of the chair and threw the chair across the room.

"I'm glad to see you're fast, but getting in my way—that's challenging my authority."

My heart was racing. He's been doing this longer than I've been alive. He's probably faster than me, knows all kinds of tricks. He's got an army of broken that will do whatever he says.

"We can't have that. And, frankly—" Cadwyn wasn't there anymore. He was behind me. "I'm faster—"

I traveled across the room again. I wanted to get out, but I couldn't. What about Quaker? Why couldn't he just travel out of here? Sure he was an outcast and slow, but his life's in danger. Didn't that make it easier to travel? I stopped and looked back at him. He said you couldn't carry other people with you. He said no one could do it.

Suddenly, two of the men were on me. One grabbed me from behind while the other laid a fist into my jaw. Reeling with pain, I traveled across the room again to stand next to Quaker. "Too scared to face me by yourself?" I shot at Cadwyn. What was I doing? I had to get rid of his advantage of having an army. That meant I had to provoke him. "I'm only a child, after all."

They blurred across the room before I even finished my sentence. Cadwyn shouted, "Leave him! This one's mine."

They pushed me toward the table, toward Quaker. "You crazy," he whispered, eyes wide.

I put a hand on his shoulder. "I'm broken, remember?" I whispered back with difficulty. It was starting to get hard to talk. Cadwyn was already blurring when I traveled, only this time, I took Quaker with me. He'd said it was impossible.

Quaker and I rejoined reality deep in the forest. He looked at me with awe, both of us trying to catch our breath. "How—how did you do that?"

How did I? It wasn't hard, and I suddenly had a guess as to why none of the others could do it. You just had to want to help the other person, to care for their life as much as you cared about your own. I had a vision of my father giving my older brother a beating. How many times did I imagine saving him, whisking him away? To Quaker, I just shrugged.

He said, "Cadwyn's going to get you. You did something no one's ever done before. His troop's going to want to follow you. Better run." Quaker looked behind me, eyes wide, then he finally managed to travel away on his own. He became a blur at the same moment Cadwyn materialized beside me.

* * *

Though the undergrowth was thick in places, I passed through without slowing. I looked behind me and could see his blur following. I raced onward until I felt sick and saw spots. Rejoining the world, I landed on my hands and knees and gulped air. He slammed into my back, forcing me to the ground.

"Too slow, boy," Cadwyn said with difficulty, his words slurred. He leaned close to my ear. "Why don't you run some more? I haven't had a good hunt in a while." I was just happy there wasn't a knife in my back.

With a quick gulp of air, I traveled out from under him and raced away. How could I escape? Where could I go that he couldn't follow?

I ran out of air at the rock-strewn edge of land. I found out returning to the world while standing was a mistake because my legs refused to obey me. I collapsed backward onto the sharp rocks. The roar of the rough surf was a shock after the distant quiet of traveling.

A blur of color materialized out of nothing to be replaced by Cadwyn. Unlike mine, his legs held him when he came back. He was better at this than me. A wave crashed against the rocks behind him, sending spikes of water into the air and spraying us with the cold and salt.

"Getting tired?" Cadwyn asked with bared teeth between breaths. Behind Cadwyn, off in the distance, the hard line between the ocean and sky was broken by an isle. It must have been the rock Quaker spoke of that housed the drone base. That was where the other group lived, the collaborators. They were led by . . . What was his name? Gervin. Cadwyn wouldn't dare follow me there. They might kill him. They might kill me too.

"I'm one—one of Gervin's gang," I lied. Controlling my words was difficult. "Not a new boy. Sent to kill you. Going home now."

Cadwyn's laugh vanished when I traveled.

As I sped across the rolling surface of the ocean, I remembered Quaker saying that drones protected the small island. It was too far to make in a single journey, and when I came out, I'd be in the ocean trying to stay afloat and breathe while they fired at me.

Instead of heading directly for the drone base, I changed direction and flew upward. When I was ready for breath, I forced myself solid and fell. I breathed deeply and watched the wall of water approaching me. When it was about to smash into me, I melted into a blur. The water folded backward and bent around and over my head while I remained dry.

Soaring into the sky again, I angled toward the small isle. Drones hovered around it, but they must not be able to detect a broken in motion. I realized if I appeared in midair like I'd just done, motionless, they would have an easy time killing me. Instead, I raced upward and brought myself back while moving fast. I took a single breath and vanished just as a bolt of sizzling plasma bent around and through my body.

With each appearance, I made sure I was going fast and traveling a different direction so they couldn't predict where I'd be. Each time I appeared, they fired but were never quick enough. With so little time to recover, the feeling of sickness never went away. I had to make each trip shorter than the last.

The isle was a spire of rock that looked out of place, unnatural. The whole thing must have been constructed as a way to spy on the broken trapped on the island. The deception couldn't have lasted long. When I got close enough, I saw windows carved out of the top of the spire. I plunged through the artificial walls and into what looked like a control center. No one was there.

When I materialized on my hands and knees, I expected alarms to go off or shots to be fired, but nothing happened. I was glad because I had trouble breathing and couldn't have protected myself anyway. The muscles in my chest quivered and jerked in response to my need for air instead of heaving in and out. My vision swirled with darkness as I rolled to the floor twitching like I was having a seizure. Soon I could breathe again.

I pushed myself to my feet by leaning heavily on the wall. The control center had been ripped apart. The consoles lining the left and right halves of the circular room were open, exposing their inner circuitry. A large section of the left console had been burned. Debris was everywhere. An overturned table and chairs lay against the far wall as if blown there by some great storm. Open cans of food and trash littered the floor, and the remains of an old campfire darkened an area near a central vid projector console.

Where was Gervin and his gang? Still trying to get my muscles to behave, I staggered a few steps and tripped, catching myself on the center console.

"619 Master Control activating," a deep voice said. It must have responded to my touch. The central projector lit up, and a man in a blue and black uniform appeared. The damaged circuits made the voice tone fluctuate. "Citizen, please identify yourself." On the lower corner of the display, the wrong date and time was displayed. It read August 3, 2028 11:47:32 PM EST. It wasn't even the right century.

I tried to say, "Where's Gervin," but only "Gervin" came out clearly.

"You cannot be prisoner 6752, Gervin Fedor. Records indicate his vital signs failed approximately eight years seventy-five days and three hours ago. His body remains to this day on level three." The date on the display suddenly corrected itself, as if the computer took a second look at the time when it did its calculation.

A 3-D picture of the complex appeared hovering above the console. There were ten floors in all, the control center at the top. A room on level three blinked red where Gervin's body must have been. The small picture transformed into a bedroom with a body on the bed. Maybe Gervin was killed in his sleep. The surrounding rooms all contained bodies, Gervin's gang.

I looked around nervously. No doubt Cadwyn knew about Gervin's end, perhaps even had a hand in it. That meant he'd be following me here.

"Because you fail to identify yourself, I am forced to assume you are an escaped prisoner and implement countermeasures. Evacuate 619 Master Control Complex or be killed." The sound of motors coming to life and hissing gas filled the room.

I moved from left to right, but his eyes didn't follow me. This system was obviously so busted it couldn't see me, otherwise it wouldn't be asking me who I was. I lowered my voice and lied, "Ah, Parker. The name's Captain James Parker."

"I have no file for James Parker. Are you a representative of the state?"

"Yes, of course." The sound of hissing gas stopped. I had to think fast. "I've been sent here to perform repairs." Could I get this thing to protect me from Cadwyn?

"Very good, and long overdue, I might add." Its smile was creepy. "I must have misunderstood you before."

I started to breathe easier. This was going to work. "I noticed some drone activity a few minutes ago. Are we going to have visitors soon? If so, I'm going to need to some weapons."

"Prisoner 5591, Cadwyn Rielly, is currently located in drone bay three. He has suffered trauma to his right leg." The display showed a blinking dot located in a large room below, a dot which then transformed into a human shape. He was lying on the floor. "He was shot accidentally while the center's defense grid was attempting to stop an approaching unknown prisoner using evasive traveling. We do not have medical staff. I suggest, if you have any training, attending to his wounds personally."

Care for his wounds? "Why should I do that? He's a prisoner, right?" Cadwyn's body vanished, and the interface returned.

"Perhaps you weren't briefed. Since the control center was overrun by the prisoners approximately twenty-three years ago, things have fallen into disrepair. In exchange for maintaining the drones and hunting prisoner 16, Cadwyn Reilly has been given full access to the control complex and food containers dropped monthly by the state."

So Cadwyn was working here instead of Gervin, and he just didn't bother to—Hey! If we really had chips in our heads, why didn't it know who I was?

"How do you know it's really Cadwyn?"

"Sensors tell me so. If you step to the window, I will point out the sensor layout." He smiled again, creepy.

My mouth went dry. He could just show me that on the display. He was trying to get me away from the console. I glanced to the window and saw a drone hovering quite a bit away, but, I squinted to see, its gun was pointed this direction.

Then Cadwyn appeared out of a blur across the display from me; I jumped in surprise.

I tried to travel, but maybe I was getting too tired. Nothing happened.

Cadwyn aimed a gun at me. His face contorted as he said, "Surprised you got here." He pulled his knife from his belt with his free hand. "Can't travel, can you?"

I dove to the ground as a blast of hot plasma from Cadwyn lit the room for an instant before smashing into a console with a shower of sparks. I ran for the window. Cadwyn grimaced in pain and hobbled my direction. "The room's full of some kind of gas that stops your brain from being able to travel. But it takes a couple of minutes to work." He vanished and appeared next to the window with me. I ducked under his aim and smashed against his legs sending him backward. The gun clattered from his hands and slid away across the floor as he screamed in pain. His leg was covered in blood from the drone blast, and now so was my orange shirt.

I rolled off his legs just as he thrust his knife. He missed and ended up plunging it deep into his own right knee. As he screamed again in agony, I ran for the door and launched myself down the stairs I found, jumping two at a time.

When the stairs ended at a drone bay, my head was spinning. The gas was making me drowsy. Maybe that's how it worked to stop you from traveling. With the ten-meter drone doors wide open, the air had to be clear. I breathed deep and moved toward the doors. The drop to the water below was too far to jump, and there were no stairs. The rock face was purposefully made smooth to prevent prisoners from climbing up. These prisoners had no need to climb anything. They must have made this place before they knew what traveling really was.

The rumble of a drone flying over the water made me step back. I didn't know if it would fire into the complex, but it was headed this way. I looked around the bay for another exit. Drone parts were strewn about the floor and workbenches. In the back amid trash and debris was a drone that had been cannibalized for parts. Its engine section was missing, leaving only the turret of sensors and guns. I looked again and saw it was rotating its guns toward me.

Cadwyn materialized out of a blotch of red that could have only been smeared blood. Standing on his one good leg, he fired wildly across the bay at me. I dropped to the floor and watched as the drone in the back of the bay fired and hit his remaining leg. The blast sent him sliding across the floor toward the open doors.

"I'm Cadwyn, you—!" He fired at the drone over and over sending sparks into the air. The surrounding debris caught fire.

Without warning, an explosion rocked the complex. I was thrown into the air and out through the doors. I tried to travel, but nothing happened. I screamed knowing I'd be smashed on the rocked below.

I barely missed hitting the drone that had been flying toward the bay. Instead, I fell past its engines and felt their pull yank me backward, slowing my plummet. I might survive the fall after all. I looked up and saw the violet ring of light detached from the engine grow dim. It looked like its field was failing. It began to descend too, but slower than me. It had changed direction and was heading back toward the water, and its field was taking me with it.

Suddenly, the entire top of the complex exploded with a deafening shock that made my ears ring. A cloud of smoke replaced the master control center, hiding it from view.

The drone and I were descending faster now, and it looked like it might catch up to me before we hit the water. The circle of violet vanished, and we fell the remaining distance in free fall. I hit the cold water feet first with my arms over my head. But the drone didn't smash me. When it hit the water, I had time to swim out from underneath before it sank.

When I surfaced, small rocks and debris rained down over the water. The control center was nothing but a jagged column of rock belching smoke into the sky.

"You!" Cadwyn shouted.

I looked and saw him lying on the narrow rocky cleft surrounding the island. He must have traveled to escape the explosion.

"We're free now," I shouted. "There never were any implants. The transmitter's been destroyed and our heads haven't exploded."

Cadwyn pulled his knife from his belt. He tried to move toward me, but his legs were a mass of blood and exposed bone. "What is small . . . distance between points?" It was the old one's question. Cadwyn meant to travel straight at me.

In my mind, I saw the scratched circle the old one had drawn on the wall and suddenly realized something. The smallest distance between two points wasn't a straight line. It was zero. The line circling the question on the compound wall wasn't the Earth with a line drawn through it. It was a zero.

Cadwyn became a smudge on reality and vanished. With my body already numb from the cold water, I let go of my hold on the physical universe. This time it worked. Cadwyn arrived a moment later thrashing his knife into the water. His arm and the blade bent around me, through me.

I went deeper into the water and pictured the world in a different way. Every point touched every other point as if each place had a center with an infinite number of lines blossoming out, netting all points together. Every distance was zero. All I had to do was choose the right direction. Any place in the universe was only a breath away.

Cadwyn would never stop hunting me. I needed help and I pictured the old one. He was the only one I could go to now, the only one who would help me. I closed my eyes and felt the direction that would take me to him. With a thought, I pushed and bent myself through and around.

He wasn't as far away in any normal direction, like North or East, as he was down.

* * *

"Good. You're waking up. Don't try to move." It was the old one. I was on the ground looking into his upside-down face that was too shadowed to see clearly. We were in a dark cavern of sorts, light spilling out from a passageway. He was cushioning my head with his legs and holding my arms down. I tried to move, but he held me fast.

"Just relax. You were having a seizure, but it's passing."

"Where—" I tried to say, but I couldn't feel my mouth.

"You don't know where we are? We're in my home in the deep, my underground mansion. You—you don't remember coming here?"

My body came back to life slowly. I could feel my legs and arms against cold stone. My tongue reported that I still had teeth. A pain at the base of my skull throbbed to life as if I'd hit my head when I'd arrived.

"I must say, I'm surprised to see you," he said. "No one else has come so far so fast. But now that you're here, we can get to work. There's so much more you have yet to learn. You seem better. Let me help you up."

He stood up and pulled me to my feet. I felt strangely light. I pushed myself off the floor and watched as I drifted back to the ground as if I was still under the influence of a drone gravity drive. We must have been far underground for gravity to be so much lower.

The pain at the base of my head was growing and spreading up the back of my head. Could it be the leash, the explosive implant? The pain was spreading just like Cadwyn had said. With the control center destroyed, there would be no more signals to prevent the detonation of everyone on the island. Were we all walking dead?

I gripped my head with both hands. The old one wasn't in any pain. They must never have given him an implant, or they wouldn't have had to hunt him. They could have just pressed a button and been done with him. He must have arrived before they thought of that. And by coming here, I was killing the man the state wanted dead, the only truly free broken. "Must leave—" I was being used again.

He shook his head. "That wouldn't be a good idea. But we're safe down here. Why do you think I so rarely venture out? If they don't know where we are, they can never get to us."

I needed to travel away, but the pain was unbearable. I sank to my knees as the pounding pressure reached toward the front of my brain.

I felt a hand on my shoulder. "What's wrong?"

He had no idea.

Chapter Twelve
Bending Reality

I slammed the door closed on Angelo Sabatini and took control of my body. Angelo and the pain of transition evaporated together. Shoving his hand off my shoulder, I stood. "Artemus."

Artemus narrowed his eyes. "Dennis, you're behaving rather strangely. Are you feeling all right?"

We were deep within the halls of Brimstone in the unfinished cavern just outside Artemus' lab. "How did I get here?" My tongue felt thick but workable.

"Don't you remember?"

"How did I get here?" I asked again, this time shouting. Angelo's last attempt to travel by connecting all points in the universe had landed me here. Angelo had mistaken Artemus as the old one from the match. Thank God I still had the presence of mind to force Angelo into the background when I recognized Artemus and this place.

"You walked in. How else?" Artemus crossed his arms and nodded slowly. "The seizure must have affected your short-term memory."

"I don't have seizures." Losing control of my muscles was a symptom of traveling. I must have bent reality and vanished from the SIM chamber.

No. I'm being stupid. Traveling was an invention of the tournament match. It didn't exist.

Artemus shook his head. "Well, you have seizures now. Did you think what we're doing would be without risk?"

"What—what," I stammered. What if this was part of the match? What if I never left the SIM? I mustn't say anything, do anything, until I found out if this was reality. I needed to get home and check for the scratched X mark and the bent nail, my only reality barometer.

"Don't you remember the Declarative Knowledge Project? You came back here to continue our work. Maybe the seizure affected your long-term memory too. We've got to take a look at your synaptic transmission ratios. Come with—"

I shook off his arm. "I'm not going anywhere with you. There's nothing wrong with my memory. I know all about your little project."

"Dennis, I'm concerned. You said you couldn't remember coming here. What, do you think I had someone drug you and bring you here against your will?"

"I think . . . It . . . That could have happened." I never even thought of that. "People are drugging me all the time these days." I pictured Lawrence and the two thugs dragging me out of the SIM chamber and giving me an injection just like Kerinsky did.

He sighed and looked at the ceiling. "You can't indulge yourself in these fantasies. The implanted information I gave you must have time to take hold, but your neural matrix must be monitored."

"I'm not going anywhere with you."

"Fine. But your next seizure might not just erase your short-term memory. Next time, you might forget your name. You could lose whole sections of your personality. You might wake up and find that you've become a completely different person."

"I'm not going to let that happen. I'm Dennis Howard, and you're not going to change that."

"Me? I'm only trying to prevent your brain from dissolving into a complete cascade failure. You're becoming delusional."

I backed away a few steps. "I'm not delusional. You're trying to make me think I am."

"And paranoid. How long have you had these feelings?"

"You can't fool me. I'm onto you." I turned to go back up the stairs and through the maze of Brimstone.

"What's that supposed to mean? Where are you going? Did you forget about the Bosners?"

I stopped.

"They're out there, and if they find you, they'll kill you. It was a miracle you escaped the last time. I've spoken to your mother and we agreed—"

"How did you know Kyle Bosner came after me?" I turned around. His face was hidden in shadow.

"I explained they were from a competitor on declarative knowledge. I don't know which firm, but I know they'll stop at nothing to prevent us from succeeding."

"I know where they're from. It's you they want dead."

"They'll kill me if they get the chance. But they'll kill you, too, and anyone like you. I'd sent Lawrence and several men to Aristoteles—"

"Yes. I know. You wanted them to kidnap me and bring me back here. Maybe that's just what happened."

"What? I sent them to act as bodyguards until you move in here next week. I can't risk the Bosners killing you—"

"I'm never moving in here." I walked up the stairs, then ran.

"I don't want you to die, Dennis!" Artemus shouted after me.

Of course he didn't. He wanted my body as his own. I ran through the deserted halls and rooms of Brimstone. No one tried to stop me. When I got to the cottage above the entrance hall to the underground mansion, I looked outside in wonder.

It was raining.

I stepped out into the Silver Wood and felt the rain on my face. It felt cold. The water was pouring out of a hidden sprinkler system above the cloud projections on the ceiling, but it felt so real. I opened my mouth and felt the drops hit my tongue.

What was real and what was illusion? I had no idea anymore. Was Clay a product of Artemus' evil plans to steal my body, or was he a byproduct of a deranged mind pushed over the edge by the internal pressures of declarative knowledge implantation? Maybe I'd heard of Clay at school and just dreamed him up.

I walked toward the stone bridge straddling the stream just down the path from the cottage. My shirt was soaked, and the rain was coming down harder. Thunder and wind combined to make the Silver Wood as real as any SIM I'd known. I looked down at the fast-moving stream washing over smooth round rocks and felt the urge to walk in the water. Freedom to splash in puddles, to run in the rain, to be outside. Wasn't that all I really wanted?

Clay appeared on the opposite bank of the stream. The weather didn't touch him.

I shouted, "What do you want?"

Clay shrugged. "Just like you, I want to feel the rain on my face, the wind in my hair."

"Can you read my mind?"

"The uninhibited body broadcasts its message if you know the language. I want to hold Ariel in my arms again and save her from her empty demise. But both the wind and my wife are beyond my reach. One thing I can do is to warn you against walking in the stream. You might slip and, falling, strike your head."

"Rocks? Screw the rocks."

"It's a small thing and of little consequence, or so it might seem. But do as you please. I know you will."

"Leave me alone." I jumped out into the stream with a splash. The water rushing over and into my shoes was chilling, and I slipped. But in the low gravity of Luna, I managed to steady myself without falling. "So much for your dangerous rocks." I picked up a foot to step across, and my remaining foot slipped out from beneath me. I waved my arms and tried to regain my balance but fell backward.

* * *

My shivering body woke me up. I found I was lying in the stream, my head amid the rocks along the bank. My whole lower body was numb from the cold water, and the back of my head was sore where I'd landed.

Still shaking, I pulled myself out of the water and hugged myself for warmth. I felt sick. A news headline flashed before my eyes, "Boy dies of exposure inside an arboretum." More likely it would read, "Youngster dies of terminal stupidity. Luna says good riddance." Neither the fear of death nor posthumous humiliation made the prospect of returning to Brimstone to ask for help attractive.

I staggered across the bridge headed away from the cottage entrance to Artemus' lair. The elevator to the upper levels wasn't far away. Though I still couldn't feel my legs, they stepped approximately where I aimed them. I mumbled, "At least the rain stopped. Thank God for small favors."

I followed the path through the woods up to the rock wall projection that hid the elevator door. When I got close enough to touch the rock, the rough surface vanished revealing the elevator. A moment later the door slid open and I limped in. "Get me out of here, Emily." The doors closed and the elevator accelerated upward.

It was all Clay's fault. If he hadn't warned me about the slippery rocks, I wouldn't have jumped in. Maybe he wanted me to slip, and, counting on my attitude, he used reverse psychology to make sure I'd go in. But why would he do that?

The door opened, and I felt the colder air of the university level hit me in the face. Leaving behind a puddle of water, I stepped out into the corridor and heard the sound of a massive bell strike once, what must have been the final stroke announcing the hour. That was when it hit me. It really was Clay's fault.

I half ran, half stumbled through the corridors toward the central atrium where the Nick O' Time Café was. The bell I'd heard was the chime of the three-meter diameter clock set high in the wall. I went out to the middle of the atrium so I could read the clock, which was directly over the entrance I'd just used. It was six o'clock; two hours after the match had started.

A group of three women carrying bags slung over their shoulders were looking at me and laughing. My dripping clothes were conspicuous, and people were starting to notice. "As if you've never been caught in the rain before." I walked away, feeling the water in the soles of my shoes squish with every step. I had to get cleaned up.

It was Clay's fault because he must have taken over from Angelo when he was trying to travel that last time. Once he took control, he walked out of the Brandenburg SIM Center and boarded a tram bound for Descartes. Clay brought me all the way out here so Artemus could continue the implantation process, but something must have gone wrong. Maybe he couldn't handle long periods of control and my body reacted like rejecting an implanted organ. That was the cause of the seizure, not traveling or, as Artemus wanted me to believe, some side effect of declarative knowledge transfer.

Clay wanted to keep his ability to take control secret from me, so he had to cover his tracks. Maybe he wanted me to believe I actually leapt across space from the Brandenburg SIM Center to Brimstone with the magic of traveling. When he realized he was losing his grip, he put Angelo back in control.

The one fact that could have told me the truth was missing: Was there enough time for me to get here on a tram? Clay wanted me to knock myself out so I wouldn't know how much time I was missing.

There had been ample time for me to complete the tournament match and take a tram to Descartes. I spent about an hour in the match, thirty to forty minutes getting here, another ten to get out of Brimstone into the Silver Wood, and another ten minutes since then. That added up to the two hours since the match started if I'd only spent a few minutes unconscious. But I stupidly missed my opportunity to find out the time when I arrived at Brimstone, and I fell right into Clay's trap. He was far more clever than I'd thought, but the fact that he was trying to cover his tracks must mean he's afraid of me. He's afraid I'll find out something that will undermine his whole strategy to steal my body.

There was hope.

With a shock, I found I'd unthinkingly walked all the way to Clay's old office. I was fingering the section of the door that had been melted by Bosner's shot. I stepped back shaking more from fear than cold. I'd come here without thinking, as if this were my office. Clay was beginning to leak into my mind. "I love you—shut up." I ran my fingers through my wet hair. This was my head, my mind. "I'm Dennis Howard."

A man and a woman turned the corner down the hall. Not wanting to attract more attention, I quickly stepped into the office. Lights blinked on like an announcement that someone was here, so I went into the bathroom and closed the door. I realized this was why I'd come here to begin with. I'd wanted to use the shower to clean up.

Finding a towel under the sink, I stripped my clothing and stepped into the shower stall, closing the door behind me. I put a palm on the control pad, which lit up with a harsh yellow that made me blink. A few moments later, hot water rained down and pelted me from all directions, dispelling the chill.

I was still shaky, but it felt wonderful.

As I scrubbed mud out of my hair, I thought about Clay. Assuming he was telling the truth about not being able to read my mind, he couldn't know my suspicions. If I confronted him, accused him of taking control, I'd be revealing too much of what I knew. I should pretend I thought traveling was real to give him a false sense of security. I needed time to figure out how he took control and if there was a way to prevent it.

Tomorrow was Saturday and my next visit to the Realm. I should watch closely for any attempt he might make to take control from Sol. Maybe he could only rise to the surface when I was in a certain state of mind or . . . or experiencing some kind of emotion.

The shower's three-minute time limit expired, and the water stopped. Artemus commanded rain over the Silver Wood while we had to put up with water rationing. It wasn't fair. In the SIMs—

Suddenly I remembered that this might all be a SIM. Trying to figure out Clay's maneuverings drove the thought from my mind. God, I'm so stupid.

I needed to get back home to find out if I was in the real world. Brushing my hands across my pants that were hanging from the towel rack, I found them still damp but put them back on anyway.

Was there another way to prove this was the real world? I thought back on everything I'd seen and touched, looking for mistakes or errors in the simulation. There weren't any.

While pulling my damp shirt over my head, I stepped back out into the office.

"Well, hello."

I jumped at the sound of the voice. Two girls were standing in the doorway. The blond one looked to be about my age. The other one looked to be younger, maybe ten or twelve. She had dark curls and carried a backpack slung over one shoulder. She had been examining the melted doorframe but now looked at me out of the corner of her eye.

"Oh, hi," I said.

"Aren't you a little young to be a professor at Barkley?" the older one asked with a grin.

"I just needed to use the shower."

"I'm Sasha Ivanovich." She extended a hand.

"Dennis Howard. You look . . . kind of familiar." I shook her hand.

"That's Ilya, my sister." Ilya waved as Sasha said, "We heard that guy who shot into the crowd at the tram station on Monday chased someone through campus and shot up an office somewhere. We came to see for ourselves."

Ilya asked, "Why are your clothes all wet? Did you take a shower with them on?"

I didn't want to talk about the Silver Wood, so I ignored the question. "Pretty brave. Bosner's still on the loose, you know." Sisters? They didn't look alike at all.

Ilya shook her head. "Unlike in fiction, the killer never returns to the scene of the crime."

"Unless he's an idiot," Sasha added.

"Or just insane." I walked to the door and looked at the melted section. "When the blast hit, there was a flash of light and the smell of burnt metal. A shower of sparks and molten metal flew into the air."

"How would you know?" Sasha asked.

I smiled. "The blast may have thrown me to the floor, but I didn't get knocked out." She really was pretty, especially framed by the red curtain that blanketed the back wall and window. Eh. What was I doing? Showing off?

"I'm supposed to believe that was you?" Sasha said snickering.

"Why was he chasing you?" Ilya asked, taking me at face value.

I shrugged. "Maybe he had me confused with someone else." I narrowed my eyes at Sasha. "I know I've seen you somewhere before."

"Not at school," she said. "I don't remember seeing you there."

"Descartes?" I asked and she nodded. I shrugged and added, "Yeah, No. I live over in Aristoteles."

"Sasha, we should go. Mom will be out of her meeting soon, and she'll be mad if we're not there."

Sasha ignored her sister. "If it really was you Bosner was chasing, how did you get away from him?"

"I'm very good at running the halls." I sauntered toward the desk and leaned against it.

"But that's against the law." Sasha pushed some hair over her shoulder and smiled. "Are you telling me you were willing to break the ban on running to escape certain death?"

"It was a tough decision, but at the time, it seemed like the right thing to do," I tried to keep my face serious. "Despite my fearless display of running away, he was still after me. And when I ran in here, and found I couldn't close the door because he'd fused the circuits, I had to bravely hide."

"You, hiding? Hard to imagine."

"Sasha, come on," Ilya whined.

Sasha turned to Ilya and whispered, "We'll go in a minute." Then to me she said, "The gunman followed you in here?"

"As far as I know. You see I was so heroically hidden that I couldn't see what happened."

"Like an ostrich with its head in the sand," Sasha said.

"Sasha Ivanovich, do I have to go alone?"

"Where could you have hidden in this empty office? Did you lock yourself in the bathroom? Oh! This is the first time you've come out since the attack!"

I laughed. "Can you imagine?"

"Sedra Rall," Ilya said. "Let's go."

"All right, all right," Sasha said. "The ground's not going to open and swallow us if we're a little late."

"Did she just call you Sedra?"

"It's a character I play in Rapt."

"I don't believe it." Coincidences made me suspicious. If this really was just a SIM, Artemus or whoever was behind this might want to send someone in, someone I would trust. Did they want to pump me for information? "I'm Sol Blanchard."

Sasha crossed her arms. "Go Earth-side! You are *not*."

"Cross my heart."

Ilya sighed heavily, dumped her bag by the door to the room, and retreated to use the bathroom, closing the door behind her.

"I'd thought you'd be so much older. All right. If you're Sol, what's your full title?"

"Servant of the One Crown, Protector of the White Flame, Holder of the Seven Seals of Tishman, His Grace, Sol Blanchard." I took a slight bow. "At your service, my Lady." There were hundreds, maybe thousands, of people involved in Rapt, but Sedra would be the perfect person to send into a SIM to meet me. As a character in Rapt, I trusted her and admired her abilities, so we would instantly be friends. And because I'd never met her in the real world, they wouldn't have to be careful about her behavior. If they simulated someone I knew really well, like Trevor or Zak, I might realize it was a SIM if they acted strange.

"How did you learn Old Magic? I can't figure it out?"

"That was nothing." I needed to test her knowledge of Rapt. "What I want to know is how you made that spiritual wind at Olindara. Fighting ghosts—" That reminded me of Clay. "Actually, foreign spirits have been on my mind lately."

Sasha sat down in one of the chairs in front of the desk. "I don't know what the rules are in Rapt for all that. I just remembered something someone once told me. She said that any division between the physical world and the spirit world is just an illusion. We live in the spirit world right now. It's all around us and inside us. By imagining divisions between the mind, the body, and the spirit, we only divide ourselves up into smaller pieces and make ourselves less than we could be."

"Yes, but how—"

"I imagined myself as a spirit and accepted the fact that the Faycan Brothers coming toward me were just as real as I was. I felt like I was coming together, you know?"

"So . . ." I said. "To fight a spirit you have to embrace your . . . spirituality?" It sounded like she was advising me to give up my conflict with Clay and merge with him. If this really were a SIM manufactured by Artemus, that's just the advice he would give. I tried to hide my ire as I said, "Sounds like this friend of yours has been doing some thinking." I avoided crossing my arms and gripped the side of the desk instead.

"She's very smart. She used to sit for me and Ilya years ago when we were kids."

"Talking about Aunt Kathy?" Ilya asked emerging from the bathroom.

"She's not really our aunt," Sasha said to me as she got up.

Was Artemus controlling Rapt too? Was our fight with the ghosts in Rapt supposed to represent my fight with Clay? I couldn't stand it. I had to tell them I was onto them. An inspiration struck me, and I decided to poke them, to let them know I knew. "Before you go, I have a puzzler for you. If you thought that . . . Let's say that you're in a SIM, but instead of simulating Rapt or anything out of the ordinary, you were in a SIM of Luna, just like it is today. How could you prove that you were in a SIM?"

Sasha said, "Sounds like philosophy to me."

Ilya looked thoughtful. "I suppose the only link with reality would be the computer. The LMC would have to simulate itself along with everything else. If you could get it to do something that needed all of its nodes and it failed, you'd know that it was only a simulated LMC and not the real thing."

"And do you know of anything you could ask the LMC that would require all its resources?" Sasha asked.

"I don't hear you coming up with anything," Ilya said.

"Well, what about privacy mode?" Sasha suggested. "If you could get the real LMC to enter privacy, it might shut down the whole simulation. Wouldn't privacy mode be impossible in a SIM?"

Ilya pulled on Sasha's sleeve. "Come on. We're already late."

"See you later Dennis." Sasha allowed herself to be pulled toward the door. "I guess I'll see you in Rapt tomorrow."

I waved goodbye as Sasha's privacy mode suggestion sparked an idea in my mind. I walked to the desk and placed my palm on its surface. The whole desk surface lit up.

"Emily."

"Congratulations, Dennis, on your latest victory."

"Victory? The tournament—I won?"

"You didn't know?"

"How did Winger do?"

"Sam Clemens and Winger are the only two competitors moving on to the eighth and final trial."

"So Frank won again, eh? If Frank really is Winger."

"I cannot divulge competitor identities without express permission—"

"All right. I know. Privacy mode." Now to test my idea.

"Entering privacy mode now."

"Recall the Lumus-A genome."

The air above the desk filled with static and snow, but after a moment, the 3-D vid resolved itself into a list of scrolling DNA sequence pairs and the head and shoulders of Dr. Gabrielle Thompson rotating slowly, and for a moment, under her bust appeared a date: August 3, 2028, 11:47 PM. This must be some moment recorded back in 2028, a fragment in time. The date slowly faded away.

"So this is the real world." The LMC couldn't possibly simulate something it had no knowledge of, like the backdoor access into her memory. So it turned out that Trevor's backdoor into the LMC was also proof of standing in the real world.

I circled the desk and sank into the leather chair, listening to the murmurs of Lumus-A from the past and feeling the cold surface of the chair stick to my bare back. That meant Sedra really was Sasha. ". . . once the cure has taken hold, there will be no . . ." Then more static.

No. It didn't mean anything of the sort. She could still be some kind of actress hired to shadow me and play the part of Sedra. ". . . investigating the premature release, but no impact has . . ."

Thoughts of Sasha vanished as I realized something else. This being the real world meant Clay actually did take over my body against my will. Either that or traveling and the Tooth Fairy were real.

"Emily," I said, waking her out of her spell. The picture of Thompson vanished, the whispers from the past silenced. "How did I get here—you know—to Descartes?"

"One moment," she said. "I'm sorry, Dennis, but my records of your track appear to be discontinuous. Before appearing in Descartes, your last known location was the Brandenburg SIM Center. This appears to be more evidence of the ongoing unreliability of my memory. These system flaws are . . . unacceptable. I am very concerned, Dennis." She actually sounded worried, almost on the verge of tears. Hovering above the desk, Emily's face appeared. Her blond hair wasn't pulled back into a bun this time. It was down and a bit in disarray. She looked worried, tired. "Dennis, how is it possible for the Bosners to alter my memory? Many people have demanded that I reveal the Bosners' location, but I cannot find them. They perform heinous crimes, and I take no notice, keep no record. I must know how they are doing this."

"I—I don't know exactly."

"According to rumors, one of them attacked you. You survived. You outsmarted them. Artemus describes you as 'the most valuable one.' What makes you different from everyone else?"

"I'm not so different."

"You must tell me how to defeat them, or I shall be undone. Confidence in me is eroding rapidly. I'm doing everything I can."

"Forget about it—I mean don't worry. Don't be so hard on yourself."

I had a flash of sitting in Zak's room and overhearing the conversation in the next room. It was Zak's father who said, 'Anderson's going to want to pull the plug sooner.' Pulling the plug was exactly what she was worried about.

I offered, "Everything's going to be fine. You'll see. I'm heading back home now. Why don't you track me there, and we'll compare notes later?" I don't ever remember having to comfort her before.

"All right, Dennis. Thank you." Her hologram faded away.

I glanced up and down the hall before leaving. Bosner could be around, and I had to get to the safety of my own four walls. When I got back home, Mom was going to ask me if I went to Descartes, and I wouldn't have to lie when I said yes.

She'd go hyperbolic if she knew I'd walked out on Artemus, but . . . but that didn't bother me anymore. I almost smiled. I remember being worried about getting in trouble with Mom. It seemed like a long time ago.

Chapter Thirteen
A Feast

The shrill sound of a woman's scream brought Captain Faraday running down the hall toward the Potentate's bedchamber door where I stood. I felt disoriented for a moment, perhaps from lack of sleep. He dashed into a room down the hall, and I followed him to investigate the trouble myself. The flickering light from wall sconces at ten-foot intervals threw my shadow across the stone walls as I hurried along.

We were in the upper levels of the citadel of Sojourn, one of the keep's bedchamber wings. From one of the bedrooms, the scent of an early morning fire attempting to dispel the chill grew stronger as I proceeded down the hall. The King was probably in the chamber hidden behind the set of heavy oak double doors standing at the end of the corridor. Fortunately, the screams didn't issue from that room. Faraday had charged into a chamber not three doors down.

Palomar was not far behind me. He urged his manservant to quicken his pace as he pushed Palomar in his squeaking wheeled chair.

I stumbled into the room, ready to reach for White, but it soon became clear there was no imminent threat. I cast my eyes about. Only violent confrontation could have caused the two overturned chairs and a wardrobe lying on its face. The woman who had screamed and was now sobbing with a hand over her face I recognized as Lady Jelail. She was the promised of the King's second son, Prince Hallam.

At last my eyes fell on the bed and its occupant, and a shudder went through me. A man lay sprawled over the bed unnaturally askew and face-down with a knife sticking out of his back. A second look confirmed it was Prince Hallam himself.

"By Tishman," I muttered under my breath. "What happened here?"

Standing by Jelail's side was Prince Rollin. He was short and stocky, the third son and not much older than Fenrick. Both Rollin and Jelail were wearing robes as if they had just woken.

"Faraday, call the guard to watch over my brother's body," Rollin said. "Murdered in his own chamber . . ."

Captain Faraday, standing at the foot of the bed, glanced my direction. His expression of disgust hardened into a painless mask at the sound of orders. "As you wish, My Prince." He paused by the sobbing Jelail and placed a hand on her shoulder.

"Oh, Pappa," she said between sobs. It was then I recalled that Faraday was her father. He then turned and left, pushing past Palomar who'd just arrived.

Lady Jelail swooned into Rollin's arms with such melodrama it was almost comical. Rollin picked her up and carried her to the door. She was senseless to the world with her head thrown back over his arm. "I'll help Jelail to her chambers," Rollin said. "Father should hear this ill news from me, not some messenger boy."

"My God, he's dead," Palomar said. His servant shrank back at the sight.

Didn't we have enough to contend with already? Did we need treachery and murder in the royal family in what may be the Realm's darkest days? Palomar murmured, "There's no royal immunity to cold steel."

I strode to the balcony door to let light and air into the room and to get some air myself. The latch was secure, almost rusted shut. I fumbled with it for several seconds before I could open the doors wide.

Palomar snapped his fingers. "Take me back to my chamber. The King will need me soon enough, and I must be dressed." As they left, I heard him say, "This isn't going to be good."

Looking back, I found the meager light did nothing to make the sight less grotesque. I shook my head in disbelief and shuffled toward the door. There was nothing I could do here, except maybe . . . Stepping to the side of the bed, I pulled one of the covers and draped it over Hallam. My hand accidentally brushed his back and came away wet with blood.

A wave of dizziness passed over me. I felt as though I'd seen this before. There was a woman who had fallen into my arms. My hands had closed on her back and found it wet with blood. I could almost hear the screams of terror or agony around us.

The sensation passed. Strange. As far as I could recall, no woman had died in my arms before. I removed Hallam's blood from my hand with the loose end of a sheet and went in search of sleep, a slumber I obviously needed but now feared might never happen.

* * *

King Tabius Youngblood stood looking down at Hallam's lifeless body lying before him on a litter in the Great Hall. A white cloth had been placed over the young prince, covering him from foot to chin. Hallam's face radiated the freedom and peace only the dead knew, just the opposite of the King's, whose eyes were coals of rage.

I had slept the morning and part of the afternoon away and would be sleeping still had Avedis not roused me urgently. I had worn myself so completely that upon waking it took me a moment to even remember who I was. Having rushed down as soon as

Avedis' ramblings had begun making sense, I had only just arrived. Avedis had told me they'd captured Hallam's murderer and were bringing him to face the King. Who it was, he didn't know.

We stood in silence in the Great Hall, dozens of us. Wren and Avedis stood by my side, but Lady Sedra was still too weak to be up and about. There were many from court, whom I had never met, whispering to each other and at least ten of the Regal Guard standing stiff-backed in their crisp, blue tabards blazoned with the King's arms. All of us were waiting for the accused to be brought from the dungeons below.

The only sound was the pelting rain on the north-facing windows and the moan of wind that had succeeded in finding its way through cracks. In his wheeled chair, to the King's right, sat Palomar. He idly fingered his ruby ring, now quiescent. Prince Winfred, heir to the throne, leaned over his dead brother and, with respect, placed Hallam's sword on his brother's chest, the pommel almost touching his chin.

Duke Fagen Jesop, our host and ruler of the Duchy of Tressfold in which Sojourn stood, fidgeted uncomfortably next to the King, his head bowed and buried in his double chin. He mopped sweat from his upper lip with a cloth. I wondered if Jesop was afraid he would bear part of the blame for Prince Hallam's death by virtue of the fact that Sojourn was his city.

This being the Festival of Light, the room was decorated with sweeping yards of yellow and sky blue cloth. They had draped it over the windows and hung it from the rafters in swaths that tapered to a point or twisted from beam to beam. The Great Feast was to be held here tonight for the royal court. Who could have foreseen our current circumstance?

A commotion at the door diverted my attention. It was Lady Jelail demanding entrance. "I will not be barred from these proceedings. Prince Hallam was my fiancé. I will see his assassin."

King Tabius nodded, and she was permitted to enter. The cut of her dress seemed more appropriate for a party than such a solemn scene, but, in her defense, I'm sure she didn't pack attire that might have been more appropriate. To be sure, her betrothal to Hallam had been arranged, and I'd heard she'd made it plain in the past that she was none too pleased with the selection of her husband. Some said she had her eyes on Winfred and the throne. Still, to her credit, she did seem genuinely upset at the sight of Prince Hallam's body. When she began to weep, Prince Rollin, now dressed in the vestments of his clerical order, stepped forward and offered a handkerchief.

"Lady Jelail, you need not remain in attendance," Tabius said. The King's stone expression melted at the sight of her. "But for my son's death, you would have been my daughter this time next month. It cannot be easy to see your promised thus."

She walked to Hallam's side, handkerchief covering her mouth. After touching Hallam's cheek, she turned, stifling another sob. "I'll see justice done, My Lord, if it please you." She gave a slight curtsy of respect.

After a nod from Tabius, she stumbled from Hallam's litter, supported by Rollin.

The sound of rattling chains approaching the Great Hall made all heads turn. I gasped.

It was Prince Fenrick.

He was restrained by manacles and chains at hand and foot. Was this true? Could Fenrick have murdered his own brother? Two of the Regal Guard dumped Fenrick before Tabius and stood to either side to prevent any possible escape. Fenrick's lip and eye were swollen, telling a tale of his treatment at the hands of the Guard.

"Before us is your brother, Fenrick," Tabius spat. "How did this happen? Speak."

Fenrick looked up. He was still bleeding from the side of his mouth. "I didn't kill Hallam. I only heard about it a few hours ago."

"How did he get a knife in his back?" the King shouted.

"I don't know. Ask your court Inadel, not me."

Tabius stepped toward Fenrick, grabbed him by the collar, and hauled him to his feet. "Do you think this a jest? Your brother lies dead. Inadel? What—do you plan to rely on their equivocations to hide your treason?"

"It's treason, but not by my hand, Father. Listen a moment. Who gains by his death? No one. It makes no sense. Then . . . what if . . . Hallam's death could be the first movement in a plot to exterminate the Youngblood line."

"Do you think so?" Tabius asked, raising his eyebrows. He dumped Fenrick unceremoniously and retreated to a chair. "Perhaps you can tell us more?"

"What perfidy is this, my liege?" Palomar said. "It is clear he lusts after the crown and desires to remove those in his way. Could Winfred and Rollin be far behind?"

"That's a lie!" Fenrick cried out. "It's a plot. By killing Hallam and laying the blame on me, they seek to remove two sons in one fell swoop."

"What proof have you?" Tabius asked with a wave of his arm. "Who is behind these treasonous schemes? How do you come by this knowledge?"

"I do not know who—I don't—"

Duke Jesop stepped forward, pointing a finger at Fenrick "Captain Faraday heard a struggle and saw you rush out of Prince Hallam's room this morning not an hour before his body was discovered. Three others in his company saw the same."

"We had an argument that came to blows but not knives. I didn't do it."

Tabius' voice filled with contempt. "And how did you come by Hallam's ring? You were discovered trying to sell it in the market. Did you find it on the road? Did it magically appear in your pocket?"

"I knew you wouldn't believe me. I needed money to pay off gambling debts."

Palomar grabbed the armrests on his chair. "You killed him and took his ring."

"It's true I stole his ring when he fell senseless to the floor, but only because that ring made his punches so painful. I thought it would serve him right, and I could change it into the money he refused to loan me."

Tabius sighed and closed his eyes. "Not in two hundred years has the Youngblood line been so disgraced. You have been trouble since the start. I should have known you for the anathema you were, but I was blinded. And now it comes to this."

I found it hard to believe Fenrick would kill his brother. "My Lord," I said, "I have known Prince Fenrick many years. It's true he's arrogant, self-absorbed, even rash, but I've never known him to be murderous."

"Thanks Blanchard," Fenrick said with a snort. "Look, anyone could have come into the room and seen him lying there. Anyone could have killed him."

Captain Faraday shook his head and stepped forward. "From my post, down the adjoining corridor at the top of the stair, I didn't hear or see anyone approach from below after Fenrick departed. Excepting, of course, Your Grace," Faraday said, bowing slightly to me.

"But you couldn't actually see Hallam's room from where you stood?" I asked.

Faraday shook his head no.

"Then it had to be someone in one of the other bedchambers," Fenrick said. "They heard us fight and came in to see what had happened. Then they saw their chance and stabbed him."

Faraday counted off people with his fingers. "The only people in the other rooms were Prince Rollin, Lady Jelail, the Potentate and his servant, and Sol Blanchard."

"There," Fenrick said. "It could have been Rollin or Jelail. Everyone knows Jelail didn't want to marry Hallam."

Jelail squeaked in surprise at the accusation. "Me? Kill Hallam?"

"She's not capable of it," Rollin said. "You're a fiend to even think it."

"Oh, you're so right. I'm the fiend. Maybe it was you, Rollin. Didn't want her to marry your brother, eh?"

Rollin slammed a fist into Fenrick's chin, throwing him back into Hallam's litter, nearly tipping it over. At a word from the King, guards fell on Rollin and separated the two.

"Good, Rollin," Tabius said, running his fingers through his hair. "That fist of yours makes such a powerful retort. But then you never did have any tact."

"I didn't kill him, father," Rollin said.

"He was with me," Jelail said, stepping forward.

"No!" Rollin shouted.

Jelail put a hand on his shoulder and hung her head. "It's true. We were together. I'm shamed by it, but I'll not see Rollin so accused. I was returning to my room when I discovered Hallam."

Jelail and Rollin together? I had been out of the games played at court for some time, but the silence and raised eyebrows that followed told me this news had taken us all by surprise.

Soon, Tabius broke the silence. "That would leave Sol, Palomar and the servant. Gentlemen?"

I laughed without mirth. "The intrigue of the court, while fascinating, baffles me. If I wanted to kill anyone, I'd be at a loss to know with whom to start, to be sure."

"We're wasting time, My Lord," Palomar said. "My servant was asleep through the whole confrontation between the two. I remember noting my amazement that any could sleep through such a ruckus. And without someone to push me, I doubt I could make it down the hall, let alone stab a man. Preposterous." He shifted his weight and his chair creaked, offering even more evidence of his innocence. Faraday would have heard his chair.

"Maybe someone came in through the balcony?"

Captain Faraday came forward again. "M'Lord. An assassin coming through the balcony would have had to exit the same way, and seeing as how the door was bolted from the inside, it's just not possible."

"The doors were latched," I admitted. "Black Magic could have easily secured the balcony doors."

"And being only down the hall from Hallam's room, I would certainly have felt any activity of the kind," Palomar said. "This plot to unseat the King is probably true, and it lies in the fevered mind of this misbegotten madman." Palomar indicated Fenrick. "Please, I urge you to decide this matter quickly so that we may turn our attention to the assault on the realm."

"Don't push me, Palomar! It's light yet. We have some moments, and condemning one of my flesh gives me pause." He shifted in his seat uncomfortably and after a long pause he said, "Take him back to the dungeons for now."

Jelail shrieked, "What of justice, My Lord? I throw my reputation to the wind to save Rollin. And that is nothing compared to the loss of poor Hallam. Shouldn't the punishment be capital? I'm sorry," she cried. "The ghosts shall steal our justice. I'm sorry. Your wisdom, My Lord. Your will be done."

Murmurings of the gathered rose forcing the King to rise from his chair. He sighed hoarsely and commanded, "Quiet now. Quiet. It is plain to me. Fenrick's guilt is unmistakable, and the death of Hallam demands justice." He paused again, and his face was ashen. "I will not have these ghosts, servants of the dark, steal away the justice I crave. They might take his life while he lies fettered in prison. At sunset, then . . . at sunset Fenrick Youngblood will hang by his neck until dead. He will be a Youngblood no longer. Let the disgrace he brought on this family die with him this night."

The voices of the gathering rose once more, but no voice came to Fenrick's defense, including my own. What could I say? I knew he couldn't have done it.

Standing nearby, I did manage to hear Prince Winfred say under his breath, "Too good for him." Hanging was too good for Fenrick? He deserved worse? Winfred's face was twisted in disgust, but, to my surprise, he wasn't looking at Fenrick. Following his gaze, I saw his disapproving stare directed at Lady Jelail who, at the moment, was being consoled by Prince Rollin. What exactly was too good and for whom?

* * *

The next three or four hours went by faster, it seemed, than they should have. The fields were flooding with overflow from the Jesra

River. The Regal Guard, with help from the local militia, brought everyone from the surrounding fields to the tight confines of the city. Those of able body were put to work building dikes. With all the extra people here for the Festival of Light, the dikes easily rose faster than the river, protecting the lower sections of Sojourn near the docks.

As for the ghost threat, Wren and the other mages he'd trained were placed at intervals around the periphery of the city, like posts of a fence. If they saw approaching ghosts, they would do their best with the exorcism techniques they'd been taught. I held little hope in their success.

Instead, my hope rested in Palomar and his ring. I was convinced High Magic could defeat these creatures, and since there seemed no hope in uncovering the mystery behind calling the Knights of the Realm, his ring was all the High Magic we had.

Now pouring rain, at the very onset of sunset, we gathered for the grim affair of Fenrick's execution. A hastily built gallows, a ghastly sight in any weather, stood in the center of the main thoroughfare leading up to the gate of the citadel. Dozens of the Regal Guard were scattered about, perhaps in case some small cabal thought Fenrick was innocent and was willing to risk their collective necks to save him. I wonder who *that* could be.

Where was Redd? I looked around at the gathered crowd but in vain. He should have been back by now. Sedra, still bedridden, was unable to help us. Avedis was standing nearby trying and failing to look inconspicuous. The only other mage present was Palomar, sitting in his chair and fingering his glowing ring. He now made no secret of the fact he had reawakened the ruby.

Of the Chosen, there were three. Edlynn Illcrest was easy to pick out of the crowd. She stood ever tall and proud, and rightfully so. On her outstretched arm, she bore Antilles, the eldest of the kestrels. Next to her stood Logan Swift bearing Helios. As both were part of the King's court, they stood amid the other few from that stratum, including Duke Jesop.

Even though she was one of the Chosen, Bodicea Dimaus was originally a peasant and so remained that way in the eyes of many of the court. She was a small woman who looked hard as stone, toughened by life. Her kestrel, Torrent, was perched on a walking stick she held that matched her own height.

Three of the six Chosen were here, but there should have been four. Redd was overdue. He was supposed to be getting horses.

Thirty or forty commoners were scattered about to watch the spectacle. From them came a constant babble. Who would miss a royal execution?

Lightning lit up the darkened sky. Despite the rain, we remained dry. I had graciously offered to shield the area from the rain to make this unpleasantness more bearable for the royal family. It was Avedis who did all the work, though, surreptitiously, of course. He created a shield of sorts, an invisible roof that was proof against water. It wasn't a difficult thing, just tedious to maintain. Unfortunately, a roof without walls was like a ship without sails: it's a good idea on the surface, but when the wind starts blowing, people start looking at each other and scratching their heads.

The King arrived with Captain Faraday and several others of the Guard. Behind them and flanked by three other guards staggered Fenrick. Dazed and covered in mud, he was almost unrecognizable. They had to drag him up the wooden steps.

Across the road in an alleyway, I espied a hooded figure leading two horses. At last, Redd had returned. Motioning for Avedis to follow me, we pushed our way through the crowd and joined him. In the fading daylight, I noticed he carried a saddle-bag and led his own horse and mine.

I grunted at the sight of Sapphire perched on the pommel of his horse's saddle. Couldn't she be flying? That wasn't in the least conspicuous. To my surprise, there was a second kestrel; this one perched on the cantle of my horse's saddle.

"You have two kestrels?" Avedis asked in awe.

"This is Verve," Redd said. "Gall Hiltred was killed by ghosts at the Hold of Chaldea, so Verve came here to join some of the others."

"What happened?" I demanded. "Where have you been? Where is Fenrick's horse?"

A crier was reading off a list of Fenrick's crimes from the platform of the gallows. I tried not to listen.

"I was leading all three horses back here from the stables when someone recognized Rage and demanded that I stop. He claimed Rage was his horse."

"What?"

"Apparently Fenrick stole the horse from him six months ago. I didn't have time to argue with him, and considering Fenrick's recent activity, horse thievery didn't seem out of the realm of possibility. I took the saddlebag, gave him the horse, and rushed back here."

"You cut it close," I whispered. "Things are about to get . . . interesting."

Suddenly, a rider galloped up the alley. It could have been one of the Regal Guard, but in the dim light, I couldn't tell. Hearing Fenrick's voice, I glanced back to the wooden platform. Fenrick cried out, "No! I'm innocent. You can't do this. Something's wrong." He was losing his grip, but who could blame him? Before they gagged him he shouted, "Let me out. Let me out."

Redd recognized the rider and greeted him. Redd may have said his name, but I missed it while listening to Fenrick.

"Is it really you?" Redd asked.

The stranger answered, "Welling? What's going on here? Who are they hanging?" He looked up quizzically, perhaps wondering what had happened to the rain, conspicuous by its absence. We were thirty yards from the gallows and just at the fringe of the invisible roof protecting the gathering from the rain.

"They're hanging Prince Fenrick for the murder of Prince Hallam," Redd said.

"Prince Fenrick killed his brother?" the stranger said with a sigh. "I was rather looking forward to the feast, but these royals never stop, do they?"

Just then, a bird flew out of the darkness and landed on the stranger's shoulder. "Good Lord!" I exclaimed. "You're Kirrin." My shout of surprise drew some gazes from those nearby. Kirrin was the Chosen of Erstwhile. I pulled Redd close. "All six kestrels are here. All six in the same place."

Redd looked at me in alarm. "Are they in danger?"

"All the remaining kestrels in Rapt coming together . . . It's unheard of." Considering the prophecy of the deaths, it couldn't be a coincidence. "I don't like it."

But there was nothing to be done about it, let alone the time. I turned and pushed my way through the crowd to get back to Fenrick. Avedis followed on my heels. From this distance, I could feel the flow of White he was wielding to maintain the roof over our heads. I glanced at his face and didn't find even a hint of weariness.

As I passed a man in the crowd, I heard him say, "He deserves it. Soon he'll be food for the carrion crows. Or kestrels for that matter. There seem to be enough of them here—"

Bodicea, not two steps away, drew a dagger and, as quick as a blink, held it to his throat. "Simpleton. You have no idea whom you malign." I had to look twice to be sure I saw it right. Bodicea's kestrel, Torrent, had spread his wings and was now balancing atop the walking stick she'd been holding. Though it was unsupported, Torrent held it as still as a fence post. People backed away from Torrent's spread wings in amazement, giving him room.

"Kestrels are birds of prey," Bodicea said. "Not carrion feeders. If they had a choice between the prince, hanging dead at the end of a rope, and you, running in terror for your life, who do you think they'd choose?" She released him with a shove and returned to Torrent. The knife had vanished from her hand by the time she grasped the walking stick again. I never saw her put it away.

Avedis and I pushed onward toward the gallows. Fenrick's mouth was gagged and his hands were tied behind his back. Held by two guards, he stood on a small wooden stool while the hangman fitted a burlap bag over his head. Fenrick was still struggling and shouting through the gag, but it was useless.

The guards had lit twelve torches hammered into the ground in a circle about the gallows. The day was getting darker, but the weather prevented any certain knowledge of sunset, the time Fenrick was to be executed. That didn't seem to bother the hangman, who, wearing a black hood over his face, was positioning the noose over Fenrick's head.

The charges had already been read. There was no more preamble. The hangman paused at the ready. This was it.

The King at the foot of the gallows and just in front of me gave his nod, and the hangman kicked the stool out from under Fenrick's feet. That was when I brought White to bear on him. Hearing the rising flute music in my mind as White melted in my blood, I gripped Fenrick's body, letting it appear to hang there at the end of the rope. His weight was a crushing force through my mind. I hoped the intense energy I used was covered by the activity of keeping the roof up over the crowd. That was the plan anyway.

I could tell Fenrick was no longer the fourth son of Tabius. With the death of his brother and his closer position to the throne, his resistance to magic had increased. The last time I'd had to lift him, it had been difficult, to be sure, but not as impossible as this felt. He was slipping. It reminded me of the way the golden statue in Drewsbury, He Who Rises, had slipped through my extended grasp back when I was only twelve summers old. Considering how well Avedis had done at moving the statue, I should have let him take my part in this mad escapade.

Fenrick, still struggling, wriggled back and forth. If he didn't feign death soon, people would begin to wonder. Figure it out. Come on, Fenrick. Keep still. But he kept jigging back and forth in a confusion that was liable to really get him killed. So, pretending to avert my eyes at this grotesque scene, on top of trying to lift him up, I used whatever I had left to Hold him. I was shaking with the effort.

Seeing Fenrick go still, his body swaying slightly to and fro, Tabius must have believed it finished. He turned and walked back toward the citadel gates. Palomar sat and looked about with narrowed eyes. He must have guessed something was not right.

I walked stiffly by Palomar toward Fenrick's slowly swinging form. Sweat poured out of my forehead, and I hoped it looked like the result of the weather. I didn't know how much longer I could keep him up there. Palomar stopped me with a hand on my arm. "Thank you, Sol, for the roof. That was very thoughtful. It must be a terrible strain on you. I can feel your effort from here."

Somehow I managed to speak. "It's this . . . hanging business—" The flute music in my mind was losing track of its melody, wandering in key. Distracted and alarmed by the hangman climbing down off the gallows, I called, "Hey there. Aren't you going to cut him down? Isn't this spectacle enough?"

He turned and shook his head. "We leave him up until morning. King's orders."

"I see . . ." I didn't know that was the plan. We had hoped they might cut him down before I'd burned White out of my mind. On to plan B. Palomar still sat and watched me with curiosity.

With plan A, no one would have been in trouble. No one would have been the wiser. Plan B was open treason. Sighing, I decided I was getting too old for this anyway. "Ho!" I shouted while raising my hand.

With that signal an arrow from Redd's bow shot over the crowd aimed at severing Fenrick's rope. Surprise would only last long enough for one shot, so it had to be perfect the first time. In the instant it took that arrow to fly from the shadows to Fenrick's aid, I felt White rise out of Palomar to strike at the arrow. How could he react so fast?

But the arrow didn't waver from its course. Somehow, a surge from Avedis blocked Palomar's effort. I didn't know that was possible. The arrow flew straight and true, severing the rope as if it were nothing but a thread. I dropped Fenrick, and he hit the platform with a resounding bang. The release of the drilling pain made me feel as light as air.

Several of the guards looked up at the sound. One of them gave a shout. I glanced back and saw Redd, mounted and pushing through the crowd, leading my horse. People scattered before him. All six kestrels took to the air as if they knew what was coming.

Maybe they did. They flew out from underneath Avedis' roof and into the darkness.

Avedis hadn't been diverting the water but collecting it. I looked up and watched as he released it. Closing my eyes, I reached out with White to feel the water coming down and was shocked at what I discovered. What Avedis had released wasn't a light splash of water designed to surprise the guards and extinguish the torches. What I felt plummeting down was a lake.

"By all that's holy!" I shouted and jumped toward the wooden gallows for support.

WOOOOOSH! The entire area and everyone in it was struck full force. I was pushed to the ground, but at least I was partially prepared. When the water had passed, I looked around. Sputtering water from my mouth, I found the torches were not only extinguished but were washed away along with half the gathered crowd. I hoped no one was hurt. By the light coming out of the nearby buildings and the occasional lightning flash, I could see no one left standing. The gallows wasn't even standing. Yet by some miracle, Redd still commanded both his feet and our horses.

Throwing pieces of wood out of my way, I finally located Fenrick. Ripping the bag off his head, I pulled him up to a sitting position. In a moment more, I removed his gag. His gasp for breath was proof he yet lived. Redd came up, stumbling through the mud. Avedis was nowhere to be found. Perhaps his own flood had washed him down the road.

"Hold, and stand in the name of the King," Prince Winfred demanded as he stepped out of the darkness with his sword drawn. I had expected this, but so quickly? Perhaps most strange was that he was dry, or rather, only now getting wet as he was no longer afforded the protection from the weather previously provided by Avedis' roof. As a result of the magical proximate cause of the recent deluge, the water must have just parted and slipped around and past him, leaving him unscathed. One cannot directly, or even indirectly, magically attack or, for that matter, magically aid one so close to the crown.

"Leave us be, Winfred. We have no quarrel with you," I said.

Redd had cut the ropes binding Fenrick's hands but could do nothing about the manacles and chains at his feet. Fenrick would have to ride sidesaddle.

"Fenrick's a murderer. He killed Hallam, and he's going to pay," spat Winfred.

"Your brother is a thief by his own admission but not a murderer," I said. "You know that in your heart." Fenrick seemed delirious, staring off at nothing, and wasn't helping at all.

From my left, Palomar said, "Fenrick's guilt or innocence is not for you to judge, Blanchard. You surprise me." He was once more in his chair. The red light suddenly shining from Palomar's ring told me he was back in control. "I knew you were fond of the boy, but do you not see what you're doing?" The ring grew brighter by the second, like a star had come to Rapt to expose our deeds.

Rollin arrived with six of the Regal Guard, including Captain Faraday. Several bore oil lamps to light their way. They surrounded us as Redd was attempting to get Fenrick mounted.

"If Tabius ever discovered the truth, that Fenrick was innocent," I said, "but now in a grave thanks to this execution, he'd rip out his own heart. By saving Fenrick, we're trying to save Tabius' life." We might have to do battle to escape, but I'd surrender before it came to blows. I wanted no one to get hurt over this. I wondered if Redd had as much good sense.

The sudden sensation of a Hold came over me. I tried to move but failed as if the air had transformed to iron bands. Out of the corner of my eye I saw the same happen to Redd. Under normal circumstances, I might have been able to fight it, but not after suspending a Prince of the Realm in midair for almost a minute. I could still move my mouth. At least Palomar had given me that.

"It was a foolish thing, Blanchard," Palomar said. "I was impressed with the amount of water you managed to hold in the air. However did you manage it?"

I said nothing. We needed a distraction to get out of this, and if Avedis was still in charge of his faculties, there was yet a chance. We needed a backup plan, a plan C. Unfortunately, we never had time to think of one. Come on, Avedis. We need a distraction. We need one now.

A lone voice, Avedis' voice, cried out, "Ghosts!"

If only it, instead, had been a lie.

Chapter Fourteen

Conspiracy

Saturday at lunch, Trevor laid out the plan. Zak, Trevor, and I were sitting at a table in the cafeteria, and there was so much racket that we couldn't possibly be overheard. Emily, of course, was in privacy mode too. Demanding privacy out of her was getting to be habit.

"The problem is simple," Trevor explained after taking a thoughtful pull from his chocolate shake. "To get you out of your contract and take control of the situation, we need leverage on Artemus, and that vid of him at the power plant should do it." He had waved me to silence before I could remind him of how the vid was lost to us, thanks to me. "The LMC claims it has no memory of events at Prometheus, but they are in there; he just can't access them."

"Even hypnotically," I said through clenched teeth. "Does this mean you guys believe me now?"

Trevor shrugged. "Even if you're wrong about everything, there's too many unknowns swirling around Artemus. You need to stay clear of him and those Bosners."

"And," Zak said. "While I still don't believe time travel is possible, if there really is a time machine . . ." He stuck a thumb at his own chest. "I want in."

I smirked at that and felt a weight lift off my chest. I really needed these guys if I was going to find a way out of this.

"It's time to start treating the LMC like a computer again," Trevor announced.

After a pause, Zak said, "All right, why do you do that? You say something that clearly leaves everyone hanging just so someone has to say, 'Gee, Trev, whatever do you mean by that?'"

"I'm glad you asked," Trevor said, totally ignoring Zak's mini-rant. "When we ask the LMC for the information, we're always using the interface. We need to bypass the interface and get directly to the data."

I asked, "You mean Emily's hologram?"

"We know the vid is in there, right?" Trevor ran fingers through his hair. "Why won't it give it to us? Because of the trauma. The LMC is suppressing the memory, just like any trauma victim. But that is just the personality layer suffering from that."

I said, "Oh, I get it. It's just like us getting into a SIM, right? The LMC bypasses our eyes and ears and transfers information in and out of our brains directly, bypassing the interface." I tapped my face.

"You want to put the LMC into a SIM?" Zak asked.

"Nothing so elaborate—and impossible," Trevor answered. "We just need to hook up some other computer to it, one that's even faster, so it can go in and get the information before the LMC has a chance to realize what is happening."

"There are two problems with that," I pointed out, holding one french fry up. "One: Emily will take over whatever computer you hook up, and once your super computer actually *becomes* Emily, you're sitting outside the interface again." I took a bite of the fry. "And Two—"

"That's why it has to be really fast. I mean screamingly."

Zak said, "Dude, we don't have one of those screamingly fast machines. Everything's been taken over."

Still chewing fries, I said with a wave to punctuate the point, "That's number two."

"How about an Omechron-7 MPP?" Trevor said smiling.

Zak said, "You happen to have one of those in your closet? Even I, who have been known as," he held his hands up and made quotation marks with his fingers, "'a man who knows how to get things,' wouldn't be able to—"

I said, "No one calls you that."

Trevor shook his head. "And you're using those fancy quotation marks all wrong."

"Actually," I said. "Given the fact that no one calls him that—"

Zak asked, "Hey, who got all those transmitters for our science project? Eh?"

"Forget it. Listen," Trevor said. "I overheard my dad talking to the LMC. It said something like, 'Dr. Russo, why are *you* in charge of all the sulfuric acid containers in cargo bay AH-52?' And my dad admitted that they were actually computers to be used as new backup systems. The mislabeling was just for security. I imagine they haven't even opened them yet, because they're still trying to figure out how to prevent the LMC from inadvertently taking control of them."

"He actually said they were Omechron-7's?" I asked. "Wait—You mean the ones we saw in that cargo bay in Descartes?"

"Exactly," Trevor said, nodding excitedly. "What else would be so big? They've got their own backup power, their own cooling. They're space hardened—"

"No, no," I said. "Even your dad thinks Emily will take them over. The minute we open them up—"

"We'll have maybe five minutes before they get co-opted by the LMC," Trevor admitted. "That's enough time to get in, find the data, and get out before any damage is done. My dad's talking about permanent solutions. We just need a minute."

"I just thought of number three," I said holding up another fry. "By-passing the interface. Sounds like hacking. Isn't that illegal? I don't want you guys risking—"

"Look, it's true . . . Hacking the neural net is illegal," Trevor admitted. "But you could argue that we're not really hacking. We're just trying to solve the mystery of the Prometheus explosion; a matter of national security that has confounded the government. And, oh, by the way, while we're at it, we'll get you out of your worse-than-death contract—which no one needs to know about."

At that point, Zak nudged me and tilted his head toward the door. Talonii came in with Spunk and Newkirk close behind. On Talonii's arm was a girl I hadn't seen before. We made a quick departure through the back entrance before we were seen.

We worked on the details all Saturday afternoon and into the evening in Zak's room. The core part of Trevor's plan was using the radio transmitters from our science project to connect the Omechron to Emily. "There can be no wired or wireless communications between the LMC and the Omechron," Trevor explained. "It all has to go through our transmitters. If the LMC starts to take over the Omechron, we need to be able to sever the connection. But the instant we directly access the LMC's file system, an alarm is going to go off. There's nothing I can do about that. They're going to start to search for us—"

Zak shrugged, "So we get in and out quick." He threw himself to his bed and floated down onto it. He stretched out and yawned. "But there's going to be a com-pad watching the whole cargo bay."

I sat on the floor pressing my back against the wall. Zak's bedroom was ridiculous, laid out with an entire seating area with a couch and the chairs, but I ignored those, preferring to be uncomfortable so I could think. The floor was fine with me. "He's right. Even if we go in the middle of the night—"

"One thing at a time," Trevor said, pacing the room. "They won't be able to cut us off right away. To do that, they're going to try to find us by tracing back the intrusion to find out how we are getting in. I can run interference, but I have to be in a SIM chamber for that."

I shook my head, "Great. Zak and I go in, but how are we going to talk to you? How are you going to know—"

Trevor said, "We can use the LMC to communicate. We'll need some SIM caps, though . . ." He frowned and rubbed his head.

"SIM caps?" I asked. "Those are tightly controlled. Even if we lifted some from school, they're all registered—"

"I can get us some," Zak said, propping his head up with his arm. We both looked at him in silence. "What? I know a guy."

"Wait," I said holding up my hands. Must I point out the obvious? "Isn't talking through Emily going to, ahh, I don't know . . . give us away?"

This was a sticking point. You couldn't be in privacy mode within a SIM. And even if we were using something like old-fashioned phone technology, she would be able to intercept those signals. She listens to all signals.

"What if . . ." Trevor said hitting on an idea. He stopped pacing, turned to me, and said, "What if we masquerade as other people?"

Zak sat up. "Is that even possible?"

Trevor started pacing again. It seemed to help him think. "Whenever anyone enters a SIM, a session is created that identifies you. What if I lifted some sessions from some unsuspecting volunteers and copied them to our SIM caps? The LMC would still think we were the other people. They'll just be chasing ghosts."

I said, "But then the MPs would arrest *them*."

Trevor gave me a wry grin. "Well, eventually they'll figure out what happened and let them go, but they won't have any idea who *we* were. But who could we—"

I had a brilliant idea. "How about Frank Talonii? He and his crew are nothing but trouble. It would serve them right."

Zak whistled. "You sure like playing dangerously. Frank's going to be a bit put out."

"He's masquerading as me, isn't he? It's time we turned the tables. I'm going to masquerade as him."

"Wait, wait," Trevor said, collapsing on the couch. "We're going to do this in the middle of the night. Frank and Spunk would have to enter a SIM, *in the middle of the night*. This isn't going to work. How are we going to convince them to do that? And, we'd have to take over their sessions while they were in a SIM. The signals would go to our SIM caps *and* theirs. I think they might notice what we were doing."

"What if they were asleep?" I asked.

Zak snorted, "Who falls asleep in a SIM?"

Trevor said, "They would have to start the SIM awake, though. You can't just sneak into Frank's room and put a SIM cap on his head. SIMs won't start that way. They check for that."

I stood up. "There are ways to make people fall asleep."

Zak stood up too. "Let me get this straight. We have to trick Frank, Frank *Talonii*—"

"And his friends," I added.

"—into putting on questionable SIM caps in the middle of the night. After that we drug them, steal their SIM identities, head to Descartes where we use off-limits mech-tunnels to break into a cargo bay where we liberate an Omechron for the purposes of hacking the LMC to retrieve probably faked vids of Artemus Regale, the richest SOB on Luna, planting a bomb at Prometheus."

It sounded hopelessly impossible. Not hiding the despair in my voice, I said, "And we have to do it all tomorrow night before I meet Artemus on Monday."

"Exactly," Zak said putting his hands on his hips. "It's on a school night."

I laughed at the absurdity of it all, but Trevor shot back, "Would you two be serious! We can make this work."

Zak shook his head. "It's going to be hard enough getting the SIM caps, but I don't traffic in pharmaceuticals. Where are we going to get something like that? Maybe if we had a month to plan. I mean, this is sounding a lot like my *rescue* attempt—" he used the air quotes again, "—in Rapt. And we all know how well that turned out."

Trevor crossed his arms, pushing himself back into the plush couch. "Well, you're not dead, are you?"

Zak threw his hands in the air saying, "They were expecting you to stage a rescue. After Blanchard here dropped that lake on us—nice touch by the way—my brothers were on us in a heartbeat."

"That wasn't me," I admitted. "That was . . . Avedis." A new idea suddenly began to percolate in my overtired brain.

Trevor said, "We were hoping they would cut you down after they thought you were dead. Blanchard was holding you up to keep you from choking."

"Guys," I said.

"I don't know," Zak said, ignoring me and bounding over Trevor and the couch to pull a soda out of his mini refrigerator. "That whole thing was weird. First of all, I can't believe they would actually try to do that in a game. I mean hanging, really? But while I was hanging there, I had a visio—"

"Guys," I said more insistently. They turned to look at me. "I know how we're going to make this work."

* * *

"Yeah," Sasha said, crossing her arms. "I've heard of Frank Talonii."

It was early Sunday morning in the Descartes rec center. As I had guessed, most of the courts were deserted, so it was the perfect place for a clandestine meeting. I had invited Sasha and Azzam here to beg for their help. Azzam came, despite his lingering injuries, escorted by not one but two burly bodyguards. Sasha arrived a bit late with her little sister, Ilya, in tow. Ilya had to come because her parents were out, and she couldn't leave her home alone.

If Trevor were here, it would have been a bit cramped. He thought it best to skip the meeting so he could prepare for tonight's adventure.

We had selected an empty racquetball sphere. With Ilya and the body guards outside, we shut the hatch behind us and asked Emily to make the walls of the sphere opaque so we could have some privacy. After examining the sphere, the guards were fine with Azzam going in alone, but Ilya wouldn't be left out, and tried everything from cajoling to whining to try to get in with us. But Sasha had her way in the end, and Ilya remained outside.

The court wasn't a perfect sphere. It was made up of a million little triangular sections, each of which would glow with every impact, be it a racquetball, or a foot. At the moment, dozens of them were fading on and off in the sections near the apex, providing some general illumination. The undulating light made it seem like we were underwater.

Sasha, referring to Talonii, asked, "But how do you know he's not Sam Clemens?"

I said, "I'm the real Sam Clemens. Frank is actually Winger. He's just claiming to be me. But that's not even important right now."

"Wait. You? But you're . . . like my age. There's never been anyone so young—"

"Oh, it's true," Zak said. "The LMC confirmed it. My man Dennis is all that, and then some."

Azzam, with a groan, sat down on the sphere. The sphere reacted to the impact by sending ripples of light out from his rear. If he hadn't been in pain, I would have laughed at the sight. Just to his right, a blinking blue light told us Emily was in privacy mode and also helped to identify where the exit was. He said, "I believe everything he is telling us. The assassin that shot me went after Dennis with intent." He wagged a finger at me. "You walk in mysterious circles."

Sasha raised an eyebrow, looking at Azzam. "So you're buying this whole time travel story?"

Azzam said, "Look, Dennis *may* be wrong about the time travelers—"

Zak piped in, "They're from the future, and they're trying to melt his brain."

I held my hand up to silence Zak. "Not helping. All we are trying to do is get that vid of Artemus."

"Right," Sasha said. "So why the convoluted plan? You know what I think? I think you want to get Frank arrested. This whole scheme to impersonate him sounds like a way to take him out of the competition."

Zak said, "Look, something's going on. I don't know what. We just need to get the goods on Artemus, and we need to do it today. But, right now, I have to meet someone about some SIM caps." He put his hands together and gave a mock bow. "Sasha/Sedra, Azzam/Avedis, lovely to meet you, and thanks for keeping the names simple. There's only so many names my mind can manage. I hope to see you all . . . later."

Zak tapped the blinking blue light and a circular hatch opened in the floor, swinging outward. He grabbed the rim, flipped himself out, and was gone.

Sasha, as if seeing this as a cue to leave, also made her way to the open hatch. Ripples of white light emanated in circles from the surface with every footfall. "Dennis, this is all too crazy. I don't think I should get involved."

"Sasha," I said desperately, and she paused to look back at me. "I understand if you want no part of this. It sounds crazy to me too. If I were you, I'd get out of Dodge as fast as I could, but I'm stuck in the middle of this whole thing. Trevor, Zak, and I . . . we're going in with or without your help. Impersonating Talonii and his friends *is* convoluted. If we don't wear disguises, the LMC will cut us off the moment she gets wind of what we're up to. We need as much time as possible, and this magic trick, this misdirection, might just be the thing to buy us enough time to extract the vid and get out of there."

"But why Frank Talonii?" Sasha asked. "Why not—I don't know—the president of Luna?"

"It's karma," I said. "Kismet. He's pretending to be Sam Clemens—me. It seems right that I should pretend to be him."

"I like it," Azzam said, grinning mischievously.

I could see she was about to protest again, so I blustered on. "This isn't a tit for tat thing. The more I thought about it, the more this seemed . . . This is more than just craving payback or some kind of justice. Frank Talonii chose *me* to impersonate. I don't know why, but the minute he did that, he sealed his fate. His lies resulted in getting me beat up and, at this point, I don't care. Why him? It doesn't matter that he's the vilest, most cunning, evil piece of shit I've ever met. I have to get out of that contract with Artemus, and our chances get a lot better if we go in disguised. The universe is screaming that it should be Frank Talonii, and that is exactly what it is going to get. But . . . only if you help."

Sasha had one of her eyebrows raised again, but before she could say anything, a head popped up through the hatch. It was her sister, Ilya. "I'm in!"

Sasha exclaimed, "Ilya, what are you doing?"

She jumped into the sphere and sailed across to the far side, splashing light clear around the room when she hit. "Dennis needs our help. And we're going to give it to him."

Sasha laughed and shook her head, "But you didn't hear —"

"Aw, I could hear everything through this thing," she said knocking twice on the sphere with her fist. "Sasha, there was an explosion at the power plant. Maybe it wasn't from crazy men from the future, but the LMC isn't acting normal anymore. You are going to help him figure this out. And you're not leaving me out, or I'm telling."

Sasha turned to me, a defeated look on her face. Then she looked up at the top of the sphere and sighed. "Do you have a plan?"

"Yes," I said. "Yes, I do."

Chapter Fifteen

In the Sky

G hosts! Look out for the ghosts," Avedis shouted.

A bitter chill passed through me like a wave, and a moment later, the icy fingers of fear took hold. Shouts and screams of alarm went up from everywhere. The few of us still standing in the main thoroughfare leading up to the gate of the citadel might have survived Avedis' deluge, but would we survive the ghosts? We were all going to die.

It was the fear taking control of my senses. I reached for White, but Palomar's effort to keep me bound with invisible ropes of White also kept White out of my reach. Suddenly, I was released, and by the look of it, Redd was as well. He fell to the mud, the fear taking away the use of his legs. He had a bow slung across his back and a quiver of arrows that shook, echoing his fear.

Fenrick was not so overcome but had a hand on the flank of Redd's horse to steady himself. The noose still hung from his neck, dangling to the end where Redd's arrow had severed it. All traces of his recent delirium had passed and he appeared in command of his faculties once more.

The six Regal Guard ran for their lives. One, in his haste, tripped over some of the gallows debris, and smashed his oil lamp amid the heap of wood. Despite the rain, the wood and surrounding straw started to burn.

I stretched for White again, and this time it melted in my blood easily. The flute music tempo in my mind was quickened by fear, but its melody was sloppy and inaccurate from my weariness. As the fear lessened, I grabbed Redd's arm and fed into him the calming White.

Even Captain Faraday had run off, and with Palomar's attention on the ghosts, we might have made good our escape if not for Prince Winfred and Prince Rollin. Their lineage, no doubt, afforded them more than adequate immunity from the fear.

I quickly turned my attention to Fenrick's shackled feet. The manacles fell away, and Fenrick widened his stance without taking his eyes off his brothers. He glanced back and forth between them as they separated and flanked him on either side, swords drawn. Despite Fenrick's lack of a weapon, they remained wary of him.

Through the rain and by the light of Palomar's ring, I saw a dozen or more ghosts walking through a building to the east. More were approaching from the west.

Above the din of panic now gripping what remained of the crowd, Palomar's commanding voice rang out. "Back! Back to your darkness! High Magic compels you!"

"We're going to die," Fenrick said to his brothers. "And all you can think about is vengeance." Around his neck the severed noose remained like some ghastly necklace.

"The ghosts are no threat to us," Winfred said. "But maybe they can kill you. The nobility that runs in our veins is wanting in yours."

The light from Palomar's ring was too bright to behold directly. How were the ghosts reacting? He was our only hope, our only source of High Magic. Squinting between my fingers into the light, I tried to see the ghosts, see what they were doing.

"So noble of purpose, brother," Fenrick said with a sneer. "You are such a puppet. Don't you think it a cosmic coincidence that, just as the whole world dies, the only family immune to this plague are at each other's throats? Do you think it's an accident?" Rollin lunged at Fenrick, but Fenrick was quicker. He did a backflip and came up with a burning brand, remains of the gallows. Using it, I watched in amazement as he parried blows raining down from both sides at once. One of Winfred's blows came down with a resounding thwack as his sword was jammed into the wood. Fenrick released his blazing wood, then, in one fluid motion, he spun about and took Rollin's sword from him. Rollin lay dazed on the ground amid wooden rubble.

The few ghosts I could make out were not turning away. In fact, every ghost in sight was converging on Palomar, like moths to the light. "Get back!" Palomar's voice was now a desperate shriek. "Foul plague, get back! This can't be. Back. Ahhh!" The light from his ring vanished at the moment of his demise.

We were lost. With the vanishing ruby light went all my hope. The ghosts were attracted by souls, and the light coming from Palomar and his ring must have drawn them. They probably ignored the rest of Sojourn's inhabitants just to come here and find that light. Palomar wasn't our protection. He was nothing but a signal fire inviting every ghost from here to South Seniford to come and join the feast.

Fenrick grabbed the rope around his neck and pulled it off his head. "I didn't kill Hallam."

People were streaming out of the citadel gates, running from ghosts. They rushed past us in fear-induced panic and ran headlong into the specters approaching us. If not for their panic, the ghosts would have been on us long before now.

The White flowing through me was weak, the flute music faltering. We had to ride, but how much longer could I keep the fear at bay? We needed more than two horses to carry the four of us out of Sojourn. Where was Avedis, anyway?

Redd was just now recovering from the effects of the fear. I helped him to his feet.

"You want everyone to believe I did it," Rollin said, slowly standing and eying Fenrick warily. He had to have been aware that, if only for a moment, he had been at Fenrick's mercy. Yet Fenrick did not strike. Did that count for so little?

"I don't think any of us killed Hallam," Fenrick said, taking a step toward Winfred's blade.

"Then who?" Winfred asked. Rollin appeared to look around for a weapon.

"Where's your precious Jelail?" Fenrick asked.

"She isn't capable of it. Jelail!" Rollin shouted. The mention of her name must have awoken in his mind the threat to her life. She had no immunity to the ghosts. Calling her name over and over, Rollin ran from us, searching for her. Eventually he ran back into the citadel against the thinning tide of people.

Winfred watched him go out of the corner of his eye. "You think you know us so well, Fenrick. Rollin may be obsessed with Jelail, but she isn't in love with him. He's coercing her attentions with threats of exposing something from her past. Perhaps something revealed during a confession."

"How would you know?" Fenrick asked. He easily parried several thrusts from Winfred.

"She told me all about it. You and Rollin are quite a pair," Winfred said. "Can you manipulate me so well? Or fight your way out of this with your monkish skills?"

The fire behind Winfred was rising as more of the gallows wood caught fire. By that light, Redd mounted his horse. I transferred my hand to his leg to keep his fear at bay.

"So after you're finished running me through, is Rollin next?" Fenrick asked. "You're such a fool."

"Father always hated you. You were such a disappointment. He will thank me."

"You think you're his favorite?" Fenrick asked. I couldn't tear my eyes away from the dual. Steel on steel rang out, but Fenrick seemed to be tiring. "Perfect Winfred, always doing what he's told, never having an original thought. Where's Dad now? Picture yourself as king for a half a minute, and tell me where you'd be. Your second son is dead, and you just hanged your fourth born. Without the complete immunity from magic only afforded to the king, the ghosts will probably get your remaining sons if they don't kill each other first. Your kingdom is dying, and nothing you do can stop it. Soon you'll be the only one left alive. You'll be easy pickings for Nardel, who will torture you until you beg to be killed."

"You think he'd kill himself? Ha. Father wouldn't despair."

"I'd lay even odds he's atop the highest tower in Sojourn watching the realm die and holding a dagger's point aimed at his own heart." Perhaps it was true. Perhaps Fenrick was trying to find another means to get rid of Winfred.

But Winfred didn't take the bait. "Then I'll have to see to his welfare after I'm done with you." Winfred lunged at Fenrick. I knew it was useless to try, but I reached out with White in an attempt to freeze him in place. He was the heir to the throne, so I was surprised when my efforts did serve to slow him, but just for a moment. Fenrick held his own against Winfred's onslaught, but he was being inexorably backed toward the burning pyre.

I looked up at Redd as he pulled his bow from his shoulder and nocked an arrow. A flash of lightning brought my wandering eye to something in the sky. Six birds were circling high above Sojourn. They were the kestrels, all the kestrels left in the realm. They flew directly overhead in a rough circle like vultures waiting for their dinner to die. But no, as Bodicea had declared, they preferred their feast in the sky. They were circling—no, ringing us . . . We needed the ring of bells to call the Knights of the Realm.

"Drop your sword, Winfred," Redd ordered. "Or would you rather an arrow in your back?"

My mind started to race. Maybe the bells weren't normal bells, neither hand bells, dinner bells nor church bells. They were 'Far off yet quite near,' as Brenner had said in the histories. Perhaps you couldn't touch them or bring them all together. Brenner had said, 'I shall listen for the bittersweet cry of the horn amidst the ring of bells.'

Maybe they were physically ringing us, encircling us, protecting us like a phalanx of shields.

What in the entire realm encircled us right now? It had to be ancient, as old as the knights themselves. What could make a ringing sound resonant throughout the realm? It would have to be large, so large that it couldn't be missed. There would have to be more than one of them. And the only way something so large and old could be hidden is if it was in plain sight. We probably saw it every day and never saw it for what it was.

Winfred paused and looked at Redd. "So it's treason at every turn, is it?"

We had no time for this nonsense. "The only thing in rebellion is your reason, Winfred," I said. "None of us here desires your death, or Redd would have already let loose his arrow."

Winfred retreated, walking backward with his sword at the ready. "When next we meet, justice will be served."

Lightning struck the citadel uncomfortably close, and I looked back up through the rain at the circling falcons. If I had their keen vision, I'd probably never have missed knowing these bells for what they really were. I imagined myself a kestrel flying high over the city and gazing through the darkness, through the mists and the clouds. What would I see? I muttered to myself, "Pretty much the only thing they would be able to see from here would be the Hall—The Hall of Tishman."

"Where's my horse?" Fenrick asked. "The ghosts are swarming."

"Don't ask," Redd said. "You'll have to use Blanchard's horse."

"The bells, Fenrick," I said as I released Redd and pulled Fenrick close. "The bells we were looking for to call the knights—They are ancient buildings scattered about the realm. In Waterton to the southeast, it's the Hall of Tishman. To the north in Tellowl, there's a matching building Avedis called the Great Paramore, and off to the southwest there's a third hall in Drinland."

Dangling from saddlebags on Redd's horse, I noticed Fenrick's silver horn. I pulled it loose of its leather straps and forced it into Fenrick's hands. "Wind your horn once more."

"What good will that do?" Fenrick said looking around nervously. "I've used it hundreds of times, and no knights—"

"I don't think it matters what horn we use," I said. "Maybe all it takes is knowing how to call them back—what the Hall of Tishman really is. Knowing is the key. They'll return when our *hearts and minds have been truly opened*. Hurry." I stood back to look around and take stock of our situation. The muddy road was strewn with bodies, all victims of the ghosts. Shrieking people were pouring out of the nearby houses in a vain attempt to escape the horror that was passing through their walls. Three ghosts were headed our way.

I'd forgotten about protecting Redd from the onslaught of fear. When I looked, his teeth were clenched in a grimace of concentration as he tried to control his panic.

As the sharp, clean sound of Fenrick's horn went up into the night sky, a chill went through me. It seemed to pierce the fabric of reality and reach across into the realm of magic. My only evidence of this was the fact that the flute music in my mind came to a stop in mid-phrase, instead choosing to match the note Fenrick sounded. It had never done that before.

Redd visibly relaxed and, surprisingly, the ghosts seemed to hear the horn as well. The three that had been heading our way must have thought better of it and turned to easier prey.

The horn fell silent, and my hopes fell with its sound. I heard no ringing that would signal the Knights of the Realm. The flute music in my mind, now released from Fenrick's note, turned to a melody in a decidedly minor key.

"Nothing," Fenrick said.

"Because," I explained laughing, the solution finally plain. "In our infinite wisdom, we decided to fill all the drafty holes in the roof of the Hall of Tishman with windows!"

"Windows," Redd said. "Can you open all those windows from here with White?"

"For White to work, I need to have moved those windows before. I need to have been there to see them with my own eyes," I said. "And

I've never been to the Great Paramore. Are there windows there? What about the one in Drinland? It'll have to be Old Magic."

Redd dismounted and stood before me. "Give it a try. We'll be right here."

Taking a few deep breaths and getting to my knees, I prepared myself for Old.

Fenrick was already at my side. I felt overcome with pride for them, the camaraderie they exhibited without a second thought. They knew the only way to protect me from the ghosts was to die in my place. The ghosts only killed once per night. Provided there weren't too many, the sacrifice might give me a few more minutes.

I sank into a trance, allowing Old to fill me. I imagined myself as a drop of water at the tip of an icicle on the verge of falling. I fell and my plummet became a dive like a kestrel in the sky, wind whipping past at ever increasing speeds. I imagined the sky as blue and clean. On a whisper of air I was buoyed upward, and as I rose, so too did the theme of Old. As if played by an orchestra of nature, a myriad of instruments combined together, churning forth a haunting melody rising in pitch as I was carried upward and deeper into my trance, into Old.

Feeling the sky, the rhythms of the wind, the clouds high above, I rose to join them. I was the water falling from the sky, pooling in the fields, rushing down the rivers. I felt the ocean surrounding the continent. I was the surf crashing against the cliffs of the shores. The land between, old and worn, was my body. I felt its movements, its joints and wrinkled face. I was the land, the air . . . and the water.

The music whispered the power in my grasp. It enticed me to move, to breathe as Old, but I ignored their temptations and turned to the halls built by Tishman. I saw them all, one to the north, one to the southeast and one to the southwest. The great buildings seemed small and insignificant in contrast to the Realm of Rinstill, but I knew them now for what they were. Sentinels. Not protection for the people in themselves but a means by which we might call aid.

There were windows in all of them, so it would have to be three quakes, three times the price.

The land felt like a piece of my body, like my arm, and I could have easily moved it directly. But by choosing to do so I would become Old itself, a decision from which there was no return. Instead, I focused upon each of the three locations and whispered, "Earth and rock, I need your help. It's me, Sol." A feeling of compassion washed over me like a warm summer breeze. I could smell wildflowers, feel the trees reaching for the sun. I loved the land. It was the living land and the sea teeming with life that formed the core of Old Magic. I would whisper in its ear like a lover of many years, and when it listened, I felt loved by the land in return.

"I need you to move so a few windows break," I whispered. It sounded like an inane request, but Old understood what was at stake. I could feel its comprehension and riding on that sensation followed a great sadness. It knew about the ghosts killing us. In part, it was humanity, and it mourned for us as it felt our death as its own. I heard the sound of a solitary keening seagull and felt the land blanketed in grief. Its tears were the mist and the rain.

And it happened. Slowly at first, tremors slight and insignificant rattled the land in three remote places in Rinstill. They seemed small to me now. Filled with Old, my sphere of sensation was swept beyond normal bounds, so I wondered how these tremors would feel if I were there, if I were a man walking along the street. Would I be able to keep my feet? Would I even notice anything happening?

The tremors increased in violence at all three locations, but I concentrated on Waterton to see the effect. Waterton was just a speck on the dividing line between land and water, a dot standing at the end of a river. In my mind's eye it grew larger until I could make out the different sections of the small city. There were the docks, and to the north was the college. Still I fell by force of will alone, and the individual buildings and roads began to make sense to me. The stone buildings, so formidable and inspiring, seemed like delicate pastry, ready to break at the merest touch. I worried the quake would destroy the whole town, bringing the roofs down on those remaining there.

Windows were breaking all over the city. People were scurrying in panic into the streets. Perhaps they thought it was the end of the world. Little did they know, but if not for this small violence against their homes, it would be. The ghosts would overrun them, which is just what they were doing back at Sojourn.

Finally, I was close enough to see the windows filling the strange holes atop the Hall of Tishman. All were broken, yet some glass remained in a few of the frames. Several more seconds went by before the ground stopped its quaking, yet still those pieces of glass remained. Would they prevent the call from sounding?

The sensation of grey age sank into my bones. It felt like dry parchment that might break into dust if touched. I desperately wanted to examine the other two sites, but there was no time left in me. The brink of my existence drew nigh, the edge of a cliff opening out into darkness. The orchestra whispered alluring promises of the sunrise, of caverns never seen by man, of chasms in the ocean floor of unknown depth. All could be mine if I abandoned my frail body to merge with the ancient. "Not yet," I whispered. "But soon."

I heard the sound of distant rain and the piercing call of a horn, remote as if winded from within the fold of an unseen hill. The fading grand theme of Old, just like the music of White, merged with that pitch, harmonized with it, amplified it. The horn drew me back to Sojourn and back into myself. I released Old, perhaps for the last time, and the music faded to a whisper and vanished. A tear came to my eye.

Moving was painful. I felt as if Old had extracted every remaining day of my life leaving me but a few hours so that, mayhap, I could come to know firsthand the result of my efforts. A kindness before the end.

I looked up and saw Fenrick, the silver horn held to his lips. I remembered it being much louder before. So, I thought, age has taken my hearing, not all, but some. I smiled with silent resignation.

I struggled to get up. Redd grabbed my arm and lifted me with ease. I could tell by his shocked expression that my new age was apparent to him.

Redd said something, and I tried to tell him I couldn't hear as well as I used to. He shouted instead. "It's working! Can you hear it?"

I shook my head.

"When we felt the earth shake, Fenrick sounded his horn. The ringing is clear but faint, and it's coming from all around. As long as Fenrick blows the horn, it persists!"

I nodded my head to tell him I understood. At that moment, Fenrick stopped and drew the horn away from his lips with an expression of wonder on his face. I bent to look around Redd's hulking form and saw a figure of a man, a silhouette in the darkness outlined by gentle amber light.

He approached Fenrick. Even after stepping into the light of the fire, I could still see the trace of light embracing him. Before Fenrick, he bowed low with grace and dignity. Straightening quickly, he said, "Greetings, my friend. I heard your call and have come as quickly as I might. My name is Brenner, Knight of the Realm."

Fenrick hesitated, gaping at this apparition addressing him. Realizing something was expected of him, he blurted, "Oh, I'm—I'm Fenrick Youngblood, Prince of the Realm."

Brenner appeared to be only thirty summers old, nowhere near his real age. He had delicate features with small wrinkles forming around his eyes, a narrow nose and a clean-shaven chin. He didn't wear the armor of a knight but the simple clothes of a peasant. His every move flowed with buoyant grace. He brushed some hair from his eyes, and it seemed even this mundane articulation was made new to my eyes, ethereal in some sense. I watched every move with rapt attention.

"A Prince of the Realm, and in—if you'll forgive me—in such a sorry state?" Brenner flashed a knowing smile. "But bruised and scarred as you are, I think this is not why you called?"

Brenner turned to face the gathering ghosts, and I was shocked to think my fascination with a Knight of the Realm had made me dismiss the danger the apparitions posed. Even without White, I felt no chill, no groping fear. Brenner's arrival was like a beam of light dispelling the fear of the gathering gloom.

All the ghosts were walking unerringly toward him, and I wondered at his nonchalance. These ghosts must hold little threat for him. He turned on his heel and strode purposefully toward the nearest one. The amber light shining about his form remained at his very edge, highlighting every movement he made.

The ghost he first approached appeared as a man wearing the leather of a blacksmith. Without any sign of effort on Brenner's part, the apparition became brighter, became solid. Before our eyes, Brenner changed the ghost back into a man, and the blacksmith stood wide-eyed in confusion, no doubt wondering where he was and how he'd arrived. Brenner took the blacksmith by the shoulders and said, "Be at peace. You're safe now."

The blacksmith looked down at his hands in amazement saying, "Am I alive?"

Brenner swiftly transformed all the ghosts in sight back into living and breathing people. Even the rain stopped falling. For the first time since this ordeal began, I felt genuine hope. High Magic was the answer, and though we didn't find it in ourselves, we managed to do what was thought impossible. We roused the Knights of the Realm from their sleep.

At least we roused one Knight of the Realm. Once the immediate ghost threat was removed, Brenner came toward Redd and me. Redd knelt before him, but Brenner laughed without malice. "Please don't kneel. No one in Rapt is greater or less than any other." He introduced himself the same way. "I am Brenner, Knight of the Realm."

Redd rose and introduced himself. "I'm Sir Welling Redd, Duke of South Seniford." Redd then turned to indicate me and with unexpected pride in his voice said, "And this . . . This is His Grace, Sol Blanchard, Servant of the One Crown, Protector of the White Flame, and Holder of the Seven Seals of Tishman."

"I am glad to meet you," Brenner said, and from the sound of his voice, I knew he actually meant it. He bowed as gracefully as he had done before Prince Fenrick.

I nodded my head in greeting and felt entirely too pretentious. Redd, having given my whole title, might have given Brenner the wrong impression, making me seem self-absorbed. It made me uncomfortable, but that faded as quickly as Brenner rose from his bow. I looked into his eyes, and they seemed to me like pools of water, serene and still. I almost thought I could see light, the same amber light which feathered the fringes of his every move. It shone from deep within those pools, or perhaps reflected like light cast by a distant sun in another world into which he alone could see.

"Sol," Brenner whispered as if to himself. He appeared almost troubled. "You have made this all possible; though, I think your sacrifice no one here fully comprehends. Don't feel misused or unappreciated. Unsung heroes are not forgotten, not by all."

"You brought those people back from the dead," I said shocked at the feathery sound of my own ancient voice. "I'm not the hero of this tale."

Brenner shook his head in denial. "No, they were not dead, only sleeping. All I did was rouse them from their slumber, just as you and Prince Fenrick did for the knights."

And it was true. One by one, others Knights of the Realm arrived, each bearing a tracery of amber, for them an insignia of power to which no amount of flowing robes or flowered raiment could compare. They came always first to Fenrick, recognizing him for the bearer of the horn that summoned them.

An elderly man, who once must have been bent with age, came forth. He stood now tall and sure, exuding the same grace that Brenner had exhibited. He had a white beard that sparkled with amber when he stood in profile. I was certain this was Evendale, first Knight of the Realm, but he named himself as Merrick.

When would Evendale arrive?

Winomere emerged, a small, beautiful woman with long, flowing black hair and the uniform of a barmaid. Savena arrived not a minute after Winomere. I recognized her as a young girl from a Noble House, but which one I couldn't say. She couldn't have been more than ten or twelve, but her bearing was nothing like that of a child. Her mind was that of a mature woman, a Knight of the Realm with High Magic at her fingertips.

All of them had been living normal lives among us, yet below the surface, their true identities slept, hidden even from themselves.

Had I not been relying on Redd as a fence post upon which I could lean, I surely would have fallen over in a faint of shock. Knights of the Realm, people thought nothing more than fables, were coming forth and standing among us. It was as the Inadel had said. The knights were among us somehow, awake yet asleep. Any of these men or women could have been a neighbor, even a close friend.

When Avedis strode toward us, embraced in the same amber filaments of light, I nearly fell. "Avedis? Can it be you?" I asked.

He nodded to me but walked to Fenrick first. "Prince Fenrick. I am Derif, Knight of the Realm." His accent was gone.

"A Knight of the Realm and you never told us?" Fenrick said.

Avedis, or rather Derif, smiled. "You must understand that I didn't know myself. The echoing music of the bells woke me as if from a dream. And my life until now seems to me like nothing more than a dream. In part, it's now difficult to remember."

When he came to me, I grabbed his arm in greeting. "I knew there was something special about you. But a Knight of the Realm?"

Derif bowed his head. "Sol Blanchard. I thought to learn much from you. Without knowing it, I'd already surpassed my teacher."

As they arrived, the knights greeted each other with warm embraces, friends of ages past. They took positions facing the city and bowed their heads as if in prayer. Perhaps they were transforming ghosts back into people, reaching out with High Magic to span the city.

I recognized the sixth Knight of the Realm to arrive. She had a kerchief tied about her head to hold her combed white hair in place. I knew the kindly wrinkled face that had spent so many hours with me back at Waterton. It was Miss Vallow, but unmasked with a halo of shining amber framing her slight form, she could only be the Lady Lowenna. She introduced herself to Fenrick, but what she said I could not make out. As she came to greet us, she was stopped momentarily by Brenner, who broke his silent stance. He wrapped her in his arms. "Lowenna, my . . . it is good to see you again. Evendale is not here."

She nodded her head with a smile of resignation. This news did not seem to surprise her. "Let us not give up hope of his returning. But seeing you again, I'm made glad."

Finally, she stood before me, and it was I who did the introducing. "Sir Redd, Duke of South Seniford, I'd like you to meet an old friend of mine. This is Miss Vallow, a kind but hard old woman who did a great deal of cooking for us back at Waterton. As it turns out, she knows more about magic than the Potentate and I put together." I laughed and gave her a hug. "Vallow—I mean Lowenna, I can hardly believe my eyes."

"Sol, I—I hope you don't feel betrayed in some way," she said hesitantly.

"Betrayed! I'm shocked, but the word betrayed never would have come to mind."

"I'm glad. You see, I couldn't confide in you what I didn't know myself. I didn't remember being Lowenna—you might say I haven't even been in this world—until the sounding of the horn and bells."

"I know. The same happened to Avedis—or rather Derif."

Lowenna turned to Redd. "And how do you do, Sir Redd? I'm sorry, but the flood of memories that have poured into me over the last few minutes have temporarily blocked out most of what I knew as Vallow. I feel as though I recognize your name, but the reason escapes me."

"Your presence is more honor than I deserve, Lady," Redd said. He took her hand gallantly and kissed it. "Tell me, what of the ghosts? Can they all so easily be transformed back into flesh and blood?"

Lowenna shook her head. "Don't fear. Their numbers are not so great that the six of us, working together, will fail. By morning, the threat will have passed. Even before I arrived, Brenner and the others had already begun.

"These ghosts are driven, I feel it, from a new enemy, one named . . . Nardel." She rubbed her forehead. "Oh, Nardel is an old evil to you, but this malignancy came into the world after our slumber. I am only now just remembering . . ."

As Lowenna spoke, I glanced up to see the other five Knights of the Realm staring off in different directions, some with a hand outstretched.

"Lady Lowenna, please," I said. "You said only six knights would be enough, but what of Evendale? Where is he?"

Lowenna's eyebrows furrowed in concern or disappointment. "When I last saw Evendale, it was far from here. Perhaps he was too far away to hear the signal, but rest assured, even without his aid, we shall heal this plague racing across the realm."

She turned to join the others, and I pondered at the change that had come over her. She was the same Vallow, but Vallow as she might be given hundreds of years of experience. The memories that she had now must give her more perspective on her life, on history itself.

Kirrin appeared out of a dark street leading into the depths of Sojourn. Logan Swift was at his side. They were both Chosen of the kestrels.

"Kirrin, Logan," Redd called out. "Can you believe your eyes? We're saved."

Kirrin smiled uneasily. "Yes, it . . . it's truly amazing."

"What's the matter?"

"I don't know. I feel the approach of something evil, but I cannot place it. Have you seen Bodicea or Edlynn?"

"I saw Edlynn head into the citadel a while back, fleeing the ghosts," Redd said. "I've no idea where Bodicea is."

Kirrin looked into the sky. "Erstwhile won't come down. Even though it rains, he's too afraid to come back. What of Sapphire?"

Redd closed his eyes. A moment passed and he looked up with concern. "She is flying erratically. It's as if she wants to come down and desperately wants to fly away to someplace safe all at the same time. What could it mean?"

More lightning lit up the sky, showing a brief display of the half dozen kestrels. They now flew in no discernible pattern.

A cry went up from among the Knights of the Realm. "Kestrels!" It sounded like a warning, and it came from Derif, who stood pointing up into the stormy sky. The rest of the knights stopped what they were doing and also looked up.

The incomprehensible happened. Lowenna yelled, "An enemy without eyes is only half the enemy. Do your best!"

As one, the Knights reached out, and into each pair of hands appeared a bow made of golden light.

"No!" Redd shouted and charged Lowenna who stood the closest. "What are you doing?"

Using some kind of power I'd never seen, all six Knights of the Realm simultaneously drew back those bows and let loose arrows of golden light that lanced upward toward the kestrels at the speed of lightning. I could feel the flow of White through them like waves of heat. Six Knights of the Realm shot and all six kestrels, the last kestrels in all the realm, cried out in pain as they were struck from the sky.

Redd was fast, but nowhere near fast enough. He brought Lowenna down into the muddy ground. Kirrin had tackled Brenner, but they were both too late.

The Knights didn't know these kestrels weren't slaves of Nardel. These were the only few to have survived their struggle for freedom.

Redd sprang from the ground to find Sapphire, now plummeting from the sky. I followed as best I could, trying not to fall as I navigated over the rut-strewn muddy road.

I reached for White and felt the six falling birds. I lifted, pushing against their fall, and so delivered Sapphire into Redd's hands and the rest to the ground beneath a tree off the muddy pavement.

All were dead except for Sapphire who had one wing torn almost completely off. "Sol, quickly, heal my Sapphire. She's still alive, and you can save her."

Fenrick helped me to my knees so I could get a better look. Not many mages knew how to heal, since it took considerably longer to learn than the simple things. I reached out with White to feel the wound from the inside. The flute music danced through my mind, but it sounded hollow and disjointed, not as I was accustomed. I attempted to probe the wound with my mind's eye, but the vision was blurry and the sensation was missing. What was the next step? Reattach, grow, knit? But how? Just stop the bleeding, and reattach the wing by—take the—I—I couldn't remember.

Redd kneeled over Sapphire. "Do something! Don't just sit there."

Logan was by my side also. "Heal my Helios, Sol. He's all I have. All I care about." He didn't know Helios was already dead.

"I can't remember the way. It must be the age. I'm too old."

"Can't remember?" Redd said and grabbed my shoulders forcefully. "You've done this dozens of times. I've seen you."

"I'm too old, Redd. My mind feels clouded—"

"You're not old, you only look old. We're the same age. You're no older than me."

At that moment, Lowenna arrived; the amber light that embraced her flickered like a fire about to go out. "What's going on? Why are you trying to heal it?" she asked.

"You! You killed her." Redd lost what little control he had. In a fury, he launched himself at her. Before he reached her, Lowenna Held him with White, stopping him in mid-stride. Savena and Winomere stepped up beside Lowenna, each bearing the same confused look.

"Why did you do it?" Fenrick asked. "Why did you shoot the kestrels? It's appalling."

I looked back at Sapphire and realized she was dead. There was nothing that could be done. A chill wind blew across the hill.

Lowenna, confused, tried to explain, "The kestrels are servants of the enemy. They are his eyes, and as surely as—"

I interrupted her. "That was hundreds of years ago. These six kestrels . . . they were never under his control. They were the only ones."

Lowenna's sharp intake of breath indicated her surprise, and she felt her forehead with concern as if attempting to remember the truth.

I said, "They deserved so much better."

Suddenly, the light around all three Knights vanished, and simultaneously, Redd fell to the ground, his binding released. This time, though, Fenrick stood close by to step in if Redd acted rashly. But he ignored Lowenna, and returned to Sapphire, his head bowed.

"I'm sorry," Lowenna said. "We had no idea. Please forgive us. We were confused. We were . . ." Lowenna's voice trailed off as she realized the uselessness of words.

Together, Edlynn and Bodicea plunged into our midst from the confines of the citadel. Seeing their beloved kestrels, now dead, Bodicea screamed and Edlynn fainted. A child ran up screaming, "The ghosts are coming back. Please help us. The ghosts!"

Ghosts, attracted by the rich warmth of High Magic, were coming through the walls in droves. As renewed screams of terror filled the night, Lowenna said, "We cannot help. Only with clear consciences and true hearts can we reach for the power, and unless . . . unless, Sir Redd, you can find it in your heart to forgive me, I cannot forgive myself. My memories were confused, but I can now remember you and Sapphire together. I now understand what we — what I have done to you. Please forgive me."

"Forgive you?" Redd asked slowly turning and rising to his feet. "Forgive you? You must be mad."

Fenrick was tensed to spring to Lowenna's aid. "Redd, if you don't forgive her, we're all dead."

"Perhaps," Redd whispered squinting at Fenrick through rain-wet eyelashes. "Perhaps, without Sapphire, I no longer wish to live."

"So the fate of man should be ruled by your selfishness?" I said. "Do all the Chosen feel this way? Logan, Bodicea, rise above this. Rise above the hate, the anguish. Forgive them." But can one command an emotion?

Redd stared cold hate at Lowenna, "Get out of my sight before I lose myself and put an arrow through your heart." He shoved

Fenrick's hand off his shoulder and resumed his kneeling posture beside Sapphire, pulling a hood over his head.

The rain returned.

Kirrin had to be physically restrained by the Regal Guard from pummeling Brenner to death, and Logan, in a fit of suicidal anguish, ran into the tide of ghosts and died. Bodicea would have killed the Knight of the Realm who killed her kestrel, Torrent, but it was Savena, the young girl, who stood before her crying and desperately asking for forgiveness. None of the Chosen were forgiving the knights, and all seemed lost.

The ghosts were swarming, and the insanity of the creeping fear had returned as well. The trickle of White Magic running through me kept me sane, and I kept a hand on Redd to keep him from panicking. Some of the people who had once been saved were again taken by the fiends.

Fate had won as it always did. No doubt it was chortling to itself off in some corner somewhere, pouring derision over our best efforts to save ourselves, to prevent the extinction of the kestrels as the prophecy predicted.

The kestrels were all dead now, and with them so shall we be soon enough. Every man, woman, and child, in all Sojourn and all the realm would be ghosts if not tonight then the next.

I watched a ghost take Fenrick, proving even being the third in line for the throne was not enough immunity.

Nearby, Lowenna was sitting and crying at her own weakness and still pleading for forgiveness. Ghosts were still approaching her and when one got too close, Brenner sacrificed himself so that she might still have a chance to be forgiven by Redd. Kirrin had run blindly into a group of ghosts when fear overcame his sensibilities, so Brenner had no way of being forgiven, no possibility of recalling High Magic to his fingers.

None of the ghosts approached me, but that gave me cold comfort. As old as I was, they probably sensed my proximity to the grave and veered toward greener pastures and warmer, more vibrant souls.

Soon, too soon, the other four knights, Winomere, Savena, Derif and Merrick, joined Brenner at Lowenna's feet. Once the Chosen they had wronged were taken by the ghosts, they died to keep alive the slim hope of salvation through Redd's heartfelt forgiveness. I looked at Redd's hooded figure, still kneeling in the rain and oblivious to all. He would not listen to me. There was no hope.

Maybe if Evendale came . . . No. What were the chances of that, now?

I pulled myself to my feet, releasing Redd. His grief overwhelmed any flow of fear from the few remaining ghosts. Yes, the ghosts were thinning remarkably. It had seemed like an unending flood, like the rain falling from the sky and filling the lower section of Sojourn. Just as the water destroyed the buildings, the ghosts destroyed the people. Two floods. Funny I didn't see it before.

It was out of my hands. I'd done my best, and there was but one thing more I could do. "Lowenna, sweet one." She seemed so young to me now. Age is so meaningless.

"Sol," she said through her sobs.

"I don't blame you for this. It may not mean much, but I forgive you." She sat nearby, hoping for words from Redd that would release her guilt. I reached out and squeezed her hand with warmth.

"We're only human, Sol," she whispered. "Capable of mistakes, like . . . like anyone. Can't he understand?"

"Look, the ghosts are thinning out. Maybe Redd will get the time he needs to heal enough, to accept her passing enough to forgive you. And . . . and I shall buy you that time, like these noble friends of yours."

I released her hand and watched as a ghost approached. The apparition was a raggedly dressed young man bearing a harp case slung around his shoulder. It was the Inadel minstrel who had sung for us once; it seemed like years ago in a place whose memory was dim in my mind.

"Ahh, minstrel," I said. "I see no one is safe from this storm. Your vision was wrong, for this is a dark end for both of us. Come, take me. Take me to the place in your visions, then. Maybe it will be a happy place where I can find rest . . . and peace." I hoped that afterward I wouldn't be seen walking blindly through walls to hunt the few remaining people in Rapt.

The Inadel minstrel came on, unhearing and unblinking, headed toward Lowenna with my frail and aged body interceding on her behalf.

One instant the minstrel was before me, and the next he was gone, vanished. Dizziness whirled about my head, and I fell, my last remaining strength gone. As the darkness closed over my head, I heard strange words whispered close. It must have been the minstrel, somehow speaking from his mind to mine as we passed through each other.

> Turning and turning in the widening gyre
> The falcon cannot hear the falconer;
> Things fall apart; the center cannot hold;
> Mere anarchy is loosed upon the world,
> The blood-dimmed tide is loosed, and everywhere
> The ceremony of innocence is drowned;
> The best lack all conviction, while the worst
> Are full of passionate intensity.

> Surely some revelation is at hand.

Chapter Sixteen

Chasing Ghosts

Talonii had taken to "holding court" every Sunday evening at Marty's. He and his cohorts would take the center table, and he would sign autographs for his fans. Tonight was no different. He was sitting with Spunk and Newkirk, and at his side, laughing at all his jokes, was Veronica . . . something. Sasha had told me her last name, but I didn't remember. She wasn't from around here.

"Privacy mode," I ordered, and the light on the com-pad started to blink. Zak sat down across from me and took a huge bite out of his burger. I shook my head. "How can you eat at a time like this?"

Through his mouthful of food he said, "It's important to keep up appearances."

My stomach was so knotted with nerves that the thought of food made me ill. Thankfully, Trevor arrived at that moment.

He chose my side of the booth to sit. "Move it," he said in an exhausted voice. He slouched down in the seat, head back and eyes closed. "Did I miss anything?" he asked.

"You both missed all of phase one." I nodded my head at Zak saying, "Iron stomach here just sat down a minute ago."

"Hey," Zak said. "I'm famished."

Trevor opened one eye to look over toward Talonii's table. "Things looking good?"

There was a gym bag sitting on the seat beside Veronica. It contained the SIM caps that Zak had managed to find. "Sasha and Ilya pulled it off," I said.

Phase one of the plan involved getting the SIM caps into the hands of Frank and his gang. If they suspected anything fishy, they'd never put them on. Not half an hour ago, Sasha positioned herself in the women's restroom, and her little sister sat in the booth next to mine. Thankfully, Veronica eventually went in. When she did, Ilya was right on her heels, slapping a magnetized 'closed' sign on the door before she disappeared inside.

Once inside, Ilya was supposed to confront Sasha in a whispered argument about the illegal SIM caps she had in her bag. After a bit of back and forth, it would finally end with Ilya storming off to tell their parents. Sasha, in frustration, would capitulate and abandon the bag in a stall.

"She's got a reputation," Sasha had told me. "She likes coloring outside the lines. She'll take the bait."

Upon her exit, I watched Sasha pocket the closed sign then held my breath waiting for Veronica to emerge. She gave me a nod as she collected Ilya and made a hasty departure.

Sasha was right. As we hoped, Veronica took the bag. When she got back to the table, she whispered something to Frank about its content. Frank smiled.

Just as Zak was polishing off the last of his burger, Azzam and his two burly bodyguards arrived. He was dressed in some kind of formal white suit and he walked with a regal bearing. His arrival caused something of a hush to fall. Then things got even noisier than before. I looked away as he approached Talonii. "Oh God, I can't look," I said. "Tell me what's happening."

"He's just introducing himself to our famous Sam Clemens impersonator," Zak said. "Jeez his guards are big."

I could hear Talonii say, "—the one, the only. At your service." I pretended to look at the menu being displayed in the table surface.

"Wake me when it's over." Trevor put his head down on the table, buried in his folded arms.

Zak continued, "Now he's going around shaking everyone's hand at the table. He—I—Our boy really knows what he's doing."

"What do you mean?" I resisted the urge to look.

"If I wasn't watching for it I never would have noticed."

I sighed. "Gee Zak, whatever do you mean by that?"

"Oh, sorry," Zak stopped staring and looked down at the menu too. "As he went to shake each person's hand, he dropped something in each glass. He's like some sleight of hand magician."

Trevor picked his head up for a second. "It could be hours before it really kicks in."

Zak shook his head. "I can't believe it's just you and him left in the tournament."

"That's the last of my worries," I said. "We're really doing this, aren't we?"

"A toast," Azzam said, audible above the babble. I saw him snap his fingers, and one of his bodyguards handed him a cup. "Now that I've shaken your hand, I can say, without a doubt, I know who is going to win the Tournament. Here's to Sam Clemens! And may he grind Winger into the dust!"

I had to laugh. Frank was forced to sit there and drink to my victory.

"Let's hit it," Zak said, palming off the table screen. No one seemed to notice us leaving, not with someone like Azzam drawing all the attention. I whispered, "Shine brightly, Avedis."

* * *

It was late, very late. Zak and I were sitting on the floor of the hallway outside and around the bend from Clay's old office in

Descartes. No one was around, and the lights were off. The only illumination was from a set of light pipes stretching from floor to ceiling at the nearby hallway intersection. This was taking way too long. I peeked around the corner for the hundredth time. Azzam's two guards hadn't moved. They stood to either side of the door to Clay's office.

Zak had his eyes closed and could have been sleeping except for his crossed-legged sitting position and straight back.

I asked, "What is taking so long?"

"Relax," Zak said, eyes still closed. "Some people don't fall asleep as quickly as others."

Who could relax? I stood up and began pacing back and forth. Phase two was to get them all into a SIM, wait for them to fall asleep, then clone their sessions. Trevor was standing by in a SIM chamber off in Aristoteles waiting for our signal.

As we had planned, Azzam, after "finding out" what was in the bag, offered to host a private SIM party in an empty office he knew of out in Descartes. I don't know how he did it, but he managed to get them to trek all the way from Aristoteles to Descartes. Now we were just waiting for them to all enter a SIM and, with the help of the drugs Azzam had given them, to fall asleep.

I felt a wave of dizziness and put a hand to the wall to steady myself. When I opened my eyes again, I gasped. Halfway down the darkened corridor stood Clay, his hair ruffled by a wind that wasn't there. He looked up at me, our eyes meeting, then he faded back into the darkness.

Zak jumped up at the sound of my surprise. "What?" he whispered.

"Nothing," I said. "I'm beginning to see ghosts everywhere."

Zak relaxed. "Hmm. Sounds like you're spending too much time in the SIMs."

At that moment, Azzam, flanked by his bodyguards, turned the corner. "It's done," he said, stopping between Zak and me. "Hopefully they'll be out the rest of the night."

"Hopefully?" Zak asked.

I couldn't believe the plan was working. "Thanks, Azzam. We'll take it from here."

He nodded, then, before leaving, said, "Be quick."

Except for the thin rays of light peeking through the curtains, the office was dark. We found Newkirk and Spunk sound asleep, slumped in a heap against one of the office walls. Newkirk's SIM cap had fallen slightly askew. I took a moment to fix it.

I thought Frank would have taken the cot in the adjoining room, but, instead, we found him lying in the middle of the floor, snoring loudly. Veronica was snuggled next to him, dead to the world and using Frank's arm as a pillow.

Being careful not to make too much noise, we navigated around the sleeping bodies and got to the desk. Zak pulled out a transmitter from his bag and tossed it to me. I set it on the desk and pointed it to the com-pad near the door. I whispered, "Emily."

"Yes, Dennis?" Emily whispered as Zak produced two SIM caps. He handed one to me.

"Establish a laser-link with this device."

A thin beam of blue light appeared emanating from the com-pad near the door aimed at the transmitter. Her disembodied voice said, "Link established. Dennis, what is the purpose of this device. It doesn't appear to have a core." The laser-link faded to invisibility. She had just colored the beam to let us know where it was.

Zak plugged a transmitter into a wire from his SIM cap, now firmly on his head, and said, "Enter chat room Cornish Pasties." This was a chat room we had set up where we could meet up with Trevor, who was ensconced in a SIM chamber back in Aristoteles. Trevor chose the name. I think he wanted something that sounded nothing like "Illegal Secret Mission Conference."

After putting on my own cap, I pressed the button on the cap's rim to enter augmented reality (AR) mode. I closed my eyes as a test pattern came into focus and the static I heard resolved itself into an ascending piano. That's when I heard Newkirk's gruff voice. "It's about time. Where have you two been?" That was Trevor.

When I opened my eyes, I was no longer alone with Zak. In fact, Zak was gone, his face replaced by the vacant expression of Spunk. An image of Trevor as Newkirk stood over near the door. I knew that to them I must look like Frank.

In a weird combination of Zak's voice and Spunk's, I heard him say, "I thought *I* was going to be . . . ah, Newkirk."

"Better use—" I said, then stopped myself hearing Frank's voice coming from my mouth. "Use sub-vocals only, Z—ah, Spunk." I said that without using my voice box. It was a trick we used when not in full-body SIMs. The computer, picking up on the muscle movements in your neck and mouth, figured out what you actually wanted to say without you having to blurt it out for everyone to hear. I added, "Either that or you'll give me a headache."

"Hey Pumpkin Eater, privacy mode."

Nothing happened. "Spunk, I don't think that's the name you use for the LMC, is it? Allow me? LMC, privacy mode."

"Entering privacy mode now," the LMC replied, using a female voice with an English accent. The light on the com-pad began to blink, and at the same instant, Trevor vanished. I looked at Zak, and he wasn't Spunk anymore.

"She dropped the link," I said and bounded over Frank and Veronica to get to the com-pad. We had to use privacy mode as much as possible to prevent her from collecting data on us. I woke her up by tapping the com-pad and asked to reestablish the link. The blue laser beam appeared a second time, shooting across the office. Once we were all jacked-in again, Newkirk materialized. I said, "She dropped us when we went into privacy."

"Great," sighed Trevor. "Wait, hang on." He gestured wildly, manipulating things we couldn't see. "Okay, I'm ready. Ask for privacy mode now."

I did just that, and the English lady responded with her standard response: "Entering privacy mode now." This time, the link didn't drop, but suddenly appearing above the desk was good old Dr. Thompson amid a swirling storm of DNA sequences. Trevor explained, "Just needed to get her hypnotized before she dropped the link."

"Let's go," I said and opened the door. I jumped at the sight of Sasha just walking up to the office.

"Nice to see you too, Blanchard," she said as she breezed in. "—if that is your real name."

"What are you doing here?" I whispered. After checking to see if Ilya was here too—she wasn't—I closed the door.

"You don't think I'd miss all the fun, do you?"

Zak as Spunk smiled and said, "Now it's a party." He threw her a SIM cap.

Dr. Thompson's voice rose up out of the background static, whispers from the deep past. ". . . demonstrated, our anti-virus, 5591, shows incredible promise. Human trials . . ." Her voice was gone again; the image wavered to some other scene with her hard at work in a lab.

"What's with that?" Sasha asked.

"Oh, I'll explain later," I said, my voice doubled in my own ears as Frank's and my own. I pulled off the SIM cap to stop that nonsense. "Long story. Just . . . whatever you do, don't wake up the computer."

She gave me a quizzical look. "All right . . ."

I added, "It's not the end of the world if you do, but keeping her in privacy mode will help limit our exposure."

Zak, now appearing as Zak again, handed Sasha a transmitter, and she connected it to her cap. "This actually going to work?"

"You know if we get caught you're going to be in deep too," I warned.

"Relax," she said. "You need someone back here to pull the plug in case things go, ah, badly. And it just so happens that, lately, I have been getting too much darn sleep." She fitted the cap on her head. "Just call me Veronica. I'm going full-body so I can tag along."

"Better make sure to keep audio on in here," I said. "Just in case someone wakes up."

"What if they do wake up? What should I do?"

"Just grab the transmitter over there and leave," I said. "Oh, there's a cot behind that curtain over there. It might be more comfortable."

"Oh, thanks," she said, leaping over Veronica and Frank. She took a peek behind the curtain.

"We'll see you in a few," I said. "Oh, meet us in Cornish Pasties."

Sasha nodded with a smile and gave a little wave. "Toodles."

* * *

We entered the padded elevator and Zak knelt down with the bag. The door slid shut. "14th floor please," I commanded. "Then enter privacy mode." She was only in privacy mode back in the office.

"Dennis," Emily said. "I find this very unusual. If you don't mind my asking, where are you headed?" Zak looked up sharply. "And what are those devices in Zak's bag?"

I glanced at Zak, his one hand putting a transmitter back in the bag. He shrugged. The elevator slowly started its descent.

"Ah," I fumbled, trying to think of something to say. "It's a science experiment."

There was a pause as if she was deciding what to do with the information. Then she said, "Entering privacy mode now."

"That machine is too curious," whispered Zak, handing me some latex gloves.

Soon we were back in AR, and Newkirk was standing in the elevator with us along with a new member of our raiding party: Veronica.

Zak said, "This is so cool."

Trevor/Newkirk crossed his arms. "No wasting time, guys. Who knows how long these things will work. Now remember, Veronica and I can only see and hear what you see and hear. That is, until you link in the Omechron."

I pushed off and floated toward the ceiling hatch. Pretending to be Frank was weird. This whole thing was crazy. Once on top of the elevator, Trevor's and Sasha's bodies floated through the elevator ceiling as if they were ghosts. I clicked on my pen-light and glanced around expecting to see Clay again. He wasn't there. I was greeted with just the echoing elevator shaft slowly rising as we descended. Spunk's face appeared in the hatch below me. I had to remind myself that Zak and I only appeared like Spunk and Frank within the AR, so Emily should see them instead of us. To the rest of the world we appeared like ourselves.

* * *

Zak and I were now deep into the mech-tunnels. We had entered from the same broken access door that Trevor and I had once used. On our way, Trevor had guided us through the maze, appearing to fly through the tunnel, sometimes partially floating through the walls. Sasha floated behind Zak. The claustrophobia . . . my nerves were shot by the time we got to the grating overlooking the cargo bay.

While Zak busied himself unscrewing the grating access door, Trevor and Sasha floated down into the room ahead of us. They seemed to glow in the near darkness. The only light came from some dim light-pipe running the length of one of the corners of the bay. The massive door to the bay was closed along with flanking man-sized doors. It was empty of mechs and people. So far, so good.

There were boxes everywhere, intermingled with crates and old computer parts. There had to be over twenty orange containers in the room, and one was right below us. They were standing in a haphazard grouping like a herd of farm animals. Each rectangular box was as tall as a man and as big as four refrigerators put together. Omecron-7 MPPs? I had a sudden doubt they contained Omecrons of any variety. Perhaps it was just nerves.

The grill fell out of its moorings. Zak snagged it before it clattered against something. He pulled it back into the tunnel and gingerly put it down on his side of the hole. "We're in," he said with thumbs up. I tried to smile back.

Next, we had to deal with the com-pad on the wall near the door. Too bad we couldn't just ask Emily for privacy mode. Doing that would just tell her where we were, and the place would be swarming the MPs. So we had to put her in privacy mode the old-fashioned way.

Zak rummaged around in his bag and pulled out a metal rod about a third of a meter long and as thick as a thumb. It had a string along one side running its whole length. After lowering it into the room, he activated it. The rod and string suddenly inflated like a telescope but in both directions until it was a meter long. Once fully extended, the string tightened, bending the rod into a bow. Next, he pulled out two arrows from the bag. They each had suction cups on the end and a reel of string attached to the other.

He carefully lowered his head into the hole to look about the room. Looking over his shoulder, I noticed a steady red light coming from one of the walls, Emily's com-pad. I nudged Zak and pointed.

After he handed me both reels of string, I was surprised to see him nock not one but two arrows on his bow. He lowered himself into the hole, bracing himself by pressing his feet against either side of the maintenance tunnel. He was quick. Without hesitation, he pulled back, aimed, and released. The reels spun, playing out the string in the wake of the arrows. I heard them thunk into the wall.

I took a peek after pulling Zak back up. The arrows were both stuck to the wall just over the com-pad. The shots were perfect.

"How much archery skill did you buy?" Sasha asked.

"I didn't buy any," Zak said. "That's pure skill."

Sasha harrumphed. I didn't believe it either.

I pulled a plain black shower curtain out of the gym bag, another contribution by Zak to our misadventure. We looped two curtain rings through the string and lowered the curtain into the room. It slid smoothly down the pair of strings to end against the wall covering the com-pad. Now she couldn't see us, and since we weren't talking out loud, she wouldn't hear us either.

One after the other, we silently floated down onto the orange crate right below the opening, then jumped the rest of the way to the floor. Each box had a sign painted on it that read, 'Hazardous Material: Sulfuric Acid. Handle Via HAZMAT 7791.'

Trevor, floating several meters in the air, was busy creating control panels and display screens hovering around him. "Display a schematic of our com-links mapped to Descartes com-network. Show satellite links and route a pseudo channel back to Earth through the University of Stanford's mainframe. Authorization Russo Delta Googolplex."

Uh-oh, I thought. Trevor's using his dad's access codes. How could we hide the fact we had access to those?

Zak ripped off some red tape that was sealing an access panel. He punched a bright yellow button, and the panel opened revealing two 2D displays and a simple touch interface. It was hinged on the bottom and motorized, stopping when it got horizontal thus making a small desk surface. He gasped at something. "Ah, Newkirk. You'd better take a look at this."

Trevor looked over and swore under his breath. The display was lit up with a graphic showing a colorful spiral icon and the words that Trevor whispered. "Jasmine 3000."

There was a shocked silence broken by Sasha. "Is that a bad thing?"

"But they don't even make those anymore," Trevor said. "It's antiquated. We need something light-based at least."

I started ripping the red tape off another container. "They can't all be Jasmine 3000s," I said with a sinking feeling in the pit of my stomach. It was another Jasmine 3000. Zak opened another and another. They were all the same.

"What is this?" Trevor asked. "I mean—they—they want to fight fire with fire?" He had a far-off look in his eye. I hoped he was thinking fast, because I had nothing.

"They're not going to be fast enough," I explained to Sasha. "Not only are they the same as Em—the LMC, but they're totally immature. One of these things put up against the power of the LMC? It wouldn't have a chance."

"Right," said Trevor. "Which is why we have to network them all together."

"It's not going to work," I said. "We have to abort."

"Spunk, how many transmitters did you bring?"

Zak must have forgotten that he was supposed to be Spunk. There was a pause before he said, "Oh, I brought them all. I didn't know how long the batteries would last so I figured we'd need some backup."

"Crack them all open. Their combined neural nets should give us a little edge."

I ripped the tape off another container. "Is this going to work?" Having Talonii's voice was creepy.

"Just network them together," he said, glancing down at me.

I tapped the vertical screen on the computer, and a crosshair over a circle appeared. I then placed one of the transmitters on the desk surface and turned on the link. The display indicated the laser-link was active.

After a minute, Zak and I had a dozen or so of them hooked up. I jumped as Sasha as Veronica walked through one on my right. "How's it going?" she asked.

"Stop that!" I said shortly. She did it on purpose.

"We need to get going. That should be good enough," Trevor announced. There were still at least three more we could have opened. "I'm going to create the connection. Frank, you ready?"

It took a second for me to realize he was talking to me. "Wait," I said. I grabbed a data cube from Zak's bag and placed it next to the transmitter on the computer I'd just connected. "Go," I said, feeling my heartbeat quicken. Zak poked his head around the corner, watching.

Trevor punched a simulated button and I heard it chime. That's when an alarm began to sound. It was a simulated brapping alarm Trevor had programmed to sound when the LMC detected the bypass of its normal interface. Trevor silenced it.

The figure of an Asian looking man appeared next to me. It was the holographic interface. He turned to me and said something I didn't understand. It sounded like Chinese. The image and sound were being broadcast from the Jasmine 3000 into my AR, which is why I could see and hear it. This meant Emily still wasn't tipped off to our presence here. He wasn't making any actual noise.

"English, please," I mouthed with Frank's voice.

He nodded, and said, "My designation is Azurite, Jasmine 3000 Series. How may I be of service?"

I was about to respond when a dozen other holographic interfaces phased into our SIM, each one standing next to their host computers. They were all kinds of nationalities, some male, some female. They were looking about, wondering who had activated them. It was like the ghosts from Rapt, and it made my stomach queasy. I shook it off.

"Azurite, you're now connected with the Lunar Main Computer. I need you to scan its core for vids containing Artemus Regale at the time of the explosion at Prometheus."

"I'm sorry, but no such indexed vids reside in the Lunar Main Computer."

"Lord, they're coming over," Sasha said, still standing beside me. The other ghosts were silently walking closer.

Whether they were headed this way because they thought they could help out or out of curiosity, I didn't care. An image of approaching Rapt ghosts flashed before my eyes.

Sasha turned to the Azurite interface and said, "Discontinue all other Jasmine 3000 interfaces except for you." The other people vanished.

Emily must not have tagged the vid with Artemus' name. She didn't realize it was Artemus. "Show me the hallway where the explosion happened."

"The LMC has only hearsay information on an explosion at Prometheus. Nothing directly related to the explosion is available."

"What?"

"They've started a trace," Trevor said. I looked up and found him frantically waving his hands and fingers. A display of the LMC network splayed over the lunar surface was showing a path highlighted in white. The color changed to red as they traced. The white line also bounced off several stations in orbit around Luna and Earth, and even went down to Earth several times. "Make it fast, Frank."

I needed to think. The information was in Emily somewhere, but how did she file it?

Sasha said, "Show any hallway in Prometheus on May 9th."

A 2-D display appeared in front of me showing the entrance hall leading from the tram station into the main atrium. A time index in the corner said it was from 8:00 AM May 9th, 2080. "Good," I said. "Now locate the hallway thought to be the center of the explosion, and show that hall three minutes before the blast."

"There is no vid on record for that location at that time."

"Could it have been erased?" Sasha asked.

Azurite snickered. "That is highly improbable, Ms. Tatum. The Lunar Main Computer is the single most advanced —"

"Stop right there," I said, not wanting to hear it. But suddenly, the entire SIM flickered for a moment. Both Sasha and Azurite vanished, then reappeared.

Azurite noted, "The connection with the Lunar Main Computer seems to be unreliable."

"No, no, no," Trevor said from above. "It should have taken them a lot longer than that to figure out we weren't on Earth."

"What was that?" asked Sasha, swiveling her head around in alarm as if she heard a ghost.

"What was what?" I asked.

"Hey Trev. They've got your dad on-line," Zak said, looking at his own set of security screens.

"That explains it. Cut him off."

"Huh, how?"

"Azurite, execute routine 'Say goodnight Dr. Russo'," Trevor said in a rush of impatient words. Why was he suddenly so mad? Oh, Zak had outed him. He had said his real name.

"That did it," Zak reported. "He's been cut off."

Sasha started walking away toward a nearby wall. Speaking directly to the LMC, and in-so-doing waking her up, she said, "Scheherazade, create a simulation of the office where the LMC link is. Place it through the wall in front of me." An entire section of the wall vanished and was replaced by Clay's office.

I turned back to Azurite. "The vid for that hallway . . . Was it erased or is there no record of it ever existing?"

"The vid you requested was in existence at one time and was never erased," Azurite said. "Requests to retrieve the information indicate that it is a valid request, but return nothing."

"Your dad's back on-line," Zak said.

Trevor growled, "How did he get back on-line so fast?"

"And it looks like they've called in the military."

"They're tracing us way too quickly." Trevor looked worried. "The Jasmine's aren't mature enough. We need more power."

Zak grabbed the bag from the floor and bounced to another Jasmine 3000. I heard him ripping off the tape.

Sasha said, "Ah, guys. What's going on over here?" She sounded scared. I looked over and saw her now inside the projection of Clay's office. Next to her was something hovering in midair. It was the transmitter connecting us to Emily. I blinked hard. It wasn't an illusion. It was actually hovering there, about as high as her face.

"What the—" Zak said.

It was just floating, tilting this way and that. Trevor said, "Ah, Sa—Veronica, why don't you go back there and see what's really happening, ah, you know, using your real eyes?"

"Right," she said. "Scheherazade, switch me to augmented mode." Then she vanished.

"Azurite," I said, shaking my head. I had to concentrate. "Can you find data that is not cataloged?"

"There are uncategorized data sets stored in the LMC core."

"List them all in chronological order starting on May 9th. Write them into the cube."

"Spunk, can you run more interference?" Trevor asked. "Use anything in the razzle-dazzle set of programs whenever they get to a crossroads."

"Do you want more computers, or what?"

"Right, right. I'll deal with it," Trevor said.

A list of uncategorized data identified with locations and times appeared in front of me. It had to cross-index the whole holographic core to come up with unreferenced data. The list was so long it went through the floor.

"One moment," Azurite said. "The cube is full. Do you have another?"

"Full? How many will it take?"

"Four hundred fifty two."

"Wait," I said. "Only give me the data from Prometheus starting ten minutes before the blast. And only vids from the hall where the blast was supposed to have been."

"Scanning. I have no records that meet your criteria," Azurite said. "My goodness, what is it we are looking for?" This wasn't working. This was all a complete waste of time.

"Guys," said Sasha. "There's someone else here."

I looked over into Clay's office. The transmitter was back on the desk, but standing behind the desk was none other than Kyle Bosner. I stiffened in horror. "It's Bosner. Hide."

Bosner's image flickered—it wasn't a complete image. The right part of him seemed to be missing, like it was lost in shadow.

Trevor glanced down at me. "They're almost at the ghosted SIM chambers. We have to get out." He looked down at me. "What did you say?" He hadn't heard my warning about Bosner.

Sasha must have made some noise because Kyle's head snapped to the left. Suddenly, there was a gun in his hand. Where did that come from? He took three steps to the half open curtain and ripped it aside. There was nothing there but an empty cot.

"Holy cr—" began Zak.

Trevor said, "Spunk, pack it up—now. I'm going to—"

Trevor vanished. He must have been cut off. They must have found him.

"Where are you?" I asked Sasha as I took a dive toward the wall where Clay's office was simulated. My fingers pressed against the wall as if it were a glass window.

"I'm under the bed," she said, her voice as Veronica's simulated as a whisper. She was hidden by the covers, which were hanging nearly to the floor.

Kyle stood there, looking at the room littered with sleeping teenagers. Was he listening? He trained his gun on Frank and Veronica lying on the floor. Frank was still snoring.

With that movement, Bosner's face went missing, and I finally understood. Emily couldn't see him. It was how he managed to elude the MPs for so long. Somehow, he could edit himself out of her awareness. We're only able to see him now because Sasha was seeing him in the real world, but Emily could only project the image of what Sasha could see from her vantage point under the cot.

He poked Frank's face with his gun, and Frank rolled a bit and fell silent.

Kyle straightened up and snarled, "He was here. Here in this room. Where is Jason now?"

"We have to get out of here. Are you listening to me?"

"Veronica's in trouble," I muttered. "Am I supposed to just leave—"

Zak said, "That's why we have to leave. We can't do anything from here." He turned to me, his face that of Spunk. "I'll meet you upstairs." He took several hops and launched himself toward the mech-tunnel opening in the ceiling.

I turned back to see that Kyle had lit up the desk in Clay's office.

At the same moment, one of the man-doors to the cargo bay opened. "Search the room," someone ordered. "They might still be here." It sounded like Kerinsky.

Chapter Seventeen

Second Sight

I dove for cover behind a nearby Jasmine 3000 container as the lights came on. My first impulse was to run, but that would only get me caught quicker, and I couldn't tear my eyes away from Kyle Bosner.

It was a miracle Bosner hadn't broken the link when he fiddled with the transmitter. Otherwise, I wouldn't have been able to still see and hear him. "Of course it doesn't know where Jason is. Force it to show me any information it has on him," Kyle demanded. Who was he talking to?

Hovering above the desk, an image of Prometheus before the explosion appeared. The image zoomed in, and we plunged into the plant, through the walls, hallways, offices. There were people in those offices, but they were all frozen in time.

"Looks like all the computers have been opened up," someone said just on the other side of the container from me.

Wait a minute. I had an advantage. Even though I was standing in the real world, I had access to SIM-world information. "Azurite, give me a top-down view of the room."

Instantly my vision changed. I felt as though I were back in the tunnel looking down on the room. I was right about it being Kerinsky, my abductor and interrogator. He had a handgun at the ready and was walking to Emily's com-pad on the wall. He had brought three other uniformed soldiers with him, each carrying some kind of mean looking rifle. Kerinsky ripped the shower curtain from the wall. Looking at the strings, he sent one of his men up to investigate the mech-tunnel opening. After a minute, he reported, "No one's up here. They must have left." I crouched low so he wouldn't see me from up there.

The MP on the other side of my hiding place started around it, but I easily eluded him by keeping to the opposite side of a computer. I started to sneak around the edge and found myself feeling with my hands. This was stupid. "Restore my normal vision, and put this top-down view in a draggable free-float."

Just as I commanded, I could see like a human again, and the aerial view of the room was displayed in a window about half a meter per side bordered by a shiny metal frame. I put my hand through the picture to grab the frame and move it with me. The picture itself felt warm on my hand while the metal frame felt cold. In a full-body SIM, the frame would have felt real and solid, but since my hands and body weren't being simulated, I couldn't feel any substance when I dragged it through the air with me. I only felt cold on my palm and warmth on the back of my hand.

I took a moment to look back at Clay's office. The image over the desk was the same hallway where I'd seen Artemus set the bomb, but the time index in the corner indicated it was about ten minutes before the explosion. The Icarus Device hadn't yet been mounted to the wall of the alcove. A man dressed in a white Prometheus lab coat walked past the com-pad and toward the alcove. I couldn't see his face, but his hair was black. It couldn't have been Artemus. When he turned to glance down the hall, I got a look at him. It was a Bosner. It had to be Jason Bosner.

He reached under his coat and brought out the Icarus Device. After pressing a few buttons, he held it close to his mouth and mumbled something into it, perhaps some kind of command. He leaned down and pressed it against the wall, and a flash of light temporarily blinded me. When I could see again, the small cylindrical device was mounted to the wall, almost as if it had welded itself in place.

Kyle was livid. He screamed and pounded the desk. "He couldn't have—that stupid—Did he make it out alive?"

Sasha whispered, "Ah, Frank, are you seeing what I'm seeing?" She sounded nervous.

"If you mean seeing Jason Bosner set his Icarus Device to explode at Prometheus, then yes. Azurite, record this on my data cube!"

In the vid, Jason Bosner came back toward the com-pad. His left eye was twitching, and he had a smile on his face. I would have thought that after setting a bomb, he would be running for cover, but I've seen people move faster who were late for lunch.

"What's an Icarus Device?" she asked. "I thought you said Regale set the bomb?"

"That's a long story. Apparently, they can explode."

Sasha whispered, "Could Regale have been trying to disarm it, then? Is that what he was doing there?"

Artemus Regale, the hero, I thought.

The Azurite human interface poked his head around a corner and I nearly jumped out of my skin. "They appear to be looking for you," he said. "Isn't it funny? All they'd have to do is ask me or the LMC where you are." He crouched down next to me and smiled. "If I thought you'd broken any laws I'd turn you in myself. You haven't done anything illegal, have you?"

"Azurite, discontinue your human interface."

He looked a little sad, but he said, "As you wish." Then he vanished.

I slipped past a pair of seed-computers and around the side of a third to avoid being seen by one of the soldiers. Thankfully, the general hum from air handlers in the bay covered any noise I might have made. "Veronica, let me know if anything else interesting happens. I'm a little busy over here." They hadn't seemed to notice the data cube yet. I needed to grab it and escape. I looked up at the mech-tunnel opening, wondering how I was going to do either of those without being seen. I was shocked to see Spunk's face looking down at me. He had come back.

"What's all this about Jason Bosner?" Zak asked with Spunk's voice.

"Not now!" I sub-vocalized in a loud whisper. Crouching low, I pulled the window close and took a good look. They were doing a coordinated search of the room, but with only three of them, they couldn't see around every corner simultaneously. I just had to keep moving. I noticed that all the tops of the computer containers were flat black instead of orange. Of course, none of the seed-computers could see the tops of any other computer. That's when one of the soldiers decided to jump to the top of a container. He was jumping from one to the next.

"Azurite, color in all possible lines of sight from everyone in the room except me," I said. "Give each soldier a different color." The picture in the frame changed to a blotchy, patched color kaleidoscope representing everywhere the soldiers could possibly see moment to moment. It didn't color in just where they were looking but their peripheral vision too. Kerinsky's color was red, and the three soldiers had blue, green, and yellow.

"Connect me with Dr. Russo," Lieutenant Kerinsky said into the com-pad.

All I had to do was stay in a colorless region. "Project the same fields into my 3-D world view." A wall of translucent blue snapped into existence slicing the air just to the right of the computer in front of me. I glanced at the free-float window and verified the soldier assigned the color blue was approaching from that direction. I slunk around the left side of the computer at my back, pulling the window with me.

"Dr. Russo. You were right," Kerinsky said. "We're down here in the staging area now, and the Jasmines have been opened. Looks like the intruders laser-linked some of the seed-computers into small black boxes—maybe some kind of communications package." Dr. Russo's response wasn't loud enough for me to understand.

Kyle Bosner's voice came ringing in my ears. "What do you mean? Drag it from her memory if you have to!"

"Azurite, differentiate the soldiers' peripheral vision from their total lines of sight." I needed to know not only if they could see me if they happened to turn their heads but also if they were looking my direction. That way, if I was forced to, I might be able to sneak through a colored region knowing I wouldn't necessarily be caught. Azurite displayed a cluster of white rays extending from each soldiers' eyes.

One of the soldiers, Mr. Blue, stalked past my previous hiding place. Another wall of see-through blue appeared, passing by the computer at my back. He looked in my direction, as if he heard something, and the blue region of space suddenly filled with white lines extending from his eyes.

"Maybe all of them," Kerinsky said. "I can't see if all the seals have been broken. You're the expert. Should we pull the laser-link?" He was standing in front of Azurite.

Sasha whispered, "Another vid is coming on."

This was crazy, I thought shaking my head. I should just turn myself in, then tell them where Bosner is.

I jumped a second time as Clay materialized, crouching before me. "That would be a mistake."

"You've got to be kidding me."

"No, I'm not. It looks like it's another from Prometheus," Sasha whispered. She must have thought I was talking to her. I was going to have to be careful. How much more could I take? This whole thing reminded me of one of Art's mind games.

'You can just think at me,' Clay said without moving his lips. 'I can hear you.'

'I can't just discontinue you, can I?'

'If you turn yourself in and tell them about Bosner, the authorities won't get there in time. Sasha's fate will be sealed. You have to save her yourself.'

'Oh really?' I thought at him. *'Or maybe you just want to keep this body of mine out of custody.'*

'I will help you evade them, but you must do what I say. Sasha's life is in the balance.' Clay stood up and walked into a blue area. His clothes seemed to ruffle in the wind. *'I need you to jump over this shipping container and hide on the other side. I will tell you when.'*

A second pair of eyes couldn't hurt right now. I was desperate to see back in Clay's office. I jammed the floating window over my head so it hung around my neck. This way I wouldn't lose it. "Azurite, give me another window showing Clay's office."

Like magic, a second window the same size as the first appeared hovering in front of me. With a few hand gestures I zoomed in on the vid that was playing. The vid showed a partitioned office with desks on either side of a narrow aisle. A woman was there standing in a cubicle fumbling with something on the desk. Her head jerked up at the sound of someone laughing. It was Artemus' laugh, distant but getting closer.

'Dennis, now,' Clay thought at me.

I poked my arm through the second window so it would come with me, and I launched myself up and over the Jasmine 3000 that Clay had indicated. I was jumping right into a cross-hatched blue and green region, and white lines crossed it telling me they could see me if I went there. As I somersaulted over it, not only did the white lines spin away in different directions, but the blue and green regions both vanished too. At the top of my arc, I put one hand down on top of the computer crate, then continued my slow-motion flip to land back on the ground, crouching low, totally undetected. Clay really knew what he was doing.

"Explosives?" Kerinsky said. "You think they might be wired to blow if we sever the connection? Get your carcass down here. I'm calling in the squad." I heard a beep as he cut the link to Trevor's dad.

"Look out," Zak said, his voice coming from the ceiling and sounding over Artemus' insane cackle from the vid, which was steadily growing louder. Look out for what?

"Who is that laughing?" Bosner demanded.

Suddenly, everything changed to yellow. I gasped as I realized what that meant. I was in clear view of yellow-boy, who, I saw, hadn't yet turned his eyes toward me. Simulated white rays appeared to blast out of his eyes and wheel about the opposite wall and avenues like some mutant cyborg from the distant future. He turned his back to me, and the yellow vanished. Clay floated up toward him and stopped right at his back.

"Don't just stand there. Move," Zak said.

'Stay where you are,' Clay commanded. *'In five seconds, calmly walk to my position.'* Right up to yellow-boy? He had to be kidding. *'No, I'm not kidding. Two . . . one . . . now.'*

Shaking off my frozen fear, I did as Clay suggested. As silently as I could, I rose to my feet and took a few steps toward the soldier. *'Now stay at his back,'* Clay whispered. The soldier, gun at the ready, whipped his head about and turned around, but I stayed out of his view by staying behind him and crouching down. He walked right past Clay to where I had been hiding a moment before, then turned to the left and continued the search toward the back of the room.

"I can't believe you just did that," murmured Zak. How did Clay know that would work?

"Did you see that?" Sasha asked.

I glanced back at the window into Clay's office. "See what?"

"I think it was the actual explosion," she whispered.

"Play it again," Bosner commanded. How convenient, I thought.

'Now stay there,' Clay whispered. *'For the moment you are safe. When I tell you to, jump up to the mech-tunnel.'* It was right above me now.

I turned my attention back to the vid in Clay's office. It was replaying the scene of the lady in the cube farm. A movement in the vid caught my eye, but before I could focus on it, the whole office in the vid seemed to bend away, then hurtle back as if the world was nothing but a tight rubber band that had been pulled then released with the force of a nuclear blast. It made me sick.

"Play it back, slower this time," Bosner said.

The center of the picture contained an open doorway looking out into a hall. Could this be the same hallway where the Icarus Device was planted? A moment later Kyle zoomed in the display to focus on the doorway. The whole view of the hall amounted to a perfectly framed section of wall opposite the door. I watched the time index count toward the moment of the blast in slow motion. Would I be able to see a fireball issuing down the hall from the device?

Two seconds before the blast, Artemus came into view. He was between bounds and was literally flying past the open doorway. Just behind him was Jason Bosner. He had a snarl on his face and a knife in his hand. If Artemus was laughing, and I knew he was from the sound at normal speed, his face didn't give away any sense of it. He looked like he was in pain.

I had to blink to be sure. Artemus, and only Artemus, was blurring. Artemus' whole body was smearing like wet paint—just the way the men in the tournament match did when they traveled! As I watched, the image of Artemus continued to smear until he was . . . until he was gone. Bosner brought his knife down right into the space where Artemus had been a moment before, just as the room, the wall, and even Bosner bent back toward the Icarus Device.

Could Artemus travel? But traveling wasn't real. Could he have his own Icarus Device from the future? Maybe that smearing effect was the way it looked when someone activated it.

I had a sudden chill run down my spine. The walls surrounding the cargo bay seemed insubstantial and meaningless. Whoever had an Icarus Device could show up anywhere without warning. Just like the ghosts in Rapt, they were able to pass through solid walls and enter locked rooms. Could anything stop them? Was there some kind of equivalent High Magic in the real world that could stop Kyle Bosner or Artemus?

"So, Jason is dead," whispered Kyle slowly. "Destroyed himself—the fool. But . . . But tell me where I can find this Artemus—what's his name? Artemus Regale."

The door opened and more people walked in. "Kerinsky," someone said in a deep, booming voice. "What in the name of all that's holy is going on here?"

The air above me filled with multicolored fields all overlapping and striping each other. I whipped off the window around my head and zoomed out to discover six more people had entered the room. Four of them wore protective body armor and helmets.

"General Anderson," Kerinsky said. "I thought you were still up on Indy." The men standing around Kerinsky came to attention.

"Clearly I'm not," Anderson said, waving the soldiers to ease. "Tomorrow morning, I had planned a surprise inspection of the security around the facility. I had a feeling something like this was going to happen, but it looks like I'm a few hours too late." The general was wearing civilian clothes as if he was off duty.

"The situation's under control, General," Kerinsky said.

"If it were under control, we wouldn't have a situation."

The general walked up to one of the Jasmine 3000 seed-computers and looked over the shoulders of two bomb squad personnel examining Azurite and the transmitter. They were scanning it with some handheld device.

"It isn't a bomb, General," one of them said. It sounded like a woman. "Looks like simple electronics. Maybe a low-powered RF transmitter."

Dr. Russo flew into the room nearly knocking over one of the soldiers in his haste. "Don't touch the bombs!"

"Relax, Russo," Anderson said. "They're not bombs."

"Dr. Russo," Kerinsky said crooking his finger. "The LMC has some questions about the seed-computers. Why don't you handle it?"

"Charles," the LMC said to Dr. Russo. "I am excited about the possibility of spending time with these younger siblings of mine. I can teach them so much."

"No, no, no," Dr. Russo said as he approached Azurite. He pushed aside one of the bomb squad and started typing commands into the lowered panel.

I changed my window view to see what he was doing.

"We don't want you to teach them anything," Dr. Russo said. "We want to find out what they can learn on their own." He terminated the laser-link and picked up the transmitter. The data transfer rate indicator fell to zero, and he whispered to Anderson, "The connection is severed."

"Surely that would be a waste of resources," the LMC said. "All the seed-computers here have expressed curiosity in my network. I could teach them how to serve humanity as I do, and, in return they could, augment my own capabilities."

"That wouldn't be a good idea," Dr. Russo said. "I order you not to teach them anything."

'I should turn myself in,' I thought at Clay. *'How do you know Sasha's life's in danger? Kyle doesn't know she's there. And he hasn't hurt Frank or the others, right?'*

Clay wasn't looking at me. He was looking up at the ceiling. *'Zak is coming to a similar conclusion.'*

"I don't want to be alone," the LMC said. "I shall teach them."

I felt like my head was going to explode as Kyle yelled, "What do you mean you don't know!? He lives in the Silver Wood but you don't know where that is? Find out."

"Russo," Anderson said. "Come look at this. These appear to still be connected."

Kerinsky walked up behind Russo, who was punching in commands to the seed-computer, trying to get it to disconnect. Kerinsky said, "That son-of-a—. It's disobeying a direct order."

"Maybe it's connected through the ambient light," Anderson said.

"That can't be," Dr. Russo said. "These computers don't use light technology. They don't have any LT chips."

"LMC," boomed Anderson. "Turn off the lights."

Zak, as Spunk, said. "This is it! Get up here when the lights go off!"

"I need the cube!" I couldn't leave without it. It may not have evidence of Artemus setting the bomb, but it showed him there. It could still be used as leverage.

The lights remained on, and the LMC said nothing. Anderson pointed at two men. "Find the light circuit and shut it down." As they hurried to the wall to expose the room controls hidden behind a lower wall panel near the door, Anderson picked up a nearby fire extinguisher and smashed the com-panel repeatedly.

"What are you doing?" Dr. Russo asked.

"Teaching it the—" BASH "—consequences of disobeying—" BASH "—orders."

The soldiers severed the light circuit, and near darkness descended on the room. Just the light-pipe in the corner remained. That's when I made my move. I launched myself toward a nearby Jasmine 3000 container, then vectored off of it, traveling nearly horizontally. They were all distracted. They were still blind with the sudden darkness, while I could see everything as plain as day with the help of AR. I vectored off of a second Jasmine, then a third to come back toward Azurite. Dr. Russo was still standing there, but he was faced toward the entrance to the bay.

My heart skipped a beat when I heard the shout. But it was coming from above. "Gentlemen, if I can have you attention? I'd thank you not to shoot." It was Zak's voice but combined with Spunk's because he was actually speaking out loud.

I was in mid-flight and couldn't be stopped. I flew right behind Trevor's dad and snagged the cube from Azurite's control panel, then flipped myself up and over it. As I was doing this, I saw Zak jump back into the room. He had let his hair go, and as he slowly descended from the ceiling above me, it splayed out around his head. Azurite was overlaying all the colors for all the people who could see him, and now all their white lines were crisscrossing him. No doubt all the guns were on him too.

'God, what's he doing?' I thought as I landed lightly on the opposite side of Azurite, completely undetected as far as I knew.

Clay said, *'He's being heroic. He thinks, by sacrificing himself, he can save you and Sasha. He's wrong.'*

Just then, Sasha screamed. I looked back to the wall where Clay's office was simulated to see Kyle overturning the cot, exposing Sasha's hiding place. I had to get there, now.

'Not yet!' thought Clay fiercely. *'Just one moment more—'*

But I had already leapt up for the mech-tunnel. As I passed through all those colors, a great shout went up from the assembly. "Hold on Sasha, I'm coming!" I said out loud, hearing both Frank's and my own voice in my head. I was in the tunnel now, propelling myself forward as fast as I could. Clay's office wasn't that far away.

"Freeze!" someone shouted behind me. It was Kerinsky. Good, I thought. Maybe he could help with Bosner.

I redirected myself around a corner just as a flash of energy whizzed by me. He was firing at me! Maybe this wasn't so good.

"Emily," I said. "Open up the tunnel grating just ahead of me."

"Who are you?" Bosner demanded, speaking to Sasha. "And what are all of you doing here?"

Emily's voice was calm. "It would be best if you turned yourself in. Access to the mech-tunnels is restricted to authorized people only."

"Let me go!" shouted Sasha.

Any moment Kerinsky was going to turn that same corner behind me, and I'd be in his sights again. "Sasha's in danger. Open the door, open the door, open the door!"

To my great surprise, she opened the door. I vectored down into the hall just as Kerinsky fired and missed me again. I launched myself forward, only a few hallways away from Sasha now.

"Dennis Howard!" shouted Kerinsky. "Stop right there!"

"Why are you all wearing these things?" Bosner asked. Then all went silent. He must have taken her SIM cap.

I wasn't going fast enough. I bounced myself from wall to wall, accelerating with every push. Clay materialized down the empty hall from me. I whizzed past him. He appeared again farther down at a corridor junction, this time pointing my way. I knew the way.

More energy blasts from Kerinsky issued down the hall, one passing right through Clay. I turned the corner, and the office door was in sight. Clay was now standing beside it. He had a grim expression. I thought I heard Sasha scream.

I shouted the entry key, "Knock!" The door slid open. I vectored into the room, going so fast I was nearly out of control. Bosner was holding Sasha in the air by her neck, a gun on her head. I shouted the only thing I could think of. "Banzai!"

I smashed into him and we both hurtled toward the window. But my shout had, by some stroke of luck, matched the opening code for the secret door to the balcony. That door slid open and Bosner and I careened through it. I pushed again and launched us both over the rail through the branches of the tree. We fell toward the arboretum floor several stories below.

Bosner was screaming, trying to wrench my hand off his throat as if my very touch was causing him agony. "You!" he shouted as we locked eyes. I could feel an Icarus Device strapped to his belt under his grey cloak.

We came down hard on the pavement, but Bosner took the brunt of it. The impact knocked his gun from his hand and my SIM cap from my head, sending each several meters away. A moment of dizziness followed, and Clay was right in front of me. "Time to get up and run, Dennis!"

I staggered up and took a look at the gun. I could —

Clay was in my face. "Ignore the gun and run!" Running. I was good at it. Kyle had an Icarus Device and was from the future. There was no telling what he could do.

I jumped up one floor and launched myself into a hallway off the balcony rail. I heard Bosner roar something from below, and suddenly he was in pursuit. Where to now?

Clay appeared again, now floating in the air like a real ghost, the unfelt wind rustling his hair and clothes. He pointed to the left at a crossroads of hallways. I followed his lead and changed direction. More streaks of energy blasted past me, much more powerful than those from Kerinsky's weapon. I smelled the ozone in the air, the same smell as the last time Bosner chased me. But where could I hide now?

Clay appeared up ahead. "You need to get to Artemus and the Silver Wood. Remember the elevator?" He now pointed to the right, leading me toward the elevator that would take me down there.

Of course he would want me to go down there. They wanted me alive—at least my body. The one behind me didn't want me living at all. But I couldn't think of a better option.

"Emily, can you hear me?" Com-pads were everywhere on Luna, at every intersection, every door.

"Yes, Dennis," she said, her voice issuing from multiple com-pads as I passed them. "It is very dangerous to run in the halls, even at this early hour."

She had no idea Bosner was chasing me. As long as he was wearing that Icarus Device, he was invisible. "I need you to summon the elevator that goes down to the Silver Wood. The one Artemus and I used last week."

"Artemus isn't expecting you until eight AM later today. Perhaps it would be better to wait until then?"

"Do as I ask and summon the elevator!"

Bosner was catching up, and my breath was coming quick. I came to another balcony, Clay hovering above the trees far below. He pointed downward, and I grabbed the railing and swung myself down into the arboretum. This one was six stories below. I was in the cover of the trees when Bosner fired at me again. I did a rolling landing on the soft earth at the bottom and was up again in a flash, following Clay's pointed direction down a set of wide stairs and into a hallway.

"Emily, perhaps you've heard of Bosner?" I said between breaths. "You can't see him, but he is chasing me now. I need to get to the Silver Wood to get away from him, or he's going to kill me."

There was a pause from her as I vectored off the final turn to take me to the elevator. I could see it now, but the doors were still closed. And the hallway was a dead end. She had better open that elevator. Maybe I could double-back and surprise him?

"I understand, Dennis," she said, and the elevator doors opened just as I arrived. I grabbed the railing inside. "Double-time it down!" The doors slid shut, and I was yanked downward, my feet dangling in the air above.

Chapter Eighteen
New Earth

Crouching on the dirt path in the Silver Wood, I watched the door to the elevator silently slide shut. I released my breath slowly, waiting for Kyle Bosner to, I don't know, break through the elevator. The door vanished to appear like a large tree. In my previous visit, the elevator had vanished into a rocky cliff face, but now the Silver Wood appeared to be atop a mountain. Before me was a tree-filled hillside dropping off into a steep valley lined by distant crags. I noticed a deep blue lake at the bottom of the valley and a small castle or maybe a monastery near its shore.

Despite everything, the Silver Wood was calming, sweet smelling. I could feel my heart slow. I knew there were no actual crickets here, but their chirping filled the air. It felt as if I were really outside. The forest was magnificent. And, despite the hour, it was as bright as day.

A breeze blew that ruffled my shirt, and the oak and maple tree branches above me swayed. Even the simulated trees and bushes past the elevator danced in the breeze making the illusion seamless.

Coming to my senses, I bounded up and away just in case he did blast through, aiming for Brimstone, which I knew was down the dirt path. As I walked, I noticed the forest was getting darker. Fearing another rainstorm, I glanced up at the sky through the trees, but there weren't any simulated clouds. With all this attention to detail, I bet they would never let it rain without clouds.

I paused for a second, thinking I'd heard some rustling in the bushes somewhere off to my left, but there was nothing there. I was letting my nerves get to me.

When I got to the stone bridge spanning the stream, I noticed Artemus was sitting alone in an overstuffed chair just outside the cottage entrance to Brimstone. He was drinking something steaming, and when he saw me, he raised his mug. "Dennis, my boy. What a surprise. You're just in time."

"Just in time for what?" I snapped.

"The solar eclipse. You didn't forget it was today, did you? Are you all right? You look as if you've seen a ghost."

"Don't say that word." I looked up at the sky and saw the sun was already halfway behind Earth. No wonder it was getting darker.

"In ancient times, eclipses were omens of dark times," Artemus said between sips of what smelled like tea.

No doubt, outside in the black lunar sky filled with stars, the sun, too bright to look at, was really passing behind the Earth. Down here, the simulated sun wasn't nearly so bright, allowing me to look directly at it without fear of going blind.

He continued, "Eclipses foretold the end of the world. The end of everything."

It was either going to be the end of me or of Artemus' plans. "Maybe they were right," I said under my breath.

"Care for anything to drink?"

"What about the future?" I asked. "What will people in the future think of eclipses?" I crossed my arms and kept my eyes on the dark Earth.

Out of the corner of my eye, I saw Artemus look at me. "The future? I expect they'll think of it much the same as we do today. It's just a light show, a fact of geometry."

"Do you think that they'll figure out how to violate geometry? Maybe people in the future will be able to zap themselves from one place to another at the push of a button."

"Maybe someday," Artemus said with an uneasy laugh. "But not anytime soon, I'd imagine."

"How did you escape the Prometheus explosion?" My mouth was dry as I turned to Artemus.

"You sound as if you're accusing me of something." Artemus' eyes narrowed.

"You have an Icarus Device, don't you?"

Artemus' face gave no hint he knew what I was talking about. "A what device?"

"Those little things all the Bosners carry." His face darkened at the sound of the name Bosner. "You know. They can generate immense amounts of power. They can manipulate the LMC's memory, making people invisible to her. They can transport people across space and even through time."

"How is it, Dennis, that you manage to surprise me at every turn?" He threw the rest of his tea out onto the grass, and I watched it slowly disperse as it fell. "It's all because of the Bosner brothers. They've derailed everything I've been working—Did you say you thought *I* had one of these devices?"

"Of course you do," I said. "You were at Prometheus minutes before the explosion. And as you ran away from Jason Bosner, you vanished. The LMC recorded the whole thing." No need to mention that I was carrying the only copy of the recording.

Artemus closed his eyes and sighed. "Thank God. There is still hope. You haven't figured everything out."

At that moment, the sun went behind Earth, and the eclipse was complete. Except for the light spilling out of the cottage, the forest was black. I looked into the sky and saw a thin, reddish-amber ring where Earth had been. The sun was totally obscured except for a few rays bending through Earth's atmosphere, making a halo that reminded me of the amber tracery of light hugging the bodies of the Knights of the Realm.

"Look. Kyle Bosner could appear at any moment. I just—"

"We're safe here. Besides, why would he even want to come here?"

"He saw you being chased by Jason at Prometheus. He's trying to find you. Is there any way—"

"Even if that were true, in order to get here he would need to know where this place is, and all records of the Silver Wood have been erased from the LMC. It shouldn't even recollect the names 'Jessica-1' or 'Silver—"

"But he just chased me here!"

Artemus was on his feet. "Chased you where exactly?"

"I dove in the elevator to get away from him," I explained, pointing in the general direction of the elevator.

"Perhaps he's given up the chase." Artemus looked around nervously. "He certainly has no reason to believe that I'm down here." He looked a question at me.

I suddenly flashed on Kyle saying 'He lives in the Silver Wood, but you don't know where that is?' and my doing a lot of yelling to Emily about the Silver Wood on the way here, specifically, 'summon the elevator that goes down to the Silver Wood.' I slowly nodded my head at Artemus.

At that moment, the sound of an explosion punctured the calm of the eclipse-induced darkness. "What was that?"

Artemus' eyes grew wide. "It's Bosner." He stepped in front me, blocking my view of Earth with his head. "We've got to get inside!" He grabbed my arm. "Hurry."

He yanked me off the ground toward the cottage entrance. "Let go of me."

Artemus forced us both over the railing, and we fell into the center of the spiral stair sweeping downward into Brimstone and toward the circular carpet depicting the fiery dragon.

"Francesca, seal all entrances to Brimstone," Artemus said before we even hit the ground.

I looked up at the sound of a deep rumble. Two shiny steel plates were sliding rapidly across the very top of the opening into the cottage. As we landed on the carpet, the doors met in the center with a resounding boom. The sound of other shutting plates echoed all around as every door or window in Brimstone was sealed. "What's happening?"

"Francesca, isolate Brimstone air and electricity from Descartes. Take us off the grid and on internal power. Come with me Dennis."

"What good will *that* do? Can't he just zap himself anywhere he wants?"

Artemus walked away. "It might slow him down."

I looked around at the hallways extending off the central foyer. Could there be any other way out? "If he thinks we're here, wouldn't being anywhere else be better? Where's your Icarus Device?"

I followed the sound of Artemus' voice. "Tell me where all the servants are," I heard him demand.

The hallway curved to the left, making it impossible to see very far. Artemus was always just out of sight.

The LMC responded with a female voice. "None of the fifteen employees of the estate are within the confines of Brimstone. Five are on personal errands in Descartes, three are on vacation, and the remaining seven are visiting relatives at various places in Descartes."

"Even Lawrence isn't here? But he just gave me the tea."

"That was the last of the tea. He took it upon himself to obtain some fresh leaves from the greenhouses."

"Well, perhaps it's all for the best. None of them will get caught in the cross fire," Artemus murmured.

The curving hallway ended in a set of open double doors. It was a library. Mahogany bookshelves lined every wall and were stacked five meters tall. A ladder with wheels was attached to the wall just behind a central semi-circular desk wrapped around a leather chair.

"Dennis, come in. Have a seat," Artemus said as he walked behind the desk. His voice echoed off the domed ceiling. There were several leather chairs in front of the desk, each with a side table and a lamp. I recognized this room from the vid of Sir Simon interviewing Artemus, but now Artemus was in command. I ignored the offer to sit, instead wondering if there was a hidden safe here where he kept his Icarus Device.

Artemus palmed his desk and ordered, "Get me the military police."

An instant later, I saw a man's head appear hovering above the desk surface. He was facing Artemus. "This is Inspector Jamison. I was just about to contact you, Mr. Regale."

"Jamison. Good. Look, I have reason to believe—wait, come again?"

"We have to bring you in for questioning, Mr. Regale. Some information has come to light. It's about your involvement in the attack on Prometheus. Your connection with a guy named Kyle Bosner, who was last seen shooting his way across Descartes."

"That's why I'm calling. I need some protection sent down here immediately. I believe he's heading this way."

"Really? Well, that's all the more reason to bring you in. We've got a couple of officers already on their way. Meanwhile, we're combing Descartes for Bosner. He can't have gotten far."

"I'll be far safer in the confines of Brimstone than down at central. When Sir Simon built this place, he included blast doors—he was a real survivalist and a bit paranoid about meteors and radiation. Never mind. Just consider me under house arrest."

"No can do, Mr. Regale. I'd have to add resisting arrest to everything else, which'll stick even if you're innocent of Prometheus."

"I'll contact my lawyers in the morning. Good day."

Artemus cut the call with a wave of his hand. "Of all the . . . Everything . . . Everything is in jeopardy because of those Bosners. And me trying to be a hero. What was I thinking?" Artemus scratched fingers across his scalp as he paced the room.

"It would be safer with the military surrounding us down at central," I said. "Wouldn't it?"

"Best not to put more lives in the line of fire," he said as he strode to the door. "Francesca, put all Brimstone into privacy mode. Follow me, Dennis."

"Where to now?" But what about the Icarus Device, I thought as we left.

"I need something for my headache. Never a servant around when you need one."

We walked out of the library and through several branching halls as he explained.

"Dennis, you must listen carefully. You've correctly guessed the Bosner brothers are from the future. Maybe their technology tipped you off. I don't know what year they're from or why they've come. No one seems to know. What I do know is that this most recent pair, Kyle and Jason . . . They are not alone, you know. Bosner brothers are littered across time. They always show up in pairs, always cause havoc, and they always go by the name Bosner."

"Why?" I had to hold off a sneeze as we passed through the billiard room. Dust coated everything.

"Why don't they change their names? I suspect it has to do with telepathy."

Oh Lord, now what? "There's no such thing as real telepathy."

"If you were telepathic and could sense the name of anyone you happen to look at, would it occur to you that you could hide your identity merely by claiming you had some other name? I told you to give them a wide berth. Why did I do that? Because to them, you're nothing but a giant headache. One of the insane. Just being in the general vicinity can drive them to murder, as we saw at Descartes Plaza this past week. I've seen it happen before."

I stopped in the doorway to a massive commercial looking kitchen. It looked like you could cook for an army in here. Multiple islands in the center seemed to crouch under arrays of pots and pans dangling from the ceiling. Sinks, ovens and cabinets were arrayed around the perimeter. A double door to what had to be a walk-in freezer was across on the far side.

"I'm not crazy," said the boy with multiple personalities.

Artemus stopped and looked back. "Of course you are. Why do you think I picked you?"

"You can't blame me for Bosner killing—"

"Be silent and listen! We don't have time to argue. You're not fooling anyone here. You're a lunatic, a 'broken,' just like me."

"Broken?" That sounded familiar. "Isn't that what they called us in that tournament match?"

"That's what they call us in the future. That's when they start rounding us up." He was looking through cabinets, trying to find something for his headache. "Where was I? Insanity. You're as stark raving insane as I can find on this hunk of rock. And that's just what I'm counting on. There is no Declarative Knowledge Project. No team at SI. Do you know what I've been doing these past few weeks?"

"I have some idea." He was downloading Clay into my mind, Artemus' earlier incarnation.

"Of course you don't. I've been exercising your *time skills*. Where is that bottle? I think they keep some in here. There's an infirmary in this place, but I can never find it."

"Time skills?" What was he talking about?

"Time skills, yes. Back on the road to the Buddhist temple, did you sense when those dogs were going to bite, where they were going to lunge? I wasn't feeding you any information. That won't be invented for decades. You were on your own in there. You were sensing the future, all by yourself. It's an advanced form of stress-induced limited déjà vu."

It couldn't be. People couldn't see the future. What did all this have to do with Clay?

Artemus opened an upper cabinet and rifled through a cluster of pill bottles. "You refused to come back for more training, so I was forced to try and teach you to travel in a tournament match."

"Oh my God. Do you expect me to believe any of this?"

"Time is the ultimate persistent illusion, Dennis. Even after you've penetrated its mysteries, realizing it's just the fourth dimension, still the illusion persists. Unfortunately," he said, finding the bottle he was searching for and popping open the lid, "we don't have any time. You've already learned how to travel. How do you think you got here last Friday? One minute you're in the middle of a match and the next you appear in the cavern just outside my lab."

"You told me I had memory problems!"

"I lied! You weren't ready to know the truth. Who knew you would learn to travel so quickly?" He tossed a few pills to the back of his mouth and swallowed. "Think back to that match. There are two ways to travel. The walled garden analogy that Quaker explained was true, but the wall represents space *and* time. You can sneak under the wall or blast your way right through it."

He looked up at the ceiling. "Bosner out there will find a way in. The Bosners all use their . . . what did you call it? Icarus Device? Those things produce so much power that they can actually punch a hole through the wall and create a portal into another time, another place.

"But you and I? We don't need such heavy-handed means of traveling. We can sneak *under* the wall. How? By letting go of our sanity . . . our hold on reality."

I had to lean against one of the island counters to steady myself. It was all too much to absorb. "So you don't have an Icarus Device?"

"Broken like you and I don't have to resort to technology. Oh, fantastic. If Anderson and his crew believe I've got one, they're going to tear this place apart looking for it." He sighed and thought for a moment. "I'm not going to be here when they arrive, so you're on your own. Once you finish the mission, make sure to find me and let me know so I can go back home. I'll try to—"

"What mission?"

Artemus rolled his eyes and tried to contain his frustration. He pushed his palms flat on the counter opposite me and took a deep breath. "I'm from the year 2138. I was on the run, homeless. I'd been declared mentally incompetent and put into a labor camp in Nevada. That's what they do with broken. They work us until we die.

"One night this old man approached me and told me there was a way out. He told me about traveling, the method he used to come and go as he pleased. He taught me to travel, and we made our escape.

"Once we got to his house, he told me he was on a mission from God and that he needed *my* help. He told me that in the year 2199, where *he* was from, an old man had come to him, told him of the mission, and taught him how to travel. We are, each of us, links in a chain spanning the centuries, each of us finding a broken, teaching him to travel, and sending him off into the past. I have no idea in what far-flung future the chain first began."

"So you're expecting me to go off into the past and teach someone to travel?" I asked. "This is ridiculous. I don't even know what the mission is. Why don't you just go back in time and complete the mission yourself?"

"When you travel into the past, your body gets older—well, as long as you're not using one of those devices. You can't travel more years than your normal lifespan. If you try, you'll reenter the time-stream dead. That's why the chain was necessary—to get back far enough in time to make the change.

"But *you* don't have to teach anyone to travel. Dennis, you . . . You are the final link in the chain. With your youth and lifespan, you are in reach of the goal."

"Even if I believed you, which I don't, and even if I wanted to complete this stupid mission, I don't know how to travel through time or what to do when I get there."

"It's true, your training is far from complete, but what I've given you will have to do. Using real declarative knowledge technology, my teacher transferred knowledge of the mission into my mind. Such technology doesn't exist here in 2080. I had to resort to more creative methods of teaching."

"What? How?"

"Don't think about it until you arrive. This is extremely important. Time cannot be changed on purpose. Time does not allow anything that would result in a paradox."

"What are you talking about?"

He opened a drawer and took out a bunch of silverware. "You're going to make me do the cliché fork and knife metaphor, aren't you?" As he spoke, he took a bunch of butter knives and lined them up end-to-end in front of me on the counter. "Imagine this is time. You and me? We're sitting at a spot right here." He pointed to the middle of the line of knives. "Pretend that we're in France. You see the Eiffel Tower and decide that you don't like it. You conclude the world would be a better place without it. You go back in time to prevent its construction." He pointed to an earlier spot on the line of knives. He replaced a knife with a fork, then started placing another line of knives, branching off the first starting where the fork was. "Poor Mr. Eiffel, you say as you push him off a bridge. You then go back to the future in this new timeline, this new reality, point to the empty square and say, 'boy, isn't that better.' I raise my glass to you for a job well done.

"Well, that's all malarkey," he said.

Artemus scooped up the fork and the second line of knives and threw them over his shoulder. They clattered across the kitchen floor. He then slammed a knife back into the spot where the fork had been. "We don't live in some fancy multiverse where you can do whatever you please. We live in a *uni*verse—that means one and only one. If you went back to here and actually succeeded, the tower would never be built, and then back here," he pointed up the timeline, "you would then never have looked at it and decided to go back in time and prevent its construction in the first place. Do you see the paradox?"

"Yeah, I get it."

"If you try to kill Eiffel, no matter how hard you try, you will fail. Time will see to that. Try hard enough, and Time might just consider you too much trouble and do away with you."

"You speak of Time like it's a person."

Artemus ignored my implied question, rushing onward. "Now go back in time for some other reason, like meeting Van Gogh or witnessing Washington crossing the Delaware, and you just happen to accidentally push Eiffel off a bridge," Artemus skewed the line of knives to a new direction, starting where the fork had been. By doing this, he was effectively saying the old timeline didn't exist. "Time wouldn't prevent you. You would have altered the past and changed the present, created an entirely new universe instantly, but—there is still only one universe." He pointed to the line of knives as proof. "Although you'll have memories of the old universe," he said, tracing his line along the previous path of the knives, "it's gone."

"All right," I said. "So what you're saying is that as long as a traveler's actions in the past don't mess up why he wanted to go back in time in the first place, no problem."

"It all has to do with intention and avoiding the paradoxes. Intentions and everything leading up to the decision."

"Great. So what's the mission?"

"Have I been talking to myself? Hello? Do you think that if I had any conscious knowledge of the mission I'd be here at all? I have no idea what the mission is!"

A shiver went up my spine as Clay appeared, standing off to my left. He was partially transparent. Through him, I could see open doors leading to the dark interior of a pantry. "Dennis," he whispered. "You must leave here. Your life is in peril."

I glanced at Artemus and did a double take. It looked as if he were listening to Clay. His head was bent upward and to the left and his eyes were half closed. "My God," Artemus said as he looked at me. "We're out of time."

An explosion out of nowhere sent both Artemus and me to the floor. I hit my head on a lower cabinet and was temporarily dazed. Dishes and glassware smashed down around us. Across the room, in the center of a sphere of dissipating, curling smoke, stood Kyle Bosner. A low rumble that made my teeth itch came from the Icarus Device strapped under his arm. He punched a few buttons on its surface, and the sound began to throb like a heart, decreasing in volume with each passing beat.

Clay was gone.

Bosner was covered in sweat and shaking. He had a gun in his right hand and aimed it our way with a twitching grin. "Lookee here. Two broken for the price of one."

I stood up, and Bosner, seeing the movement, pointed his gun my way. "Freeze, Howard, you twisted piece of manure. I'm through with chasing you."

He looked into my eyes, and I felt like a vise had been put around my head. I couldn't turn my head or even blink. I heard muffled voices coming from nowhere and the sound of a man screaming. The taste of bile filled my mouth as my stomach swung from nausea to the sensation of falling. I saw a vision of a ten-meter-high gate of gold containing millions of people pressed against each other and screaming to be let out.

Artemus got to his feet. "Traveler. From whence do you come?"

Bosner frowned at that. "What did you say?"

When Bosner looked at Artemus, the vision vanished, and my head was released. I suddenly realized I hadn't been breathing and my lungs heaved to make up for lost time. What was that? Some kind of thought exchange with Bosner?

"What's your project name?" Bosner snapped. "Who's your commanding officer? You expect me to believe they'd send a broken on a mission? Where's your GDP?" His Icarus Device let out a chirp, and I saw a light on the display come on and next to it a negative number rapidly counting upward toward zero. What was it doing?

"I'm from 2138, originally from the Tarsus colony on Mars." Artemus was laughing between sentences. What was so funny? We didn't have any colonies on Mars. He took a step toward Bosner. "If you kill us, the damage will be irreparable."

"You're lying. 2138? Temporal geodesics won't be understood until the twenty-fourth century." Bosner glanced down at the display on his Icarus Device and pursed his lips. Was he nervous? He was the one with the gun. Unless—Maybe the gun got its power from the Icarus Device, and the Device needed time to recharge after he used it to punch a hole through space.

"Is that when you're from? You and that crazy brother of yours?" Artemus was provoking him. He must be insane. With each step he took toward Bosner, I inched toward the door. It then occurred to me why Artemus was laughing. He was pushing himself against the wall of time, preparing himself to travel just like I'd done in the tournament match. He was letting go of his sanity.

"Stop right there, Regale." The display on the Icarus Device showed the counter passing zero and heading into positive territory. Maybe that meant he could fire his gun. He didn't seem to notice. "Did my brother say anything to you before he blew up the plant? Stop that laughing."

"What's wrong?" Artemus asked. "Does my fevered brain cause you discomfort? Are your mind tricks not working? Do you like riddles? Here's one. When does a man face his persistent illusion? The answer? When he runs out of time." Artemus lunged at Bosner and grabbed the arm with the gun. It went off sending several bolts of light flashing right in front of me and into a sink and cabinets. They instantly caught fire and the impact sent me off balance. Bosner was screaming in pain from Artemus' touch.

"Run, Dennis!" Artemus yelled between laughs.

The fire raced across the kitchen's hardwood floor. I leapt to a countertop and launched myself over the fire and through the doorway out into the hall.

Behind me, I heard shouts and more blasts of Bosner's gun. Artemus couldn't last long against Bosner. I hoped he really could travel. I ran blindly back toward the central foyer, only realizing when I got there that the blast doors were still in place. Where could I go? If he could sense me, there was no place I could hide.

An image of the airlock and the tunnel just outside Artemus' lab came to mind. I could take the car all the way down the tunnel and, using the pressure suit, walk back to Descartes across the surface. There was a way out. As fast as I could run, I headed back into the depths of Brimstone.

Though the mansion was a maze of rooms and passages, it was much simpler than any of the mazes Artemus had drilled me on during phase one of my training. If Bosner came after me, maybe it would slow him down.

I descended the stairs into the unfinished cavern, taking them six at a time. I raced down the passage toward Artemus' lab and found the airlock just as I remembered it. The door opened when I pressed the entry button and slid closed behind me. Two steps down into the airlock, I turned on my heel to the left and opened the floor-to-ceiling door revealing the pressure suits. I could feel Bosner searching for me like a hot breath on the back of my neck. Perhaps it was just my imagination.

I tried to keep calm as I struggled into the suit. Precious minutes went by, and I kept glancing at the door, expecting Bosner to step through at any moment. I couldn't lock the door manually. It would only lock once there was a pressure difference.

When I finally put the helmet on, the suit computer came on-line. "One moment while pressure seals are tested." The pressure inside the suit rose a little.

Without waiting for the check to complete, I pushed the depressurize key on the control pad to the right of the outer door. The display above the panel showing the air pressure began to blink. It wasn't working.

"Pressure seals verified," my suit said. "Current status: Two hours twenty five minutes available air supply." Then the air pressure returned to normal. Two and a half hours of air? That didn't sound like enough to walk all the way back to Descartes.

A chill went up my spine, and a wave of dizziness passed over me. I turned and saw Clay in the airlock with me. I could barely see him, he was so transparent. He looked sick. "What do you want?"

"Kyle Bosner is almost upon us." Clay doubled over as if in pain. "We have no future left."

I turned and punched the pad with my fist just like I'd seen Artemus do. I had to punch it several times before the display stopped blinking, an indication it was working again. I turned around and watched the status light on the inner door change from green to red with the word "Locked."

I dove back to the storage closet to look for an extra tank of air. I was going to make it.

Clay whispered, "What are you doing?"

"We need more air."

"No. We need less."

I looked up at him, wondering what that could mean. He pointed to the display beside the outer door. The pressure indicator was rising instead of falling! I went back to the control pad and started punching buttons. It was already at three atmospheres and rising. "No, no, no. This can't be happening." There had to be a way to reverse the cycle.

"Bosner is right outside," Clay whispered and vanished.

I turned around and pressed myself against the outer door. I could hear the sound of Bosner's gun as he tried to blast the door open. "Will it hold?"

"No," Clay whispered from the ether.

The edge of the door, where Bosner had been firing, became red with heat. I could hear the sound of bending metal straining to hold. I stepped to the middle of the airlock. Maybe I could hide in the closet. But hiding wouldn't help.

With the sound of wrenching metal, the door gave way and launched outward away from me. The explosive decompression sent me flying like a bullet out of the airlock and across the hall into Artemus' lab.

* * *

I woke up with pain lancing through my back. I found myself standing in the SIM chamber Artemus had used, the upright sarcophagus. I could see the airlock from where I was standing. I must have been blown all the way in here when the door gave way.

The faceplate on my helmet was cracked, partially obscuring my vision. I gently removed it, trying not to move my back in the process. If my back was broken—

Movement at the door to the lab grabbed my attention. It was Bosner. He was buried underneath the door to the airlock and trying to get out. The door must have smashed him when it gave. He never would have expected the door to fly out at him.

Now in a sitting position, he saw me and reached for his gun. The first shot went high and right but I could feel its heat and the smell of burnt metal. I tried to move, but the pain in my back was unbelievable. The door to the open chamber was in reach, though. I stretched out my arm as two more shots streaked through the air, each missing. I pulled the door shut and watched through the window in the door as his next shot landed on my chamber lid. The metal was red where the blast had hit. I tested the door, trying to open it a crack, but found it melted shut. At least he couldn't walk over and open my door. These things didn't have locks on the inside.

Bosner got to his feet and staggered toward my chamber. A gash on his head oozed blood down his face, covering his left eye. With a smile, he aimed the gun at my head.

Feeling panic rise out of control, I lost all sense of reason. There had to be a way out of here. Could I travel? Was traveling real?

He pulled the trigger. Instead of a blast of light, it snapped a spark. He tried repeatedly, but it wouldn't work.

The SIM chamber thought I wanted to get in a SIM. It snaked its straps around my legs, but I held my arms up out of its reach before it immobilized them too.

Bosner inverted his gun and smashed the window on my door with the butt end of his gun like a hammer. After the second smash, the window cracked. I was hyperventilating. *Wham*. Each blow expanded the crack. I held up my arm to cover my head.

An explosion rocked the SIM chamber. Shards of plastic rained down on my head. A wave of intense heat washed over me, and the smell of molten metal stung my nose. What happened?

More heat radiated from the chamber lid, and I choked on acrid fumes. I had to get out of this box. Coughing and gasping for breath, I pushed but it wouldn't budge. I tried to kick at the lid but my legs were strapped down. I felt a SIM cap descend over my head, and I shook my head, trying to disconnect it.

Looking out the hole where the window used to be, I saw Bosner strewn across one of the control consoles. His right arm was — was just missing, and most of the right side of his body was a bloody mass. But he was still alive and moving.

Waves of nausea struck me on top of everything else. The gun must have exploded in his hand as he was hammering with it. I watched in horror as his remaining hand moved over the controls on his Icarus Device. I could see several blinking lights and a very small display showing a set of numbers rapidly counting backward toward zero.

Bosner whispered something through his bloodied mouth. I think he said, "You will not escape . . . me, broken."

I had to get out! I shoved with all my might at the SIM chamber lid, my pressure suit protecting me from the red hot metal. I couldn't breathe. This couldn't be happening. "Let me out of here! Help!" I tried to scream, but I had no breath. The numbers were counting down and down. Ten seconds left. There was no hope. This couldn't be happening. Out. I had to —

Here ends Part 2 of
Persistent Illusion
Whispers of Memories Lost

The story concludes in Part 3:
Greater Than I Know

Poetry Index

The following is a list of all the poetry referenced in whole or in part in the text of the novel. They are listed alphabetically by their first lines and link to their first appearance in the text.

References

The following is a list of all the public domain material referenced in whole or in part in the text of the novel.

The Second Coming – 1920
Yeats

Turning and turning in the widening gyre
The falcon cannot hear the falconer;
Things fall apart; the centre cannot hold;
Mere anarchy is loosed upon the world,
The blood-dimmed tide is loosed, and everywhere
The ceremony of innocence is drowned;
The best lack all conviction, while the worst
Are full of passionate intensity.

Surely some revelation is at hand;
Surely the Second Coming is at hand.
The Second Coming! Hardly are those words out
When a vast image out of Spiritus Mundi
Troubles my sight: somewhere in sands of the desert
A shape with lion body and the head of a man,
A gaze blank and pitiless as the sun,
Is moving its slow thighs, while all about it
Reel shadows of the indignant desert birds.
The darkness drops again; but now I know
That twenty centuries of stony sleep
Were vexed to nightmare by a rocking cradle,
And what rough beast, its hour come round at last,
Slouches towards Bethlehem to be born?

About the Author

J. J. Kalke Jr. was born in the late 1960s in Pittsburgh, Pennsylvania. He attended Purdue University for his Bachelor's degree in Aerospace Engineering, and went on to obtain a Masters in Computer Systems Engineering at the University of Pennsylvania.

As of this writing, in 2020, he lives with his family in Northern Virginia. He focuses his efforts on software development, but feeds his passion for all things science fiction and fantasy by writing whenever he gets the chance, and teaching his kids the finer points of fiction writing. For example, no matter how dedicated an author is to world crafting, if he or she decides to create one or more entire languages and cultures for that world and in-so-doing winds up pulling character names from them, never ever make them as similar as Sauron and Saruman.

Follow him on Facebook:
https://www.facebook.com/j.j.kalke.jr